"A TECHNO-T[...] [...]E HE-MA[...]

Thundering Praise for Ward Carroll and his *Punk* Novels

"Carroll has the rare ability to draw the reader into the cockpit. . . . [His] ability to portray the men and women of the U.S. Navy should engross anyone who has an interest in aviation, the sea, or military life."
—*Proceedings*

"Carroll's account of modern naval aviation reads like *Top Gun* on steroids . . . will delight the military-techno audience. . . . Aerial dogfights, nighttime in-flight emergencies, downed aircraft, pilots captured and rescued, court-martial and some nifty flying sequences keep up the pace . . . loaded with testosterone. . . . Carroll's debut speaks volumes about military careerism, aviation technology, naval operations in harm's way, and the men who fly and fight for a living." —*Publishers Weekly*

"Carroll has written an entertainment of a very high order. The airspeak is dead-on, the missions plausible, the myriad levels of control and command deftly conveyed."
—*The Philadelphia Inquirer*

"For your bookshelf to rest alongside *The Caine Mutiny*, *The Bridges at Toko Ri*, and *Run Silent, Run Deep*."
—*The Hook*

"A rousing debut tale about the jet-flying set in which heroism, high-tech expertise, and a warts-and-all look at the Navy get equal measure . . . written by a man who spent fifteen years flying Tomcats, and who has served as a consultant on such films as *The Hunt for Red October*: a convincing, often amusing, surprisingly unflinching account." —*Kirkus Reviews*

continued . . .

MILITIA KILL

WARD CARROLL

A SIGNET BOOK

SIGNET
Published by New American Library, a division of
Penguin Group (USA) Inc., 375 Hudson Street,
New York, New York 10014, USA
Penguin Group (Canada), 90 Eglinton Avenue East, Suite 700, Toronto,
Ontario M4P 2Y3, Canada (a division of Pearson Penguin Canada Inc.)
Penguin Books Ltd., 80 Strand, London WC2R 0RL, England
Penguin Ireland, 25 St. Stephen's Green, Dublin 2,
Ireland (a division of Penguin Books Ltd.)
Penguin Group (Australia), 250 Camberwell Road, Camberwell, Victoria 3124,
Australia (a division of Pearson Australia Group Pty. Ltd.)
Penguin Books India Pvt. Ltd., 11 Community Centre, Panchsheel Park,
New Delhi - 110 017, India
Penguin Group (NZ), cnr Airborne and Rosedale Roads, Albany,
Auckland 1310, New Zealand (a division of Pearson New Zealand Ltd.)
Penguin Books (South Africa) (Pty.) Ltd., 24 Sturdee Avenue,
Rosebank, Johannesburg 2196, South Africa

Penguin Books Ltd., Registered Offices:
80 Strand, London WC2R 0RL, England

First published by Signet, an imprint of New American Library,
a division of Penguin Group (USA) Inc.

First Printing, July 2006
10 9 8 7 6 5 4 3 2 1

Copyright © Ward Carroll, 2006
All rights reserved

 REGISTERED TRADEMARK—MARCA REGISTRADA

Printed in the United States of America

1

Bobby Redmond had never even heard of the Bureau of Alcohol, Tobacco and Firearms until he'd strolled through a job fair during his final semester in college, but besides the U.S. Army, ATF had been the only organization to invite him for a follow-up interview. There was no way he was joining the Army, even as an officer, so off he'd gone to the ATF human-resources offices in Phoenix, clinging to the hope not only that there was a job in the offing but that it might be one suited to his personality. He swore to himself during the drive south that he wouldn't pretend to be someone he wasn't, and he didn't pull any punches during the half dozen interviews that followed. He'd given it to them straight, told them that he was talented and energetic and willing to work hard but really didn't want to be part of a huge bureaucracy. And didn't they shake their heads and adamantly insist that they wanted leaders, not followers— independent thinkers who would take the organization into the twenty-first century?

He recollected the signing of the final job contract across from the row of beaming smiles—set up as surely as the wrongdoers he'd ambushed over the last five years. It wasn't so much the job itself. What red-blooded American male wouldn't have wanted to wear the title of special agent? Hell, few occupations offered such clarity of purpose. Good versus evil, straight up. But the road toward the pursuit of that clear-cut mission had been riddled with potholes.

Early on, during his first field assignment, it was the constant oversight of his supervisor, a knucklehead who couldn't have made ice cubes without the recipe. Redmond wasn't allowed to wipe his ass without submitting a request in triplicate. Then he spent the next few years buried under a mountain of paperwork at the St. Paul division headquarters. And just when he thought he was on his way back to the field he was informed that he would be attending a year's worth of training courses at locations throughout the country. That news had been the final blow to the tenuous relationship he'd managed with his girlfriend—the only woman since college to wear that title.

The training hadn't been all bad, though. At an abandoned military airfield in Washington state he'd learned how to fly an unmanned aerial vehicle, or UAV in military parlance—a remote-controlled airplane with cameras and other devices strapped to it, one prong in the Bureau's plan to update its arsenal of crime-fighting equipment. Throughout the four-week syllabus Redmond had shown a knack for aviating, earning record high marks during both ground school and the flight phase of the training. And although his feet never left the ground, when he coaxed the joystick and watched the results on the portable instrument panel, he felt a kinship with pilots everywhere.

But sure enough, the first time he'd requested the use of a UAV to assist in an investigation, he'd been denied. First the do-nothings in St. Paul had claimed there weren't enough assets available and when he'd proved to them that there were, they'd changed their story, inventing a new policy about the amount of evidence required before the UAV could be employed during an investigation. It was then that he'd nearly turned in his badge.

But he didn't. He couldn't. Regardless of whether or not being an ATF agent was the ideal metaphysical fit for him, Redmond had long since accepted the pragmatic reality that life seldom fit together so neatly. He'd passed the point where the job had come to define him. Administrative irritations notwithstanding, he was an enforcer of the law, and to enforce the law he needed a UAV. So he set about obtaining more evidence.

But the Badlands Militia wasn't an organization given to easy access. Every bit of knowledge Bobby had managed to glean over the months he'd been on the case was the result of his round-the-clock determination—or dumb luck. Occasionally a militia member would slip and actually use the word "guns" or something else equally damning, and in time the wiretaps yielded the argument he needed to win his airplane.

Now Redmond had the eyes inside the compound that he needed. He split his concentration between the instrument panel and the laptop's screen and gently stirred the joystick, looking for something, anything that might put the final nail in the militia's coffin. Over the last few weeks he'd watched the trucks come and go under the cloak of darkness; he'd heard the chatter of automatic-weapons fire and even the occasional rumble of explosions. There had to be quite an impressive stockpile of weapons among the compound's myriad buildings, illegal goods stacked high, just waiting to be seen by an electronic eye in the sky.

Did the militia members know that the high-pitched whine above them might be signaling their doom? And even if they did know, what could they do about it? Nothing. That was the beauty of the UAV.

Redmond chuckled to himself as he thought of the militia's leader, Devon Hite, being ushered in handcuffs from a van into the perp's entrance of the federal courthouse. Wouldn't that wipe the self-absorbed smirk off of his narrow face once and for all? Although Redmond had never met the man, he felt he knew him, in many ways better than he'd ever known anyone.

Now Redmond studied the computer screen. He pushed a button at the base of the joystick, increasing

the magnification of the infrared camera tucked under
the nose of the UAV. He could see people streaming
out of the main hall, adjourning from yet another of
Hite's evenings of holding court, no doubt. Fools. Redmond looked closer and saw several women trailing
Hite. Rumors of bigamy among the militia had spread
through Fairly along with the stories about great caches
of weapons. At one of the local diners, Redmond had
overheard a trucker mention something about a tank
and the trucker across the table had done the other several better by saying that he had it on good account that
the militia was in possession of a nuclear device. "More
power to 'em," the first one had returned.

Rumors were all the ATF had at this point. That's
where Redmond and his UAV came in. "Control, are
you getting these images?" he asked into his headset.

"Yeah," a man's voice intoned in return. Sounded like
a young guy. Probably some rookie technician, maybe
even a civilian. They were outsourcing everything these
days. Bobby wasn't even sure where the man was. All
he knew was he had been given a strange Internet address and several sets of numbers to enter into the handful of blank fields on the home page. A few seconds
after filling the blanks and selecting SUBMIT he was
seeing images from the UAV's infrared pod. Another
second after that his cell phone had buzzed and the
man's voice greeted him with, "Mission Five underway."
No introductions; no small talk.

Redmond almost asked the man where he was located
but knew it wouldn't have been professional to get too
chatty over the line. Besides, it didn't matter where on
earth the guy was as long as he was getting the images.
He could be in the Philippines or Sri Lanka just like all
the 24-hour toll-free-hotline operators.

Redmond noticed something on the screen, distinctive
shapes. "Crates," he mumbled.

"What?"

"They're stacked behind that warehouse in the center
of the screen. Do you see what I'm talking about?"

"Yeah, I think so."

"They look like weapons containers, like the kind rifles might be shipped in."

And then Redmond saw something strange. Away from the procession a cloud formed, blossoming in the upper right corner of the computer screen. He watched the cloud grow, mesmerized by its changing shape, and from it came a thin column of white smoke that corkscrewed into the sky. At that moment a realization hit him.

"They shot a SAM at us!" he cried into the headset.

Redmond's sense of technological invulnerability suddenly vanished. He hadn't been trained on dodging surface-to-air missiles, so he just went with his gut. He pushed the joystick hard left and focused on the airspeed and altitude readouts on the instrument panel. Out of the corner of his eye he noticed the computer screen go black. The gauges were erratic, and then they froze altogether.

"It looks like we've lost the UAV," Redmond said. There was no response from the other end of the line. "Control, do you copy?" Still nothing. He looked at the phone and saw they were no longer connected.

A shadow passed over him. He instinctively reached for his gun, but before he could pluck it from the holster, hands were on him. He was thrown on his back, and as he struggled against his attackers he felt the sting of a needle as it plunged into his biceps. Whatever they'd injected him with worked fast. Soon he couldn't move. His vision was dimming, a gray haze creeping in from the sides. The last things Redmond's brain registered before things went totally black were that there were four masked men standing over him and above them the South Dakota sky was incredibly blue.

2

A stiff breeze greeted Lieutenant Ashton Roberts IV as he stepped off the commuter jet in Rapid City. Walking across the tarmac Ash took in his surroundings and wondered how long it had been since he'd gone outdoors during the trip between the airplane and the terminal. He scanned the horizon in all directions. Nothing but rolling flatness. So this was South Dakota. This was his purgatory.

At the rental car counter he asked the attendant, a corpulent woman with bad teeth and cotton-candy hair, if she had a map.

"Where you going, hon?" she asked in return.

"Fairly."

She pointed through the sliding glass doors beyond the luggage carousel and said, "You go out there and find your car in Spot Six. Then you follow the sign that says EXIT. Then you come to a road. Take that road."

"Which way?"

She grimaced. "Which way what?"

"Which way do I take the road?"

"Take it to Fairly. Didn't you say that's where you're going?"

"So do I turn left or right on the road?"

"Left, of course. There ain't nothing to the east, unless you're going to Sioux Falls or all the way to Minnesota."

Ash found his car, a shiny red econo-box that reeked faintly of cigarette smoke, and followed the attendant's directions. He quickly realized that her guidance had been complete in spite of the concerns he'd had walking out of the terminal. Roads in these parts ran north-south or east-west. And they were all ramrod-straight.

The first road sign he passed read FAIRLY 67, so he breathed a sigh of relief and decided to use the drive as decompression time. He cracked the window a tad and turned on the radio, searching the dial for something remotely familiar. He finally settled on a classic-rock station out of Lord knew where. He was in a contemplative mood and each new tune brought with it a host of memories.

His cell phone buzzed at his hip. "Ash is up," he answered.

"Hello, homo."

The classic greeting rendered by only one man: Lieutenant "Wild" Willie Weldon. Wild and Ash had been together through the basic SEAL training phase; more recently Wild had joined Ash for the final phase of his adventures as an admiral's aide. But what was he doing on the phone?

"Where the hell are you, boy?" Ash asked.

"I'm in Maryland," Wild replied.

"Maryland? I thought you were in Anbar Province working with the Marines."

"I was."

Ash recognized the tone of his friend's voice. Something was wrong, and the first thing that came to mind considering Wild's mercurial personality was that he'd punched some colonel out because he didn't like the orders he was giving. "Where in Maryland are you?"

"Bethesda."

"Bethesda, as in the hospital?"

"Yeah."

"Jesus. What happened?"

"Oh, nothing much, really. I just tangled with a roadside bomb, that's all."

"Were you wounded?"

"Sort of . . ."

Wild's voice trailed off. Ash feared the worst. The silence over the line was deafening. What should've been a joyous connection had turned rapidly sour. "So what—"

"I lost the bottom half of my right leg, no big deal," Wild said. "Hey, I'm alive. Two other guys in the Humvee with me weren't so lucky."

Ash felt a cold wave wash over him. Wild, the work-out king, the man who could outlift, outrun any SEAL, was now an amputee? He pulled the car to the side of the road and came to a skidding stop. "I don't know what to say, Wild."

"How about saying that you'll buy me a beer next time we get together," Wild returned. His ebullience made the situation seem all the more tragic to Ash.

"So what are they going to do with you?" Ash asked.

"Throw me on the trash heap with the rest of us wounded vets, I guess."

"How long are you going to be at Bethesda?"

"I don't know. A few more weeks, I guess. I'm going through rehab. They're going to fit me with a prosthetic leg pretty soon, too. They've got a bunch of different models, all made of space-age material. I'll be the bionic man before you know it."

Wild's glass was always half full, and his attitude gave Ash a perspective he'd lacked minutes before. He may have been crazy but he still had all of his limbs intact. "So what's up with you?" Wild asked.

Ash was sure the SEAL community was too small for Wild not to have heard about his situation—although he hadn't heard about Wild's plight until this phone call. Whatever. The things he might have complained about before seemed trivial now.

"I'm headed to Thaedt University," Ash said. He noted the absence of shame in his own voice.

"Where the hell is that?"

"Fairly, South Dakota."

"Sounds like your kind of place, all right."

"Not a lot out here, as far as I can see. But I just got here."

"Are you near Mount Rushmore?"

"I think that's farther west than where I'm going."

"I've always wanted to visit Mount Rushmore. I'll bet it's amazing in real life."

"I'll bet you're right. We'll have to see it together. Make plans for a visit as soon as you can."

"I would assume they have handicap ramp access, right? After all, it is a federal facility."

Ash never thought he'd hear those sorts of words coming from Wild, and each one of them further twisted the knife in his guts. "Look, don't worry about coming to see me," Ash said. "I'll come to you."

"You're busy getting settled in out there," Wild returned. "I'll be fine."

"I'm coming out to see you this weekend, and that's all there is to it."

"Okay, sure." His voice had a resigned tone about it. "Come on out. I'm not going anywhere for a while."

"Do you need me to bring you anything?"

"As a matter of fact, I do: They confiscated my porn."

"Is there a rule about that?"

"I guess. All I know is I had a couple of choice offerings carefully stashed by the bedside and now they're gone."

"All right, I've got you covered. I'll stop by your favorite newsstand on the way in."

"You're cheering me up already. Don't forget I like the girl-on-girl stuff best . . . and not the bull dykes; get the lipstick type."

"Got it."

"I have to go now. Heidi, my favorite nurse, is here to give me my pills."

"Is she hot?"

"No."

"She's right there, isn't she?"

"Yes."

"So she's nasty?"

"That would be more accurate. She's making me hang up."

"I'll see you soon."

"Sure."

Ash pulled back onto the road with his mind racing. He pictured Wild and him on the charter flight bound for Iraq, fresh from breaking up an international smuggling ring that specialized in breaking UN sanctions. Vice Admiral Brooks Garrett, the man Ash had been the aide for, had seen them off with deep thanks and best wishes for a successful deployment. How foolish their optimism had been. Now, a year later, Ash had been banished by the SEAL community to the great nothingness of South Dakota for what had been nothing more than a momentary loss of temper during a mission in the Arabian Gulf. And Wild was missing half a leg. Go figure.

Twelve classic-rock songs later, Ash came to the Fairly exit. As with the simplicity of the road structure out of the airport, there weren't many options for which way to go. The two-lane road off the highway fed into what Ash assumed was downtown or a Hollywood movie set replicating the cliché of a simple Midwestern downtown. There was the city bank and trust, white columns gleaming. There was the hardware store labeled simply HARDWARE. There was the grocery—no supermarket, but a simple grocery. But where was the university?

Ash saw a lone figure seated on one of the benches in the town square, a large dark-skinned man with straight black hair that fell well beyond his shoulders. He rolled the driver's-side window down a little more and called to him: "Excuse me, sir. Can you tell me how to get to Thaedt University?" The man didn't respond so Ash repeated the question. Still the man sat without answering, apparently on a trip to some other planet. But then his head lolled, and Ash realized what the problem was: The big man was drunk.

Another man, an old codger with an arched spine and

a cane, ambled by and, noting Ash's situation, offered, "He's drunk."

"I can see that," Ash returned.

"He's always drunk."

"Oh . . . say, do you know how to get to Thaedt University?"

"You're not from here."

"No, but I will be working at the university."

"I knew you weren't from here because I've never seen you before."

"Right. So do you know how to get to the university?"

"Where are you coming from?"

Ash was trying not to lose his patience with the elderly gent, but he wasn't in the mood for light conversation. He was eager to get to the new office and see what was going on. It was almost four-thirty in the afternoon, as well. He feared everyone he needed to meet might be gone by the time he got there.

"I'm from the East Coast," Ash answered simply.

"I've been there," the man replied. "It was many years ago, but I've definitely been there."

The man started to walk away, so Ash hailed him again, "Sir, I'm wondering how to get to Thaedt University. Can you help me?" But the man just continued walking away, step by deliberate step.

Ash shook his head and continued to drive, hoping something in the small town might lead him to where he needed to go. He rolled a block, looked in all directions at the intersection, and decided to go left, since there didn't appear to be anything but clapboard houses and open fields straight ahead and to the right. A few blocks up there were signs of promise: a brick wall topped with a black wrought-iron fence. Trees, full and newly green with the spring.

A quarter mile later Ash came to the entrance to the campus, marked by a large concrete slab with THAEDT UNIVERSITY carved into it. A banner with the words SOUTH DAKOTA'S ROAD TO TOMORROW on it was strung across the street at the entrance. Entering the grounds

had the feel of entering another world. The grass was
greener, the trees were fuller, and the road was better
paved. The atmosphere was generally fresher than that
of the surrounding town.

Ash saw a sign pointing toward the administration
building, and he figured that would be as good a place
to start as anywhere, since he had no idea where the
ROTC building was or even if there was a separate
building for the unit. His ignorance reminded him that
he had made this long-distance move with very little information, and that, in turn, reminded him that he'd lost
the standing that demanded precise information; he was
not a SEAL anymore—not an active one, anyway. And
inactive SEALs weren't of much use to the nation except
as novelists and movie technical advisors. He didn't feel
like writing a book, and Hollywood wasn't calling.

No, he was in South Dakota and currently wondering
if he shouldn't get out of his mufti and into his uniform.
He figured that could wait for now. He didn't want to
attract undue attention until he got somewhat better ori-
ented. He parked the rental car and made his way into
the administration building.

Inside he approached the first counter he came to,
manned at the moment by a thin woman with a shock
of white hair carefully coifed in an attempt to hide her
female pattern baldness. She looked up from her tabloid
and offered a forced smile. "May I help you, sir?"

"I hope so," Ash returned. "I'm just showing up
here."

"Are you a student?"

Ash chuckled. "No, I'm going to be the officer-in-
charge of the ROTC unit."

The woman's brow furrowed. Ash continued his explanation. "Your ROTC unit? I believe you currently
have a Master Chief Fernandez running it? Have you
heard of him?"

"So are you faculty?"

Ash shrugged. "I'm not a student. I guess that makes
me faculty."

"Very good. On behalf of Dean Williams, let me be the first to welcome you to Thaedt University. Which department will you be teaching in?"

"Whatever department the ROTC unit falls under."

The woman paged through a directory, methodically at first, then maniacally. Suddenly she stopped and let out a long breath. "Here we go," she said. "It's not ROTC. It's NROTC. Is that the same thing, you think?"

"Yes," Ash nodded.

"What's the difference?"

"NROTC is the Navy Reserve Officer Training Corps."

"Navy, huh?"

"Yes."

"I wonder if we have Army here, too?"

"Maybe. I'm just worried about the Navy, though. Can you tell me where the NROTC is located on the campus?"

"Doesn't it seem strange to have a Navy outfit in the middle of South Dakota? I mean, the nearest ocean is thousands of miles away."

"About now I couldn't agree with you more, ma'am. Now if you'd just tell me where the NROTC office is I'll be on my way."

"Not so fast," the woman returned. She reached under the counter a produced a stack of papers. "I need you to fill these forms out before you move on."

"Can I do this later?"

"I'll give you the directions to the NROTC office as soon as you finish." She pointed across Ash's shoulder. "You can work on them over there at that table."

Ash begrudgingly took the forms while gauging her expression. She wasn't kidding. He ambled over to the table and quickly worked his way through the forms, realizing in the process that he had no idea where he'd be staying in Fairly. At the same time he caught his reflection in an adjacent mirror and noticed that he needed a haircut. First impressions with his new charges would be crucial in setting the proper tone.

"Here you go," Ash said as he plopped the forms in front of the woman a few minutes later. "I don't have a local address yet."

The woman looked up with her penciled-on eyebrows dramatically arched. "Where are you staying then?"

"I don't know. Is there a hotel in town?"

"Yeah, I wouldn't recommend staying there though, unless you're a bum."

"Some of my ex-girlfriends might say that's the perfect place for me."

The woman giggled and offered, "There's another place outside of town, a motel the truckers like."

"Is there someplace to get a haircut nearby?"

"Only one place that I know of: Sven's. It's on the square. My husband goes there although I don't know why. He's almost completely bald. I think he just likes to talk with the other bald guys who still think they need haircuts."

Ash smiled and said thanks. Having finally wrestled the location of the NROTC offices from the woman, he headed back for the car. Just before backing out, he caught his reflection in the rearview mirror. He definitely needed a haircut.

He drove back off the campus grounds and into town, circling the square twice before spotting a barber pole next to a small hand-painted sign with SVEN'S scribed on it. He parked across the street at the curb of the square and spotted the silent Indian he'd encountered earlier. The big man was still seated on the bench, head bobbing slightly. The few passersby gave him no notice.

Ash walked into the barbershop and was greeted with curious stares by all inside. As he scanned the faces he almost laughed out loud. Both barbers and all three patrons were by and large bald. He nonchalantly plucked a shopworn magazine from the nearby rack and took a seat in the line of plastic chairs, pretending to read while eavesdropping on the conversations around him.

"You been out yet?" the closest barber asked of the man in his chair.

"No, not yet," the wrinkled gent replied.

"Still got the same dogs?"

"Oh, yeah. Got a new pup, too, but hadn't had time to train her yet. She got good instincts, though, I can tell that already."

"Numbers are up this year," the far barber said.

"That's what I hear," the fat man in the far chair added. "Should be easy pickings."

"What's the limit this year?" asked the thin man waiting for his turn.

"Five."

"You think they'd raise it, population being up and all."

"That makes too much sense for DNR, you know that."

With a laugh the far barber removed the sheet from about the fat man's corpulence. The man struggled to get out of the chair and then plodded out the door with a wave and without paying. Neither of the barbers seemed to care.

The far barber shook the sheet and gave Ash an expectant stare. Ash looked at the man waiting in the chair next to him, but the man shook his head. The SEAL dutifully returned the magazine to the rack before easing into the barber chair. Without a word the barber tossed the sheet across Ash and drew the string taut across his neck. The barber remained mute as he fired up the clippers and took to his new victim's skull.

"You know how I want it?" Ash asked reflexively.

"You want a haircut, right?" the barber returned.

"Yes."

"Okay then. I'll give you a haircut."

The patron in the adjacent chair got up and left as quickly as the man before him had. Another man coming in passed him in the doorway. The new arrival was younger, taut and lean—all business. He had a full head of black hair.

"Hello, Sheriff," the barbers sang out in unison. Only

then did Ash notice the man's uniform, highlighted by a gold star-shaped badge above one of his chest pockets.

"Howdy, fellows," the sheriff returned. "How's everything today?"

"Oh, just fine," Ash's barber said. "We were just talking about the season."

"Been out yet?" the sheriff asked.

"No, you?"

"No, I'm going out this weekend, though."

"Where you going?"

"I got an invitation from Devon Hite to hunt his place."

In the mirror Ash saw the barbers exchange furtive glances. Silence followed for a few beats. "You been out there lately, Sheriff?" the next barber asked.

"Was out there a couple of hours ago," the sheriff replied. "Actually took the ATF chief from Saint Paul out there for a look-see."

"ATF from Saint Paul?" Ash's barber said. "What the heck was he doing in Fairly?"

"Seems like he lost a special agent. The chief was sketchy with the details, of course, but from what I could gather, this agent was keeping an eye on the militia."

"And the chief thought the militia had something to do with the agent's disappearance?"

"I think so, yeah."

"Is he still here?"

"No, he flew back to Saint Paul in an ATF bugsmasher."

"So what did you find out there?" the ever-waiting patron asked, looking up from his battered issue of *Field and Stream*.

"Nothing, really," the sheriff said. "Devon showed us his new storage building, then took us into his conference room along with a bunch of new arrivals."

"They're coming in every day, I hear," Ash's barber said.

"No limit on loonies in this country," the other barber said.

"Loonies? What's loony about doing what you want? The militia isn't bothering anyone; they just want to be left alone."

"That's not what I hear. I hear they're doing all kinds of wild stuff over there."

"Yeah? Like what?"

"I hear that Hite fellow's got three wives, all lookers, too."

"Three wives? He can have that, even if they are lookers."

"I also hear they got trucks showing up at all hours of the night."

"What kind of trucks?"

"I dunno. Eighteen-wheelers, I guess."

"Wonder what's in 'em? Did you see anything when you were out there, Sheriff?"

"I didn't see any eighteen-wheelers, if that's what you're asking," the sheriff replied.

Ash suddenly felt the string around his neck loosen. "There you go, son," the barber said as he tugged the sheet off of Ash, dumping most of the clippings on his pants in the process. Ash dusted his pants and reached for his wallet, asking, "How much do I owe you?"

"You're new in town, aren't you?" the barber asked back.

"Yeah, just got here, actually."

"Just passing through?"

"No, I'm going to be in charge of the NROTC unit over at the university."

"Oh, you working for Etan Fernandez?"

"Master Chief Fernandez? I believe he'll be working for me, actually."

"He's a master chief, you know," the other barber said. "A master chief who doesn't get enough haircuts, by the way."

"And I'm a lieutenant," Ash returned. "So how much do I owe you?"

"You're a lieutenant in the Navy?" the barber said.

"Yes."

"I only ask because there's a big difference between a lieutenant in the Navy and one in the Army."

Ash just nodded.

"So what did you do in the Navy? Were you on ships or a flyer?"

"I was a SEAL." Ash paused for a second, considering what he'd said, and then corrected himself: "I *am* a SEAL."

"SEAL, huh?" the other barber said as he pulled the sheet from the front of the sheriff's torso. "My grandson's got that video game, I think. You ever played that?"

"I don't think so," Ash said.

"Oh," the other barber said disappointedly. "I was wondering if it was realistic. Seems like it is."

Ash focused on his barber once again, asking, "How much do I owe you?"

"Were you in the war?"

"Which one?"

"Is there another one I don't know about going on out there?"

"Well, I was in Afghanistan, too."

The barber shook his head in disbelief and muttered, "You qualify."

"For what?"

"For free haircuts." The barber extended his hand. "Welcome to Fairly. I'm Sven." He pointed to the other barber. "That's Mel." Ash returned the other barber's wave.

"Great to meet you guys. Thanks for the hospitality."

"So where are you staying?"

"I haven't figured that out yet."

"There's a hotel across the square, but I wouldn't stay there if I were you."

"That's what they told me over at the university."

"You got anything against truckers?" Mel asked.

"Not really."

"Motel out by the highway. Sven, do they still do that free breakfast bar over there?"

"I think so, yeah," Sven replied.

"I'll check it out right after I check in with Master Chief Fernandez," Ash said. "Thanks again, fellows. Appreciate it."

Ash slipped out the barbershop's front door and into the quickly dimming sunlight. The long shadows reminded him he still had a lot to do that day and not much daylight to do it in. Better to figure out the lay of the land before it got dark.

"You're a SEAL, huh?" a voice said from behind Ash.

Ash turned to see the sheriff just coming through the barbershop door. The sheriff extended his hand, saying, "I was a Green Beret."

"I have a lot of respect for Green Beret," Ash returned, working to match the firmness of the sheriff's handshake. "I've worked with them a couple of times."

"Name's Dominic Bolo," the sheriff said.

"Ash Roberts."

"So you're taking over the ROTC unit?"

"Yeah."

"I just saw some of your folks a few hours back. They were having a little party over at the master chief's apartment."

"Oh." Ash wasn't sure what to say or how to read Bolo's wry smile.

"The master chief is quite a character," Bolo added.

The two men stood quietly on the sidewalk until Ash said, "I'd better get back to the university. Sounds like I might have a challenge running down the master chief."

"What are you doing for dinner?"

"I don't have any plans," Ash shrugged.

Bolo pointed across the square. "I live in that house right there on the corner. Why don't you come over at, say, seven o'clock?"

"Okay."

"Do you like pheasant?"

Ash hadn't had pheasant for years, not since the formal Sunday dinners that his parents used to force on his brother and him during his youth. "Sounds great."

Bolo rendered a casual salute and said, "See you at seven."

3

A few days before Ash Roberts arrived in Fairly, Bobby Redmond regained consciousness. He had no idea where he was. The room was pitch-black. He sat up and shivered against the cold and, wrapping his arms around himself, realized he was naked. He attempted to stand but was hit with a stabbing pain between his eyes that sat him back against the hard wooden slab. The cinderblock wall behind him was rough and damp across his back. How long had he been out? He wondered what time it was and then wondered what had become of his watch—and his clothes.

Redmond thought back to his capture, remembering what little he could. He'd been too focused on flying the UAV, and he felt the fool for allowing himself to get jumped. His left arm ached, and he ran a hand along his biceps and felt where the needle had pierced his skin. What had they injected him with? Slowly he lifted his arms and repeatedly clenched his fists, checking whether he had dominion over his body. He was thirsty. His shivering intensified.

A metallic clicking split the room and then a rapidly growing sliver of light blinded him as the door to the cell was pushed open. The lights were switched on—fluorescent, stark, and brighter still. Through eyes that had not caught up to their surroundings, Redmond saw the outline of a man in a lab coat approaching. He drew in, hovering close enough for Redmond to see his reflection in the small round lenses of the man's glasses. Then he was blinded again by a penlight shining into his eyes.

"So, how are we feeling?" the man asked.

"Where are my clothes?" Redmond asked back, voice cracking slightly from thirst and lack of use.

"I asked you how you were feeling."

"I'm cold . . . and I could use some water."

"I'm sure you could," the man said.

"Who are you?"

"I'm the person who asked you how you were feeling," the man said as he pulled back, face split with a toothy leer.

Redmond looked to the crook in his arm and asked, "What did you inject me with?"

"Nothing with any long-term affects, at least none that I know of."

"Are you a doctor?"

The man laughed. "That depends on who you ask. If you ask the state of South Dakota, I'm not." He waved a bony hand, fingers like green beans. "Enough questions. Open your mouth."

Redmond recoiled as the man reached out, which caused the man to suddenly lose his temper. He tried to backhand Redmond across the face, but Redmond parried his thin arm away while drawing his own fist back. Before he could deliver the punch, the other produced a stun gun from one of the pockets of his lab coat and pushed it against Redmond's thigh. The jolt of electricity caused Redmond's body to stiffen momentarily before he fell limp against the wooden slab.

"I'll ask you to be polite while you're here," the man seethed.

The door opened again and through the pain Redmond managed to loll his head around enough to see another man enter the cell. As he worked his eyes up from the approaching jeans and black T-shirt he saw who it was: Devon Hite, the leader of the Badlands Militia.

"What's going on here, Doc?" Hite asked. "Is our new friend being an unruly guest?"

"Nothing I can't handle," the other replied.

"Oh, you're a real tough guy, all right," Hite said, taking possession of the stun gun. "As long as you have this in your hand." He turned and hovered over Redmond. "How are we doing, Robert? Do you go by Robert? Bob? Bobby?" Redmond sat still and mute. "Not a talker, huh? Well, I'll just call you Robbie. I like that. Robbies are nice guys. They like to talk. Come on. Talk to me, Robbie."

"Where are my clothes?" Redmond slurred.

"You won't be needing them for a while," Hite said. "But that doesn't mean you have to hang around buck naked." He moved to a corner and picked up a bundle from the floor. "Here, put this on."

Redmond lethargically slipped a light blue smock over his head. The garment seemed to be made of paper and reminded the agent of those worn by hospital patients. Hite took a step back, which gave Redmond his first good look at him. Hite was shorter and more slightly built than the bios and stats and hundreds of photos had led the agent to believe he would be. The lines on his face were more chiseled, eyes a more piercing blue. His head was shaved and he'd grown a small tuft of beard along his bottom lip. Hite produced a plastic bottle of water and handed it to Redmond.

"How long have I been here?" Redmond asked after taking several gulps from the bottle.

Hite looked at his watch and said, "A day or two, I guess." He smiled and drew close. "I know what you're thinking: You think your men will be looking for you. They'll be wondering why you haven't checked in. Here's a news flash: You have been checking in, and your home office is convinced your little stakeout or whatever it was you were doing is going fine." He threw his head back. "You ATF boys need to work on your computer-network security. My IT guy figured out your password in no time."

Redmond was trying to stay cool, trying to think, but as he brought the bottle to his lips again, Hite slapped it to the floor. "That's enough," he said. "It's time to get down to business." He looked over to the doctor and asked, "What will it be to start?"

The doctor arched his eyebrows and returned, "Movies?"

Hite shrugged. "Why not?" He refocused on Redmond and asked, "I've got a question for you."

Redmond tried to stay mute, but Hite slapped his cheek and repeated, "I've got a question for you."

"What?" Redmond said, trying to ward off Hite's hand.

"Why were you spying on us?" Redmond didn't answer so Hite continued: "We're not doing anything here."

Hite moved across the room and stood with his back against the door. "You think you're serving the right cause but you're not. You're serving something so evil, so insidious, that if you knew the truth as I do, you'd claw your eyes out to blind you from your deeds." He tapped his chest. "The militia represents freedom, the real stuff. That's why they sent you." His eyes went to the ceiling as he lost himself in thought for a time before snapping out of it. "Movies it is, Doc. You prep him, and I'll get the projector ready." He slipped through the door.

The doctor wrapped his hand around Redmond's biceps and ushered him into a padded chair that he hadn't noticed in the opposite corner of the room. Before he could react, a strap was drawn across his chest and arms.

"This is all some kind of sick joke," the agent said as he struggled against his bindings.

"I assure you this is no joke," the doctor said, inspecting a large syringe at close range.

"Of course not," Hite said as he reentered the room. "This is very serious business—the *most* serious of businesses, in fact."

"Kidnapping an ATF agent is a federal offense," Redmond said.

The other two laughed. "We didn't kidnap you, Robbie," Hite said. "We've detained you for trespassing—a citizen's arrest." He pointed to the needle in the doctor's hand. "Besides, pretty soon you won't be an ATF agent; you'll be one of us."

Hite stepped directly in front of Redmond and took his face in his hands, saying, "You've studied me, haven't you? You think you know me." He patted the agent's cheeks. "You don't . . . but you will."

As Redmond continued to his futile struggle, the doctor swabbed his upper arm, saying, "This won't hurt a bit," before plunging the needle into the agent's flesh.

4

Ash's mind was racing as he drove back to the Thaedt University campus after getting his haircut. He thought about the down-home hospitality of the barbers; he thought about having dinner with Sheriff Bolo; but more than anything else, he thought about the night in the Gulf no more than a week before.

On the night that now lived in his personal infamy, Lieutenant Ashton Roberts IV sat on the upper bunk in the cramped two-man stateroom and opened the letter he'd just received from his father, Ashton Roberts III. Ash's father was the lone snail-mail holdout among those with whom the Navy SEAL regularly corresponded. All the others had long since abandoned pen on paper and taken advantage of the now well-known fact that the younger Ash had a Navy-assigned e-mail account that was easily accessed from his current domicile—a warship steaming in the northern Arabian Gulf. But the senior Roberts, the third Roberts to stand as president and CEO of Roberts International, was more than an old-school traditionalist; he was a man who presaged each thought and deed as being somehow captured in his biography or maybe even in a museum after his death. The letters, written in flowing cursive on heavy bond company letterhead, would certainly have looked good under glass.

Over the years Ash had come to believe that in many ways his father was a man born sixty or seventy years too late. He was an incurable romantic, a man of style. The New York City he worked in was something out of a Margaret Bourke-White photograph, an elegant black-and-white place of steel rivets, ticker tapes, pocket watches, and round-rimmed spectacles. Which wasn't to say he hadn't thrived in the digital age; he had in spades. He'd taken Roberts International to new fiscal heights—diversifying, multiplying, rightsizing. But underneath his business savvy was an unspoken yearning for the days when gentlemen wore white when playing lawn tennis in the passing shade of overhead zeppelins.

"Your mother and I have become quite concerned for your safety of late based on what we've read in the *Times*," the letter began. "Each day this war seems to get more complicated, and I know that must be hard on you and your charges."

The body of the letter was family news, most of which the lieutenant had already received from his mother via e-mail, including the fact that his younger brother, Winston, had been promoted within Roberts International once again and now wore the title of *executive* vice president. Ash grimaced. As much as an expression of pride in his younger brother, that tidbit was a question directed at him: "So what are you doing in the Navy . . . and *at war*?"

Ash knew he didn't have an answer that would reso-nate with his father, just as he hadn't had an answer when his father wanted to know why he was attending Annapolis instead of Princeton or why he was selecting SEALs as his warfare specialty once he accepted his commission. And after spending as much time away from the USA as he had during the past few years, quite frankly, Ash wasn't sure he had an answer that would've resonated with himself.

He was sure that he had another headache. They were coming more frequently now and the eight-hundred-milligram Motrin tablets didn't seem to be working any-more. He thought about visiting the ship's doctor but always seemed too busy to get around to it. Tomorrow, maybe. Or maybe he'd tough it out for a few days, see if the pain went away.

Ash sat up and winced. What the hell was wrong with him? Was it serious or just a byproduct of the stress?

It couldn't be stress. He was a SEAL, dammit. His life was no more or less stressful than it had been since the first night of the war—this war, not to be confused with the other war or any of the dozens of contingency operations he'd fought. Stress had been part of his life since the beginning of his military career. That was what he loved about it, for crissakes.

Ash looked back at the hair that had collected on his pillow, hair that had recently been attached to his scalp. There was no denying there was more there each day; the question was whether or not it was merely a function of growing older. He doubted it. He was a few years short of thirty, and even the most elderly of the men in the extended Roberts family still had full heads of hair. But as with the headaches, he didn't want to worry about it. He didn't have time right now. Long ago, in the earliest days of Basic Underwater Demolition School, he'd learned to ignore pain. His body would take care of itself.

The stateroom door flew open and Ash's roommate, Lieutenant Xavier Kirko, appeared, fresh from the bridge where he'd stood four hours as the officer of the deck.

"What's up, X?" Ash asked, trying to sound friendly. He'd snapped at the younger officer a few hours earlier after Kirko had become a bit too chatty.

"I did my best to run this stinkpot aground, but ultimately I failed," Kirko replied after a moment's hesitation. He gauged Ash's reaction, seemingly pleased that the senior man appeared to be in a better mood if not ready to make amends. Kirko moved over to the steel sink and checked his brown face out in the mirror before looking over at Ash. "What's that you're reading?"

"A letter from my father."

"A letter, huh? I think I saw something about those

in a history book somewhere." Kirko looked back into the mirror, focusing on a smudge on his chin. "The captain's in rare form tonight."

"When isn't he in rare form?"

"Good point."

"So what did he do tonight?"

"It wasn't one thing, really. He just seemed edgier than usual. He was jumping on me for every little thing."

"Edgy, huh? I know the feeling."

"You edgy? No way. You're the coolest of cucumbers." Kirko, a surface warfare officer, was enamored with the mere notion of a Navy SEAL and flattered to have one as a roommate—as long as he didn't bite his head off without warning.

"I don't feel like it," Ash returned, which caused the other to turn away from the mirror and consider him with concerned countenance.

"You're probably just tired," Kirko said as he plucked a palm-sized digital music player from atop his small fold-down desk. He flopped across the lower bunk. "In fact, you haven't been yourself for the last few days, if you don't mind my saying so."

"Look, I apologize for snapping at you earlier. I just needed to concentrate on something right then, that's all."

"No, it's more than that, I think. Oh, well. Maybe you're just tired. Why don't you try to get some shut-eye?"

"I will after I finish reading this." Ash felt the ship roll slightly, the first motion he'd noticed in hours. "How's the weather out there?"

"Sea was like glass for most of my watch," Kirko replied, "but I think the breeze is picking up now. I was talking to the navigator on the way down, and he said the weather guessers were calling for frontal passage sometime during the night."

Ash nodded to himself and refocused on the letter. The tenor of it remained uncharacteristically downbeat throughout, and the closing was strange, if not an insult:

"Maybe it's time to stop putting off your real life," his father wrote. Ash pushed his head deeper into his pillow and stared into the small fluorescent light mounted above the head of his rack. Why couldn't his family accept the choices he'd made? Every time he thought they had, things like his father's letter proved they were only waiting him out like parents waiting out a kid's affinity for electric guitars or souped-up cars. To them jumping out of a C-130 into the night sky over Baghdad or descending on an insurgent stronghold in broad daylight was the stuff of movies, not something an adult might do for his full-time occupation. In spite of his entreaties that spoke of leadership and valor and—dare he say it— *military* service as their own rewards, his family was incapable of grasping the appeal.

And now doubt crept in. Was it possible they were right? Although Ash attempted to take the high ground in justifying his choices, was he simply in denial? Maybe, for all of his courage under fire, glowing fitness reports, medals, and other awards, he was merely fighting fate or the natural order of things. Roberts family men did not join the military. They might sit on the board of some nonprofit foundation dedicated to assisting the military in some tangential way, but they themselves were not given to actually donning a uniform.

Suddenly Ash had a vision of himself as the impudent boy his father was tacitly representing that he was, and the image startled him. He'd never pictured himself in that light before, so why did his mind allow it now? Could it be his fighting edge had dulled?

Ash thought back over the months he'd been in theater, starting with the first night of the war when he'd parachuted into Iraq as part of Task Force Bravo, charged with taking the deputy minister of information into custody. Four of the men who'd been with him on that mission were dead now. Since that night, with the exception of an ill-conceived and complicated few weeks as the aide to a three-star in the Pentagon, Ash had devoted all his energies to fighting the war firsthand. No two missions had been alike and, while he'd never failed to meet his tasking, none of them had been easily accomplished. Maybe the months of stress were taking their toll. Maybe he was human after all. He involuntarily whooshed out a long breath.

"You okay?" Kirko asked tentatively from below.

"I'm fine," Ash replied.

"Hey, have you ever noticed something? These digital music players are awesome and everything, but at the same time they're kind of scary."

"How's that?"

"You remember that movie *Dreamscape*?"

"No."

"It was about a group of scientists that made a helmet that allowed the wearer to see and feel other people's experiences as if they were his or her own. In this one scene an older guy looped the tape of this younger guy screwing his girlfriend so all he saw and felt was the guy's orgasm over and over. The old guy had a heart attack."

"I'm sensing this is one of those too-much-information stories of yours," Ash said.

"No, I'm not talking about orgasms, per se; I'm talking about the way the human mind works. This digital player makes it too easy. First off, unlike my old CD player, this thing is only loaded with songs I like—or used to like. Little by little, over the cruise I've narrowed what I feel like hearing to a handful of songs and then a couple of songs and then one song and then it's a certain part of that one song. Pretty soon I'll just be lying here listening to the same note over and over, or not even a complete note; just a semitone. I'm like the old guy in the movie who looped the orgasm."

"I see," Ash said. "X, you might want to call up to the bridge and have them check the coffee you guys are drinking up there."

Kirko's chuckle was interrupted by the speaker in the passageway outside their door crackling with a static-laced command: "Now weigh the boarding team. Now weigh the boarding team. Boarding team leads muster with the TAO in Combat; I say again, boarding team leads muster with the TAO in Combat."

Ash groaned and mumbled, "So much for getting any sleep." He shoved his father's letter back in its envelope and hopped down from his rack onto the cold enamel floor.

"What do you think is going on?" Kirko asked.

"Beats me," Ash replied as he zipped his black form-fitting jumpsuit to its upper limit under his chin. "Maybe the captain got bored with messing with the guy who relieved you and now he wants to mess with me."

"Whatever it is, good luck."

Ash slipped a black knit watch cap onto his head and considered his roommate's earnest expression for a beat. "I'll be fine," he said before slipped through the state-room door.

Ash hustled up a ladder that fed to the starboard passageway on the main deck and worked his way aft, pushing past his slower shipmates as politely as possible considering his haste and the lurching of the ship. He arrived at the hatch to Combat joined from the opposite direction by one of his SEALs, Gunner's Mate First Class Jamie "Surf" Herd, who was also garbed in black from head to toe. Herd was a big man with the tousled-blond-haired, sun-kissed look of the California surf-scene alum that he was.

"Drill or the real deal?" Herd asked as he pushed up on the bar that secured the hatch.

"We'll know pretty soon, I guess," Ash replied.

The pair entered Combat and discovered they were the last two members of the eight-man boarding team to arrive. Once the tactical action officer spotted Ash he moved to the large screen that faced the TAO station and ran a finger along where brown turned to blue on a computer-generated depiction of the northern end of the Arabian Gulf.

"As you all know by now, smugglers bound for Iraq tend to hide in the littorals," the pudgy, red-faced lieutenant with a shaved head said. His nametag read MCFADDEN, but the other junior officers called him McCracken, which apparently was a running joke based on a mistake the captain had made several times in the weeks after the lieutenant had first joined the crew. Swaying against the ship's rolls, the TAO tapped on one of the symbols among the profusion that populated the screen and said, "This contact right here has been tracking along the Iranian coastline, well inside the normal shipping lanes. We've tried contacting her over UHF and VHF fleet common frequencies but got no response."

The TAO moved his girth around the edge of the station and plopped into his high-backed leather chair. "So we're hauling ass over that way," he said. "The captain has informed the carrier striking-group commander and Fifth Fleet ops reps that we're on our way to conduct a maritime interdiction. The navigator anticipates we'll be within striking distance in forty-five minutes or so."

"What does the navigator consider to be striking distance this evening?" Ash asked.

The TAO raised a thin eyebrow and offered a wry smile. "Tonight it might be a little farther than usual," he said. "We got two things working against us: the sea state, and this guy is tracking closer to the coast than any other contact we've dealt with since we entered the Gulf. In fact, I'll be surprised if this stinkpot doesn't run aground before we get there."

"Any idea of the size?"

The TAO shook his head. "You now know everything I know. I wanted a P-3 for a flyover, but the air-warfare boys told me none were available. They're too busy making the admiral's geedunk runs out of Bahrain, I guess."

Ash studied the screen for a moment before running his eyes across the rest of the boarding team and saying, "All right. Let's go brief."

"I'll relay any updates," the TAO called to Ash's back as the team made its way out of Combat.

"That'd be nice," Ash mumbled in return.

The cruiser continued to pitch and roll with ever-increasing amplitude, and the line of eight bounced off the bulkheads as they made their way aft to the former paint locker that was now the boarding team's briefing room. The room had been chosen by the cruiser's executive officer for two reasons: It provided easy access topside and was the only space available.

Once there, Ash mashed a few buttons on an adjacent cipher lock and pushed through the door. Although the space had been transformed into a briefing room several months earlier, it still retained a strong hint of its former self. Try as they might, the team had been unsuccessful in ridding the room of alcohol and thinner fumes. Early on Ash had complained to the XO who had countered that the space had been thoroughly inspected by the ship's first lieutenant, who was trained in matters of occupational safety, and deemed to be acceptable for extended human exposure.

Ash moved to the front of the tiny space as the others took their seats. He switched on a laptop computer and the projector attached to it. Once a slide labeled STANDARD BRIEFING ITEMS appeared against the front wall, he said, "Let's hit some of the high points while we wait for more information. This is going to be a nighttime maritime interdiction operation against a surface target, size unknown at this time. We've got our standard package this evening: six SEALs and two Swicks. After we brief here the SEALs will get geared up while the Swicks get the RHIB in the water." Ash looked over to the senior man of the two Special Warfare Combatant Craft Crewmen—"Swicks"—and asked, "Is Deck Department ready to assist, Biker?"

"That's affirmative, sir," Engineman First Class Hank "Biker" Hendricks replied, stroking the mustache that nibbled at the corners of his mouth, flirting with regulation grooming standards. Fleet scuttlebutt had it that he'd spent some time as a member of the Hell's Angels before enlisting, a rumor further fueled by his muted refusal to refute it. "I talked to them just before I motored down to Combat. They're prepping the dolly as we speak."

The phone at the back of the room rang, and Hull Maintenance Technician Second Class Marcus Thompson answered it, sleeves of his jumpsuit rolled up and "Born to Hip Hop" tattoo on prominent display against the brown skin of his biceps. After a quick "Yessir" into the line he extended his arm and said, "It's for you, Lieutenant."

Ash took the phone: "Lieutenant Roberts."

"Roberts, we're still too far out for the MARFLIR to pick up any detail," the TAO said, "but the word I'm getting from Surface Plot is it's big, a tanker of some sort would be my guess."

"Speed and heading?" Ash asked.

The TAO paused; Ash heard the shuffling of papers in the background. "Looks like ten knots or so," the TAO said. "Course is almost northwesterly. She's following the coastline."

"Is the datalink up?"

"Yeah."

"Okay." There was a pregnant pause over the line. "Anything else?"

"No. Whoops, I've got to go. The captain's on the other line." There was a click through the earpiece as the TAO abruptly ended the call.

Ash walked back to the front of the space and directed the red dot of his laser pointer over the word WEATHER about halfway down the first briefing slide. He paused, studying the word for a second, and then stepped over to a small television mounted against the upper left side of the front bulkhead. He switched the channel from the cruiser's inertial navigation data to the latest weather information. "Current observation shows clear skies and a half moon, which will be good for using our NVGs. Winds are fifteen to twenty knots, gusting to thirty. Seas are four feet and will probably build as the night goes on." He looked at Hendricks and asked, "What kind of speed to you think we'll be able to get, Biker?"

"It ain't going to be thirty knots," Hendricks shot back, which caused a ripple of muted chuckles. "Maybe half of that, at best."

Ash nodded and refocused on the slide. "Like I said, after the brief the SEALs will get geared up and the Swicks will do their thing. Once the RHIB is in the water and Biker clears us to board, we'll climb down and be on our way.

"We'll look for good UHF and datalink connectivity with the cruiser before we get too far away. Loss of radio comms at any time during the mission is a show-stopper. I'm not sure how far away we're going to be, but you all heard the TAO: It's going to be farther than normal, so strap everything down and hold on. It should be quite a ride."

The phone rang again, and Ash waved off Thompson and walked back and answered it himself: "Roberts . . ."

"We managed to get one of the carrier's S-3s to come over and take a look. They got a couple of decent passes with their synthetic-aperture radar and ID'd the contact as a large tanker."

"How large?"

"Five hundred feet or so."

"How far away are we going to be when the RHIB launches?"

The TAO paused before saying, "I still don't know. I can tell you the water gets shallow fast up here and in these seas the captain isn't going to mess around."

"Doesn't a tanker that size draw more than our cruiser?"

Another moment of silence was followed with the TAO intoning, "We don't know what the tanker draws; we only know what our ship draws."

"Yes, of course," Ash returned dryly. "Anything else for us?"

"No, that's it for now. We'll keep you posted."

"Thanks."

Ash addressed the expectant expressions that surrounded him on his way back to the front of the space: "It's a tanker," he said. "They're estimating it's about five hundred feet long, which is good for us. A ship that big won't be moving around too much."

The phone rang again. Ash whooshed a loud exhalation and gestured toward Thompson. Once again, the sailor picked up the phone, and once again he held the receiver out to the lieutenant, only this time he said, "It's the captain."

Ash's eyes widened a bit as he put the phone to the side of his head. "Lieutenant Roberts, sir."

"How you doing this evening, Lieutenant?" the captain said. Through the phone Commander Anthony Napoli sounded every bit the Brooklyn-reared city boy that he was.

"Fine, sir," Ash returned.

"That's good." Ash heard him slurp something; coffee, no doubt. "You guys ready to do this?"

"We're getting there, sir."

Another slurp, this one followed by a pronounced swallow, which reminded Ash of Xavier's assertion that the captain had been awake since the cruiser's last port call. Ash had no reason to dispute the claim since he seldom went to the bridge and each time he had Napoli had been conscious if not wide awake, perched in his leather chair elevated above everything else.

"Got a little chop out there tonight, you know," Napoli said.

"Yes, sir."

"Take your time with everything."

"We will."

"Don't be afraid to make the call."

Ash momentarily wondered if he was missing something obvious, and then asked, "Which call is that, sir?"

"The call to abort the mission," Napoli said. "Fifth Fleet seemed pretty excited about running this guy down, even with the sea state, but that shouldn't keep us from being smart, right?"

More than any ship's CO he'd ever sailed with—or

any leader he'd served under, for that matter—Captain Napoli was a master of framing direct orders as seemingly reasonable and conscientious questions. "We'll be smart, sir," Ash replied.

"Good." Two more swallows were followed with, "I hate to launch you into these seas, but if we don't get this guy tonight, he'll be gone."

"Then we'd better get him tonight."

"Are you all right, Ash?"

The SEAL was momentarily taken aback by the sudden shift in the exchange, and he paused a beat before saying, "Yes, sir. I'm fine."

"You sure? You sound a little bit down."

"I assure you I'm fine, Captain." Ash noticed he was drawing furtive glances from the rest of the boarding team.

"If you say you're fine, you're fine," Napoli said. "I'll let you get back to your brief then. Oh, one more thing: I don't know if the TAO already told you this, but we're not going to be able to get as close to this contact as we normally do. I don't know how this guy is doing it, but by all accounts he should already have run aground."

"The TAO did tell us that, sir."

"Again, don't be afraid to make the call."

"I won't, Captain."

"Good luck." Napoli hung up.

Ash returned to the front of the space surrounded by inquisitive expressions. One of the SEALs, Hospital Corpsman Third Class Heath Chance, asked, "What did the captain want?"

"The captain wanted to find out if we're ready to do this," Ash replied.

"What kind of question is that? Of course we're ready." When the lieutenant didn't second the motion, Chance, the team's medic and youngest member, followed with, "Aren't we?"

"We'll never be ready if we don't get through this brief, Doc," Ash said as he tapped the keyboard and advanced to the next slide. "Okay, backing up a second.

Before we start the RHIB heading for the contact, let's make sure everything is strapped down tight. Be extra careful with your weapons. We don't want any inadvertent weapons discharges happening tonight."

Ash flipped to the next slide, titled RULES OF ENGAGEMENT, and said, "A quick review of the ROE for this evening. Although this vessel is behaving suspiciously, the crew is not hostile until their actions dictate they are. I know we've been over this a million times, but are there any questions about that particular matrix?" Ash scanned the room and was greeted by impassive expressions and silence. "So, until one of these gomers pulls a gun or a knife, the term 'neutralize' means secure with zip ties, okay?" More silence and a few nods.

"Once we get visual on the contact, we'll attempt to establish radio contact. If the ship's moving we'll order her to stop. If she still doesn't respond, Surf will put a few rounds from the minigun across her bow. Once the ship's screws have stopped turning, we'll close to boarding range. Roping the bitch is going to be sporty in these seas. We'll pull up alongside, near the stern, and look for a suitable place to launch the grappling hooks. Once they're seated, Sweep one will expedite up the ropes, followed immediately by Sweep two and the security team." Ash worked an index finger around the room, pointing at each man as he broke the mission responsibilities down: "Sweep one will be Surf and me. We'll comb the deck and head up to the bridge, neutralizing anyone we happen to meet along the way.

"Sweep Two will be Smitty and Corndog. After we pass 'all clear,' you guys see what's going on in the engineering spaces. At the same time the security team, the chief and Doc, will clear the berthing compartment of any remaining crew members."

Ash flipped to the next slide. "Once we've got the personnel situation under control from a security standpoint, we'll muster everybody on the bridge and ask them the usual questions. If they don't speak English, Spanish, or Arabic then we're into the talky-pointy rou-

tine. The ship's registry should be written in English.
The first thing we want to figure out is why they're operating so far outside of the shipping lanes. We'll assume
they're up to no good, but at the same time, we can't
rule out the possibility they might just be incompetent."

"That excuse has always worked for me," Boatswain's
Mate Second Class Kendall "Corndog" Corn quipped.

"In your case that's no excuse," said Chief Intelligence Specialist Anh Dung Lam, the team's number-two
man. "That's the truth."

Amid laughter from the others, Ash offered a bemused smile and continued: "Regardless of what the paperwork says the ship is carrying, Sweeps one and two
will give the cargo holds a good going-over. Keep your
eyes open for booby traps and other self-destruct mecha-
nisms. If you spot one, stop what you're doing and let
the rest of the team know about it. Don't try to solve
something by yourself unless you don't have any other
choice."

The next slide was titled DISEMBARKING. "We'll retro-
grade in the opposite order that we got on with one
exception: I'll be the last off. Once you commit to the
rope, that's your focus. We want to be as safe and expe-
ditious getting back into the RHIB as we were climbing
out of it."

Ash closed the laptop and leaned against the side of
the table with his arms crossed. "It's no secret this team
is light a couple of people compared to standard
boarding-team doctrine. That's tough. Everybody does
his part and then some. We've done this before. Let's
act like it."

The phone rang again; Thompson answered it. He listened only briefly before hanging up and saying, "It
looks like our boat ride is going to be even longer than
they thought . . ."

Now in Fairly, South Dakota, the red light turned
green, snapping Ash's mind back to the present. He
eased the rental car forward and started the left turn
back onto the Thaedt University campus.

5

Five hours before Lieutenant Ash Roberts reentered the Thaedt campus, Master Chief Etan Fernandez ran a hand through his slicked-back jet-black hair and stared blankly at the navigation problem shining against the white board at the front of the Naval Science classroom. With a bemused grin he strolled to one of the windows that lined one side of the room and considered the view across the campus. He stood, rubbing the wide expanse that was his belly, and asked, "Does anybody else here hate being indoors on a beautiful day as much as I do?"

The question was received with wide smiles from the ten senior-class Naval Reserve Officer Training Corps midshipmen seated before him. Without a word they gathered their textbooks and calculators and queued up behind him at the classroom door.

Fernandez glanced over his shoulder, finger to his lips, and said, "Keep it down, okay? We need to move out of the building Indian-style."

The corpulent sailor turned the knob and slowly drew the door open, doing his best to keep the hinges from squeaking. He peeked around the door frame and, seeing no one, slipped into the hallway. The midshipmen followed.

Through Benjamin Hall's west side bright sunshine and an uncharacteristically light breeze, considering the wide-open spaces that surrounded the Thaedt campus, greeted the group. Fernandez took a deep breath and said, "I've spent too many days stuck in the guts of too many gray hulls to waste another day out of the sun."

In spite of their uniforms, as the eleven continued down the main walkway between rows of majestic buildings it was unlikely that those who might have observed them from a distance would have recognized them as a military unit. Billed caps were perched at jaunty angles if they were worn at all. Shirttails hung out. Two of them wore white socks with their black unshined shoes. And leading them in khakis was a man whose outline suggested Santa Claus more than naval leader.

"I thought the dean said no more classes in the grasses, Master Chief," Midshipman First Class Gerhardt Skoskstad said with a shake of the spiky, frosted hair that made him look like a refugee from the New York underground scene.

"You know I've never listened to that asshole, Skinny," Fernandez replied, using the nickname given to Skoskstad because of his wiry frame.

"The master chief don't care about nobody," Midshipman First Class Keith Oslo added. Oslo liked to be called Bruno, presumably because he had become an Italianophile through modern-day Mafia movies and television shows. And when a starting linebacker elected a name, those who preferred not to be on the receiving end of his gigantic fist generally called him by it.

Fernandez took a seat on a circular bench hidden from the administration building offices by a bandstand and a hedgerow. Scattering books and backpacks, the midshipmen spaced themselves out so that they occupied the full circumference of the bench.

"So where were we?" Fernandez asked.

"We were working on a bullshit navigation problem," Midshipman First Class Ingrid Hansen said, running strands of her frizzy collar-length blonde hair behind her ears. As was her tendency, she slouched in her seat, attempting to hide the fact that, at six foot one, she was the tallest among them. They called her Spike because she was a starter on the varsity volleyball team.

The master chief scanned the midshipmen surrounding him and said, "Oh, yeah. Celestial navigation. Do you really think you're ever going to need to look at the stars to figure out where you are?"

All of them shook their heads in response.

"What about our damn grades?" Hansen asked.

"I wouldn't worry about those," Fernandez replied. "You'll all be officers before you know it."

"I don't want to be an officer," Oslo said.

"Why not?" asked Midshipman First Class Chuck Enrich, whose oversized head—made to appear even more so perched atop a thin neck—had earned him "Globe" as a nickname. "Officers are in charge. They get to tell people what to do."

"Officers are wimps."

"I can't say as you're wrong, Bruno, but what are you going to do?" Fernandez said. "They paid for your college education. Now you got to be one of them."

"Why do I have to be an officer?"

"Because they don't pay the big bucks to make enlisted men, son. Face it: They want you to be in charge."

"But I don't want to be in charge. It's like you said: Only wimps want to be in charge."

"That's right. Only wimps *want* to be in charge. There's a difference between wanting to be in charge and earning the right to be in charge. Never forget that."

"But you don't have to be an officer to be in charge."

"That's true . . . but it's easier if you are."

"I still don't want to be one."

"Well, it's too late. You're going to be one."

"I could still flunk out."

"Don't."

Silence followed as each midshipman was left to his or her thoughts for a time. "How about a sea story, Master Chief?" Hansen finally asked, to which the others added a chorus of encouragement.

"A sea story, huh?" Fernandez looked to the sky. "Sea stories are best told over a beer."

"We've got almost a full keg left over at my frat house," Oslo volunteered.

"Iced down?"

"Yep."

Fernandez checked his watch and said, "Do you think you could get it over to my apartment in, say, ten minutes?"

"No problem."

"That's my kind of can-do right there, shipmates. Let that be the lesson for today. All right, then: Class will reconvene at my place. Be there with beer in hand in ten minutes."

"What the hell about being outdoors on a beautiful day?" Hansen asked.

Fernandez considered her while growing a sly smile and said, "Good point, Spike. We'll sit on my patio."

6

The day before Lieutenant Ash Roberts arrived in Fairly, South Dakota, Hank Howard sat at his desk, hating the fact he wasn't allowed to smoke there. How he longed for the old days when a man could light up at will anywhere, anytime. Now he stood with his lanky frame hunched under a tiny wooden gazebo stuck in the middle of the courtyard behind the ATF's field office in St. Paul, huddled with the other smokers. Hank had long since learned to ignore the derisive stares of the non-smokers as they passed. He knew their air of superiority was a lie. They all had vices—drinking, porn-watching, wife-beating, whatever—it was just that his forced him to stand out in the open like some sideshow freak.

At least the weather was nice. Minnesota wasn't known for nice weather. In the last six months he and his smoking companions had suffered through bitter cold and wind that eventually turned into stifling heat punctuated by violent thunderstorms, not to mention the presence of the biggest, bitingest flies this side of the Australian outback. And through it all, Hank had made his way to the gazebo five or six times during the workday, depending on the number of meetings he was required to attend or how long he'd been stuck on the phone. Yeah, he appreciated a beautiful day more than the health nuts could ever imagine.

"You see that game last night?" Phil Andersen asked following a long drag on one of those brown cigarillos that looked as if it were nothing more than a small stick of wood. Phil laid claim to football greatness during his college years but whatever muscle had allowed him to play linebacker had long since turned to fat.

"Of course I did," Hank said. "I never miss Monday Night Baseball you know that."

"Twins are tough this year."

"Yeah, they are."

"Think they'll go all the way?"

"By God, I hope so. But you know they always seem to screw it up somehow or another in the end."

"I hear you there. I lost big money on them last year. Won a bundle on last night's game, though."

"Hope springs eternal."

"Don't it?"

Hank's cell phone rang and he fished it out of the front pocket of his trousers, careful not to flick ashes on himself in the process. "Hank Howard . . ."

"Mr. Howard, it's Kevin." Kevin Duluth was Hank's assistant, an earnest kid with a criminology degree upon which the ink had not yet dried. "Are you nearby?"

Hank sighed. He'd just left his desk five minutes ago. "I'm in the courtyard," he replied.

"Oh, of course. I'm sorry, sir, but can you come back to the office?"

"What's going on?"

"We have a bit of a situation. Or maybe we do. You probably need to hear it in person."

"I'll be right in."

Hank took one last drag and crushed what remained of his cigarette in the sand of the ash can. "Something going on?" Andersen asked.

"I'm about to find out, I guess. See you later."

Andersen looked at his watch and with a fellow nicotine addict's savvy said, "I'll see you in about two hours."

Hank hurried across the courtyard, through the double doors, and down the long corridor that fed to his office. Inside he found Duluth standing with Terry Goodwin, the woman consistently victorious in the "inspector I'd be most willing to wreck my life over" poll informally conducted by some of the guys from time to time. As well as being judged as *Sports Illustrated* swimsuit-model beautiful, Ms. Goodwin was known for her choice of clothing, a fashion sense that suggested that she was proud of her body. Today's outfit was no exception, and as Hank approached his desk he found it hard not to stare and wonder how much damage the buttons on her blouse would cause once they yielded to the stress.

"What's up?" he asked, flopping into the high-backed chair behind his big mahogany desk.

"Terry just got a phone call from the field office in Phoenix," Duluth said. "They said—well, you tell him, Terry."

"The Phoenix office was monitoring Mission Five's images," Goodwin said. "They think somebody may have shot down the UAV."

Hank shook his head in confusion and said, "Remind me what Mission Five is?"

"Surveillance of the Badlands Militia compound outside Fairly, South Dakota."

"When did this supposed shootdown happen?"

"Two days ago."

"Two days ago? And we're just now hearing about it?"

"Apparently there was some confusion about which field office had the lead. Phoenix started an investigation on their own and didn't tell anybody else."

"Shit," Hank spat. "Who's working that one?"

"In Phoenix? I don't know."

"No, who's working the mission for us? Who's out there?"

"Special Agent Redmond," Duluth said.

"Have we heard from him?"

"Yes and no." Duluth held up several sheets of paper. "Here are printouts of Redmond's reports from the field over the last two days. Our analysts have taken a look at them and they say they look normal."

"Has anyone talked to Redmond directly?"

"We tried calling his cell phone but just got his voice mail. He may be in the middle of something and unable to answer the phone."

"Or maybe he's ignoring the calls," Goodwin offered.

"I don't like it," Hank said. "I don't like it a bit." He flipped through the printouts, skimming the reports to see if anything jumped out at him—a word or phrase that might have signaled that the mission had been compromised—but found nothing. After a few moments of contemplation, he looked at Duluth and asked, "Is the Cessna available?"

Duluth shrugged and replied, "I think so. Why?"

"I think I need to take a little trip to Fairly, South Dakota."

7

Three hours before Lieutenant Ash Roberts returned to the Thaedt University campus after getting his haircut, ten first-class midshipmen and one master chief petty officer formed a circle around the keg of beer perched in the center of the patio behind the master chief's apartment nearby. They'd been there for more hours than any of them could remember when the sun disappeared behind the adjacent convenience store, and by that time they'd consumed enough beer that the keg was nearly floating in the large tub of ice water that surrounded it.

"So you don't believe in God?" Midshipman First Class Oslo said.

"I didn't say that, Bruno," Midshipman First Class Bryan Hendricks said. "I said I didn't find much use in going to church."

"Only the people who don't believe in God don't go to church."

"Why would you have to go to church to believe in God?"

"Because that's where you pray."

"Why can't I pray anywhere I want?"

"Because you can't. God hears you best when you're in church."

Hendricks laughed and said, "Where did you get that?"

"It's how I was raised." They had the attention of the others now, although by this point *attention* was a relative term. The ROTC unit's brainiac—also a relative term among this knot of academic underachievers—had the jock against the intellectual ropes.

"Well, is it working for you?" Hendricks asked.

"Is what working for me?" Oslo asked back.

"Praying to God."

"I guess so."

"I'll bet it isn't." Hendricks let the thought hang until the linebacker's expression evinced maximum confusion, and then asked, "What religion are you?"

"Christian."

"Of course Christian, dumbass. What denomination?"

"Methodist."

"Can you imagine how many Methodists there are out there praying? And they're all using the same frequency. It's all jammed up. Nothing's getting through."

"You got a better system?"

Hendricks nodded and said, "I've got Geordie."

"Who the hell is Geordie?"

"He's the direct line to my spiritual side. All my prayers go right to him. No clutter."

"Does it work?"

Hendricks spread his bony arms and said, "Look at my grade point average. Look at my girlfriend. For crying out loud, look at the peace on my face."

Oslo studied Hendricks's freckled countenance. "I've got to admit, Boy, you've got a peaceful face."

"Well, there you go. All you need to do is find your own Geordie."

Oslo nodded slowly, then put a finger to his temple and said, "Why don't I just pray to Geordie?"

Hendricks winced. "You can't."

"Why not?"

"Because if you pray to Geordie it defeats the entire purpose of me creating him."

"But he works, right?"

"Right, but—"

"I'm praying to him, then. What's one more guy?"

"Don't do it, Bruno."

Oslo looked across the patio to where Master Chief Fernandez was prepping the grill and asked, "What do you think, Master Chief? Should Boy let me pray to his guy?"

Fernandez shook his head and said, "Uh-uh. I'm old-school, shipmates. I learned a long time ago to never talk politics or religion in the chief's mess."

There was a momentary lull in the conversation until Midshipman First Class Hansen slowly raised her wrist and let out a long groan and uttered, "I'm in deep shit."

"Why?" Oslo returned before a huge belch erupted out of him.

"I missed two damn classes this afternoon."

"So what?" Several smaller aftershock burps followed.

"I had an exam in one of them."

"Which one?"

"Western Civilization something or other."

"So what?"

"So what? If my fucking professor finds out I skipped he'll give me a fucking F, that's so what."

"You've got some nice language for a woman, Spike," Midshipman First Class Enrich said.

Hansen stood and hovered over her smaller classmate, "I'm sorry if I fucking offended you, Mr. Sensitive. And don't call me a woman, either."

"Yeah, Globe, don't call her a woman," Oslo added before tossing back what remained in his mug, one of the master chief's collection adorned with the crests of ships upon which he had served during his twenty-five-year career. "And don't even think about those big tits hanging in your face."

Hansen gave Oslo the finger and plopped back onto the tattered deck chair she'd occupied for most of the afternoon.

"Don't worry about your exam, Spike," Master Chief Fernandez said. "You missed it due to circumstances beyond your control."

"What circumstances?" Hansen asked.

"Your Naval Science lab went a little long."

"My damn poli-sci prof won't believe my sorry butt."

"I'll give him a call and explain the situation with my apologies," Fernandez said with a wink and a hoist of his mug.

"Yeah, baby," Oslo said, clicking his mug against Fernandez's. "The master chief has the power."

"And what good is power if you don't abuse it?" Fernandez said.

And the others joined in raising their mugs.

8

Ash parked the rental once again and walked up the long path toward the administration building. His uniform was sheathed in thin plastic and draped over his shoulder. He remained absorbed in his thoughts, so much so that he didn't notice the stares from the handful of coeds he passed going the other way. He only saw what was in his mind's eye. The scenes came to him at light speed, irrepressible.

That night in the Gulf he had put on a float coat and snatched his gear satchel from the floor at his feet. The others were already dressed, and the lieutenant queued up at the end of the line of SEALs as they pulled their rifles from the weapons rack along one of the tiny gear locker's steel bulkheads. In front of him Chief Lam, nearly a head shorter, turned and gave the lieutenant a wink and a broad smile.

The chief was a fireplug of a man, nearly as wide as he was tall, a physical trait he readily attributed to his grandfather, a black man who'd fought the Vietnam War as a U.S. Army rifleman. Lam was also quick to admit he'd never laid eyes on the man. His own parents had met as teenaged Vietnamese refugees aboard an evacuation flight bound for the United States. His grandmother didn't make it out and was never heard from again. These facts the chief would present with a historian's detachment rather than any sort of bitterness, which Ash figured was a function of the additional fact that Lam's parents had fared pretty well once they had gotten their feet planted on American soil.

Lam suddenly did a double take over his shoulder, "You're okay, right, Lieutenant?"

Ash looked down at himself and returned, "Why is everyone asking me if I'm okay tonight?"

The chief shrugged. "Just want to make sure, sir. You just looked like you were zoning out a little."

"I'm fine. I'll be even better once I get a little salt spray in the face."

"You'll be getting more than a *little* salt spray tonight."

The SEALs pushed their ways out of the gear locker and into one of the cruiser's myriad passageways. Sailors caught in the rush hit the bulkheads to either side, honoring the mere sight of the armed men garbed in black and in a hurry. Ash overheard one of the crew ask another, "They're not going out in this stuff, are they?"

Through the side hatch, the stiff breeze quickened Ash's pulse, the same feeling he used to get at the Academy while standing on the lacrosse field waiting for the first face-off. He quickly scanned to the horizon and back. The whitecaps were many, standing out against the darkness. He then joined the others in leaning across the lifelines and looking down at the waterline while he adjusted his headset mike to his lips and asked, "Are you ready for us, Biker?"

"Come on down, sir," the senior Swick replied, adding, "But be careful. We're banging around pretty good."

One by one each SEAL picked his way down the boarding ladder dangling over the side. It was a slower go than usual. Even with Thompson standing in the RHIB attempting to hold the ladder taut, each step down made itself a matter of concentration and timing. The waves repeatedly threw the RHIB against the cruiser's hull, each collision causing a racket like a giant banging a scale gong.

As Ash's feet hit the RHIB's gunwale, Hendricks

shouted for Thompson to release the bowline while he did the same to the stern line. Seconds later the RHIB was untethered. Hendricks slowly advanced the throttles; the throaty bellow of the twin diesels grew.

Ash braced himself against the center console and plucked the UHF handset from its mount. "Victor five hotel, this is Skunk alpha, how do you read?" There was no response, so Ash repeated his request: "Victor five hotel, this is Skunk alpha, how do you read, over?"

After a few seconds, Ash was about to tell Hendricks to pick up a circular course when a voice crackled over the speaker mounted near the helm: "Skunk alpha, Victor five hotel reads you loud and clear. How me?"

"Skunk alpha has you loud and clear," Ash said. "We're under way. Request initial steer."

"Roger. Initial steer: zero two four for twelve point three."

"Did he say twelve point three?" Chief Lam asked just before the first wall of seawater splashed over the bow and rained down on them.

"Yeah," Ash replied. "How's the datalink looking?"

Hendricks pushed a button on his console and said, "It looks like it's tight. They're showing the contact just over twelve miles away."

"Let's get going then."

"Roger that, sir. Here we go."

As Herd strapped himself to the minigun mount forward and the others found their positions for the bumpy ride, Hendricks turned northeast and began his search for the speed of approach they'd be afforded across the rough Gulf waters. He worked the throttles with a jerky cadence, powering up on the front of the waves and throttling back on the backside of them. Occasionally the motors' RPM would race as the screws came out of the water, rising pitch serving as a signal for the rest of the team to brace for the impact with the next wave.

"How's our speed?" Ash called over his shoulder after a few minutes of allowing the helmsman to get stabilized.

"Twenty knots," Hendricks shouted back.

Ash did some quick mental ciphering and said, "That'll have us there in forty minutes or so."

Forty minutes. It was going to be a long ride in the RHIB, the longest of the deployment so far. And it would be made across the roughest seas.

Others were contemplating the same facts. "At least it isn't raining," Thompson said from the lookout position on the bow, his toothy smile beaming through the seawater-filled darkness.

"You just jinxed us, you dipshit," Doc Chance cried out from behind Ash.

"Jinxed us?" Thompson returned. "You're a man of medicine, Doc. I didn't think you had any superstitions."

"I got plenty," Doc said.

With that the chatter ceased and each man withdrew to the place he went inside himself during the downtime that preceded the heart of a mission. They swayed in synch, at once with and against the violent motion of the boat, like fundamentalists at prayer. This was a collection of veterans: Experience had taught them when to peak and when to relax and how to endure.

For his part Ash let the arrhythmic pounding of the RHIB against the waves take him half a world away. His first thoughts were about the letter he'd just received from his father and those led to introspection about his family. While they'd always put on a good show of support, the Roberts clan had never really agreed with Ash's career choice. He was the oldest son, heir to the Roberts universe, and life as a military man was never in the offing. Even now Ash could vividly recall the look on his father's face when he told him he wasn't interested in going to Princeton and wanted to attend the Naval Academy instead. As his father had assimilated the news his expression hadn't been one of disappointment but rather of absolute confusion.

That's what the letter was all about, wasn't it? It wasn't a commentary about the state of the war but a stern petition for Ash to cease his youthful adventure—dalliance, even—and return to the Greenwich, Connecticut–based fold. The caste to which the Roberts clan belonged, along with the Withers, Trumborough, and Perchant branches of the family, didn't join the military, or at least they hadn't since the Vietnam era when the ugliness had made it passé. And even if 9-11 had allowed the idea to be revisited, it hadn't given a green light to making a *career* out of it.

Ash wondered if he'd ever be able to return home. He thought of when his younger brother Winston asked him if he'd ever killed anyone and his expression—muted but shocked nonetheless—when Ash answered that he had. The distance between them had grown since then, with Winston rising up the corporate ladder and Ash earning medals for actions he couldn't talk about.

"Surf, you never finished that story the other night," BM2 Corn shouted from Ash's right. "Did you ever nail that playmate or not?"

"What do you think?" Herd said over his shoulder, working to keep the harness taut against the small of his back.

"I think you got shut out."

"You'd like to think that, wouldn't you?"

"So did you?"

"Let's just put it this way, Swick boy: Hef and I have one thing in common, and it's not that we both like to wear pajamas during the daytime."

Another wave across the bow short-circuited the conversation. When the spray cleared Ash found himself in mind of a girl of his own. It had been nearly two weeks since Melinda's last e-mail, an uncharacteristically long time for him to go without hearing from her. Had she finally had enough?

Their romance had been a whirlwind, a year's worth of activity and emotion crammed into the only two months he'd had stateside since the Iraq War had kicked off. He was acting as the aide-de-camp to a Navy three-star attached to the Joint Chiefs of Staff. She was an intelligence analyst in the Pentagon, and not only was she a hard-bodied, attentive lover, but she had helped

him solve a mystery that threatened his life. But by the
time the authorities put the collar on the multinational
conglomerate responsible for, among other nefarious
dealings, murdering four of Ash's former special-
operations teammates, he was ready to get back into the
action for which he'd been trained.

But now as he thought about her he wondered if he
shouldn't have stayed on the admiral's staff a bit longer.
His father's letter, or rather his reaction to his father's
letter, was merely another symptom of something he'd
never wrestled with before. Missions had never been
questioned. Actions were automatic. There's a time
when every warrior realizes he's been at war too long—

Ash spat a short string of profanities, loud enough
that Chief Lam looked over and asked, "All right,
Lieutenant?"

"Yeah," Ash returned. "Just thinking about
something."

"Need to talk about it?"

"Nah, I'm good." Ash held his face up to the howling
wind and let the spray wash over him. He had to clear
his head and focus on the present, not to mention the
chief's comment was the second or third instance that
evening of someone questioning his state of mind.
Toughen up, dammit, he thought.

"What's the range, Biker?" Ash asked.

"Just over six miles," the helmsman replied.

"Bearing?"

"Still about zero two zero."

Ash plucked the handset from the bracket: "Victor
five hotel, this is Skunk alpha, confirm range and bearing
to the contact." No reply from the cruiser. "Victor five,
Skunk alpha, how do you read?"

"Skunk alpha, this is Slayer six zero two, how do you
read?" a female voice asked over the net.

An H-60 helicopter? "Slayer, Skunk alpha has you
loud and clear. Understand you're airborne?"

"That's affirmative," the pilot said. "We've been refragged with comm relay and whatever other support you might need."

Support, huh? A ride to the tanker might have been nice about now, although the helicopter was probably an F model, an antisubmarine warfare bird chock full of gear. All the SEAL-friendly H models had been flown to Kuwait. Maritime interdiction missions took a back-seat to land warfare. All the same, it was nice to have air support, however limited it might be.

"Are you armed?" Ash asked.

"That's affirmative. Two Penguins."

"Any guns?"

"Negative."

So much for close air support. The Penguins were probably overkill for tonight's mission, unless someone in the chain of command decided to sink the tanker. Ash was more concerned about dealing with the crew itself.

"Do you have dolly?" he asked.

"Roger," the pilot replied. "Dolly sweet. Showing contact zero two three for five point niner miles."

"Copy. How's your FLIR working?"

"It's up."

"Let us know when you see the contact, please."

"Roger. How's the ride down there tonight?"

"Just another pleasure cruise."

Ash returned the handset to the bracket and stood up, bracing himself against the center console. "Thompson, do you see anything yet?"

"Negative, Lieutenant," the junior of the two Swicks replied.

"She's going to be tough to see because I'm sure she doesn't have any running lights lit."

Ash put his own night-vision goggles to his eyes and scanned across the horizon, which was a trick consider-ing how the RHIB was pitching. "Range now?" he asked.

"Just under four," Hendricks replied.

Still nothing. They should have been able to see some-thing by now.

"Slayer, do you see the contact with the FLIR yet?" Ash asked.

"Negative."

They were getting too close not to have sight of the tanker. Ash waved an arm toward the helmsman and said, "Throttle back for a second."

The motors went from a roar to an idling purr, and the occupants braced against the sudden deceleration. Sitting dead in the water now, the RHIB continued to move with the seas but much less violently than it had while traveling at twenty knots.

"Everyone get goggles on the horizon," Ash commanded. "Let's find this bitch before we accidentally ram her."

The rest of the team, including Hendricks, did as Ash ordered. "Tanker ho!" Doc Chance cried.

"Where?" Ash asked.

"Just off the starboard bow."

"Yeah, I've got it," Corn said.

"Me too," Smith added.

Ash twisted his neck back and forth but still saw nothing. "Where the hell is it?" he asked, frustration evident.

Chief Lam extended an arm and said, "There."

Ash followed the extended line of the chief's arm and then broadened his scan around that general direction. "Got it," he said with a heave of his chest. "She's a big one, I think."

"I concur," the chief said.

Ash picked up the handset: "Slayer, do you have FLIR on the contact yet?"

"We just got it," the pilot replied. "Tanker, estimate four hundred feet in length. We're beaming the images back to the carrier for ID and further analysis. Stand by."

"Copy. Can you raise the tanker on the fleet common frequency?"

"Negative, Skunk alpha. We've been trying both UHF and VHF, but no joy."

"All right," Ash returned. "Please relay to Victor five hotel that we're closing to contact range."

"Victor five hotel copies," replied another voice, presumably that of the TAO on duty in the cruiser's Combat Decision Center.

"Victor five, understand you can hear Skunk alpha?" Ash asked.

"Off and on," the TAO replied.

Ash waved toward Hendricks and then shouted toward the SEAL manning the minigun: "Let's go. Surf, get ready to rock."

"I was born to rock," Herd shot back, following the line with a toss of his head and a loud cackle.

Ash's perception had the tanker going from distant silhouette to looming mass in short order. As if on cue, Hendricks reached into a compartment at the base of the steering console and produced a bullhorn, which he handed to Ash. Ash put both elbows against the center console and steadied the bullhorn in front of his face. He keyed the mike, sending a loud series of electronic beeps toward the tanker's superstructure, and then flipped a switch near the handle and spoke through the mouthpiece: "Unidentified vessel, this is a component of Task Group Fifty-Five, the Maritime Interception Force of the United States Navy. Your movements are questionable. By the authority of international law, I order you to stop."

Ash waited to see if the ship was responding to his command, focusing on the disturbed water that flowed under the stern. After thirty seconds or so it was obvious the tanker wasn't going to stop. Ash raised the bullhorn again and repeated his line: "Unidentified vessel, this is a component of Task Group Fifty-Five, the Maritime Interception Force of the United States Navy. Your movements are questionable. By the authority of international law, I order you to stop."

Again he waited and again the tanker didn't stop. "Maybe they can't hear us," Thompson offered from the bow.

"They can hear us," Chief Lam said. "They're ignoring us."

"Drop back, Biker," Ash said. "Let's put the spotlight on the stern and see if we can get the name of this thing."

The helmsman did as the lieutenant asked while BM2 Corn readied the spotlight. When the RHIB was far enough aft, Corn brought the light on and did his best to shine it against the back of the tanker.

"Polska Marholvski," Thompson read aloud.

Ash picked up the handset: "Slayer, relay to Victor five the contact is the *Polska Marholvski.* I'd guess that was Polish, but there's no country or city of origin labeled on the stern."

"Slayer copies," the pilot returned.

"Victor five copies," the TAO added.

"We attempted to hail the contact with the bullhorn, but got no response," Ash said. "We're moving forward to fire warning shots across the bow."

"Stand by, Skunk alpha," the TAO said. "Let me get approval for that."

"We have standing approval," Ash said, doing his best to suppress his growing frustration.

"Let me talk to the captain anyway," the TAO said.

Ash directed Hendricks to speed out ahead of the tanker as they waited for the TAO to come back with the captain's ruling. The team had done forty-three boardings in the last two months, and it seemed to Ash that the procedures had changed for each one of them. He chuckled instead of losing his temper. How the surface warfare officers liked to regiment everything—like the Army with boats. He'd kidnapped foreign officials with a shorter vetting chain.

"Warning shots are approved," the TAO reported. "Keep us apprised."

"Skunk alpha copies," Ash said before shouting toward the bow: "You heard him, Surf. Light it up across the bow."

"Roger," Herd replied. He yanked the cocking mechanism swiftly back and used his thumbs to mash the fifty-caliber minigun's twin triggers. The rapid thumping of the minigun shook the sailors' chests, and the incendiary tracer rounds whizzed several hundred yards in front of the tanker's bow, snuffing out as they hit the water some quarter mile away. The tanker didn't stop after the first burst so Herd fired another and then another.

With the end of the third string of bullets, Ash noted the churning cease behind the *Polska Marholvski*'s rudder. "Look's like she's stopping," Ash reported into the UHF handset.

"Roger," the TAO replied. "Understand you're boarding now?"

"Give us a sec, here," Ash returned.

Hendricks maneuvered the RHIB abeam the tanker's port quarter while Corn and Smith readied the grappling hooks and Herd trained the minigun toward the superstructure that towered a dozen stories above them.

"Hooks away," Ash commanded.

The two SEALs stationed fore and aft balanced themselves against the motion of the RHIB and swung the grappling hooks in ever-faster circles before letting fly toward the tanker's port rail. Corn's seated immediately, but when Smith tugged on his rope it went slack and the hook hurtled back toward them, hitting the water perilously close to the RHIB's hull.

"Watch that," Chief Lam spat.

"I've got it, Chief," Smith replied, fishing the hook from the rough seas. In short order he had the hook traveling in a speedy arc around his closed fist and quickly thereafter he tossed it skyward. Ash watched it fly into the night—a lifetime, it seemed—and waited with a grimace as the petty officer gave the rope another tug. This time it held.

Ash moved the boom mike from his headset over his lips and said, "Intercom check. Sweep one alpha's up."

"Sweep one bravo's up," Herd said.

"Sweep two alpha's up," Corn said.

"Sweep two bravo's up," Smith said.

"Security alpha's up," Chief Lam said.

"Security bravo's up," Chance said.

"Boarding the contact at this time, Victor five," Ash said into the handset.

"Roger, Skunk alpha," the TAO replied. "Slayer, request you remain overhead."

"Slayer's overhead," the pilot said.

Ash slinked to the starboard side of the RHIB, around the minigun and toward the bow, and took the rope from Smith. "Cover me, boys," the lieutenant said before giving it one last tug and beginning his hand-over-hand climb up the rope dangling across the tanker's acres of freeboard.

The world was a steadier place out of the small RHIB, which made for a smoother trip up the rope. Ash grasped the railing along the edge of the tanker's deck and pulled his body up. He hooked his right heel over the top of the railing and started to roll across it but stopped himself. The low light from the superstructure caused just enough of a glint to cue the lieutenant that there was something unusual below. But he couldn't hang on the rail and analyze the situation forever; Surf was dangling on the rope a few feet below, waiting for his chance to climb aboard.

"Stand by," Ash said into his headset. "There's grease spread across the deck."

"I guess they knew we coming after all," Surf puffed between breaths.

Ash eased himself onto the deck and gingerly made his way across the shallow pond of grease, crouching as he walked to lower his center of gravity. Behind him Surf scrambled over the rail and stepped across the deck, nearly losing his footing a couple of times before joining Ash past the obstacle.

"Sweep one's headed for the bridge," Ash said.

"Two copies," Chief Lam said with a grunt, obviously working his own way up the rope. "How much grease is there?"

"Not too much. Be careful with your first steps."

Ash pulled his M4 rifle from across his back and led Herd to the ladder up the port side of the superstructure. As they reached the first landing, a bald-headed man stepped from around the corner. The SEALs raised their weapons, and Ash firmly intoned, "Halt."

The man threw up his hands and cried, *"Nie strzela! Nie strzela!"*

Ash flashed a palm and, speaking slowly, asked, "Do you speak English?"

With his hands still raised, the man vigorously shook his head and said, *"Nie mowi angielski."*

Ash pointed toward the bridge and asked, in his best faux-Polish, "Cap-e-tan?"

The man nodded and said, *"Tak, tak. Kapitan jest tam."*

Ash smiled as he patted the man on the shoulder and then quickly spun him around, planting the Pole's face into the superstructure's steel bulkhead. Herd held the man's wrists behind his back while Ash retrieved a plastic zip tie from one of his jumpsuit pockets. In one fluid motion the Pole's wrists were bound.

"One copies," Ash replied. "We've tied up one crew member already and are now going to the bridge. Security team, are you aboard?"

"On the rope," Chief Lam transmitted.

With their new captive leading the way, Ash and Herd continued their ascent, taking in every detail as they climbed the corrugated steel stairs, ready for the next chance meeting with a crew member. No hostile moves from the first guy, but that didn't mean they could assume the entire crew was going to roll over for them. *Remember the ROE,* Ash continued to repeat in his brain.

A handful of steps past the top of the ladder, Ash moved the crewman aside and sneaked a glance through the small porthole that looked in on the bridge. He spotted two people, neither of whose body language suggested he was ready to mount a defense.

Using the first crewman as a shield, the two SEALs

were through the door in a flash, weapons trained on the two merchant seamen inside. As their crewmate had several minutes before, both of them raised their hands without any prompting. The site of the big Americans garbed in black tended to elicit that response.

"Cap-e-tan?" Ash asked the one who was older-looking by virtue of leathery skin and a bushy gray beard.

The bearded man's face momentarily contorted in confusion before his expression brightened with understanding. *"Tak, tak,"* he said, pointing at himself. "I *kapitan.*"

"You speak English?" Ash asked.

"Tak. All *kapitans* speak English. Language of the sea, you know."

Chief Lam's voice crackled through the headset: "Security team is aboard, headed for berthing."

"Sweep one copies," Ash said. He motioned for both of the crew on the bridge to keep their hands in the air before patting down the captain while Herd did the same to the other man. "What is your name, Captain?"

The captain stood a bit more erect and proudly replied, "I am Captain Miloslovak."

"Captain Miloslovak, I am Lieutenant Roberts from the United States Navy. My team has boarded your ship because your movements are suspicious and you refused to answer the radio calls asking you to identify yourself."

"Is not true," Miloslovak replied, pointing toward a radio mounted above his head. "No one has called us for days."

Ash was unmoved. Convinced the captain was unarmed, he scanned the console in front of the helm and pointed at a digital chart displayed there.

"Why are you out of the shipping lanes?"

The captain offered another quizzical look and replied, "No, not out of shipping lanes. Inner channel here."

"No," Ash returned, "no inner channel here." He

searched for a depth finder, asking, "How deep is it here?"

The captain shrugged and said, "Good deep here."

"No, you run aground here. What is your destination?"

"Kuwait City."

Ash furrowed his brow and said, "You're pretty far north to be headed for Kuwait City. What is your cargo?"

"No cargo. Picking up in Kuwait City."

"You're riding pretty low in the water for a ship without cargo, Captain."

"No cargo."

"Why did you put grease on the deck?"

"We must defend ourselves. Many pirates in these waters."

"I've heard nothing of pirates in the Gulf."

"*Tak,* they are here."

Ash and Herd cut quick glances toward one another before Ash refocused on the captain and said, "May I see the vessel's registry papers?"

"*Tak,*" the Polish captain returned. "I get them."

Ash kept a close eye on the man as he walked over to a table on the far end of the bridge and rooted through a stack of papers. A few seconds later, the captain returned wearing a placid smile and handed a folder over to the SEAL.

"You see, everything is okay," the captain said. "Everything is fine."

Ash extended his free arm and said, "Captain, I need you to stand a few feet back, please." He cut his eyes toward Herd and murmured, "Let's get zip ties on these two."

In spite of the Polish captain's objections in his native tongue, Herd carried out the order as Ash scanned the documents in the folder. He noted that the registry was current, although an up-to-date Polish registry didn't mean much from his point of view. The lieutenant knew firsthand that many Polish companies had wantonly violated U.N. sanctions before the Iraq War, activity that had hazarded his life and those of his men in the early days of the conflict.

Ash adjusted the boom mike at his lips and said, "Corndog, how's it going down there?"

"The plant could use some work," Corn replied. "It's a mess, but other than that everything looks on the up-and-up."

"How many crew members are down there?"

"Three."

"Round them up and bring them to the bridge."

"Roger."

Ash looked back toward the captain. "We need to take a look in your cargo holds."

The Pole's eyes widened enough that Ash took notice, and then the captain said, "I tell you already we are empty."

"Yes, I know, sir, but we would like to take a look, all the same."

"Is impossible," Miloslovak spat. "You have caused much delay already. We must be in Kuwait in a few hours and cannot be late."

"You won't be late, Captain, as long as you cooperate."

"You insult me with plastic ropes. This is no way treating a captain."

"It is merely procedure, Captain. I mean no disrespect. Again, if you cooperate, we will be on our way very quickly."

Petty Officers Smith and Corn came through the hatch with three grimy crewmen in tow, each bound at the wrist.

"Where are you, Chief?" Ash asked.

"We're just coming out of berthing," Chief Lam replied.

"How many guys?"

"Three."

"Understand the rest of the ship is secure?"

"Affirmative."

The UHF circuit came alive for the first time since the SEALs had boarded the vessel. "Skunk alpha, this is Slayer six zero two, how do you read?"

"Read you loud and clear, Slayer," Ash replied. "How me?"

"Same," the pilot said. "We hadn't heard from you in a while. Victor five wants to know how it's going."

"Initial sweep is complete. We're in the process of consolidating the eight-man crew on the bridge now."

"Roger, we'll relay."

Chief Lam appeared in the side hatch behind three other Polish crewmen. Doc Chance took up the rear.

"All right," Ash announced. "Looks like the gang's all here. Security team, keep an eye on the crew. Sweeps one and two, we're going to take a look in the cargo holds."

As all started to move, Miloslovak stamped his feet and shouted, "No, no."

Ash flashed his palm at the man. "Calm down, Captain."

"I tell you my ship is empty already. You must go now. We will be late."

"We're inspecting the cargo holds, sir, and then we'll be on our way."

"No, no!"

Although the other Poles seemed concerned, none of them was as agitated as his captain. "Bind his ankles, Chief," Ash commanded, pointed toward the captain's legs. "While you're at it, bind all of their ankles. Sit them along the forward bulkhead."

Ash headed off the bridge followed by Herd, Smith, and Corn. The four hurried back down the stairwell along the side of the superstructure and stepped onto the main deck, careful to avoid the grease pool that continued to spread.

"We'll take the first hold," Ash said, "Corndog, you and Smitty take the one forward of this one."

"Got it, L.T.," Corn returned.

"Take your time. We're in no hurry."

"But the captain needs to get to Kuwait City," Smith said with a smile.

"Be careful," Ash repeated.

Herd found the mechanism to roll away the huge iron door that covered the first cargo bay, and he asked, "What's 'open' in Polish?"

"How many buttons you got over there?" Ash asked back.

"Two."

"Try them both."

A second later a horn sounded. The big door protested with a metallic groan and then reluctantly yawned open as if it was in bad need of servicing. Ash shined his flashlight into the bay. It was empty save one small wooden crate in the far bottom corner.

"What do you think that is?" Herd asked.

"Beats me," Ash replied. "Let's go check it out."

Ash was about to step onto the ladder along the side of the cargo bay when Corn called to him: "Lieutenant, this cargo hatch is welded shut."

"You got the torch with you?" Ash shouted back.

"Yes, sir."

"Open it then."

"Roger that."

Ash continued down the ladder, followed by Herd, while the flicker of the arc-welding torch flickered across the night above them. As they descended they were greeted by a stench increasingly foul with each rung.

"What the hell do you think is in that?" Herd asked.

Ash didn't answer the question but instead directed his flashlight toward the near side of the crate and said, "You take this side, I'll take the other. Hurry up."

The two SEALs took to the wooden slats with their Bowie knives. The putrid stink seemed to intensify with each piece they peeled away. Ash gagged a few times but continued to work. Finally they'd dismantled the box enough that they were able to kick away one side. The contents oozed across the rusty bottom of the bay under their boots.

"What the hell is it?" Herd asked.

"I don't know—"

It was animal, or it had been at one time. Large chunks of flesh, fur, and bone had rotted beyond the point of recognition. Ash took a step away and lost his valiant fight against his turned stomach. But as he heaved a second time, he felt something more than simple nausea. He was disoriented. He dropped to one knee against the bay's steel floor.

"You okay, L.T.?" Herd asked.

"Yeah, I'll be fine," Ash replied. But he wasn't sure that was true. He suddenly felt very fatigued. His body ached all over. He took a few deep breaths and slowly rose to his feet.

"What do you think happened to that thing?"

"Who knows?" Ash said, wiping the corners of his mouth with the back of his jumpsuit sleeve. "Maybe it was a meal they forgot about."

"Or a recreational companion," Herd offered with a leer.

A horn sounded above their heads, signaling that Sweep two had managed to open the forward cargo bay. Ash and Herd picked up their flashlights, and Ash struggled to keep up with the junior man as he scurried back up the ladder. Ash still felt extremely light-headed and at one point had to stop his climb until the stars cleared. He'd paired vomiting and physical activity before, but the combination had never had this sort of effect on him.

The helicopter pilot's voice came over the UHF circuit: "Skunk alpha, Slayer six zero two, anything to report?"

Ash wanted to tell her to shut the hell up. He now felt his nerves starting to fray, which alarmed him as much as anything else. It was too early in the mission for irrationality, as if there was ever a good time for it. He took another deep breath and replied, "The aft cargo bay contained the remains of an animal. We're guessing it was a goat. We're just now looking into the forward bay."

"Did you say a goat?" the cruiser's TAO asked.

"Affirmative."

"And it was dead?"

"Very."

"Victor five hotel copies. Keep us posted."

By the time Sweep one reached the top of the aft bay, Corn and Smith were leaning over the edge of the forward bay, flashlights in hand.

"What do you got?" Ash asked as he approached.

"Boxes of something," Corn said.

"Does it stink in there?"

Corn stuck his head inside the opening and said, "No, not really. Why?"

"Ours stunk so bad the lieutenant puked," Herd offered across Ash's shoulder.

"You puked, L. T.?" Smith returned. "Damn, that's fucked up. What was down there?"

"A dead goat."

"That's truly fucked up." Smith looked over at his sweepmate and counseled, "Make sure it really doesn't stink down there, Corndog."

Corn didn't reply, having already disappeared into the tanker's forward belly. He stood on the first stack of boxes and shouted back up to the other three SEALs peering over the cargo bay's edge, "Come on down and bring your pickaxes. These boxes are sealed tight."

"We don't have any pickaxes," Smith returned.

"Bring your knives then."

Ash led Herd and Smith down the ladder to where Corn stood. By the time they reached him, Corn had managed to cut several of the thick packing straps from around the plywood box and started to lift one of the corners. Ash joined in and together they peeled the top off and threw it to the deck several dozen feet below. Meanwhile, Herd and Smith hopped over and began to work on the adjacent identical plywood box.

Inside the box were smaller cardboard cartons sealed with tape, which the SEALs' knives made short work of. Ash ripped back the lid of the first smaller box and found it was packed tight with plastic cases. He inspected one of them at close range. It was a DVD, but the cheap packaging indicated that those who had rights to the title hadn't manufactured it.

"This one's full of movies," Herd called from the adjacent box. "And brand-new ones at that."

"This is the cargo?" Ash asked rhetorically. He didn't know if it was the nausea or his fatigue in general or what, but as he dug through the box, he suddenly felt himself growing angrier with each additional DVD. He heard the voice in his head saying *Stay cool,* but his body wasn't listening. Adrenaline coursed through his veins. His heart pounded in his eardrums as his mind raced with other thoughts—his father's letter, Captain Napoli's voice over the phone, the rough ride across the stormy Gulf. By the time he reached the bottom of the first cardboard box, he couldn't contain his rage. He let out a yell as he grabbed two discs and sent them flying across the cargo bay like errant Frisbees. With a loud crash against the steel wall they broke into pieces.

"What the hell, L.T.?" Herd asked, ducking away from the debris.

"This is it, huh?" Ash said, nearly shouting now. "This is why we busted our asses? To protect the peace-loving people of Iraq from pirated DVDs?"

"It's just a thing, Lieutenant," Smith said. "Let's stay cool here."

Without another word, Ash scrambled back up the ladder, unaware and uncaring that the others followed him closely. In short order he was across the deck, up the stairwell, and back on the bridge where he went right for the Polish captain. He balled his fists into the bearded man's flannel shirt, pulling him to his feet from among the rest of his crew compliantly seated along the bulkhead.

"What else are you carrying?" Ash asked, drawing his face close to Miloslovak's as he shook him.

"Whoa, Lieutenant," Chief Lam said from across the bridge. "Easy there."

"I want some answers *now*," Ash said in return, now turned toward the chief while maintaining his grip on the Pole. "You're telling me that this ship is running dangerously close to the shore in order to protect a load of bootlegged DVDs?"

"I don't know, but . . . take it easy, L.T."

"Sure, I'll take it easy."

Ash turned to reface the Polish captain but not in time to notice that Miloslovak had drawn his head back, and before he could react, the Pole slammed his forehead square against the bridge of Ash's nose. Ash saw a flash of light in his eyes and then felt a shot of pain through his face as he staggered backward.

The space was immediately enveloped in chaos. At once the crew leapt to their feet and rushed the SEALs. Ash tried to keep his vision clear. He fought to stay on his feet but stumbled to the deck. He tasted blood and felt it warm and wet against his face as it pooled under his cheek. He tried to get to his feet; his head was spinning. He heard fighting all around him, the thud of punches and bodies slamming against bulkheads.

With bleary eyes Ash saw a figure—the captain, he thought—hop to the control panel and throw his body across the throttles. The ship started to move. A shot rang out and a body fell across Ash's feet. It was one of the Polish crewmen, a big guy garbed in yellow foul-weather gear who had somehow managed to free his hands and feet from the zip ties.

The melee ended as quickly as it had started. "Get against the wall, all of you!" Chief Lam said. "Surf, pick the lieutenant off the floor."

Ash felt the petty officer take him by the arm, and as he was getting to his feet, both of them were thrown forward, along with everyone else and all the loose gear on the bridge.

"The ship's aground," Ash slurred, still fighting to clear his head. "Reverse the engines."

Smith carried out the order, pulling the throttles to their aft limits. The ship shuddered, fighting the churning from the screws around the aft hull, but ultimately did not budge.

"We're hard against the bottom," Chief Lam said.

Ash let out a long breath and leaned against the console. The helicopter pilot's voice returned to the UHF circuit: "Skunk alpha, Victor five hotel is looking for an update. How's it going down there?"

Now Ash opened the door to the Thaedt University administration building with a shake of his head and a sardonic chuckle. It hadn't gone well.

9

Three days before Ash first entered the Thaedt University administration building, Bobby Redmond sat up on the bed in his room, feeling warm and content, like a baby wrapped in a downy-soft blanket. As long as he was there, no harm would come to him. He knew this because Devon Hite had told him so, and everything Devon said was true. Devon predicted the wind and the rain. Devon knew how the animals moved across the grassy plains. And most of all, Devon would protect him from the men who wanted to steal his freedom.

They were out there, these men. They populated the so-called government and had an insatiable appetite for power and control. Left to their own devices these men would see to it that the average citizen wouldn't be able to so much as brush his teeth without filling out some form in a big building downtown somewhere. These men wanted the land, the water, and the sky. They wanted the dwellings and the wives and the children and the livestock. They wanted everything.

There was a fumbling at the door, the sound of keys clinking, and then a rush of light. Redmond had learned to love the rush of light. It meant that something good was coming, and in this case it was better than good; it was Devon himself.

Bobby dropped to his knees and said, "Thank you for coming to see me."

"My pleasure, Bobby," Hite replied. "Please get up.

Our doctor tells me you're progressing nicely. In fact, I have a surprise for you. Would you like to hear what it is?"

"Yes, I would."

"He thinks you're ready to meet the others."

Redmond's eyes twitched and one corner of his mouth tugged downward. "I don't know . . ."

"You know I'd never make you do anything you don't want to do. But I would like you to get to know the others. After all, they are my family. I'd like for you to think of them as yours, as well."

"But . . ."

"What is it, Bobby?"

"What about the government?"

Only then did Redmond notice the rifle in Hite's hand. "I won't let them get you, Bobby. As long as you're with us I won't let them get you."

"I want to stay with you forever, Devon."

Hite smiled and took Redmond by the forearm. "Come now. It's time to meet the others."

10

Just after lunchtime on the day that Lieutenant Ash Roberts arrived in Fairly, Hank Howard studied the ground nine thousand feet below the Cessna 182 he was piloting. The badlands of South Dakota didn't look that bad from the air, he thought. No thick forests; no steep mountains. Just miles and miles of tans and browns punctuated by the occasional black.

He could see for miles and miles because it was a beautiful day crowned by the most cerulean of skies. Flying was always a pleasure to Howard, but it was even more so when the weather cooperated, and today it was cooperating in spades. There was even a bit of a tailwind pushing the plane, and there was *never* a tailwind for a pilot heading west around these parts. Life away from the office was good.

At the same time he wondered what he might find once he got to his destination. Although he had no reason, evidence-wise, to believe something was wrong, he had long since learned to trust his instincts. Sometimes instinct was all a lawman had.

"November six two alpha, contact Fairly tower on frequency one two five point two," the approach controller transmitted.

"Six two alpha is switching Fairly tower," Howard replied. He twisted a knob on his VHF radio and said, "Fairly tower, November six two alpha is checking in," into his headset microphone.

"Roger, November six two alpha," the tower controller replied in a soothing baritone. "Report the runway in sight."

Howard scanned the expanse in front of the spinning propeller. There it was, almost indistinct. It was an asphalt strip, wasn't it? No telling in this part of the country. Could be made of cow dung for all he knew. He quickly flipped open the airport reference pub to the FAIRLY REGIONAL listing. Yep, it was asphalt, all right. It sure didn't look like it from five miles and two thousand feet.

"Tower, six two alpha has the field in sight."

"Roger, November six two alpha. You are cleared to land on Runway two four."

"Copy Runway two four."

About a minute later Howard crossed the runway threshold at just over one hundred feet. He focused on the far end of the tarmac as he pulled the power to idle, timing his flare perfectly. The main wheels kissed the runway simultaneously just before the nose gear touched. A textbook landing. Howard was happy to see that his skills hadn't eroded over the weeks that he'd been chained to his desk.

"Do you know where you're going, November six two alpha?" the controller asked.

"Sinclair Aviation," Howard said, spotting the company's large sign as he spoke. "I think I see it."

"Roger, that's it straight ahead. Are you meeting anybody?"

Not exactly the sort of question an air traffic controller had ever asked him before. "I'm supposed to meet Sheriff Bellows," Howard said.

"Bellows?" the controller said with a laugh. "You mean Bolo?"

"Bolo? I guess that could be it."

Howard heard the controller say something away from the mike and then heard others laughing in the background. "Sheriff Bolo will be right over there," the controller transmitted. "In the meantime, go ahead and park anywhere you like."

Howard stopped a polite distance abeam the only other plane on the flight line, a crop duster so beat up it didn't look flyable, and shut the Cessna down. By the time he finished his postflight checks and started to climb out, a squad car had pulled up, followed directly by a fuel truck that appeared to be of the same vintage as the crop duster.

Howard climbed out of the plane and reached behind the pilot's seat, grabbing his charcoal-colored suit coat and slipping it on. Then he threw the wheel chocks around the left tire. He kicked the chocks snug and looked across the fuselage, spotting two men approaching, one tall and trim, the other short and extremely fat.

The tall one hailed him from a dozen yards away: "Chief Howard?"

"Yes?" Howard returned, readjusting his tie snug against his neck.

The man was silent until he reached the horizontal stabilizer, and then he said, "I'm Sheriff Bolo." He gestured toward the big man who was having trouble keeping up with the sheriff's quick pace. "This is Mr. Nesby, the airport manager."

"You spending . . . the night?" Nesby asked, out of breath. He was close enough now that Howard could see his face was beet-red, his shirt drenched with sweat in spite of the moderate temperature and slight breeze.

"I'm not sure," Howard replied, looking at Bolo. "What do you think?"

"You might as well plan on it, Chief," Bolo said.

"Please, it's Hank."

"Dominic." They shook.

"You want me to fill 'er up?" Nesby asked, tugging a thumb over his shoulder toward the battered fuel truck.

"Sure," Howard said. He pulled a hanging bag from behind the copilot's seat, suddenly gripped by the urge for a cigarette. After locking the Cessna he turned to

Bolo and asked, "Is there anywhere I can catch a quick smoke?"

Bolo seemed a bit thrown off by the question and stood with his brow knit until Nesby puffed, "There's a smoking lounge in Sinclair's building over there."

"Okay, great," Howard said. "Is it labeled?"

"Yeah: MEN'S."

Howard chuckled and noted Bolo's expression, judgmental, obviously not a smoker, as the sheriff said, "I'll meet you around front."

Howard ignored the man's judgment and started for the Sinclair building. He wasn't new to such attitudes. No smoker in the twenty-first century was.

Inside he stood over the sink and took a handful of long draws on his Marlboro. Obviously Sinclair Aviation was saving money by skimping on janitorial services. The bathroom stunk of misdirected urine. He studied his reflection in the mirror and came to the conclusion that he looked a bit tired, perhaps, but not pathetic. Then he wondered if his visit to Fairly would be plagued by too few opportunities to have a smoke.

Howard found Bolo waiting for him in the squad car at the head of the walkway in front of the building. He threw his bag in the backseat and climbed in front next to the sheriff. They rode wordlessly for a time. Finally, Howard could stand the silence no longer.

"Pretty country out here," he said.

"Yep," Bolo said.

"You lived here long?"

"My whole life, pretty much. Except for the nine years I spent in the Army."

"Army, huh? I was in the Army. Infantry. How about you?"

"I was a Green Beret." Of course. Bolo had the look of a special-operations guy: skin weathered and tan, hair cropped short, jaw square, and eyes lifeless—a killer's eyes. More than just athletically built, he had a rough-hewn aura of ruggedness.

"I wanted to be a paratrooper," Howard said, happy

to keep the conversation going. "I tried to get into the Airborne, but I broke my ankle when I was at Fort Benning."

Bolo abruptly changed the subject: "We were a little surprised by your call."

"We're happy you're willing to assist us with this."

"I'm not clear on what the situation is."

"That makes two of us."

Bolo momentarily looked away from the road, focusing on the left side of Howard's head as he said, "Seriously, Hank. What's the deal here? ATF agents don't just fly in from St. Paul on a whim, certainly not chief ATF agents. But you're in my jurisdiction now. You need my help. I think I have a right to know why you're here."

A female voice came over the radio: "Dom, you out there?"

Bolo plucked the handset from its mount on the dash and replied, "I'm here, Angie."

"Where are you right now?"

"Northbound on Airport Road, just about to the highway."

"We got a disturbance over in the Rushmore Arms apartments."

"You know I've got Chief Howard with me," Bolo asked. "We have some other business to attend to."

"Everyone else is over working the rodeo."

"All right," he said with muted but evident frustration. "I'm on it."

"Apartment six."

Bolo turned toward his passenger and said, "I'm sorry about this. We're just a small-town operation and all it takes is for two things to happen at once for us to get bogged down. This shouldn't take very long."

"No problem. It's been awhile since I've dealt with a wife-beater."

"I doubt this is that. Rushmore Arms is occupied by two types of tenants: college students and old people."

Bolo checked his watch. "Usually we get calls like this late at night. Maybe somebody got an early start today."

Howard noted a sign that read FAIRLY CITY LIMITS and wondered how a person would know otherwise. Besides a few scattered farms dotted by groups of run-down homes accompanied by the obligatory rusty cars on blocks in their driveways there wasn't much to indicate an actual city to the casual passerby.

"Not much to it, huh?" Howard said, thinking aloud somewhat.

"To what?" Bolo returned.

Howard snapped out of his semi-reverie. "Oh, I just mean that this place is a lot different than St. Paul."

"I'm not sure the folks around here would view that as a bad thing."

"I don't view it as a bad thing, either," Howard said defensively. "I'm just saying it's different."

A mile down the road, Bolo turned the squad car left onto, predictably enough, Main Street. A few blocks later they were at the town center, a throwback to the good old days—clean, organized, and nothing but white people as far as the eye could see. Bolo coasted along at the snail's-pace speed limit of ten miles per hour, waving to everyone as they passed.

Bolo spotted something across his left shoulder and pulled the car to a halt against the curb. Howard looked across the driver and saw what had attracted his attention. A man with spaghetti-straight black hair that flowed past his shoulders sat slumped in one of the benches in the small park—three trees and a strip of grass—in the middle of the square.

"Billy," Bolo said in a calm but firm voice. "Billy, are you asleep?"

The man stirred, and as his hair fell away from his face, Howard could see from his long, broad nose, flat cheeks, and brick complexion that he was an Indian. His eyes were blinking slits; his head lolled, threatening to topple his body.

"You remember what I said about sleeping in the park, right, Billy?" Bolo said.

The Indian stammered something unintelligible.

"I need you to go home now, Billy, okay?"

More stammering, a bit louder than before.

"Should I call the chief, Billy? Do you want Chief Eaglefeather to come get you?"

The Indian shook his head and bolted off the bench. He walked away with surprising steadiness. "He'll be fine," Bolo said to himself as he watched the man disappear behind the corner of the hardware store on the far side of the square.

"Town drunk, huh?" Howard said.

Bolo cut his eyes toward his passenger and said, "We tend to avoid labels around Fairly, Chief Howard. Let's just say Billy has had a tough life."

"Sure, sure," Howard returned. "I meant no offense."

Bolo took the next left. Three traffic lights later the surroundings changed significantly. Lines of majestic oaks on either side of the street replaced the dust and dried grass. Clapboard houses gave way to brick two-stories with manicured lawns and even a Tudor demi-mansion or two.

"Whoa, this looks like a different city," Howard said.

"In some ways it is, I guess," Bolo said. "This is Fairly's college district."

"Really? What college?"

"Thaedt University."

"Oh, that's right. I almost forgot you guys had a university here."

"You're not alone there. It seems like everyone forgets that we have a university here." Bolo pointed across the steering wheel toward a crowd a few hundred yards away. "I guess this must be our disturbance."

Bolo whooped the siren a couple of times just before he parked the squad car in front of one of the apartment complexes across from the university's main entrance. "You got a gun?" he asked Howard.

"Yeah, I got a nine-mil holstered under my left armpit," the ATF man returned. "Am I going to need it here?"

"No, I don't think so. I was just wondering."

The sheriff and regional ATF chief approached the ring of a dozen or more people unnoticed, even after using the siren. Bolo calmly but forcefully excused his way to the center of the crowd where he found a rotund man with greased-back hair on the wrong end of a double-barreled shotgun held by a skinny old woman wearing curlers in her wispy silver hair.

"Sheriff, thank God you're here," the old lady said as she spotted him. She shoved the shotgun into the man's big gut, making him flinch. "Take them to jail."

"I'm not doing anything until you put the gun down, Ida," Bolo said.

"I'll do no such thing. This group of drunks been at it all afternoon. They're so loud I can't even hear my soaps in my own house."

"We were just enjoying ourselves a little bit, Sheriff," the man explained, hands in the air. "You know, just getting part of the unit together to blow off a little steam." He pointed back at the woman. "This old bat is damn crazy."

"Watch your language, fat boy," the woman said, shoving the gun into the man's belly again. "I want this mob arrested, Sheriff, him and every one of them delinquents, especially that tall girl over there. She's been cussing up a blue streak for hours. Girl's mouth would make a trucker blush." Howard looked over at the girl in question, who was indeed very tall with mannish posture and a defiant look on her face.

"I'm going to arrest you if you don't put the gun away, Ida," Bolo said, more sternly. "*Now*, please . . ."

The old woman narrowed her wrinkled eyes and let the barrels drop. Without another word she turned on her heel and marched back into her home adjacent to the apartment complex.

Somebody tore a loud fart and the others laughed

boisterously. "My thoughts exactly," the big man said as he put his hands to his sides.

"It's time to break up the party, Etan," Bolo said. Only then did Howard realize the sheriff knew the man, and he wondered if Bolo knew everyone in Fairly by name.

The man shrugged and nodded at the sheriff's suggestion.

"Is anyone here planning on driving?"

The man shook his head. "There's no need for any paperwork on this, is there, Sheriff?" the man asked.

"Just get the midshipmen safely back to campus and get yourself inside."

"And you don't intend to speak to the dean or anyone like that?"

"No, Etan."

"Thanks, Sheriff."

"And next time I'm checking IDs."

"These are all seniors."

"Are they all twenty-one or better?"

Several of the midshipmen still within earshot quickened their paces across the street as the man mused, "I'm pretty sure they are."

The man took several steps toward his apartment before turning back to Bolo and asking, "You still need that color guard for the policemen's ball next month, right?"

"Yes, we do," Bolo said.

"Okay, Sheriff, we've got you covered." The man offered a cheery wave and headed for his apartment.

As Bolo and Howard watched him go, Bolo mumbled, "He's lucky I have a soft spot in my heart for the military."

"I'll say," Howard said, immediately wishing he'd kept his mouth shut.

Bolo cut his eyes toward the chief and asked, "What do you mean?"

The voice in Howard's head told him to shut the hell

up—he needed the sheriff's help—but he kept talking:
"I'm just wondering if you weren't a bit lenient."

"Lenient, Chief?"

"Well, it's your city, but it seems to me some pretty
major crimes were going on here: battery, communicating a threat, drunk and disorderly conduct, underage
drinking, illegal use of a firearm, et cetera, et cetera . . ."

"You're right, Chief . . ." Bolo let the words hang for
a few beats and then said, "It's my city. Now would you
mind telling me why you're in it?"

11

Ash buttoned the blouse of his khaki uniform before tightening his belt and running his fingers along the waist where his shirt was tucked, removing any creases that might have formed. He considered himself in the mirror. He looked like an officer, a leader, but he didn't feel like one. There was no denying the circumstances that had brought him to this place. Again his mind went back to the previous week.

Following the initial debrief, Captain Napoli, the U.S. Navy cruiser's commanding officer, had been satisfied that he knew enough about the mission to keep the admiral at Fifth Fleet off of their backs, so he had ordered the boarding team to get some rest before attempting any further reconstructions. In spite of his total exhaustion, Ash was unable to sleep. In between tossing and turning, he lay flat on his back staring at the cables and pipes that ran along his stateroom's ceiling.

Hours passed. The phone rang. A voice said the captain wanted to see him in the wardroom. Ash slipped into his desert cammies and made his way along the main passageway to the bow.

But as Ash sat waiting for an audience, he thought he might have arrived too soon. He could hear voices coming from behind the closed door of an adjacent space, familiar voices, and they were talking about him.

"Was it the transit, you think?" Captain Napoli asked.

"No, sir," Chief Lam replied. "The transit went fine. It was rough and everything, but he seemed fine then."

"Maybe it was the dead goat," Herd offered.

"I know Lieutenant Roberts has seen much worse than that."

"All right, gentlemen, I thank you for your time," Napoli said. Ash heard movement toward the door, so he moved away from the table and stood in the far corner as if ignorant of the discussion.

"What's going to happen to him?" Herd asked as the door cracked open.

"I don't know," Napoli said. "We'll have to wait for the chain of command above me to make the call after everyone puts the pieces together."

"He's a good man, sir. I'd follow him anywhere."

"I'll second that," Lam added.

They suddenly grew quiet as they caught sight of him. Both enlisted men acknowledged his presence with a nod before slipping out of the wardroom.

"I didn't realize you were out here, Ash," Napoli said.

"I got a call a little while ago that you wanted to see me," Ash said.

Captain Napoli knit his brow and then said, "Come on in."

Ash stepped inside and stood at the head of the table that took up most of the small meeting room's available space. A stoop-shouldered lieutenant with glasses and meticulously combed hair remained seated at the far end of the table. They made eye contact but otherwise the stranger made no effort to greet Ash. He wore the same long-sleeved khaki uniform the captain was wearing, which made Ash believe he might have been from another ship in the battle group.

"The Polish crewman is going to make it," Napoli said as he took a seat next to the bespectacled lieutenant. "An H-60 transferred him to the carrier right after we stabilized him. Thank God we have Petty Officer Chance aboard. That man's the best corpsman I've ever seen."

"What about the tanker?" Ash asked, still standing.

"Fifth Fleet is sending a seagoing tug from Manama, Bahrain to try and pull the tanker off of the sandbar. The tug should be on station in six hours or so. Until then we're maintaining airborne surveillance. We have fighters patrolling CAP stations in case the Iranians start getting itchy with us hanging out in barely international waters."

Ash winced with the thought of all those assets being employed in the wake of his fuckup. The captain noted his expression and said, "Sit down, Ash."

Ash did as he was directed as Napoli continued, "I know we went over this a few hours ago, but I want to make sure I've got a couple of details right."

Ash found it strange that the captain still had not introduced the lieutenant.

"Tasking receipt, brief, and transit all normal?" Napoli asked.

"Yes, sir," Ash said. "The brief was pretty normal, except we didn't have as much information about the contact as we normally do. The Swicks got the RHIB in the water, and the team got aboard without incident. The transit to the tanker was slower than usual because of the sea state."

"How slow?" Napoli asked.

"About twelve knots for most of the trip."

"And did that anger you?"

Ash found the question a little strange. "Anger me?" he said. "No, not especially. I prefer a fast, smooth ride—who doesn't, right? But what are you going to do about it?"

"Of course." There was a therapeutic tenor to the captain's voice, one Ash hadn't heard out of him before. "So then what happened?"

"We spotted the ship through the NVGs," Ash said. "We reattempted contact over fleet common but got nothing. At some point in there one of our helos came over the UHF and let us know they were going to be operating overhead, which was fine with me."

"Did you have comms with the TAO?"

"I don't think we had him the entire time. He might have heard us more than we were hearing him."

"But you maintained good comms with the H-60 throughout?"

"Yes, sir."

"Then what?"

"Well, we got aboard and secured the crew."

"No resistance?"

"No, not really."

"And you said the Polish captain spoke English?"

"Yes, sir, for the most part."

"And he didn't put up a fight at all or protest your presence in any way?"

"He did start to get upset when I told him we needed to search the cargo bays."

"Upset?"

"He said he needed to get to Kuwait City and that our search would put him behind schedule."

"That's it?"

Ash heaved a sigh and massaged his temples for a time before saying, "Look, Captain, it's hard for me to defend my actions based on the outcome. I've never lost my temper like that, to be honest, but I will say that I didn't think the guy was on the up-and-up. The greased deck, the cargo bay welded shut—the whole picture stunk."

"And yet all the team found was a couple of boxes of pirated DVDs." Napoli produced a folder and spread it open before him. "I reviewed your record last night, Ash. It's top-notch across the board. It would be a shame to . . ."

Ash locked eyes with Napoli as the captain's words trailed off. The tension that permeated the room was suddenly heightened. A few beats clicked off before Napoli regained his focus, extending his arm toward the mystery guest at the far end of the table and saying, "Ash, this is Lieutenant Homewood."

The lieutenant stood and said, "Please, call me Max." Ash got out of his chair and they shook.

"Lieutenant Homewood is from the fleet staff," Napoli said. He checked his watch. "I need to get back to the bridge. Why don't you two talk for a while?" Without any additional explanation, the captain walked out.

Homewood moved to the chair Napoli had just vacated and said, "He's a nice guy, don't you think?"

"Who?"

"Captain Napoli."

Ash shrugged and said, "Sure."

Homewood caught sight of a coffeepot in the far corner. "Man, I could sure use some of that."

"Go for it."

Homewood moved across the room and charged one of the mugs from the small stack next to the stainless-steel coffeemaker. "Can I get you some?" he asked over his shoulder.

"I'm good," Ash replied.

"So, how long have you been in theater?"

"What are you, a JAG or something?" Ash asked in return.

"No, I'm a doctor."

"A doctor?"

"A psychiatrist."

Ash released a nervous cackle and pushed back from the table. "What, am I crazy now?"

"No, you're not crazy."

"That's right: I'm not crazy. *Goddammit.*" As Homewood slowly stepped back to his chair and sat down again, Ash jumped to his feet. He paced along the paneled wall.

Homewood silently tracked him with his eyes for a short while, then said, "I'm just here to talk, Ash, that's it." "Talk, huh?" Ash leaned across the table. "All right, let's talk then. What do you want to know?"

"I asked how long you'd been in theater."

"This time or all told?"

"All told."

"Thirteen months."

Homewood scribbled on a notepad and then looked up and asked, "Does that seem like a long time to you?"

"Does it seem like a long time to you?"

"Actually, it does." Homewood gestured toward Ash's seat. "This conversation might be more productive if you sat down."

"I don't want to sit down," Ash said, pushing off of the table and standing with his back to the wall. "My ass hurts too bad from the pounding it took last night."

"I understand."

"Do you? Have you ever ridden in a RHIB?"

"No, I haven't."

"Then how could you understand?"

Homewood put his pen down and laced his fingers. "Thirteen months is a long time, Ash."

"Okay, it's a long time," Ash said. "What about it?"

"You're human."

"You obviously haven't talked to some of my ex-girlfriends."

Homewood chuckled politely. "Have you been sleeping well?"

"What are you getting at?"

"I'm just asking a few questions. No reason to get upset."

"I'm not upset, *Max*."

"Okay, then how have you been sleeping?"

"Infrequently."

Homewood jotted on his notepad before focusing on Ash once again. "Would you say it's stress that's keeping you up?"

"No, I'd say it's my job that's keeping me up."

"And how have you been eating?"

"On the run."

"Yes, of course." Homewood nodded as he wrote. "I see from your record that you're not married."

"No."

"Girlfriend?"

"If you can call her that."

"Is she communicating with you on a regular basis?"

"I get an occasional e-mail from her."

"So no real stress there?"

Ash considered the other lieutenant's—the *psychiatrist's*—bespectacled face. The doctor's expression was impassive, wholly professional and clinical, and that was pissing the SEAL off as much as his line of probing questions.

Ash took what he hoped would be a cleansing breath and calmly asked, "Is there a point to this, Doc?"

"A point?" Homewood returned. "What do you mean?"

"I mean I'm wondering why I'm talking to you at all."

"All right, now, Ash. Stay calm."

"I am calm. I want to know why you're here."

"I'm here to talk."

"You're here to analyze."

Homewood shrugged. "And analyze, of course."

"So, what's your diagnosis?"

The other lieutenant grimaced with confusion. "I don't have one yet. We just started talking."

Ash looked at his watch and said, "I've got a SEAL team to run, Doc. You've got one more question and I'm gone."

"One more question?"

"And that was it." Ash stood and extended his hand across the table, saying, "Good luck with your write-up. I look forward to reading it."

And the SEAL walked out.

Nearly a week later Ash stood in one of the Thaedt University administration building's bathrooms, pushing a few strands of his newly-cut hair from his forehead. He had since read the doctor's write-up, too many times to count, in fact. And each passing day had found him less convinced that the doctor's findings weren't true.

12

A few hours before Ash was to change into his uniform in one of the administration building's bathrooms, ATF regional chief Hank Howard noticed a sign that read POLICE HEADQUARTERS over an arrow pointing in the direction the squad car had just turned when Sheriff Bolo said, "Your office wasn't very clear on why you were coming down here."

"No, I don't imagine they were," Howard said.

"So what do you need from the Fairly Sheriff's Office?"

"I'm not sure yet."

"Okay . . ." Bolo brought the car to a stop and looked over at the chief. "Why don't we stop the games, Hank?"

Howard furrowed his brow, and said, "Games?"

"The games you big-city agency boys play when you come to a small town like Fairly. You haven't told me shit, Chief. Why are you here? People don't fly into Fairly just to enjoy life on the plain for a couple of days."

Howard pointed ahead. "Let's keep driving."

With some reluctance, Bolo pulled away from the curb and continued down the side road away from the town center. "You're aware of the Badlands Militia?" Howard asked.

"Of course," Bolo said.

"ATF has an agent observing them."

The strained harmony between the two men came to an abrupt end as the sheriff slammed his fist against the steering wheel. "Where does the ATF get off conducting a stakeout in my jurisdiction without me knowing about it?"

"It wasn't a stakeout," Howard said. "The agent was simply observing."

"Observing what?"

"Activity."

Howard could see the sheriff was fighting not to boil over. Bolo wrapped his hands tighter around the wheel, knuckles turning white. "I'm already tired of your visit, Chief Howard," Bolo said. "If you want to play 'I've got a secret,' play it someplace else."

Howard turned in the passenger seat to face the driver. "Calm down, Sheriff. We need your help."

"Then tell me what's going on. What was this guy observing and why? I want to know everything. I *need* to know everything if I'm going to help you."

Howard looked out the passenger-side window, watching the row of narrow two-story clapboard homes go by. "The ATF had some tipper information that the militia was stockpiling arms."

"Arms? Well, they do hunt out there."

Howard chuckled. "Oh, yeah? What do they hunt?"

"Pretty much everything: antelopes, pheasants, prairie dogs."

"Well, I don't think this stuff is going to be used for that." Howard reached into the briefcase on the floor between his legs and produced a folder from which he pulled a photograph. "This was taken a few days before we lost comms with our special agent."

Bolo tried to study the image while at the same time maintaining sight of the road. "What am I looking at?"

"It's a photograph of the Badlands compound taken from the air."

"What took the picture?"

"One of our UAVs."

"A UAV?"

"It's an unmanned aerial vehicle. A radio-controlled drone."

"I know what a UAV is, I just didn't know ATF had them."

"We don't have that many of them and the ones we have are hard to come by. Redmond came up with a good argument, good enough to get us a UAV anyway."

"Who's Redmond?"

"He's the agent who's been watching the militia."

Bolo got a fix on the road and then quickly focused on the photo. "So what do you see in this photo that makes you believe the militia is stockpiling weapons?"

Howard used an index finger to scribe a circle around the upper-right-hand portion of the photo. "Our analysts believe this white building right here was built specifically for weapons storage."

"Why is that?"

"The shape . . . the size . . . I'm not an analyst, though. I guess I trust the judgment of those who are." Howard shoved the photo back into the folder. "Anyway, that's why we had Redmond scoping out the militia."

"And now he's disappeared?"

"We haven't heard from him in several days. Our cryptologists believe someone has been falsely filing his status reports, trying to make us believe he's still in place."

"When's the last time anyone at the ATF heard from him?"

"During a UAV flight a couple of days ago. He dropped offline right after somebody shot at the drone with a surface-to-air missile."

"A surface-to-air missile? I guarantee you the Badlands Militia doesn't have anything like that."

"Really? How can you be so sure?"

The squad car came to a red light, which allowed Bolo to focus solely on Howard. "Look, Chief, you've been dealing with the militia for a few days, right? I've been dealing with them for a lot longer than that."

"What about Devon Hite?"

"I've had a number of long conversations with him over the years. I've also hunted with him a time or two."

"What do you think of him?"

Bolo thought for a time. "He's opinionated, I guess. I don't share his politics, necessarily. But I will say he's built quite a spread out there, especially when you consider that he started with basically nothing."

"You know about his past?"

"You mean the rock-star stuff?"

"That, and his relationship with Melvin C. Stewart."

"A lot of people in these parts watch 'Be Healed.' I've seen it, although I must admit I was just curious what all the fuss was about."

"I understand that Hite's sudden departure from the reverend's camp was a matter of, shall we say, dubious circumstances. Are you aware of any of those details?"

Bolo negotiated another corner, already tired of the chief's pop quiz. "I know what I need to know about what's going on out there, nothing more. They don't bother us; we don't bother them."

"So you don't view them as a threat?"

"They're just out there doing their own thing."

"We heard the IRS might be after them for tax evasion."

"That's no threat to Fairly."

"You're a lawman, Dominic. You're telling me you don't care about people breaking the law?"

Howard was pushing Bolo's buttons now. "Look, Hank, I'm the one responsible for keeping the peace between Fairly and the militia," the sheriff snapped. "And I've been doing a pretty good job over the last few years. What I don't need is you federal boys coming in here all high-and-mighty and stirring up trouble."

"One of my agents is missing, Sheriff. I want to know where he is."

"Fine. Let's go see if we can find out." Bolo pulled off of the street and onto a gravel lot. He stepped on the accelerator and put the wheel hard over, throwing the car into a rock-hurling power slide. Seconds later the squad car was back on the same street it had just left, heading in the opposite direction.

"Where are we going?" Howard asked, fingers still digging into the dashboard.

"We're going to visit the Badlands Militia," Bolo replied.

Fifteen minutes later they arrived at the edge of the Badlands Militia property, although it was impossible to tell. There were no signs posted as the squad car slowly bounced along a narrow gravel road that split a field of long honey-colored grass moving in waves with the wind.

"Shouldn't we have called first?" Chief Special Agent Hank Howard asked, one hand gripping the dashboard, the other against the padded cloth above his head.

"They don't have a phone out here," Sheriff Dominic Bolo said. "I'm surprised you didn't know that."

"No, I didn't know that," Howard offered with a bit of indignation of his own. "So how do you communicate with them?"

"They have a shortwave."

"Maybe we should have called them on it before we drove out here." Howard reached into his coat and found the butt of his pistol.

"Now stay cool here, Hank. We're just paying these folks a visit. You come on too strong and we're not going to find out shit. You let me do the talking."

Cocky sonofabitch for a local yokel, Howard thought. *But I need him right now.*

Bolo brought the car to a sudden halt. He laid on the horn for several seconds and followed that with another couple of short blasts. "That's the magic honk," he explained.

Thirty seconds later a pickup truck appeared from around the bend in the gravel road. Howard could see men in the bed of the vehicle, and as the truck got closer he could also see that they were armed.

The truck stopped and three men jumped from the bed. "Wait here," Bolo said before throwing his door open and climbing out. Howard watched closely, keying on the body language of the men walking toward the sheriff. They were all pretty well built and neatly groomed. Their dress was almost uniform save the color of their shirts. Their expressions were variations on suspicion and defiance. Howard slouched until his chest was beneath the line of the dashboard and again found his pistol near his armpit.

"Didn't expect you out here today, Sheriff," one of them shouted.

"Yeah, me either," Bolo shouted back. "I was just in the area and thought I'd see if there's anything I can do for you folks."

"Who's that with you?" another asked, pointing toward the squad car.

"That's just an associate who's visiting from up St. Paul way. Is Devon around?"

"Of course he is."

"Could I talk to him for a sec—you know, just say hello?"

The three stepped away and conferred before one of them said, "We'll take you to him."

"Can he come with us?" Bolo asked, tossing a thumb over his shoulder.

"I don't know about that," the other said. "Devon's particular about strangers."

"Devon trusts me," the sheriff returned, "and I think it would be good for him to meet my associate. It would be good for the militia."

Another quick huddle and they motioned toward the sheriff, one of them saying, "Come with us and bring him. Leave the police car."

Bolo signaled for Howard to get out and the two of them strode deliberately toward the pickup. Before they reached the bed, each was searched by one of the men, and each was relieved of his handgun. "We'll give these back at the end of your visit," one of them explained.

Bolo and Howard climbed into the pickup bed and sat across from each other on the wheel wells as the militia members directed them to. The driver said something into a CB handset and then threw the pickup into reverse, throwing gravel against the body of the vehicle. A second later they were bouncing down the road in what Howard assumed was the direction of the militia compound.

A mile later the pickup crested a rise in one of the hills and the compound came into view. Howard feigned nonchalance while he scanned the structures and tried to mentally mesh them with the overhead photos he'd seen. He thought he recognized the warehouse that the ATF analysts had said was being used for large-scale weapons storage but at the same time he wasn't sure. Things looked very different at ground level, especially from the back of a pickup that seemed to be finding every bump in the road.

The road fed into a clearing at the far end of which was a line of cars, mostly pickups similar to the one they were riding in. The pickup took its place in the line and the men jumped out of the bed. Howard took his cue from Bolo in following them.

Howard continued to scan the grounds as the group strolled for the largest among the plain wooden structures. The place looked innocent enough. Beyond the buildings were a couple of silos and a handful of barns. Closer, children played on a homemade jungle gym. Two women led horses from a stable to an adjacent rodeo ring. An elderly man drove a tractor toward the adjacent field complex. The most threatening piece of equipment Howard could see was a rusty backhoe parked next to one of the barns. He continued to reconcile his intel with the scene before him. At the same time he sensed something. Was it his heightened senses or did the activity seem choreographed? He recognized the feeling, the same one he used to get when sitting in the stands at a theme park watching the Wild West show.

Four men emerged from the large building, pushing their way through the double doors and striding down the stairs—a greeting party. Howard furtively studied each. The guy leading them was considerably shorter than the rest and only when they drew closer did Howard realize it was Devon Hite. The militia leader spread his arms wide and beamed like a nation's president greeting a visiting delegation.

"Sheriff, what a delightful surprise," Hite said as he shook Bolo's hand.

"Well, my associate and I were in the general area, so I thought we'd pay you a visit," Bolo said. "This is Chief Special Agent Howard from the ATF office in St. Paul."

Howard focused on Hite's reaction. Nothing unusual. The guy was either innocent of any wrongdoing or capable of an impressive poker face. "Very nice to meet you, Chief Howard," Hite said.

"Please, call me Hank," Howard returned.

"And you please call me Devon. So how are things in St. Paul?"

"Fine, I guess. Can't hate the weather, at least not this time of year."

Hite looked to the sky and said, "That's the truth, isn't it? So what brings you down Fairly way, Hank?"

"Oh, I just wanted to say hello to the sheriff here," Howard said, easing into the question. "And I'm checking up on one of my agents."

Still nothing in Hite's expression as he asked Bolo, "Hey, Sheriff, have I shown you the new warehouse we built?"

"No."

"Follow me."

Hite led the group around the corner of the large building and then between two others. As they approached the warehouse in question, Howard realized it was the same building that the analysts had flagged as being full of weapons. He caught Bolo's eye. Bolo nodded slightly, almost imperceptibly; he'd made the connection, as well.

The doors parted as if by magic as Hite neared them. Inside fluorescent lights came on automatically after he entered. Bolo and Howard followed, both surprised to see the warehouse was completely empty.

"Nothing in here yet, huh, Devon?" Bolo asked.

"No, not yet," Hite replied.

"What are you going to put in here?" Howard asked.

"We're not sure yet."

"Not sure yet?" Bolo said. "Why did you build it then?"

"For the sake of building. That's its own reward." Hite ran his hand across one of the beams along the wall. "Do you know anything about construction, Hank?"

"Not really," Howard replied.

"I know the sheriff does."

Bolo moved over to inspect the beam and said, "Impressive. I should have you come over to tackle some of the projects at my place."

Hite was suddenly less ebullient. "You know we don't leave militia property, Sheriff."

"Sure, Devon," Bolo returned. "I know."

Hite turned to Howard and said, "We keep to ourselves. We don't want any trouble. Just a little peace."

Howard just shrugged.

Hite eyed the ATF man for a time, as if sizing him up. He looked as if he was about to say something but instead regained his cheery disposition, looking over at Bolo and saying, "Sheriff, do you two have time for a glass of peppermint tea?"

"We probably need to be moving on," Bolo said.

"Oh, come on now. Don't rush off. We don't get to see you enough as it is. Have you ever had peppermint tea, Hank?"

"I don't believe I have," Howard replied.

"Then you must stay." Hite hailed one of the men, a frail-looking elderly gent, standing by the warehouse doors: "Matthias, set us up in my conference room." The man nodded and scurried off as fast as his old legs would allow.

Hite put an arm around each of his visitors and led

them out of the warehouse. Howard noted how the lights went out and the door automatically shut behind them as they returned to the outdoors. A simple building project, huh? Seemed a bit too high-tech by the ATF man's standards of home construction.

As they traversed the compound Howard kept his eyes moving—and the digital camera hidden up his sleeve clicking, gathering data, possible evidence, like any good lawman might. But this circumstance was different from any he'd encountered over the decades he'd been with the Bureau. Never before had he been in a situation where he couldn't simply ask a direct question of a potential witness or suspect. Now, in spite of the innocuous appearance of his surroundings, he felt not that he was behind enemy lines, per se, but that he was an explorer among a potentially hostile tribe. He knew to honor that feeling. He also knew that nothing would be more damaging at that point than putting off the vibe of suspicion.

Howard pointed to a tractor parked next to the closest barn and said, "Isn't that the new John Deere 8430?"

"You've got a good eye, Hank," Hite returned. "Are you a farmer?"

"No, not now, anyway. Maybe in the next chapter of my life."

"Or your next life. Do you believe in reincarnation?"

Howard strolled silently for a few steps, mulling over how to respond to the potentially loaded question, and then said, "I'm not sure I do."

"Are you a religious man?"

"I go to church, if that's what you mean."

Hite laughed, a forced cackle. "What does going to church have to do with being religious?"

Howard cut his eyes toward Bolo, who subtly shook him off. But Hite wouldn't let it go. "Doesn't that seem a bit artificial that the only way to get the ear of God is to sit in a special building? I mean, we're talking about communicating with the Creator of all things, the Maker."

"I guess that's a matter of personal choice, Devon," Howard said in the most stolid voice he could muster, suddenly feeling as if he were playing catch with a grenade.

"That's a cop-out, Chief," Hite said. "Spoken like a true government official."

The exchange was cut off as they reached the stairs leading into another building, presumably the one that housed Hite's office and conference room. The double doors were opened by two men who stood by them. Howard noted that all the men in the compound had the same look and presence: medium-built, relatively clean-cut though decidedly unmilitary with their facial hair and mufti, and impassive—like compliant automatons. He'd studied cults while working on his criminology masters' degree and these guys definitely fit the bill.

At that point it also struck Howard that he hadn't seen very many women in the militia compound. After hearing rumors of polygamy and orgies he figured the place would be full of females, but there were few to be found. He almost asked the question but let it go. He kept his eyes open.

Hite showed them to a conference room and invited the two visitors to sit at a large wooden conference table. As Howard took his seat next to Bolo he noticed two rows of men seated along the far wall, like a jury. Hite noted his curiosity.

"Those are our newest arrivals," Hite explained, moving over to them. "They've only been here a few days."

"How often do you have folks join you?"

"All the time. Our numbers continue to grow as the word of the Badlands Militia spreads across the country. We welcome all."

Howard ran his eyes across the rows of men. They looked somewhat dazed, as new recruits might look during the early days of boot camp. "You mind if I ask them a few questions, Devon?" Howard asked.

"You can ask them anything you'd like, Hank."

Howard stood and pointed to the center of the back

row, singling out a man with white hair and a broad nose who was staring at the floor. "What brought you here, sir?"

The man sat rock still. "He won't answer you," Hite said.

"Why not?"

"Each group of newcomers has one of three initiation rituals to choose from: fasting, celibacy, or silence. This group chose silence."

Howard used Hite's statement as a bridge to another question, the one he'd avoided asking just minutes before: "I think I'd choose celibacy."

"Why is that?" Hite asked.

"Well, I don't see any women around here."

"I assure you we have women among us, a large number, in fact. They're currently gathered at the other end of the compound. One of my wives is leading an awakening session."

"How many wives do you have?"

Hite demurred: "I meant to say 'wife.' My mistake."

"What's an awakening session?" Bolo asked.

"A class of sorts. We've developed our own curriculum. I'm afraid it wouldn't make much sense to you."

The one called Matthias entered the conference room carrying a tray of glasses filled with ice and a large pitcher. He distributed the glasses and charged each one full.

"Now you taste that, Hank," Hite said, "and you tell me that its not the most refreshing thing that ever crossed your lips."

Howard studied Hite's expression for a few beats before tentatively putting the glass to his lips. It was as refreshing as Hite demanded it was yet surprisingly unsweet. Howard lowered his glass and saw that the militia leader was staring at him, awaiting a ruling.

"It's very good," Howard said.

"I told you," Hite said. He leaned back in his chair and laced his fingers behind his head. "So tell me again what brings the ATF out this way?"

"You say that like it's unusual for us to be in this area."

"I don't remember any ATF presence in Fairly before."

"Oh, we're here, all right. We're all over the country."

"Of course you are."

Howard narrowed his eyes, but otherwise let the jab go without comment, instead saying, "I'm just here saying hello to Sheriff Bolo and checking up on one of my field agents."

"Oh, that's right; you said that. How long has he been missing?"

"I didn't say he was missing."

"I guess I just assumed he was missing. You wouldn't happen to have a picture of him on you, would you?"

"Actually, I do." Howard reached into his shirt pocket and produced a copy of Redmond's official headshot. "Here he is."

"He must be missing," Hite said as he studied the photo. "Authorities don't carry around photos of their subordinates unless they're missing." He looked up at Howard, who stood nonplussed, and said, "Handsome fellow, huh?"

"Sure," Howard shrugged.

"What, you don't know if a man is handsome or not? And what are you saying, that I'm weird because I do?"

Hite was truly aching for an argument. He was obviously bored out of his gourd talking to the automatons that surrounded him.

"I will say that he's one of our up-and-comers," Howard said, working hard to dodge the showdown Hite seemed determined to effect. "I know a couple of the higher-ups at the Bureau have got big plans for him."

"Well, I haven't seen him." Hite handed the photo to the leftmost man in the first row of new arrivals and said, "Pass that around. See if anyone recognizes that face." He turned back toward Howard and explained, o"They've only been here a couple of days. They might have run into him on their way here."

Howard raised his eyebrows to the possibility and watched the men quickly pass the photo among each other. None of them spoke; of course not. They had taken a vow of silence. Beyond that, each stoic visage evinced nothing.

Hite took the photo from the last man in the back row and studied it again for a short while. "This one's got a mischievous light in his eye, don't you think, Chief? I'll bet he's run off with the circus."

Howard allowed a polite laugh. "That's every boy's dream, right?"

"Not mine," Hite returned. "I'm living my dream right here." He took a long draw from his glass and brought it down with a refreshed exhalation. "How about you boys? You all living your dreams?"

"I've got no complaints," Bolo said.

"Me either," Howard said.

"Are you sure about that, Hank? ATF's a pretty big machine, isn't it? You have to have some complaints."

"Not really."

Hite released a shrill whistle and said, "Flag on the play. Look, Hank, you and me aren't going to get very far in the trust arena if you refuse to tell me the truth."

"I am telling you the truth."

The tenor of Hite's voice shifted, suddenly deeper, more dramatic, as if he were behind a lectern instead of on the other side of a conference table. "The nature of government is not to enforce the social contract but to seize power," he said. "Little by little matters of liberty and individual rights are marginalized and then destroyed altogether." He lowered a finger and alternately pointed toward the two lawmen across from him. "That's the business you are in."

Bolo polished off the last of his tea and pushed his chair away from the table. "Thanks for the tea, Devon," he said. "It's always nice to see you."

Hite continued his polemic, either unaware or uncaring of the fact the sheriff had grown uncomfortable with the conversation—like a relative at a holiday dinner determined to get something off of his chest. "Your greatest fear is that I might succeed," he said. "If I find my freedom the country won't need either of you."

Howard was about to say something else but felt Bolo subtly tug at his sleeve—a signal to shut up and leave.

"It was nice to catch up, Devon," Bolo said.

"It was, Sheriff," Hite said. "Hank, I hope you find your agent very soon."

"Thanks," Howard said. "I'm sure we will."

Hite's gaze went above their heads, into a mythical distance, as he said, "I look across the fields and wonder why we can't just live and let live." He stood in a dramatic pose for a few beats, and then his posture softened. "The pickup will meet you out front and take you back to your car."

As they left the room, Howard thought he heard something, a muffled voice perhaps, from the rows of new arrivals lining the far wall, but when he turned to look in that direction he saw nothing but blank stares.

13

Bobby Redmond felt anxious in the line of men. He was told they were his new friends but they didn't feel like friends. He only had two friends: the doctor and Devon Hite. The doctor could make the pain stop and the bad dreams go away, and Devon would order the doctor to do so.

Redmond was happy for the vow of silence. He didn't like it when there was talking. Devon said talking was dangerous for new arrivals and that it was better to listen. Devon was right. Devon was always right.

Inside the building some of the tension in Redmond's body went away. He would had come to see walls as a sign of security. When walls surrounded him nothing bad would happen. Some of his new friends seemed to like the outdoors but he didn't. There was trouble on the wind. The sky was full of spies, men who wanted to control his brain and take his freedom away. Devon had told him so and he believed him.

Redmond followed the man in front of him as he walked down the hallway and turned into the big room. They sat along the bench as they had many times before. This was where Devon talked to them most of the time. This was where they would learn the things that would make them happy and safe.

He sat down and averted his eyes as he was told, but as he did, he couldn't help but notice there were two strangers in the room. The anxiety hit him again. He didn't•like strangers, especially not when they were men dressed in uniforms or suits. He saw the flash of a badge from the taller one's chest just before he shifted his focus to the toes of the running shoes that Devon had given him. They were comfortable and had Velcro straps so he didn't have to worry about tying them.

Redmond tried not to listen to the conversation Devon was having with the men. Then one of the strangers moved toward them. Out of the corner of his eye he could see that it was the one wearing a dark suit.

"What brought you here, sir?" the man asked.

Redmond wanted to break his vow of silence and tell the man to go away. He wanted to tell him he had no interest in his filthy need to control everything. But he sat still, feigning calm, not letting his emotions get the best of him, as Devon had taught him. Redmond would honor his vow.

"He won't answer you," Devon said, thankfully drawing the man's attention away. Redmond went back to his silent contemplation, not worrying about the discussion going on in front of him. Someone else entered the room: It was Matthias, the one closest to Devon, even closer than the doctor. Redmond felt a twinge of envy, but suppressed it. Envy was a bad impulse. It was best to want for nothing . . . except freedom. And as long as he was with the Badlands Militia he would have his freedom.

The two men were leaving now. Good. Redmond continued to focus on his shoes and the shiny floor beneath them. He leaned forward, ever intently staring at his reflection, and just then he noticed his hair. When had it turned white? And why was his nose so wide?

Redmond was hit by an ache in the pit of his stomach. His body was revolting against something but he didn't know what it was. Something was trying to emerge from deep inside his gut. He felt as if he might vomit. He sat upright and covered his mouth with his hand, and as he did, he caught sight of the strangers just before they walked out. It suddenly struck him that he knew the man in the suit. He started to cry out but stopped himself when the man next to him grabbed his forearm. Redmond sat like a statue. He felt the strangers' eyes on him. Finally they walked out.

Redmond wasn't sure what had happened, but he hoped Devon hadn't noticed. His hope was quickly destroyed as Devon poked his head back around the doorway and lowered a finger in his direction, seething under his breath but audibly to those along the wall, "We will deal with you later." Devon disappeared again, surely to escort the strangers off of the compound. Redmond rubbed his upper arm, almost subconsciously. More shots were coming.

Devon Hite stood in Bobby Redmond's cell, glaring at the doctor, fighting the impulse to slap him across the cheek with the back of his hand. The doctor had failed him, and he didn't tolerate failure. Failure was weakness and Hite was not going to tolerate weakness. Not within his organization. He had seen what it did to others. His band, the Baron's Itch, had fallen prey to the lure of drugs, drugs that exploited the weakness in his bandmates. That's what had kept the band from making it big. And weakness had punctuated the next chapter of his life, plaguing the ministry of televangelist Melvin C. Stewart, in spite of the preacher's fire-and-brimstone rants to the contrary. Stewart's weakness had driven his wife into Hite's arms. She'd seduced him, not the other way around, as Stewart had accused in private quarters.

Hite had read a book by General Irwin Rommel, the German Army's legendary "Desert Fox" during World War II, in which the general put forth the notion that the way to a sound organization was to set high standards right from the beginning and then maintain those standards over time. That idea resonated with Hite; plus, there was a fantastic black-and-white photo of Rommel inside the back dust-jacket flap that showed the general looking boldly into the sun, face windblown, rugged behind large round-lensed shades. He had his tall Vermacht hat at a jaunty angle on his head, a look that screamed *leader*. Hite wanted his mere presence to evoke in others the feelings he felt in himself when he studied the general's photo.

It all started with wiping failure from the face of the Badlands Militia.

"I want to know what happened in there, Doc," Hite seethed.

The doctor tried not to flinch. He'd seen his fair share of Hite's temper tantrums, but as he considered his countenance and read his body language he knew he was about ready for maximum boil-over. The doctor offered, "Some recognition mechanism must have been triggered."

"I thought you said he was ready. I thought he was all ours now."

"He is, Devon. He just needs a minor . . . *adjustment,* if you will."

Bobby Redmond sat on the edge of the metal table, hearing the words but not fully comprehending their meaning. He saw the movement, colors against colors, but his mind registered no recognition. Then came the shot, the sting he'd grown accustomed to in the last days, and soon the cold was traveling about him, up his arms and through his torso. Then he saw nothing.

But how his mind danced. His was suddenly a world without time or dimension. He felt joy as he floated through space. But then he heard something, something he had come to recognize: the hissing of a rattlesnake. It was faint at first, as it always was, but then the noise grew. There was more than one of them out there, but he couldn't see them yet. All his life there was nothing he'd hated more than snakes.

Redmond felt dry scales rubbing against the flesh of his forearm. The undulations were unmistakable. The same feeling hit his other arm, then his legs. The snakes were all around him. He turned to see them, but he still couldn't.

Then he did see them, their heads rearing, fangs

bared. They were going to bite him. He tried to get away but couldn't. His arms flailed wildly, his legs pumped in the vast nothingness. He screamed for all he was worth.

He heard a voice. It was the doctor saying, "It's going to be all right, Bobby. You're with us now." And the snakes disappeared.

Another brief sting and more coldness flowed through him. Now Redmond wasn't floating. He was lying on a mattress big as the plains of South Dakota. The mattress was covered with a white down comforter that flowed in waves. In the distance he saw a man walking toward him, and as the man got closer he saw it was the doctor.

"Are you ready to join us again, Bobby?" the doctor asked.

"Why are you asking me that?" Redmond asked in return.

"Because you did something that made us think you were leaving. Do you want to leave?"

"Where did the snakes go?"

"They're out there."

"Will I see them if I leave?"

"You might."

"And you won't be there, will you?"

"No, Bobby, I won't."

"I don't want to leave."

"That's good, Bobby. That's good. Now are you ready to sleep?"

"Yes, I think I am."

"Sleep well, Bobby." And everything went dark in Redmond's world.

"Don't get sloppy on me, Doc," Hite said as he leaned over Redmond, now supine on the operating table.

"Sloppy?" the doctor shot back, swagger sufficiently regained with their guest compliant once again. "I assure you there's nothing sloppy in my technique."

"Just make sure he doesn't go astray again. This little experiment is all fun and games until someone pokes an eye out."

The doctor knit his brow and said, "What are you talking about?"

"This boy almost sang on us."

"Maybe we shouldn't have paraded him in front of that ATF agent and the sheriff like that."

"Don't get skittish on me, Doc. Parading him was the whole point, remember? Now what is Chief Howard going to do? He's going to go back to Minnesota and report that he inspected the compound like a real badass and didn't see anything noteworthy."

"I guess you're right."

"Of course I'm right." Hite leaned in closer, studying the center of Redmond's slack face. "This nose disguise was kind of lame, though. I mean, it looks real and everything—I'll grant you that—but why are we using putty? What is this, a high-school play or something?"

"What do you propose?"

Hite stood up and took a few steps away from the table. "You've done some cosmetic surgery, right?"

"It's been a few years."

The militia leader reached down and peeled the putty that formed the artificial nose from around Redmond's real nose. "Well, it's time to give it another shot."

14

Ash dropped his civvies in the car and walked across the Thaedt campus to the NROTC office. The notion of offices put him in mind of all the offices he had been in recently. He'd spent the last week waiting to enter conference rooms and offices, or so it seemed.

Watching the movement of his long shadow before him, a by-product of the setting sun, Ash thought back to when he'd sat in the outer office of Captain Lane Bennett, the senior SEAL in the Middle Eastern theater, flipping through a months-old edition of a sports magazine, thinking about the recent flurry of events that had sent his life into chaos. The moment's inattention; the Polish crew rushing them; the shot and one of them falling. The meeting with the psychiatrist and his subsequent ruling, a ruling that certainly had the potential to ruin his professional reputation if not his career altogether. Then he thought back to earlier that morning when he'd walked to the helicopter waiting to take him to Bahrain, and how he'd passed another SEAL lieutenant just arrived aboard the cruiser—his replacement?

But one image appeared in his mind's eye over all others, in spite of his attempts to suppress it. It was the face of his roommate, Xavier, expression evincing more than simple disappointment. His countenance was one of pure heartbreak.

"How long are you going for?" he'd asked as Ash packed his duffle.

"I don't know," Ash had replied.

"You'll be back, though, right? I mean, they're not blaming you for how this tanker thing went down, are they? You're the best SEAL they've got."

Captain Bennett's door opened and the captain appeared, tall, tanned, fit—the perfect image of a career SEAL, a man who'd grown older with style. His hair was terminally windblown, blond, and almost too long for a military man's. If the rows of ribbons on his chest could talk they would've captivated their audience with tales of missions accomplished with limited resources against incredible odds. But as many of those missions were still classified, for now those tales would remain untold. Ash didn't need to hear them, anyway. He'd lived a couple of them himself.

"Come on in, Ash," Bennett said. "Let's talk for a bit."

The captain's office was spartanly appointed: He sat behind a simple metal desk surrounded by nothing—no family photos, no unit plaques, no memorabilia of any kind. The only thing posted was a large map of the region that was affixed to the dingy cream-colored wall with duct tape. Ash took his place in the folding chair in front of the desk, the only other piece of furniture in the room.

Bennett opened a folder, the same folder Captain Napoli had paged through the day before, Ash's official record. "You've got great paper, Ash," Bennett said, with a heave of his chest. "Great paper." He closed the record and tossed it aside before picking up another folder, the doctor's report. "You've read this?"

"Yes, sir," Ash said.

"And?"

"And I don't know how that guy could have come to that conclusion based on the short discussion we had."

"Discussion?" Bennett opened the folder and flipped through several pages. "It says here you were argumentative and that you walked out before the doctor was finished with the interview."

"The interview was BS," Ash said.

"BS, huh?"

"Very respectfully, sir, I don't see where that guy gets off diagnosing me with combat fatigue based on a single incident."

"Captain Napoli said it was more than a single incident. He said everyone he talked to on the ship said your behavior had changed over the last few weeks. Even your roommate said so."

Ash rubbed his eye sockets with the bases of his palms and muttered, "Fucking X."

"I know this is all pretty new to you, Ash; hell, it's new to all of us, but did you ever consider the possibility that the doctor is right?"

Ash didn't want to believe what he was hearing. "SEALs don't get combat fatigue, sir."

"Maybe they do."

"Well, maybe they do, but I don't have combat fatigue."

"Then how do you explain your actions two nights ago?"

Ash paused, running his thumb and forefinger along his eyebrows as he thought about how best to frame his response, a response he'd attempted numerous times over the last hours without the desired result.

"A combination of factors," Ash said. "Not the least of which was the nature of the mission itself."

"We don't question our missions, Lieutenant," Bennett said, leaning back in his chair.

"We don't?" Ash shot back. The words just leapt out of him.

Bennett's eyes widened slightly with the junior man's comeback, and then he said, "I'm not saying a leader doesn't have a responsibility to ensure a reasonable chance for success."

"Exactly, sir," Ash interrupted. "And that's the only thing I can think of to explain why I lost my temper."

Bennett ran his eyes across the report. "You did more

than just lose your temper, Lieutenant. You hazarded your men."

"None of my men was hurt."

"You hazarded your men!" the captain forcefully returned. "You snapped, you lost it, you freaked out . . . use any words you like, you failed."

Ash's head dropped, in spite of his desire for it not to, and Bennett continued: "I've known you for some time, Ash. The entire SEAL community knows you. You're not the kind of guy who fails. You were handpicked for a crucial joint op the first night of the war, for crissakes, and you got it done. No, there's only one explanation for your actions the other night."

He agrees with the doctor, Ash thought. *He thinks you're burned out.*

Ash shook his head as the captain went on: "It's understandable, Ash. You've been at war for a long time. Stress is a tricky thing. People deal with it in different ways."

"I'm fine, Captain," Ash said, even as he heard the doubt in his voice.

"No, you're not." With that Ash looked up and locked eyes with Bennett, waiting for the axe to fall. And it did. "We need to reassign you for a while."

Ash sat processing the words for a time before he asked, "Where?"

"I'm not sure, to be honest. I talked to the Personnel Bureau yesterday and nothing was jumping out at them. They asked that you call your detailer today as soon as we're done here."

Ash got out of the chair and slowly walked to the far wall. He ran a hand across the smooth surface as his mind tried to process his fate. Even yesterday they had been talking about him, trons flying between Bahrain and Tennessee. "So am I done?"

"With me?" Bennett said. "I guess so."

"No, sir, am I done as a SEAL?"

The captain arched his eyebrows and flipped open Ash's record again. "If you hit the ground running with this new assignment, whatever it turns out to be, I would think you'd be back on track."

Ash was suddenly overcome by anger, a feeling similar to what he'd experienced aboard the Polish tanker. He wanted to punch the wall or kick the folding chair. He wanted to get in Bennett's face and challenge how vigorously the captain had gone to bat against those in the chain of command above him. Bennett knew him. Why had he sold him out so easily? Navy SEAL, huh? Bennett was nothing more than a goddamn politician. That's how he'd made captain.

But the growing flame inside was extinguished by a sense of resignation that hit Ash just as quickly as the other emotions battling for control of his thoughts, words, and deeds. He came to attention and excused himself from the office. There was nothing for Ash to do now but call his detailer.

Ash listened anxiously as the phone buzzed through the earpiece. He looked at his watch and did the Bahrain-to-Tennessee time-zone math. His detailer, the man responsible for writing his orders, should have been at work by now. He was about to hang up when a man's harried voice materialized on the other end of the line.

"Lieutenant Schoenstein."

"Lieutenant Schoenstein, this is Lieutenant Ashton Roberts calling from Bahrain," Ash said.

"Bahrain? In the Middle East?"

"Yes."

"Cool. What's going on over there?"

Ash was in no mood for lighthearted banter. "I was told to call you about orders."

"Really? Who told you to call me?"

"Captain Bennett, the ranking SEAL in the region." Ash didn't hear recognition in Schoenstein's tone although they'd dealt with each other a couple of times, before and after Ash had spent several months as the aide to Vice Admiral Brooks Garrett in the Pentagon— a job that had challenged the SEAL in ways he'd never expected when he'd reluctantly accepted it. "I'm not sure if you remember me, but—"

"Sure, sure, I remember you." Ash heard the tapping of a computer keyboard as the detailer thought aloud: "Okay, just hold on here a sec . . . there we go. I've got you attached to SEAL Team Two out of Little Creek, right?"

"Yes, but right now I'm over in the Gulf."

"That's right, I see it here. It looks like your last fitrep was written by the commanding officer of a cruiser."

"Captain Napoli, right; but I'm not on the cruiser anymore."

"Where are you?"

"I'm in Bahrain."

"Oh, that's right. You told me that. So, what can I do for you?"

Ash rubbed his temples. The long day was growing still longer. "I was under the impression you'd already know the answer to that."

More tapping on the keyboard was followed by a few seconds of silence. "I don't see anything on my screen here. Why don't you tell me what I'm supposed to know already."

Ash let out a long breath. He had been hoping to be spared the ignominy of reviewing the details with the detailer. "I was diagnosed with combat fatigue," he said matter-of-factly. "They want me to go somewhere and chill out for a while, I guess."

"Chill out, huh?" A flurry of tapping. "I'll see if we have anything on a tropical island somewhere. Do you like coconuts?"

"Not really."

Schoenstein chuckled. "I'm just kidding. Oh, hold it. I do have something on you here in the notes section of your file. My boss must've just put it there. Gotta love this computer network we have here at the Bureau."

"What does the note say?"

"Not much, just 'Roll to low-stress shore duty.' "

Ash hated every second of this. It was completely contrary to everything he'd ever wanted out of his Navy career, everything he'd worked so hard to earn. "So what qualifies as low-stress shore duty these days?" he asked.

"I'm not sure, to be honest," the detailer replied. "We're not really specializing in low stress these days, if you know what I mean."

Great. Now a guy sitting behind a desk in Millington, Tennessee was telling Ash what was what in terms of operational tempo. "Nothing's jumping out at me," Schoenstein continued. "Are you at a number I can call you back?"

Ash searched the face of the phone but found nothing. "I'm not sure what the number is here." He searched the conference room walls for a list of phone numbers but again came up empty.

"I need to check with some of the other detailers real quick," Schoenstein said. "Can you just hold on for a minute or two?"

"Sure."

The line went silent and Ash was left with his thoughts. Combat fatigue. A badge of dishonor. What would the rest of the SEAL community think when word got out? What would his best friend Lieutenant "Wild" Willie Weldon think? Maybe word was already on the streets. Ash imagined the conversations in hooches across the planet and felt like puking.

"Ash, are you still there?" Schoenstein asked.

"I'm here."

"It looks like I'm sending you back to Little Creek."

"Little Creek? What job?"

"I'm not sure exactly. We're just going to send you back there to take it easy for a while. I'm sure one of the SEAL teams will have something for you to do. Or maybe they'll have nothing for you to do. Either way it's a good deal for you."

"How's that?"

"You're going home, shipmate. What could be better than that?"

The detailer had no clue. He wasn't a warfighter. He was a desk jockey. He'd never felt the exhilaration of success in combat. His idea of a challenge was getting some sucker to agree to shitty orders.

And now Ash was that sucker. He pictured himself sitting in a cubicle at SEAL Team Headquarters, avoiding eye contact with anyone who might happen through the door. He used to be the one they talked about, the model special warrior. He was the one who'd done the hardest jobs well. He'd been awarded medals that he couldn't talk about because the missions were still classified. Now he'd be the one they whispered about: "He, you know . . . *lost it.*"

"I guess I don't have much of a choice here, do I?" Ash said.

"No, not really," Schoenstein replied.

"You don't have any other billets available, anything anywhere?"

"Like what?"

"I don't know, War College, some sort of fellowship, something like that."

The detailer paused for a few beats, and for a moment Ash thought he might actually be looking for a billet along the lines he had suggested. But when he started to speak again, the SEAL heard his fate loud and clear, not so much in what Schoenstein said but in how he said it: "Ah, those jobs are for, you know . . ."

"What, people who haven't been diagnosed as crazy?" Ash said. He felt his temper flaring.

"We're going to help you through this."

Great. Now he was leaning on his detailer in Millington, Tennessee for orders *and* psychological advice. All Ash could think to say was, "Whatever."

No talking but tapping on the keyboard. "Hello, what is this?" Schoenstein said. "Well, I think we might be in luck. Let me ask you: Where are you from?"

"Old Greenwich, Connecticut."

"Oh . . ."

"Why?"

"Well, it's always nice when a job is located near where you're from. We detailers like to keep folks happy if we can."

"What job are you looking at?"

"Do you have a master's degree?"

"No."

"That's fine. You don't really need one for this, I guess. This job's been gapped for a couple of years now, but we might be able to open it back up just for you."

For some reason Ash didn't feel lucky; what he did feel was frustrated. "What job is it?" he asked, very much trying to keep his cool, something he'd been consciously working on since that fateful night a few eons back. Now everything seemed different. He was off balance, unconfident, nowhere a SEAL should be.

"Officer in charge of the Reserve Officer Training Corps at Thaedt University."

"Thaedt University? Where the hell is that?"

"Hold on . . . here it is: Fairly, South Dakota."

"Where is that?"

"It's where Thaedt University is." The detailer laughed at his attempt at humor. "I don't know where it is exactly. I'm an East Coast guy myself."

"This ROTC unit has been without a lieutenant for a couple of years, did you say?"

"It looks that way."

"So who's in charge there?"

Still more tapping on the keyboard, a noise that Ash found increasingly grating with each stroke. "A master chief petty officer, best I can tell from the information I have here."

Ash took another deep breath and asked, "So that's my only other option, huh?"

"It looks that way," Schoenstein returned. "When the reason for the orders is your sort of medical situation, the choices are limited, obviously."

Silence followed. Finally, the detailer said, "I've got another call I need to take here. What do you think? Will South Dakota work for you?"

"I guess it beats having people talk behind my back while I'm pushing paper for the SEALs at Little Creek," Ash said.

"What?"

"Never mind. I'll take the orders. When do I have to be there?"

"You're already late." The detailer let out a nervous whinny. "No, I'm just kidding. How about showing up a week from now?"

"Sure. What else am I going to do?"

"That's the spirit." With that the detailer hung up.

Walking across the Thaedt University campus some days later, Ash remembered sitting with the phone to his ear, in shock and disbelief. The South Dakota wind whistling past his ears reminded him of the static he'd heard through his cell phone's earpiece after the detailer cut the connection—static, the soundtrack to his future.

15

Ash continued his walk several hundred yards across campus to the building that hosted the NROTC offices—the same building, he discovered, that was also used to store the equipment used by the university's intramural sports teams. As a result, the building had a nagging air about it, the underlying scent of dirt, grass, and sweat. It reminded him of some of the oldest gyms at the Naval Academy.

Ash went door to door along the tile of the main hallway reading the signs and looking for clues. At the far end he saw over a closed door a poorly-stenciled banner that read simply NROTC OFFICE. Unsure of what might be on the other side, Ash knocked.

"What?" a young male voice said from inside.

Ash cracked the door open and peered in, saying, "Is it safe to come in?"

"I guess," the other returned. Ash entered and saw a young man with close-cropped black hair leaning back in a chair behind one of the handful of desks in the room. He had his feet propped up on the desk and one hand behind his head while the other worked a computer mouse. He was wearing a uniform much like the one Ash had on except with fewer ribbons and no gleaming gold SEAL pin over the pocket. Ash also noted a single small anchor pinned to his right collar, indicating the young man was a third-class midshipman—a sophomore.

The midshipman didn't move as he asked, "What can I do for you?"

Ash waited a few beats, amazed that the midshipman didn't rise as he entered the room. Once he could stand no more, he asked, "Don't you normally come to attention when a lieutenant enters a room?"

The midshipman wheezed a *pshaw* and pushed back from the desk. His legs fell heavily to the floor, hitting with a loud slap. He begrudgingly stood, feet apart, arms dangling, and shoulders slumped. His eyes defiantly locked with Ash's.

Ash moved forward until his thighs were touching the front edge of the desk and firmly intoned, "That's not attention."

The midshipman rolled his eyes, and with a heave of his chest got to a halfhearted position of attention. Though unimpressed, Ash elected not to press the matter further at the moment. He had other work to do. "Are you the duty officer?"

"No."

"No, *sir*."

"No, sir."

"Who *is* the duty officer?"

"What's a duty officer?"

"The person manning this office."

"We don't have one of those."

Ash made a short tour of the room, taking in the disorganized mess of files, magazines, and video games that surrounded him. "Where's Master Chief Fernandez?"

"I don't know," the midshipman responded.

"You don't know?" He saw the midshipman's eyes widen slightly. Whether or not he knew that there was a new sheriff in town, the kid was beginning to realize that the man in front of him wasn't kidding around.

"Well . . . I know, but I don't think I'm supposed to tell anybody."

Ash felt his blood starting to boil. "You're not the duty officer?"

"No . . . sir."

"What are you doing here then?"

"Surfing the Web."

Ash leaned across the desk and glanced at the screen. "Porn?"

The midshipman's eyes darted wildly as he said, "The master chief doesn't care. He says all this stuff about no porn is just politically correct BS. He's old-school Navy. And I want to be old-school Navy, too."

"What is old-school Navy?" Ash wondered aloud before tugging his thumb across his shoulder. "Shut that off and come with me."

"Where are we going?" the midshipman asked.

"You're going to take me to the master chief."

The midshipman reflexively shook his head no.

Again, Ash felt his temper rising and again he elected to stay calm. "What's your name, son?" He'd never addressed anyone as "son" but it seemed like an appropriate way to set the tone at the moment.

"Henry Harrison."

"Well, Henry, I'm Ash Roberts—Lieutenant Ash Roberts. I'm the new officer-in-charge of the unit."

Harrison's grip was weak and clammy. "I didn't know we were getting an officer-in-charge," he said.

"That doesn't surprise me."

"So where's Master Chief Fernandez going?"

"I don't think he's going anywhere." Ash started for the door.

"Then why are you here?"

"Because a ROTC unit is supposed to led by an officer, not an enlisted man."

"But in some ways a master chief outranks an officer."

Ash turned and considered the youngster. "Who told you that?" He waved his hand. "Never mind. I think I know."

Ash led Harrison back down the hallway and out the door. The midshipman lagged a step behind as they made the walk to the lieutenant's car. "So which way?"

Ash asked as the midshipman flopped into the passenger seat.

Again Harrison seemed reluctant to answer, but as Ash locked his eyes on him he yielded: "He lives in the apartment complex right across from the university's main entrance."

Ash backed out of the parking space and drove down the main road through the campus and out of the gate. It was almost dark now. The last traces of daylight barely lit the buildings across the street. At the intersection he turned to Harrison, who still seemed reluctant to provide information, and he asked, "Where is it?"

Harrison tilted his head and mumbled, "Over there."

"Where?"

The midshipman finally raised his arm and said, "That apartment complex right over there."

Ash swung the car around and parked the car at the curb. He jumped out and took a few steps toward the complex before realizing that Harrison wasn't behind him. "Let's go," Ash said.

"I want to stay in the car," Harrison returned.

"Negative, you're coming with me. I need you to show me which apartment it is."

"It's one-oh-five."

"Get out of the car."

Ash saw the passenger door slowly swing open. Harrison slid out and trudged to Ash's side, head hung low. What was he hiding?

Ash followed Harrison through the Spanish-style portico, which seemed strangely misplaced among the rolling hills and open fields of South Dakota. Ash pulled on the main door but it was locked. "You have to get them to buzz you in," Harrison explained. He hunted among the rows of buttons and then pushed one of them. There was no reply, so he pushed the button again.

A static-laced voice crackled through the tiny speaker at the top of the stainless-steel panel. "What?"

"It's Harrison."

"What do you want?" Ash could hear other voices in the background.

"I need to see the master chief."

"He's busy." Laughter. "And no underclassmen allowed here."

"I have someone here who wants to see him."

"The master chief wants to know who it is."

Harrison looked over his shoulder, a petition for Ash to identify himself through the intercom. Ash leaned forward and said, "It's Lieutenant Ash Roberts. I'd like to introduce myself to Master Chief Fernandez."

Silence followed. Something was very wrong. Ash felt his warrior senses kicking in, the same ones he employed when taking down an insurgent stronghold in the Anbar Province or a suspicious ship in the Arabian Gulf. A woman passed through the door and Ash used the opportunity to feign chivalry before slipping inside with Harrison in unwilling tow.

Ash saw a sign on the wall with an arrow and 101–110 over it, so he headed down the hallway. Odd numbers were on the left. Even before he got past the second door he could hear the voices. He heard someone shout, "Turn the goddamn music off," and the rhythmic thumping ceased echoing against the walls. As he read the number on the door he heard people speaking in loud whispers and the tinkling of glasses. Ash pictured a hasty cleanup operation in progress.

He knocked. No response. He knocked again.

"Yeah?" a voice—deeper than the one that had blared through the intercom—said from behind the door.

"It's Lieutenant Roberts," Ash said. "I'd like to say hello to the master chief."

"Who's are you?"

"Excuse me?"

"Did Captain Nelson send you?"

"I don't know Captain Nelson."

"You're not from the regional headquarters?"

"What regional headquarters?"

"The NROTC regional headquarters."

"No."

"So where are you from?"

"What do you mean?"

Silence, and then, "Why are you here?"

"I'm here to be the officer-in-charge of the Thaedt University NROTC unit."

More silence followed by a long, loud groan. The door cracked open and a dark-skinned face appeared. "So they finally sent an officer to Thaedt, huh?"

"Are you Master Chief Fernandez?" Ash asked in return.

The man didn't answer but disappeared from the opening. The opening widened. Ash saw the big man walking down the hall deeper into the apartment. "All right, you no-loads," the man shouted. "We've got company so do your best to get your shit together."

Ash interpreted the open door as an invitation to enter the apartment. He walked in, stepping over various forms of trash—bags, cans, and bottles—along the way. At the end of the hall he came to the gathering, almost a dozen midshipmen lounging about in the cheap furniture along with the older guy who still hadn't introduced himself but who Ash assumed was Master Chief Fernandez. No one, including the master chief, bothered to get up. As he scanned the room, Ash could see several of them were very drunk.

Ash walked over to the man and extended his hand, saying, "Master Chief?"

"Uh-huh?" the man returned, taking Ash's hand without rising from his chair.

"I'm Ash Roberts, the new OIC here. Can I talk to you alone for a second?"

The master chief shrugged, got out of the faux-leather lounger and ambled over to the kitchen. "What can I do you for, Lieutenant?" he asked, leaning against the refrigerator.

"What going on here?" Ash asked.

"Just a little morale-builder with the first-class midshipmen, you know, the seniors."

"Nothing wrong with that, I guess. It looks like a few of them have had too much, though. How long has this party been going on?"

Fernandez looked at the ceiling, trying to recount how long the midshipmen had been hanging out at his apartment, and said, "A few hours. They came over after the Naval Science class I was teaching them."

"So none of them had any other classes after that?"

Fernandez paused, pinching the bridge of his nose, and then said, "You'd have to ask them."

"No," Ash returned. "You'll have to ask them." He gestured toward the adjacent room. "This party's over. Get everybody back to campus."

"Why?"

Ash did a double take. "Excuse me?"

"They're not hurting anybody. I'm sure you appreciate the sort of bonding that's done between shipmates in informal settings."

Ash moved a step closer to the other man, who was a head shorter but had at least fifty pounds on him. "Master Chief, let me tell you this right up front," the lieutenant said. "We're going to get along a lot better if when I give you an order you carry it out. Now get the midshipmen back to campus."

"Whatever . . ."

Ash glowered at the master chief.

"Oh, what," Fernandez returned. "You're one of those 'yes, sir' guys?"

"Look, Master Chief," Ash said. "You've been at it here for a while; you're tired. I don't want to start off on the wrong foot with you, if I can help it. Why don't you simply end the party and get some sleep? First thing tomorrow morning I'd like to see the entire unit in formation in front of the NROTC building."

"What do you consider first thing?" Fernandez asked.

"Zero six thirty."

"Wow, that's kind of early."

"Not by my standards, which are soon to be your standards, I hope."

"And tomorrow's Friday. That's not a normal drill day for the unit; in fact, they don't wear their uniforms on Fridays."

"What day do they wear their uniforms?"

"Tuesday."

"When do you PT?"

"PT?"

"Physical training . . . when do you work out as a unit?"

"We do the physical fitness test every six months . . . in accordance with Navy instruction, of course."

Ash shook his head in disbelief. "All right, have the unit form up wearing PT gear."

"Tomorrow?"

"Master Chief, am I going to have to repeat myself a lot with you, because I'd rather not."

Fernandez only mustered a shrug.

Ash walked out of the apartment, grabbing Harrison, who was standing stiffly with his eyes darting as he continued to draw derisive stares from the by-and-large inebriated first-class midshipmen. They were certainly blaming him for the lieutenant's sudden and unannounced arrival on the party scene. Ash avoided making eye contact with any of the seniors. He'd begin setting the tone tomorrow.

16

Bobby Redmond stood among the others in the final glow of the day, listening to the grinding of gears in the near distance. He smelled the diesel exhaust in the air even before he spotted the big truck coming around the last bend before the militia compound. Redmond felt his heart pounding. He was excited because Devon Hite had told him he should be.

The truck came out of the haze. It was always hazy around the compound—even indoors. Redmond had learned to see through the haze. He'd also learned to hear through it, and now he heard the voice of the truck's driver as he leaned out of the cab and asked, "Where do you want it?"

"Around the back of that new storage building," Hite shouted back. He ran toward the shed like a child trying to get ahead of the circus as it rolled into town. The truck passed Redmond, and then he saw that it was dragging a trailer with something huge on it covered with a silver tarp and strapped down tight.

"Stop, stop," Hite ordered, waving his arms. The truck stopped.

The driver bailed out of the cab and jumped to the ground. "If you want this to go quickly, some of you are going to have to help me."

Hite snapped his fingers at the group of new arrivals and barked, "You guys get to work."

Redmond joined the others in grabbing a strap and

working it loose. Soon the straps were off. The truck driver started to tug on the silver tarp, so Redmond joined in. The tarp fell away, revealing what the trailer was carrying: a tank.

"Isn't that beautiful, Doc?" Hite asked.

"I know it was expensive," the doctor returned.

"No more expensive than all that shit I let you buy for your lab." Hite spread his arms out and announced like a narrator for a car commercial, "This is a genuine Russian T-72."

"All right, you guys," the driver said. "Help me get the ramps in place and we'll back this beast off the trailer and let your boss drive it around a bit."

"I still don't know what the hell you think we're going to do with this thing," the doctor said. "We're already treading on thin ice with him."

Redmond saw the doctor was pointing at him, but he had no idea why. He knew that it was best not to be noticed. He moved to help the driver although he could still hear the conversation between Hite and the doctor.

"So what is it for?" the doctor asked.

"It's our ace in the hole, Doc," Hite returned. "Our security blanket. With this we have an equalizer, one that should keep them in check."

"So you're going to let them know about it?"

"Of course not. Why would I do that?"

"It's hard for something to be a deterrent for the enemy if they don't know about it."

"Who said anything about a deterrent? I'm talking about an equalizer."

The exchange was suddenly drowned out as the driver fired the tank up. It was loud. Redmond could see the driver poking his head out of a small hatch at the front of the tank under the large barrel of the gun. The treads clanked as he slowly drove the tank down the twin ramps. The ramps groaned. Redmond thought they might break, which he knew would make Devon mad. He prayed that the ramps would hold up, and then remembered that he wasn't supposed to pray, at least not to God.

The noise subsided slightly as the driver allowed the tank to idle. "You want to give it a shot?" he shouted toward Hite.

"Hell yeah, boy," Hite shouted back before jumping on the turret and disappearing down into the tank. A second later his head appeared where the truck driver's had just been. With a burst of exhaust smoke the engine revved. The tank pivoted in place and then took off between the buildings and into the nearest field, nearly running over some of the new arrivals along the way.

Redmond watched as the tank bounced through the field. He thought he could hear Hite cheering. It was good that Devon was happy. Suddenly the gun erupted with a boom and a blast of flame. A few seconds later the far side of the field exploded in an orange-and-black cloud.

"Damn, he's crazy," the doctor said.

17

The long day threatened to go deep into the night. Hank Howard's domain had been invaded within hours of his return to St. Paul. With the first whisper of discovery high-ranking ATF officials from all over the country had descended on the lesser-known half of the Twin Cities. Now all of them, this gathering of Monday-morning quarterbacks, sat in a low-lit auditorium passing judgment on Howard's actions. It was galling; he was the one who'd taken action, as opposed to those who sat on their asses in distant locales and did nothing. But that fact didn't keep them from pointing fingers.

"How is it you let Devon Hite know you were surveilling him?" asked Mel Ferguson, the corpulent head of the Seattle division. Howard noted the nods that surrounded him.

He fought not to boil over as he replied, "He didn't know I was surveilling him, Mel, because I wasn't surveilling him."

"Why did you go there, then?" asked Keith Fredericks of the Kansas City division. Howard had counted on this stringbean of a man to be more sympathetic. Fat chance. It had become a feeding frenzy.

"Because the local sheriff took me there." Harrumphs and snickers all around. As soon as he'd said it Howard had realized how stupid the explanation sounded. But all the same it was the truth. And they hadn't been there.

"This sheriff is a good man," Howard continued.

"He's the man on the scene in Fairly, knows more about the Badlands Militia than anyone, I'd say. In fact, we should bring him into the mix here. Make sure we use his information in our planning."

"We're not bringing a town sheriff into our process, Hank," Ferguson said. As the senior man present, he'd taken it upon himself to talk the most. "Our intelligence resources are far superior to anything Fairly, South Dakota could offer." He looked around with a goofy leer, petitioning agreement and coaxing laughter as he added, "What do they use to communicate with each other anyway, smoke signals?" More snickers. More nods.

"I didn't see anything while I was there that would've led me to believe that Redmond was there," Howard protested.

Ferguson directed a chubby arm toward the huge screen in front of them that currently hosted an image from a digital camera, one that Howard had surreptitiously snapped during his tour with the sheriff. This particular shot showed the rows of new arrivals that had lined the wall. "Zoom in on that white-haired guy in the center of the back row again," he said. The high-resolution image allowed the tech at the computer controls at the back of the room to zoom in. A second later, Redmond's altered visage dominated the screen.

Ferguson turned toward Howard once again and said, "The man was right in front of you, son!"

Son? It was almost more than Howard could bear. But he took a deep breath and worked to stay calm. "He'd been disguised. I mean, look at the guy. You tell me he looks anything like the brown-haired, thin-nosed man in his official photograph."

"He has the same eyes," Ferguson countered.

Howard slapped the table and said, "With all due respect, I'm throwing the bullshit flag on that, Mel. The fact our people can do ocular comparative analysis using digital photographs and high-powered computers doesn't mean I can casually glance at somebody's eyeball from ten feet away and make a positive ID."

"Of course not, Hank," Ferguson said patronizingly. Howard thought he heard laughter behind him, but as he wheeled around he was greeted by nothing but stony expressions.

Ferguson waved his meaty hands and changed the subject: "All right, so what do we do here?"

As the lights came up the room was silent; faces scanned other faces in petition, but no one spoke. Finally Pete Pervis, a gaunt, near-translucent gent from the Houston division, said, "Well one thing is clear: We have to get our man out of there . . . right?"

A few nods, slow at first, and then Ferguson said, "Yes; yes, of course. We've got to get that guy out of there." Howard was struck by the fact the fat man didn't use Redmond's name.

"How do we do that?" someone asked from the back.

"We go in," someone else said.

The discussion grew animated quickly. Words flew and Howard had a hard time figuring out who was saying what.

"What do you mean, 'go in'?"

"What else are we going to do, just sit here?"

"Nip it in the bud."

"Quick and decisive."

"We need more information."

"Just do it, *dammit.*"

Then one voice rose above the noise, clear and resonant: "Make no mistake, gentlemen. This is a crucial moment in our history."

Howard watched as the man emerged through the gaggle at the back of the room. He was short with thick-rimmed glasses that looked too big for his face and thick gray-flecked hair split in a militantly straight part along the side of his head. Unlike the others in the room, he'd refrained from removing his suit coat.

The man moved to the front of the conference room with the confidence of someone who thought he belonged there. Howard glanced furtively around the room; from the expressions it was obvious he wasn't the only one without a clue as to who this guy was.

Ferguson must have sensed it too, because he stood up just before the man began to speak again and said, "This is Douglas Feint. He's on retainer from the Schaffer Foundation, a think tank that I'm sure most of you are familiar with. I asked Dr. Feint to join us today for this very reason." He gave a slight bow toward Feint and said, "Please, sir."

Feint bowed in return. He cleared his throat and called to the back of the room, "Please lower the lights and put up my first slide."

The room went black again and the slide appeared on the screen, or "smart board," as they called it—a space-age gizmo that did everything but make the coffee. Howard was happy to let the others run the controls. He still hadn't figured out how to work his plasma TV at home, not to mention this contraption. He liked things simple. All he needed in his life was an airspeed indicator and an altimeter—and good old-fashioned steam gauges at that. No "glass," no digital stuff.

Feint directed a laser dot on the slide. "Here's a map of the United States, obviously," he said. "Now watch this."

New shapes appeared, colored red against the light yellow of the continental U.S. "These shapes represent land occupied by militias in 1993." He pressed a button on the controller in his hand. "Compare that with this." To Howard's eye it seemed that twice as much red now occupied the slide.

"The growth continues basically unchecked," Feint continued. He offered a slight smile. "And these are not nice people. While each group might have a different foundation, a different theme, if you will, they all share several traits." A new slide outlined the traits as he spoke. "They are all led by males. Their ages vary, some have criminal records, some, like Devon Hite of the Badlands Militia, have failed in other walks of life, but all are able to woo unfortunates, people down on their luck . . . losers, as we say."

A new slide appeared. "But even though they might be considered losers, they can also be considered a threat to society. These are some other trends we have observed: These militias—separate societies, if you will—are not at all beyond wanton disobedience of federal laws or Judeo-Christian mores. Many of these groups practice witchcraft; many believe in bigamy. Some traffic in drugs. Some stockpile illegal weapons, and worse. We think that the Badlands Militia has the latest generation infrared SAMs." Feint jerked a thumb over his shoulder. "One look at our captive special agent also makes me think they might be into thought control, as well. Overall these groups pose a great threat, an imminent threat, to our way of life." He raised a hand toward the back of the conference room. "Lights, please."

The room grew bright once again. "So, what should we do?" Feint asked. "Do we wait for them to kidnap another agent? Do we wait for them to acquire more weapons? Do we wait for them to sell more drugs to our children?"

"We need to shut these bastards down," Ferguson said, joining Feint at the front of the room. "What else would we wait for?"

"Proof?" It just popped out. Howard was surprised by the question, even though he was the one who asked it.

"Proof?" Ferguson asked back, glaring at the other division chief.

"Yeah," Howard said, more firmly now. "We're lawmen. We need proof, Mel."

"You heard the analysts. They made an ocular match. That guy right in front of your nose was Special Agent Redmond."

"Okay. Why was he there?"

"Because they kidnapped him."

"Are you sure? Maybe he joined them voluntarily."

Ferguson let out a belly laugh. "How well do you know Redmond?"

"Not very well."

"Well, that's problem number one, I'm afraid. A good leader gets to know his people. But never mind that. Does it seem likely to you or anyone else in here that a career ATF agent would suddenly decide to cash it all in and join the Badlands Militia?"

No one answered. Howard noticed everyone was looking at him as if he should.

"I grant you it's an unlikely explanation, and I'm not saying that that's what I think happened. My point is—"

"Irrelevant," Ferguson interrupted. "We need to get our agent out immediately. And beyond that we need to make an example of these guys." He looked over to Ralph Trimble, head of the San Francisco division, who held the collateral billet as national strike lead. "Ralph, let's get the planning team together. I want something on paper before midnight tonight."

"Roger that, boss," Trimble returned, stroking his thick white mustache as his mind immediately started to work in overdrive. "Can you give me a ballpark for scale you have in mind here?"

"No limit. Overwhelming force."

"Air support?"

"Yes. Air support. Armor. Whatever you need to take them down hard and fast."

Howard couldn't believe his ears. "What are you talking about? Why don't you just send in a couple of sedans and tell him you know he's got Redmond and you want him back?"

A handful of the others joined Ferguson in a chuckle. "You think that would work, tough guy?" he asked.

"I think its a proportionate first step. There are women and children living in the militia compound."

"I didn't see any in your photos."

"They were in the fields doing something."

"What were they doing?"

"I don't know. Hite said something about a retreat."

Ferguson smiled. "You're the best agent the militia ever had, Hank."

"Look, Mel, it's a well-known fact that there are women and children living there."

"Oh, you're right. They're bigamists, like the doctor said."

"They're innocent."

"I'm not convinced. Anyway, that's not our focus right now. Right now I want Ralph to start putting the plan together."

"I'm on it," Trimble said, before starting out of the conference room.

"Hold it, Ralph," Howard said. "You need to get Sheriff Bolo on your planning team."

"Who's he?" Trimble asked.

"He's the local sheriff. He knows the militia better than anyone."

"Are you shitting me, Hank?" Ferguson said with a wince. "We're the *ATF*. We don't need the local sheriff."

"I think we do."

"No, we don't. We've got you. You've been in there same as the sheriff." He pointed toward Trimble. "Ralph, add Hank to your team."

"Roger." Trimble looked at his watch and then at Howard. "Hank, I'm going to make a few calls to get the team assembled. Join us in the planning cell at fifteen thirty."

"I'd like to invite the sheriff," Howard said.

"No goddamn sheriff," Ferguson bellowed. "You got that?"

Howard could see there was no having an intelligent exchange at the moment, so he muttered, "Yeah, I got it."

"I'm serious, Hank. This is a secret operation. I don't want a word breathed to anyone, least of all the local sheriff."

"What about the FBI?" someone asked from the crowd at the back of the room.

"Yeah, and the South Dakota National Guard?" someone else added.

"Execute as our standing instructions dictate," Ferguson snapped. "Come on, everybody. Let's act like professionals here. This is the ATF's time to shine."

As the meeting was breaking up, Douglas Feint, Ph.D., took it upon himself to add a final thought: "Future generations will thank you for dealing with this in your time instead of theirs."

And Ferguson nodded. It was the ATF's time to shine. It was *his* time to shine.

18

Sheriff Dominic Bolo's home had a warmth about it that quickly put Ash at ease. Between the generous use of quality hardwoods in the walls and floors and the scent of roast pheasant wafting from the adjacent kitchen, he was comfortable with his surroundings for the first time in days. The cold beer in his hand helped his state of mind as well.

Bolo's wife, Little Feather, an attractive and young-looking Native American with roots in the Sioux tribe, emerged from the kitchen cradling a platter that hosted a nicely browned bird. "Dinner," she sang.

"Fantastic," Bolo said. Ash followed him from the den to the table. As he sat in one of the sturdy wooden chairs he caught sight of a rifle butt mounted to a plaque halfway up the near wall. The wood on the small end of the butt was splintered, as if it had forcibly broken away from the rest of the rifle.

"What's that?" Ash asked, pointing toward the plaque.

"That was a gift from my platoon," Bolo replied as he spooned a lump of mashed potatoes onto his plate.

"How did it break?"

"Against the side of a VC's head."

"But it's wood. Last I checked an M16's stock was plastic."

"It wasn't my rifle. It was the gook's rifle." He cov-

ered his mouth and shot a furtive glance toward Little
Feather. "She doesn't like me to use that word."

"Cool gift."

"Yeah. I didn't realize my platoon sergeant had
picked it up. He didn't present it to me until four months
later, just before I rolled back to the States."

"How long were you in Vietnam?"

"Ten months."

"I thought tours were a year long back then."

"They were."

Ash could see that Bolo caught the confusion on his
face. "Have you ever heard of Mi Chu?" Bolo asked.

"As in the Mi Chu Massacre?"

"Yeah."

"What about it?"

"I was there."

Ash locked eyes with his host, unflinching, waiting for
him to go on. Bolo took a sip of beer and continued:
"By the middle of my tour operations had started to get,
well, messy. We were Green Berets, but we weren't
doing Green Beret missions. More and more we were
doing these 'sweep and destroy' missions, and more and
more we weren't finding anything. The VC were smart.
They knew the land, and that knowledge made them
faster than we were. We were frustrated, but more than
that, the brass was frustrated. They wanted results. The
pressure was mounting from Washington. The protesters
were getting louder, more violent."

The sheriff sliced into his pheasant but instead of
eating just stared at his plate for a time. "The day before
we walked into Mi Chu we lost two guys. One guy
stepped on a land mine and the other took a grenade.
We never saw the enemy. We fired at noises and
shadows."

Bolo stuck a slice of the roast bird in his mouth and
chewed slowly. His eyes were unfocused. After another
bite of food he spoke again: "I said that I'd only been
in Nam for ten months; what I left out was that tour
was actually my third rotation in four years. As I think

about it now it seems unbelievable, but at the time I thought I could hack anything. After all, I was a Green Beret, right?" He looked over and Ash gave a nod, wondering where the story was heading.

"Maybe we should talk about something else," Little Feather said as she reached over and patted her husband's hand.

"No, I'm fine," Bolo returned. "I want to talk about it. It's been a long time." He took another swig of beer. "Anyway, by the middle of my third tour over there I was burned out, but I didn't recognize it. And if I did recognize it, I didn't want to admit it. Plus, the war had become . . . confusing. During my first tour we thought we could win. The Tet Offensive took a lot of the swagger out of our step and things didn't get any better after that. And I'd been home just long enough to see how pissed off the American public was. I didn't want to wear my uniform when I walked around town because I was afraid someone would spit on me or a fight might break out. I mean, have you ever been afraid to wear your uniform?"

Ash shook his head and said, "No, not really."

"You're lucky."

Little Feather passed the platter of pheasant to Ash and asked, "Would you like some more?" She exuded calm. Her dark brown eyes had a beautiful sadness about them. Her long black hair shimmered in the orange-yellow glow of the dining room.

"I'd love some," Ash replied, taking the platter and plunging his fork into several slices.

"Have you ever had pheasant before?" she asked.

"A few times, yes; but never this good."

She smiled. At the same time, Bolo refused to take his wife's cue for a new topic, determined to finish his thought. Ash could see at once that it pained him but he needed to get it out. "We weren't sure who the enemy was anymore," the sheriff said. "By the time we walked into the village of Mi Chu, we'd lost our ability to discriminate between combatant and civilian. Every-

one who wasn't one of us was one of them, the enemy."
His voice grew even quieter as he rubbed his forehead.
"So we got our orders: 'Level the village and neutralize
anyone found there.' I wasn't sure what headquarters
meant so I radioed back. I got Major 'Swede' Swenson
on the line. I'll never forget the conversation, if you can
call it that. He said, 'Carry out your orders, Staff Sergeant Bolo.' " He laughed, a disturbed chuckle. "I had
my orders, all right. We went in there and started firing.
Men. Women. Children. Pigs. Goats. Chickens. It didn't
matter. We had stopped being men. We were machines
of death. I didn't see the blood. I didn't hear the
screams. I tuned all of it out.

"When it was over we torched the buildings. Then we
walked five clicks and waited for the helos. We sat
around and smoked and chatted like we'd just played a
company softball game or something." He shook his
head with the memory. "Unbelievable."

The three of them sat in silence for a time. Ash knew
it would have been best to let the subject drop but now
his curiosity got the best of him: "So what happened
when you got back to the base?"

"The platoon leader and I debriefed the mission,"
Bolo said.

"And what did they say?"

"They said, 'Well done.' What they didn't realize, at
least until we made the cover of *Life* magazine, was that
there was a photographer with us. Only then did the shit
hit the fan."

"Court-martial?"

"Yep, a very high-visibility one. I was a popular face
in the news for a while. Of course, this was all before
you were born."

"What did they convict you of?"

"Nothing. It was one of those 'what works against you
works for you' deals. Plus, I didn't give the order, and
I wasn't the senior man present."

"So they hammered the platoon leader?"

"No. He was just following orders."

"So they nailed that major at headquarters?"

"No. When he gave the order he didn't mean for us to waste innocent civilians."

"Who did they convict?"

"Nobody. The Army politely suggested that I leave, but by that point that wasn't really a punishment."

"So you got out and came to Fairly?"

"More or less," Bolo said. "I grew my hair long and bummed around the country for a few years. I tried to be an actor. I tried to be a professional baseball player. I tried to get into law school. Eventually I wound up on the police force down in Wyoming, of all places. A few years after that I came up here. At first I was a security guard at the casino on the Indian reservation a few miles out of town. That's where I met Little Feather. Her dad still manages the place. Then three years ago I ran for sheriff and darned if I didn't win."

"And the rest is Fairly history," Ash joked.

Bolo's mouth formed the most imperceptible of smiles. "You know, I haven't talked about my experiences in Vietnam for years."

"I'm sorry," Ash replied, unsure of what to say in response to the sheriff's revelation.

"No, it's fine. I probably need to talk about it."

"I don't think you do," Little Feather intoned.

Bolo reached over and put his arm as far around her narrow shoulders as it would go without leaving his seat. "She protects me more than a Beretta ever could," he said.

"I can see that," Ash said.

"I guess the fact you're a SEAL brought these stories out," Bolo said. "I haven't been face-to-face with another special operator for many years now. Needless to say, I don't keep up with my buddies from the units I served with in Vietnam."

Little Feather summarily rose from her chair and began scooping up plates and platters as she commanded: "Why don't you two go back to the den and I'll bring coffee."

"Good idea," Bolo said. "Ash, are you a coffee drinker?"

"Never ask a Navy man if he's a coffee drinker," Ash quipped.

Bolo laughed and started for the couches where Ash and he had been seated before dinner. "I guarantee you, regardless of where you've been, you've never had coffee like the stuff Little Feather makes." He called toward the kitchen: "In fact, Little Feather, you may want to only give Ash a half-mugful. See how he reacts to it first."

"I'm okay, Dominic," Ash said. "I've had a lot of exotic coffees over the years—Turkey, Saudi, UAE, even the local brew in Baghdad. I'll tell you, some of the strongest coffee I ever drank was aboard the cruiser I was just assigned to."

"So why are you in Fairly?" Bolo asked.

The sudden shift in the conversation caught Ash a bit off guard, and he paused a moment to collect his thoughts. "Now it's my turn to tell a story, I guess." He flopped back on the couch and released a long breath. "That was a great dinner, by the way."

Bolo nodded and said, "Get to the story."

"Since 9-11, like most folks in the military, certainly most special-operations folks, I've been overseas a lot. That's not an excuse; it's just a fact."

Bolo raised his hands in surrender. "Easy, Tex. I'm unarmed."

"Sorry," Ash returned. "I'm sort of in the opposite situation from you with my story. I've been telling it a lot lately, or at least I've been listening to others tell what the story was."

Little Feather placed a tray of coffee mugs on the table between the two men and then withdrew to the kitchen without a word. "Give that a taste," Bolo said, pointing to the mug nearest Ash.

Ash complied, a bit tentatively at first as he gauged the temperature of the liquid, but then he allowed a good amount into his mouth. The coffee was rich and complex.

"That's good," Ash said.

"It's addictive is what it is," Bolo said. "So go on with your story."

"Where was I?"

"You were telling me about how much you were overseas since 9-11."

"Right. So I'm in Afghanistan for ten months, then in Iraq for the first few days of the war."

"Only a few days?"

"Yeah, I got called to be an admiral's aide in DC." Ash saw the confusion in the sheriff's eyes. "That's another story."

"So what did you do the first few days of the war?"

"A snatch-and-grab on the first night. Jumped out of a C-130 and drove into Baghdad to take the Iraqi deputy minister of information into custody."

"Kidnap?"

"We don't use that word."

"Right. So you start the war kicking ass and then get called to be an admiral's aide?"

"Yeah. I was only the aide for a couple of months, though. I discovered the hard way that the admiral's staff was using him to run an international smuggling ring that short-circuited UN resolutions, among other things."

"You know, I think I read about that."

"You may have. So as payback for that flail, the admiral gave me my wish and I got orders back to the show."

"You got your wish. What's the problem?"

"Nothing, from my point of view."

"How long were you in theater the last time?"

"Almost a year."

"And that was shorter than you were supposed to be over there?"

"Yeah."

"And that's how you wound up in Fairly?"

"Yep."

The sheriff cradled his mug and took a long draw from it. He was silent.

"Aren't you going to ask me what happened?"

"Do you want me to know?"

Ash thought for a time, and then said, "I was leading a SEAL detachment on board a Navy cruiser in the Northern Arabian Gulf. Our main mission was Maritime Interdiction Operations, or MIOs, as we call them. Basically, if the battle group identifies a ship working a suspicious pattern or that they have concerns about, a boarding team does a MIO."

"How do you get aboard the other ship?"

"Sometimes we rappel out of a helo, but most of the time we drive next to the ship using a thirty-foot boat and climb up the side using grappling hooks. One night a few weeks ago we got the call that a ship was hugging the Iranian coastline and the captain wanted us to do a MIO. I had my concerns. The weather was bad; the seas were rough. But we went ahead and did it."

"How many guys are in the boarding party?"

"Eight, including the two Swicks."

"What's a Swick?"

"The special boat guys. They're all but SEALs."

"All right, you got aboard the ship; then what happened?"

"It turns out it was a Polish tanker. The captain spoke English and was playing it real friendly, but I didn't like the vibe. Something wasn't right. Although the captain claimed he didn't have anything, I decided to search the ship. I had part of the team guard the Poles and the rest of us checked out the cargo holds."

"Did you find anything?"

"A dead goat in the first one, and a bunch of pirated CDs and DVDs in the second one. Those set me off."

"The DVDs?"

"Yeah. I mean, this tanker wasn't full of weapons; it was full of DVDs. Suddenly the whole effort seemed like a waste. I lost my temper a little bit. I ran up to the bridge and got in the captain's face. I refused to believe he didn't have more serious contraband aboard. Somewhere during the course of my interrogation one of the Poles pulled a gun and started shooting."

"Anybody get hit?"

"No. But during the debrief more than one of the boarding party stated that they thought my action jeopardized the mission."

"Okay. So . . ."

"So the cruiser's captain had the battle group's shrink come talk to me. He decided that I was suffering from combat fatigue."

"Combat fatigue? Is that still a diagnosis? I thought they would've come up with a fancier name for it by now. Combat fatigue sounds kind of Battle of the Bulge-ish, don't you think?"

"It's still an official diagnosis. I have the paperwork to prove it."

"And so they sent you to Fairly to run the ROTC unit?"

"Yeah. That was actually the better option, believe it or not. The personnel bureau's first offer was a SEAL headquarters job. I wasn't terribly excited about performing the daily walk of shame, if you know what I mean."

"I know exactly what you mean. During the court-martial I was stuck in an office at Fort Bragg with a bunch of other Green Berets and Rangers. They never said a word to me."

"So what do you know about the NROTC unit at Thaedt?"

Bolo smiled again. "I know you've got your work cut out for you."

"How so?"

"You can start with the master chief and work your way down. He's a good guy, and his heart is in the right place when it comes to the students, but he's the most unmilitary man I've ever seen. And he's a drinker, big time."

"I've seen that already. After I got my haircut I went

over to check in with the unit and the only thing I found was a sophomore hanging around the office surfing porn on the Internet."

"Fernandez was throwing one of his parties with the seniors."

"Yeah. I had the sophomore take me over to the master chief's apartment. Unbelievable."

"I'm sure he wasn't happy to see you."

"No, I broke up his party."

"In more ways than one. He was the king, and now he's not, thanks to you."

"I don't want to fight him."

"If I know him like I think I do you will have to fight him. But he won't fight you head-on. He's one of those passive-aggressive types or at least he can be when he knows he can't win a direct battle. And I'm sure as soon as he laid eyes on you his survival mechanism kicked in."

"You sound more like a psychologist than a lawman," Ash observed. "Or is that just something that has come with the job over the years?"

"Maybe. Little Feather tells me the same thing. There's not much in the way of serious crime around Fairly, but there are a lot of interesting personality types."

"What were the barbers talking to you about today—something about a cult?"

"The Badlands Militia."

"What the hell is that?"

"Have you ever heard of Devon Hite?"

"No," Ash replied.

The sheriff polished off the last of his coffee and leaned forward, sawing his hands together like a raconteur poised to launch into a tale. "This is what I've been able to piece together based on some research and a lot of rumors. Devon Hite dropped out of high school and changed his name to Lafayette Slimmz. Now I'm not a big fan of rock and roll, certainly not heavy metal, but I understand that he was the lead singer for the Baron's

Itch. He bummed around Hollywood playing the bars for a few years and waiting to get famous, but it didn't happen. What did happen is he became a heroin addict.

"After a stint in a low-budget rehab facility he cut his hair and worked out of the shadows dealing drugs to other bands. But even then he had this survival instinct that kept him out of jail. He must have felt the law breathing down his neck and decided on a quick feint. With no warning he left the road midtour and used his drug money to enter a seminary in Wyoming. He came out two years later as an ordained minister."

"Rocker to preacher, huh?"

"Yep. He stumbled into work as a singer with the show 'Be Healed.' You've heard of that, of course."

"Nope."

"You're messing with me, aren't you?"

"No, I've never heard of it. What is it?"

"It's televangelist Melvin C. Stewart's TV show, of course." Ash figured his expression evinced some sort of concern, because the sheriff immediately said, "I'm not a Jesus freak or anything. I just watch the program from time to time for entertainment. Melvin gets himself all fired up and the music is pretty good."

"Got it," Ash said.

"So, anyway, Hite becomes a staple on the show and before too long his rendition of 'Peace in the Valley' turns into the high point of the show and a gospel radio hit."

"He's got it made."

"Not quite. Seems he was having an affair with the middle-aged but admirably preserved Mrs. Melvin C. Stewart. Obviously, Melvin was less than impressed. But the preacher also knew that that kind of press might take the entire machine down. Fundamentalist Christians can be funny like that. Equipped with some line about going to the country to truly find Jesus—a story provided by the televangelist's crack PR team—the singer made his way to South Dakota with a pocket full of hush money, enough money to build a good-sized complex—four hundred acres' worth—outside of Fairly."

"So how does the militia get started?"

"That's the part of the story that's a little sketchy. Best I can tell the word of free room and board got back to his former associates and fans and soon he was, in fact, the man in charge of a new flock several hundred strong. And somewhere along the way, Hite put down the Bible and picked up a rifle. He stopped preaching and started ranting against the evils of big government—the thing that he figured had conspired against him. Words of sin and salvation were replaced by a call to arms, and with the arrival of the first batch of rifles the Badlands Militia was born."

"What was the one barber saying about Hite having two wives?"

"I've heard all kinds of things like that. It might be true, for all I know."

"Didn't I hear you say you were just out there?"

"Yeah, but I didn't see anything like that. In fact, I hardly ever see any women at all when I'm out there. I just go out there occasionally to make sure things aren't getting as crazy as Sven and the boys say they are. One of my main jobs is keeping the peace between the town, the university, and the militia." Bolo snapped his fingers. "That reminds me: Are you a hunter?"

"Not really."

"But you know your way around a shotgun, right?"

"You might say that."

"How'd you like to go pheasant hunting on Saturday? I think you'd get a kick out of seeing the militia's setup out there. Plus, Devon's always got a lot of big boy–type toys around."

"I'd love to, but I'm headed back to the East Coast tomorrow after classes."

"Oh. Well maybe we can go the weekend after this one."

"Sure. Will they be hunting then?"

"They hunt every day during the season. Why are you going back East already?"

"I have a SEAL buddy who was wounded in Iraq. I'm going to see him in the hospital near DC."

"How bad?"

"He lost half his leg."

Bolo winced. "It never ends, does it?" He rolled up one of his sleeves and pointed to a large scar along his left forearm. "This is from a booby trap, Quang Tri Province, 1972. Guy on point in front of me set it off. He got the worst of it. I put him on the chopper missing an arm, bleeding badly. I said, 'I'll see you soon, Nolan,' and he smiled back at me. Guy had balls. But I never saw him again. We got word in the field a few days later that he died in the hospital in Saigon."

Another silence followed as both men considered the friends they'd lost in combat. Ash checked his watch. "Well, I'd better figure out if I can get a motel room out by the highway."

"The truckers have probably filled the place by now. Why don't you stay here?"

"I don't want to put you guys out."

"It's no problem at all. This house isn't that big but we have made good use of what space we've got." The sheriff hailed toward the kitchen: "Little Feather, can we make up the guest bedroom for Ash?"

"Okay," she sang back.

"See, no problem," Bolo said to Ash.

Ash finished off the last of his mug of coffee and said, "I don't know how to thank you for all of this."

Bolo grew a wry smile and returned, "We'll figure something out, I'm sure."

19

Ash stood before the formation of NROTC midshipmen, although calling the gaggle of forty college students a "formation" was a stretch. They stood in crooked lines in various forms of workout dress, nothing close to a uniform between any two of them. The seniors were easy to pick out: They were the ones with the bloodshot eyes and drained pallor. Several of them were having trouble standing without swaying.

"I wanted to take this opportunity to introduce myself," Ash bellowed. "I am Lieutenant Roberts, your new officer-in-charge." He heard a titter from the back of the formation but chose to ignore it. He'd make his point soon enough.

"We're going to work out as a unit three mornings a week—Monday, Wednesday, and Friday." A chorus of groans followed. "That's right. Three mornings a week. Fall in by zero six hundred. And I want you to show up in regulation PT gear, not something you found in a Dumpster on your way out of the dorm." Ash walked up to the thin midshipman at something less than parade rest in front of him. "What is your name?"

"Gerhardt," the young man returned.

"Gerhardt. Is that your first or last name?"

"First."

Ash waited for the midshipman to finish, but he stood defiantly mute. "Okay, folks," Ash said. "I can see we're going to have to start this relationship from scratch, which isn't my favorite way to go. When an officer asks you your name you give him your rank and full name," Ash said, refocusing on the midshipman. "So let's try again: What is your name?"

"Midshipman First Class Gerhardt Skoskstad."

"There we go," Ash returned. "Now we're connecting. So, Mr. Skoskstad, I see that you're a Metallica fan."

"Damn right," Skoskstad replied.

"Damn right, *sir*," Ash corrected, which caused a ripple of snickers across the formation. "How about this? When you come to morning PT, you're a Navy fan. You're all Navy fans, right?" Silence. "And Navy fans wear Navy gear, preferably matching Navy gear." He looked over at Master Chief Fernandez, who was standing off to the side in his ill-fitting khaki uniform, leafing through a newspaper. The master chief ignored him.

"I see this group needs some motivation. Squads, form up on me. We're going for a little run."

Ash jogged a few yards across the adjacent parking lot and then waited for the midshipmen to follow him. They didn't line up in neat squads but rather gathered in a disorganized mob. "Line up. Four squads. Let's go," he commanded. At the same time he noted Fernandez had not moved from where he stood casually flipping through the day's news.

After nearly two minutes of attempting to orchestrate straight lines, Ash finally gave up and decided to just start running. "Double time, ho!" he shouted, as if they had any intention of running in unison. He took off at a moderate clip.

It was a beautiful spring morning in Fairly, perfect running weather. The air was cool and crisp. The breeze was nonexistent. At the early hour the faculty hadn't arrived and the rest of the student body was still in bed. The streets of Thaedt University were deserted. Time to let the campus know the U.S. Navy had their backs.

"Come on, let's get in step," Ash shouted back at the uninspired rabble that followed him. He clapped his hands and called, "Left, right, left, right, one, two, one, two." Twenty-five yards later, the group was starting to resemble a military outfit. Feet hit the pavement in near unison.

Ash started a chant: "I want to be a Navy hero." The midshipmen didn't echo the words. "Come on, now. Let's wake up the lazy civilians." He repeated the sing-song line, louder this time: "I want to be a Navy hero."

The midshipmen chanted back in a dull murmur: "I want to be a Navy hero."

"You're kidding me, right?" Ash prodded. "You guys are out here busting your asses, and your lazy classmates are still asleep. Doesn't that fire you up?"

"They're smarter than we are," somebody returned from the middle of the formation.

"That might well be true," Ash said. "But that doesn't mean you should let them get away with it." Again he shouted: "I want to be a Navy hero."

The midshipmen repeated the line with more gusto: "I want to be a Navy hero."

"I want to be a Navy SEAL."

"I want to be a Navy SEAL."

"I want to bag a bunch of insurgents."

"I want to bag a bunch of insurgents."

"I want to hear those scumbags squeal."

Laughter punctuated the midshipmen's response, but they managed to get it out: "I want to hear those scumbags squeal."

"Left foot."

"Left foot."

"Right foot."

"Right foot."

"Hoo-yah."

"Hoo-yah."

"One mile."

"One mile."

"No good."

"No good."

"Two miles."

"Two miles."

"No good."

"No good."

"Three miles."

"Three miles."

"Getting better."

"Getting better."

There was a spring in their steps now, even for those of the hungover among them. But their enthusiasm only lasted another quarter mile or so. Soon he had a chorus of wheezing behind him.

"You're sounding pretty bad back there," he said, turning around and running backward. "I guess we'll keep it down to four miles today."

"Four miles?" a voice in the gaggle replied. "No way."

"I don't care," a well-built fellow said from near the front of the second wavy squad. "Bring it on."

"Right on," a tall female added. "Let's go for five."

Ash was impressed. "That's what I'm talking about," he said to the two of them.

The female glared back and said, "This ain't for you, *sir*." Again, Ash let it go.

As they continued, the wheezing turned to coughing. Ash looked back and saw some threatening to fall out of the formation. A few steps later, a handful of them did. "Head back to the building," he called to them. He wasn't going to herd sheep today. Today was an assessment. A test.

At the two-and-a-half-mile point the formation had dwindled to less than half its original complement, and a mile after that Ash was accompanied by only two midshipmen: the well-built male and the tall female. Ash bumped the pace up a bit.

The two stayed right with him. He sped up and then again until he was almost in a sprint. He heard the girl start to fade. Faster still. The male midshipman stayed with him, surprisingly fast for a man of his size, not to mention one most likely suffering a hangover.

Around the next corner the NROTC building parking lot came into view—the unofficial finish line would certainly be where they'd started this run. Ash sensed that the midshipman knew it, too, as he edged his way slightly ahead of him. Ash met him, and then worked his way back into the lead, although his legs were starting to feel the effects of a hard run.

Closer, Ash could see a crowd ringed around the far edge of the lot: those who'd dropped out of the run earlier, no doubt. There was no way he was going to lose what had now become a de facto race. He couldn't, not if he had any hope of commanding the unit's respect in short order. And Ash had never been one to waste time.

Ash heard the crowd cheering: "Bruno, Bruno," and he figured that was who he was racing. The two were neck and neck now. This kid was tough, but Ash had one more gear left. He just had to wait for the right moment to use it.

One hundred yards away from the parking lot entrance Ash started his kick. He got a jump but was surprised when a few strides later Bruno had caught him again. They were neck and neck, stride for stride. And then Bruno surprised him by throwing an elbow that caught him squarely in the chest. The midshipman let out a cackle in spite of his huffing as he pushed ahead. Ash tried to catch him but he was already at full throttle.

But then justice of sorts was served. Bruno tripped on an invisible bump in the asphalt and toppled in a noisy heap just before the parking lot. Ash watched him go down, crossed the threshold into the lot, and then went back to check on the fallen midshipman.

"Are you all right?" Ash asked between breaths.

The midshipman slowly got to his feet and dusted himself off. He was bleeding slightly from one knee and had road rash along his shoulder blade. "I'm fine," he muttered. "I would've beat you if I hadn't fell."

"You kind of surprised me with the elbow," Ash said. "I didn't realize we were playing a contact sport."

The younger man grinned and said, "Got to be ready for anything around these parts, I guess."

The two of them walked over to the crowd at the far end of the parking lot and Ash said, "All right, form up again." The group looked a bit confused at first, but then slowly formed into a unit. "With two notable exceptions, I'm not terribly impressed with your physical readiness. Our PT sessions will take care of some of that, but I also recommend all of you start to take a strain on your own, as well. I'd like to see the first-class midshipmen over by the building right after this. Fall out."

The crowd dispersed and the seniors ambled over to the side of the building, as Ash had directed. Master Chief Fernandez materialized at the same time, holding a mug of coffee. He lined up next to the midshipmen, across from Ash—a clear signal.

"How many of you expect to be commissioned at the end of this semester?" Ash asked. All of them raised their hands. Ash nodded and continued with, "We've got a lot of work to do then." He pointed at himself. "This is no joke. We are a nation at war, and I won't let anyone pin on ensign shoulder boards if I'm not convinced they're ready to lead troops in battle. I expect each and every one of you to be a leader." He made it a point to look at the master chief, who was staring at the ground at his feet, obviously put off by the lecture. "All right. We'll see you bright and early Monday morning. Now go get ready for class."

The seniors dispersed along with Fernandez. Ash called him back: "Master Chief, you got a second?"

"Sure," the master chief sang back with a disingenuous air. "I've always got time for an officer." He wheeled around, spilling a little of his coffee as he did.

"I'm a little disappointed that you didn't join us for PT," Ash said.

Fernandez threw his head back in a deep belly laugh. "Hell, Lieutenant, I'm forty-five years old. Why would I want to run around and get myself all sweaty?"

"Because it's your responsibility as an active-duty master chief. And while we're on the topic of responsibility, it's also your responsibility to ensure the midshipmen get the education the taxpayers have paid for. Letting them miss class to help you polish off a keg at your place is way off the reservation."

Fernandez's face drew taut, and he leaned in toward Ash, again spilling a few ounces of coffee down the side of his mug. "You've got a lot of guts lecturing me, *Lieuten-ant*." He drew the rank out mockingly. "You see, I've done a little asking around myself. I know why you're here."

"Oh, yeah? Why?"

"Because you're burned out. You see, you and I aren't that different."

Ash shook his head. "From what I've seen so far, Master Chief, you and I are very different. Now we can do this one of two ways: We can work together or apart. If you choose the second option I'll see to it you leave, and I doubt the Bureau has many shore-duty billets for you."

"I'll retire."

"At nineteen years of service? Seems kind of foolish to me."

Fernandez froze. Stymied. He muttered something and then turned on his heel and walked away. Ash watched him go, wondering which path the enlisted man would choose and afraid that he already knew the answer.

20

Ash walked along the main corridor of Bethesda Naval Hospital, convinced more than ever that he hated hospitals. His most recent experience with a doctor certainly didn't help alleviate his fears. Even as he strode across the shiny tile he harbored some concern that someone in a white coat might grab him and lock him in a room somewhere and tell him that he could never leave.

He approached the main information desk, which was manned by a handful of enlisted sailors who, in fact, wore white coats over their Navy uniforms. "Can I help you, sir?" a pretty blonde petty officer asked.

"Can you tell me what room Lieutenant Weldon is in?" Ash asked in return.

The petty officer tapped on her keyboard, furrowed her brow, and said, "I'm going to have to make a phone call, sir. Can you hold on a moment?"

"Sure."

She turned her back and dialed the phone. After a short conversation, she hung up and turned back to Ash. "He's in therapy right now."

"Yeah? And?"

"And patients can't have visitors when they're in therapy."

"When can I see him?"

"Visiting hours in the amputee ward are later this afternoon."

"How much later?"

She looked at the clock on the wall. "Three hours or so. I'm surprised Lieutenant Weldon didn't tell you that."

"I'm surprising him."

She smiled. "You can surprise him in three hours, then. There's a lounge over there." She pointed across Ash's shoulder.

Ash checked his watch. He didn't have much time, since he was catching a flight to New York to make the duty visit with his family. He wasn't leaving without seeing Wild.

As he walked toward the lounge he passed a coatrack upon which hung a couple of lab coats similar to the ones those behind the desk wore. He had an idea. It might have been one of the oldest tricks in the book, but it just might work, even though he was wearing civilian clothes and not his uniform. He glanced furtively to either side, and seeing no one paying attention, he slipped one of the coats on and swiftly made his way to the elevator.

He emerged on the fifth floor and strode purposefully down the passageway, using a lesson he learned early during plebe year at Annapolis: You could get away with almost anything if you looked like you knew what you were doing. He walked up to one of the corpsmen and asked, "Where is the therapy room for amputees?"

The corpsman eyed him and asked, "Who are you, sir?"

Ash extended his hand and said, "Lieutenant Roberts."

"And what organization are you with?"

Ash paused and said, "Thaedt University."

The corpsman's eyes brightened and he gestured down the hall. "It's the last room on the left."

Ash said thanks and continued on his way. Without hesitating he passed through the doorway and into the room.

"Hello, Dr. Roberts," a voice said from the left. He looked over and saw Wild negotiating a set of parallel bars with the assistance of a young black sailor. "Be with you in a second."

Wild turned around and started the other way down the bars, which allowed Ash to focus on his missing limb. Ash was having trouble processing the sight. Wild reached the end of the bars and turned around again. He was getting tired now. By the time he made it to the other end he was completely winded.

"That's enough for now, sir," the sailor said.

"I agree," Wild puffed.

The sailor draped a towel around Wild's shoulders and helped him into a wheelchair. Ash went over to shake his hand, but a handshake didn't seem to be enough, so he bent over and gave him an awkward hug, which Wild reciprocated as much as he could from his seated position.

"I didn't know you were coming," Wild said.

"I didn't either, to be honest. The idea sort of hit me when I was on my way to the airport."

"I'll come back in a little bit," the sailor said before focusing on Ash. "This isn't really kosher, you know, sir."

"I appreciate you giving us a little time to catch up," Ash said.

"And I appreciate you giving me some time to catch my breath," Wild added. "This guy's a motherfucker."

The sailor laughed and walked out.

Only then did Ash notice the others across the room. Another sailor assisted an amputee down another set of parallel bars. "There are a lot of us," Wild intoned.

Ash nodded, unsure of how to respond. "How are you?" he asked mechanically.

"I'm alive."

Ash suddenly felt as if his problems were insignificant, and for the next few hours he and his friend talked and laughed as if the last year had never happened.

21

Ash walked down the Jetway after the short flight from DC, happy to see another familiar face. McCaffrey had been his father's driver since Ash was in grade school. He was more than just an employee; he was a member of the Roberts family. He'd even been there the night that Ash had lost his virginity, several hundred feet away, anyway, always the master of trust and discretion. Now he stood, tall and lean, his short Afro peeking out from under his chauffeur's cap like a gray cloud over each of his brown ears.

But McCaffrey had no poker face. As they drew nearer each other, Ash could see a look of paternal concern in his dark eyes. It was an expression tinged with sorrow and perhaps a bit of disappointment, and it broke Ash's heart. Ash had always tried to be what McCaffrey believed he was, and now in the driver's countenance he saw just how far he'd fallen.

They hugged. McCaffrey muttered a simple, "Welcome home."

"It's good to see you," Ash returned.

The two men strolled to the baggage carousel where they stood in awkward silence waiting for Ash's hanging bag. Once it appeared, McCaffrey asked, "Is that it?"

"Yes," Ash said.

"Doesn't seem like very much considering how long you've been gone."

Ash offered a slight smile and said, "Everything I needed over there is still over there."

The black Lincoln was idling at the curb, guarded by a rent-a-cop, more evidence of Roberts family clout. McCaffrey climbed behind the wheel and Ash jumped in the passenger seat next to him even though he knew McCaffrey preferred his riders to sit in back. Ash didn't want to be served. He wanted to ride into Manhattan with a friend's understanding.

McCaffrey remained silent as he steered the car westward on the Long Island Expressway. Ash sensed he had questions but didn't know how to ask them. Finally, the lieutenant could take no more of the quiet.

"It's all right, McCaffrey," Ash said. "I'm not crazy or anything."

"I know you're not crazy," the driver returned. "And that's what I've been telling your father, too." He bit his thick lip and cut his eyes toward his passenger. "Not that he thinks you're crazy. I didn't mean it like that."

Ash stared blankly out the side window, watching the guardrail rush by like a long white snake. "He's never liked the choices I made. Now I guess he'll be convinced he was right all along."

"I wouldn't be too hard on him, Ash. He's very proud of you."

"I don't know about proud. I'd say confused is a better word. And I can't say as I blame him."

McCaffrey changed the subject: "I think Winston has a sort of welcome-home party planned for you tonight."

In his mind's eye, Ash saw his brother even less capable than his father of understanding his situation. He let out a sardonic chuckle and muttered, "Why?"

The tone of McCaffrey's voice shifted to one Ash hadn't heard since his time home on leave from the Naval Academy. "Don't always try to be the rebel, Ashton. Your family will always support you. Never forget that."

"If you say so."

"I do. And you know I'm right."

With that the conversation abruptly died. Ash stared pensively out the window as McCaffrey drove in silence. Like any good career driver, he could go for hours without talking to his passengers, even if, as in this case, there was much he wanted to know from them.

Then the Manhattan skyline appeared, at once a welcome sight and a reminder of the circumstances now before him. He worked his gaze southward, across the Empire State Building toward the tip of the island where the glaring absence of the World Trade Center reminded him of what had made his life so chaotic over the last number of years. Politics aside, it had been a fight well fought by his men and him. And that's what the uninitiated would never understand. The press, the pundits, the television personalities, even the politicians all the way to the commander in chief didn't get what it was that made a warrior fight to win. Ash wasn't sure that his enemy hated his freedom; he was quite certain that his enemy had killed his men, and he was willing to fight to the death to prevent it from happening again. But now the fight had been taken away from him. Or he'd lost it. Either notion made his heart sink.

Across the bridges and southward along the avenues and the car pulled in front of the entrance to Roberts International World Headquarters. Ash jumped out before McCaffrey could even think about opening the door for him and in short order was through the massive revolving door that fed into the expansive, marble-appointed lobby. It was only then that he sensed he was underdressed. To his eye, his chinos and corduroy jacket—comfortable for a long transatlantic flight—were in sharp contrast to the worsted wool suits and silk ties that now surrounded him. At the same time it didn't matter. Those who passed were in too big a hurry to pass judgment.

Ash rode the express elevator to the seventy-first floor, and when the door opened he was immediately greeted by the wide smile of Abigail Harrison, his father's personal secretary. She hung up the phone and ran around her desk, arms spread wide as she bore down on him.

"Oh my God," she said, instantly breathless. "He's home at last."

"It's good to see you, Abby," Ash returned, arms only making it halfway around her wide frame as he met her in a hug. As usual she was wearing a bit too much perfume, a thick flowery fragrance that made her seem older than she really was.

"How was it over there?" she asked. "Just horrible?" She waved her hands. "No, wait. Don't tell me. I don't want to know."

"It wasn't that bad, Abby," Ash said. "I was fine."

She nodded with concern as she asked, "So how are you feeling now?"

"I'm fine, really."

"Really?"

"Really."

She continued to stare at him, as if unconvinced. "Okay . . ."

Ash pointed toward his father's office. "Is he in?"

"Yes, yes, of course. Go right in. Oh, it's so good to have you back with us."

Ash looked over his shoulder at the woman. "I'm only going to be here for a few days."

"Really? I thought . . . didn't the Army . . ."

"Navy, Abby. I'm in the Navy."

"Didn't the Navy . . . weren't you discharged or something?"

"No. I'm only changing duty stations."

"Oh, I guess I misunderstood. Well, that's too bad."

"It's okay. I like the Navy. Or I *liked* the Navy."

Ash noted the puzzled look on the secretary's face and it made him wish he'd skipped qualifying his current thoughts about his professional standing. He didn't want to get into it, not with her, not with anybody.

The test of his ability to not get into it was about to

come. Ash—a man who'd faced down gunfire and road-side bombs without much more than the blink of an eye—felt a lump in his throat as he moved toward the office. He peered around the door frame. His father was seated in his large leather chair facing away from the desk, looking out the window that gave him a panoramic view of New York City.

Ash tried to slip into the office without disturbing his father, but the senior Roberts caught a glint of movement in one of the windows. He spun around with his brow furrowed, but then his expression softened as he recognized his oldest son. He said, "I've got to go," into the phone and hung up.

As his father stepped from behind his huge wooden desk Ash studied his face. Ashton Roberts III looked markedly older than the last time they'd seen each other during an almost-chance meeting in Washington, D.C., over a year before when Ashton Roberts IV was working in the Pentagon as the aide to a three-star admiral. In the time since then Ash hadn't bothered to keep up with how Roberts International was faring businesswise. There hadn't been time in his busy fighting life. But now, as he considered his father's full head of gray-flecked hair and tanned complexion, he figured things must have been going just fine.

Ash wasn't sure how to greet the man—never had been. He waited for his father to set the tone. The older Roberts extended his hand and clasped his son's biceps, saying, "Welcome home, son. It's good to see you."

As he was every time following an extended separa-tion, Ash was struck by how the rough texture of his father's palm belied a man who worked as a captain of industry—the king of the white-collar world. This time of year the calluses would have been earned clearing brush from the five acres that surrounded their Old Greenwich estate. In the fall they were from chopping wood, "the most rewarding work," as he often said when stacking a cord or two. "It's good to see you, too," Ash replied.

And then they stood for a few beats, both sensing that the handshake fell short of the emotion of the moment. But Ash still waited for his father to initiate the next move, and he was relieved when the senior Roberts wrapped his arms around him, repeating, "It's good to see you."

Ash followed his father into the far corner of the large office and sat tentatively on the large leather couch, across the Bolivian wormwood coffee table from where his father plopped into a wingback chair. His father, never one to mince words, jumped right into what he considered the matter at hand: "Winston and I were thinking about where your talents might best be suited in the organization, and it occurred to us that you might be most effective working with our international markets, you know, with your knowledge of the Arab world and whatnot."

"What are you talking about?"

"We assumed you'd want to work with Roberts."

"I might someday, but not now."

"Not now? What are you going to do for a job?"

"I'm in the Navy."

"I thought you were being discharged from the Navy."

"Why would I be discharged?"

His father sat back, face twisted in confusion. It was obvious to Ash now where Abby's impressions had originated from. "I thought . . . you're not completely . . . *well,* are you?"

Ash released an exasperated breath. Rubbing his temples, he said, "I'm already tired of telling people I'm not crazy, Dad. I just lost my temper on a mission one night."

His father leaned his lanky frame across the coffee table. "This is it, don't you see? This is the perfect opportunity to make your move back to the private sector, back to us."

"I'm not ready."

"Oh, that's ridiculous. You were never meant to be a

military man. You weren't bred for it. And now they've stolen your honor."

"No, they haven't."

"They've stolen your honor!" his father insisted, pounding his fist on the table. "And that means they've stolen the entire Roberts family's honor."

Ash saw movement through the door out of the corner of his eye, and he turned to see his younger brother, Winston, coming toward him wearing a broad grin.

"All hail the conquering hero," Winston called across the office. "I hope you're ready for a celebration because the boys and me have cooked up a night on the town like you've never had."

The brothers embraced. Winston was slight as ever, a full head shorter than his brother. But he had the executive look down pat, all the way down to his Cartier watch with the black leather band. His pallor was similar to his father's, and his hair was a tint or two lighter than its natural dirty blond.

"You're looking buff," Ash said.

"I've been working out," Winston returned. "They just opened this new health club on the West Side. Wait until you see it."

"I don't know if I'll have time."

Winston jerked a thumb toward his brother as he looked over his shoulder. "Get a load of this guy, will you, Dad? Always the overachiever. Trust me, Ash; we'll have time to work out. The international market is busy, but it isn't *that* busy."

"He's not joining us," their father intoned.

"What?" Winston said. "Not joining us? Who are you working for then?"

"The Navy," Ash said.

"I thought you were being thrown—er, I thought you were leaving the Navy."

"No, I'm not."

"It turns out he's not crazy after all," the senior Roberts said.

"Why would you be staying in the Navy after the way

they've treated you?" Winston asked, taking a seat next to their father. Now the two-on-one was official.

"I don't really have any complaints," Ash said. "The Navy's been pretty good to me."

"Why are you dragging us through the mud with this?" their father asked.

Ash held his hands out and said, "This isn't about you and Winston, Dad. It's about me. And even if I agree with you that they've taken my honor—which I don't— I certainly wouldn't get it back by running away. Besides the Navy's not letting anybody out right now, especially SEALs."

"I could pick up that phone right now and talk to one or two very important men. I could have you out of the Navy within the hour."

"Please don't do that."

"You've done your bit, Ash," Winston added. "Why don't you come back to the fold before it's too late?"

"Too late for what?"

As Winston tapped a finger against his forehead, Ash's cell phone buzzed at his hip. Since he wasn't enjoying his current conversation, he chose to glance down at the caller's number. He didn't recognize it, but wanted to take the call anyway. He was ready for a distraction. "Do you mind if I answer this?" he asked the two across from him. Both shrugged in response.

Ash took a handful of steps away from the sitting area and put the phone to his ear, answering with his signature line, "Ash is up."

"Where is Fairly?" It was Wild.

"Hello, Wild," Ash replied. "It's in South Dakota."

"I know that. What big city is it near?"

"South Dakota doesn't have any big cities."

"Oh."

"Why do you ask?"

"I'm just thinking."

"Thinking . . . about what?"

"Nothing. Here comes my therapist again. I've got to go. Rap at you later, dude."

Wild cut the connection.

Ash looked across the room at his father and brother, who both eyed him with looks of concern. He almost related Wild's plight but somehow a sense they wouldn't fully understand kept him from saying anything.

22

Ash noticed the cell phones and Blackberrys were coming out now. It was nearly ten p.m. and the well-paid executives of Roberts International were dialing their wives, girlfriends, or both and informing them that they'd most likely be spending the night in the city. Their expressions told of a routine oft executed, and Ash was reminded that money wasn't free, in spite of middle-class perceptions to the contrary. Many times he'd tried to tell his fellow SEALs that his father had worked at an excruciating pace 24/7 to maintain the family fortune, but none of them had wanted to hear it.

But as Ash had worked his way around the table chatting with the select group Winston had invited, he was reminded of another New York City, or more precisely, Manhattan phenomenon: Nobody had a job that could be explained in a word. In other part of the county people were doctors or ministers or teachers. In Manhattan people were futures traders specializing in the bond market or offshore investment advisors or business development executives assigned to the Far Eastern sector.

Ash was ravenously hungry. Nobody around the table seemed to find it unusual that it was ten p.m. and they still hadn't eaten dinner. Another facet of life in the city that never sleeps, he figured.

These environs used to be familiar. In high school Ash and his buddies would venture into the city as if they owned the place. Concerts at Madison Square Garden, baseball games at Yankee Stadium, pickup lacrosse games in Central Park—life was good then. But now he was an outsider, one who had turned his back on the destiny his family had expected. He wondered if his inevitable future was now catching up to him, the thing that would make his years as a SEAL the dalliance that his family considered it to be.

He thought back to the night that now lived in his personal infamy and cursed himself for losing control of the situation. He'd been trained better than that. He'd always performed better than that. Maybe the doctor's diagnosis had been accurate after all. Maybe he did have combat fatigue.

But SEALs didn't get combat fatigue. The argument raging in his brain was circular. He wanted to make it stop but seemed powerless to do so. The red wine on an empty stomach combined with his current low alcohol tolerance certainly wasn't helping things. He stared at the frames on the walls of the steakhouse—autographed pictures of famous patrons, moments in time, and paintings of racehorses—searching for ground, hoping to cling to a touchstone that would keep his mental spiral from traveling further downward.

"Are you all right?" brother Winston asked from across the table.

"Yeah, I'm fine," Ash replied after taking a second to snap out of his reverie.

"This is your homecoming celebration, you know. You could act like you're having more fun."

"I am having fun."

"If you say so." Winston grabbed a spoon and tapped it against the side of his wine glass. The *tink, tink* instantly ceased the din of conversation.

Winston stood up, glass in hand, and said, "Gentlemen, first I'd like to thank you for joining me in celebrating the joyous return of my big brother." A smattering of applause. "It's no secret Ash has taken a different path, one the Roberts family is very proud of, one that America should be very proud of. I know all of you fully support our military; in fact, I know some of you actually serve on the boards of various charities and nonprofits that support the military. So please join me in a toast to Ash Roberts." He raised his glass. "Welcome home, brother."

All around the table raised their glasses and echoed, "Welcome home."

As Winston retook his seat, Benjamin Greyson, the heir to the Greyson Fabrics empire (and the fortune that came with it), leaned toward Ash and asked down his aquiline nose, "So how was it, *really*?"

Ash had known Greyson since he was a youngster—he'd prepped with Winston—but hadn't seen him in several years. Now here he was all grown up, not just in the working world but *owning* the working world.

"You mean the war?" Ash asked in return.

"Of course I mean the war," Greyson said before polishing off what remained of his Beaujolais and than recharging his glass. "Have you done anything else noteworthy in the past couple of years?"

And there it was: the essence of corporate life in the big city. Accomplishments were only those things that registered as noteworthy in mealtime conversations at a Manhattan steakhouse. There was no hope for nuance. Subtle details would fall to the floor. All that survived were those marquee things that could cut through the noise.

"It's hard to describe," Ash said.

Greyson placed both elbows on the table and perched his delicate chin on his manicured fists: "Indulge me."

Ash studied the young exec's expression momentarily. His brain was pounding again, this time even worse than before. Maybe it was the wine, the hunger, the jet lag, but he was well out of sorts. But even beyond his current physical state, one that should have been easily tolerated by a special warrior, with each stupid question, with each modicum of civilized comfort, he felt less the SEAL. He was getting weaker. He wondered if he'd ever get back

to the teams . . . the men he loved to lead . . . his life.
How was he going to stop the descent?

Ash took a deep breath and decided there was no
running from his current setting. Winston deserved better from him, however naive he was. Ash wasn't about
to embarrass his younger brother in front of the other
future captains of industry. The only purpose that would
have served was to get tongues wagging about certain
imperfections in the Roberts family bloodline and in no
time related stock performance would begin to decline.

Ash was about to attempt an answer when one of the
waiters leaned between Greyson and him, asking, "You
had the porterhouse, sir?" The waiter held a wooden
cutting board piled high with thin slices of perfectly
grilled steak. The wisps of steam that rose from the platter were an invitation.

"Give me the whole thing," Ash said, using both arms
to wave the meat in.

"All of it, sir?" the waiter returned.

"Yeah, all of it."

"But, sir, these cuts are supposed to be for three
people."

Ash looked around and saw that the exchange had
drawn the attention of everyone at the table, including
Winston. "Just kidding," Ash said. "I'm really hungry;
I apologize."

With smiles and a chuckle or two, everyone returned
to their previous conversations. Greyson said, "So you
were saying . . ."

Ash took the first bite of steak. After months of ship's
food and MREs in the field the taste and texture of
world-class steak was heavenly. He moaned and said,
"Damn, that's good."

"You were going to tell me about the war,"
Greyson prompted.

Ash swallowed his third bite, happy to feel the burning in his stomach subside. There really was no better
comfort food than steak, he thought. He was sawing into
his fourth when he said, "War is a tricky thing, Ben. I

know you probably want to hear stories of intense battles—and I've been in a few, I guess—but all that springs to mind when somebody asks me what it was like are the faces of my men."

"Did any of them get killed?" Greyson asked.

It was an innocent enough question but with it another wire in Ash's brain came loose. "Why do you ask that?"

"I was just wondering."

Ash leaned close to Greyson and jabbed a finger into his pinpoint Oxford shirt. "No, you weren't just wondering, Ben. You wanted to be entertained. Or even worse, you wanted me to give you a story that would make you sound tough, something that you could tell your buddies after a grueling squash match."

"Take it easy, Ash."

"That's all this war is to you, isn't it? Something you talk about, something you see on CNN and go, 'Isn't that a shame?'"

Ash stopped himself. All eyes were on him once again. He looked over at Winston, whose expression was not only one of shock and embarrassment, but of pity.

"Excuse me," Ash said, wiping his mouth with a cloth napkin. "I need to use the bathroom."

Ash worked to ignore the faces around him as he calmly pushed back from the table, chucked his napkin on his chair, and made his way across the restaurant toward the bathroom. He was happy to find the place empty. He splashed cold water on his face and then stood looking at himself in the mirror. His eyes were bloodshot and the circles under them were dark and pronounced. The lines on his face seemed deeper and longer than before, back when he was sane. And he could have sworn that his hairline had receded another inch in the last few days.

He held his hand up to his face and watched his fingers shake like an alcoholic's after a bender. He ran his tongue along his teeth and thought that several of them were loose. He was on a downward slide. Regardless of how bogus the beginning of it had been, how much the overreaction to a single loss of temper, his journey into the depths was now revealing itself as some sort of self-fulfilling prophecy.

Ash splashed more water on his face and then hung over the sink. He wished he could throw up and some-how rid himself of the sickness, whatever it was. But he just hovered there, breathing deeply, trying to compose himself. Only then did he realize there was an attendant seated only a few feet away.

"Tough days," the man muttered as he extended his arm and handed Ash a cloth towel.

The towel had a pleasant scent and felt warm against his face. He suddenly felt a soothing calm as he studied the attendant. He was dressed in a white waiter's jacket with a bow tie, black slacks, and shiny leather shoes. What few thin wisps of hair remained on his head were combed straight back. He looked old, probably older than he was, but there was a softness in his crystal-blue eyes. His thin lips curled in a wry smile as he said, "Tough days is part of it, you know." His voice was deep and resonant but harsh around the edges, that of a lifelong smoker, Ash figured.

"Trust me, I know," Ash returned as he continued to pat his face with the towel.

"It doesn't look to me like you do."

Ash wasn't in the mood for a lecture, especially not from a bathroom attendant. "Thanks, old-timer," he said. "Have a nice evening."

Ash dropped the towel on the basin and had taken a couple of steps toward the door when the man said from behind, "You ain't sick."

Ash reversed himself and said, "You're right; I'm fine."

"Then why did you try to barf in the sink just now?"

"I didn't. I was just washing my face."

"Looked to me like you was trying to barf."

"I wasn't."

"Nothing came out, though, did it?"

"No."

"Because you ain't sick."

Ash took a few more steps, considering the man more closely, and the man didn't flinch, choosing instead to grow a wider smile until what few teeth remained in his mouth were displayed in all of their stained glory. The SEAL reached for his wallet and placed a five-dollar bill in the small dish near the attendant, saying, "Thanks for the diagnosis, Doctor."

"I don't need the money," the attendant called to Ash's back.

"Take it anyway," Ash returned with a wave over his shoulder.

"I don't work here."

In the mirror's reflection Ash saw the stool upon which the attendant had been seated was now empty. For a second he wondered if he'd been talking to a ghost or if the entire exchange had been in his mind, but then he heard the clanking of a belt buckle and noticed the man's shoes, tips peeking out from under the slacks and striped boxers that had bunched over them. As the stall erupted in a staccato burst of flatulence, Ash made his way through the door.

He ran headlong into his brother, who buttoned his suit coat as he said, "You may think Ben's a twerp from the old days, but now he's a very important associate of mine; in fact, all of these gentlemen with us here tonight are important associates of mine. I'd ask that you treat them with whatever kindness you can muster up at this point."

"I'm sorry, Winston," Ash said.

"Fortunately Ben has chosen not to take offense. He suggested we go out to this new place on the Upper East Side."

The others queued up behind Winston, greeting Ash with nods and forced smiles. Ash looked at Greyson and said, "I apologize, Ben. I didn't mean to get upset."

"That's fine, sport," Greyson said as he draped a silk scarf around his neck. "Let's go get a few drinks and see if we can't get laid in the process."

"Don't forget you're married, Ben," one of them said from the back of the procession.

"Details, details," Greyson quipped in return.

The group piled into three cabs that formed into a convoy as they rolled across the width of the island. Ash gazed out the window, taking in the lights of the city along with the bums, punks, addicts, and whores. He wondered what an Iraqi might think presented with the same images. Was this what the "global war on terror" wrought? Was this the freedom that the nation promised to the world?

And in the cabs sat the scions of privilege, obtusely passing among their unfortunate subjects. Their animated conversations, wisecracking smiles, and backslaps were all products of those who'd never seen a body split by a rocket-propelled grenade or the tears running down an Iraqi child's face as his house went up in flames behind him. They didn't care; their job was to run the world, not to live in it.

Ash realized then that he could never work for Roberts International, and that was unsettling. That option had always been his out, his mental release valve. At once he now saw that his choice of the path less taken wasn't just a youthful lark; it was the definition of his life.

But he was lost on the path less taken. He'd always avoided bravado but that didn't change the fact that before he was sent packing from the SEALs' world he'd ambled about with the swagger and confidence of one who'd earned his stripes under fire. He wasn't a warmonger; he was a warrior. And a warrior lives life in balance but desires victory over everything else. Ash wondered if he'd ever be allowed to feel that passion again.

The cab came to a stop and Ash followed the others to the curb and across the sidewalk. The group sashayed past a long line of people to where the doorman—a gigantic Asian guy with a Mohawk—parted the velvet rope and let them pass without a word. They entered the place through a black metal door with BLUE EYES stenciled on it, which Ash figured was the name of the club.

Ash fully expected to be surrounded by smoke, loud music, and dancers inside but he soon realized the vibe was much more low-key than that. The strains of violins and the smooth braying of clarinets and saxophones replaced the almost obligatory thumping low-end pulsing through sets of gigantic speakers. On the stage across the large room a Frank Sinatra impersonator bathed in a single white spotlight. Ash was no expert—more a rock fan than forties-era swing aficionado—but it struck him that the performer was doing a pretty decent job with "Luck Be a Lady."

The patrons were all dressed for the venue. The men looked like Rat Pack refugees—suits with narrow lapels, skinny ties, and pointed-toe shoes; and the women favored big hairdos, sparkling knee-length cocktail dresses with plunging necklines, and multiple strands of pearls around their oh-so-long necks. Ash gazed down at his rumpled casual wear and felt ever more the man who fell to earth.

At the bar Winston gestured toward his brother and shouted, "What do you want?"

"Beer," Ash replied.

Winston shook his head and returned, "They don't do beer here. How about a martini?"

"They don't do beer? What kind of bar doesn't do beer?"

Winston shrugged. "Do you want a martini or not? That's what we're all having."

"Whatever."

The drinks were served in huge conical glasses with long stems that hosted olives the size of small apples. After another toast, this one to "good friends," the execs made their way toward one of the handful of sitting areas. A thin man sporting a Caesar haircut and a turtleneck rose as they approached and extended his hand with a pronounced crook at the wrist. "I'm doing Peter

Lawford tonight," he announced with a twirl. "What do you think?"

"Sure," Ash said, somewhat dumbfounded.

"You must be Ash," the man said. "I've heard a lot about you."

"Oh . . ."

The man stood expectantly for a few awkward beats, and then said, "I'm Gerard."

"Nice to meet you, Gerard." His hand felt disturbingly soft as they shook.

"I'm friends with the girls."

Gerard stepped aside with a sweep of his arms, revealing a dozen women strewn across the couches that bordered a large Oriental rug. The execs moved without pause, flopping between the women with polite air kisses as Ash tried to figure out whether they were wives, mistresses, or just casual acquaintances.

Winston walked over with a pretty blonde wearing an Oriental-style housecoat and capri pants with very steep spiked heels. "This is Erica," he said. He saw no spark of recognition in Ash's eyes, so he followed with, "My girlfriend."

"Oh, right, of course," Ash said. "It's great to see you again."

"I don't think we've met," Erica said, shooting a curious look back to Winston.

"Are you sure?" Ash returned, attempting some measure of recovery.

"We've only been dating a few months," Winston explained.

"I'm sorry; in any case, Erica, it's very nice to meet you."

"We're all glad you made it back safely," Erica said. "It must have been terrible over there."

Ash shrugged.

"I told you he doesn't like to talk about it, dear," Winston scolded. "Why don't we go dance. Excuse us, Brother."

Ash watched his brother move away with his girlfriend

in tow. The others paired up with the remaining women and soon the dance floor was full of executives holding lithe women by their waists, all pretending they knew how to dance to the half-century-old music coming from the bandstand. Ash felt that he stuck out as he stood solo in his mufti, so he sluck over to the sitting area and slouched low in one of the leather couches.

He thoughts went to South Dakota, although he wasn't sure what to think. He'd never been there until a few days ago. As far as he knew, the only thing in South Dakota was Mount Rushmore. And why had a master chief petty officer and not an officer run this particular ROTC unit over the last few years? That didn't mean the unit wasn't squared away, necessarily. Most master chiefs that Ash had ever dealt with were better leaders than most of the captains he'd served under. But all the same, it was weird.

Ash considered his half-empty martini glass and longed for a cold beer instead. He refused to believe the place didn't serve beer, so he got off the couch and walked over to the bar.

"What can I get you, champ?" the bartender asked. He had a pencil-thin mustache and parted his hair straight down the middle like a refugee from a barbershop quartet.

"Beer, please," Ash said. "Something on tap."

The bartender shook his head and said, "We don't have beer."

"Seriously? What kind of club doesn't serve beer?"

"The same kind of club that usually doesn't allow patrons in who aren't dressed right. You're lucky you're with them." He pointed toward the gaggle on the dance floor.

"Funny, I don't feel lucky."

Ash heard laughter a few stools down the bar to his right, a female's pleasant titter. He looked over and locked eyes with a foxy brunette who said, "I know what you mean." She slid over to him and extended her hand. "I'm Veronica."

"Ash." They shook. Her hand was at once delicate and firm. Her scent wafted over him, all spices and mystery.

"I saw you walk in," she said. She took a step back and spread her arms. "I think you and I are the only two people in here not dressed right." Only then did Ash glance away from her blue eyes long enough to notice that she was wearing low-cut jeans and a T-shirt that rode up far enough to expose her navel. Her skin was tanned and looked as if it would be smooth to the touch.

"I guess I would have dressed right but nobody told me we were coming here," Ash said.

"I knew I was coming, but I refuse to dress like that." She pointed toward the group on the dance floor. "Do you work with them?"

"No. The guy with the bright blond hair is my brother. Those are his 'associates,' as he says."

Veronica smiled and said, "Alcohol and associates can be a dangerous thing."

"From what I've seen so far, I'd have to agree with you." Ash noticed her drink was empty. "Can I get you another?"

She shrugged and said, "Sure. Seven and seven."

The bartender was already on the case. He may have had an attitude, but he was efficient. The drink was served up in short order.

The music swelled and the dancers clapped. Ash leaned over to Veronica and asked, "Would you like to go someplace quieter to talk?"

"Where did you have in mind?" she said.

Ash pointed to another sitting area in the opposite corner of the club, saying, "Over there, maybe?"

"That would be nice."

Veronica took his hand without warning as they crossed the room. She led him to one of the couches and sidled in right next to him. Ash wasn't sure what to make of her signals. He was no stranger to the opposite sex, but it had been some time since he was in close company with an attractive woman. As he quickly thought about it, he realized he could pinpoint exactly how long it had been: In his mind's eye he saw a car parked in a remote end of a military terminal's parking lot. One last bout of intimacy before a long separation. Melinda.

But Melinda, for all of her pre-deployment overtures to the contrary, had proved to be a woman incapable of handling the rigors and hardships caused by lengthy separations. She wasn't alone in that regard, either. The halls of Ash's love life were littered with the images of girlfriends who'd made promises upon his departure for foreign shores only to disappear from his life forever.

It didn't matter. There was no reason to dwell on that any more than he needed to question his apparent good fortune at the moment. Ash wasn't a religious man, necessarily, but he had come to believe in a natural order. The only issue before him was how natural the order might get over the next few hours.

"So, are you from New York?" Veronica asked.

"Sort of," Ash replied. "I grew up around here. My family owns a business in town."

"What business is that?"

"Roberts International."

She gave his biceps a playful punch and said, "No way."

"You've heard of it?"

Veronica jabbed a thumb toward herself and said, "I'm a stockbroker. Of course I've heard of Roberts International. Your stock is doing very well."

"That's good to hear."

"Wait a second. Ash? Ash Roberts, as in Ashton Roberts?"

"Yes?"

"You're heir to the throne, right?"

Ash felt the allure fading from the scene. "No, I'm not."

"Why wouldn't you be?"

"Because I don't work for Roberts International."

She pursed her full lips as she processed the information, thinking aloud: "The next generation of Robertses doesn't work for Roberts International."

Ash motioned across the room to the dance floor. "My brother Winston is the next generation of Robertses working for Roberts International. Please don't start any bogus rumors about the empire crumbling because of lack of family support."

She smiled and said, "I won't. So if you don't work for Roberts, where do you work?"

"I'm in the Navy."

"Oh, like *Top Gun*?"

"No. I'm not a pilot. I'm a SEAL."

"Like the video game?"

"Which one?"

"Isn't there a video game called *Navy SEAL*?"

"I guess. I don't really know. It's been a while since I've played video games."

"Right, why play a game when you've got the real thing?"

"It's not so much that. I really haven't had the time."

"What, have you been fighting a war or something?"

"You might say that."

Veronica put a hand to her mouth and said, "I'm sorry. That was stupid of me."

Ash could see her embarrassment and feared she might elect to cut her losses and walk away. He reached over and patted the back of her hand. "Don't worry about it."

She sat back, running her hair behind her ears, quickly drained of her humor. "When did you get back?"

"Today."

Veronica narrowed her eyes, processing the information. She looked deep into Ash's eyes and asked, "Are you married?"

"No."

"Girlfriend?"

"Unfortunately not."

"Want to get out of here?"

It was the first good thing to happen to him in a week; he almost couldn't believe his luck, but he wasn't about to sit around and muse on it. "Sure."

They stood to go, and Ash held up a finger, saying, "I'll be right back." He hurried over to the dance floor where he cut between Winston and Erica with all the grace of a rocket-propelled grenade. "I'm leaving, bro."

"Leaving?" Winston asked. "Where are you going?"

Ash simply gestured toward Veronica, standing like a patient bride near the sitting area across the room.

"Got it," Winston said. "Will we see you at the penthouse later?"

"I don't know, now do I?"

"No, I guess you don't." He leaned over and lowered his voice. "Do you have a condom?"

"Actually, I don't."

"Follow me." Winston gave Erica a peck on the cheek and said, "Will you excuse us for a moment, dear?"

A minute later the two brothers were standing at the long marble basin in the bathroom. Winston produced his wallet and said, "I feel like we're in high school again."

"We didn't go to high school, remember?" Ash returned. "We went to an all-male prep school."

"I guess that's why the idea of spending the night with a woman you met fifteen minutes ago is still appealing to you?"

"Aren't you Mr. Above It All. Did you see the woman?"

"Distances can be deceiving."

"Not in this case. She's hot."

Winston placed the flat plastic wrapper squarely in his brother's palm and said, "Be careful."

"I'm fresh from the war, remember? You should have given me that advice a couple of years ago."

"I'm not talking about war danger; I'm talking about life danger."

Ash felt himself starting to snap. He'd had enough lectures from family members for one day. He clasped his brother's shoulder and said, "Thanks for the rubber. I'll see you later."

Ash was almost through the door when Winston called to him: "We are proud of you, you know."

Ash doubled back and faced Winston once again as his brother continued to speak: "You just made a choice that's, you know, hard for the family to understand."

"Even I can't understand my choices from time to time," Ash returned.

Without warning and quite uncharacteristically, Winston reached out and embraced Ash. "We'll always be here for you, brother."

"I'm not doing all of this out of spite."

"But what do you have left to prove? You've fought wars, shown courage under fire, all that Hollywood jazz. What else do you need to do?"

"Well, for starters, I need to go to South Dakota." Ash raised his arm and waved the packet Winston had just handed him like a small flag. "But even before that, I need to use this thing. Later, bro."

Ash exited the bathroom only to find that Veronica wasn't where he'd left her. He scanned the far end of the bar but she was nowhere to be found. It figured. She'd been too good to be true. There was no way somebody with his recent track record would have such a dramatic and rapid change of fortune. The natural order wouldn't support it.

He wasn't about to face Winston and there was no way he was going to sit on the couches and watch the gang pretend that they hadn't been born fifty or sixty years too late. He pushed his way back through the metal door and ran headlong into the line waiting to get in. On the other side of the line he spotted a friendly face, Veronica's face. He'd known her for less than an hour, but now a wave of emotion hit him as if they'd been lifelong lovers separated for months. Without any hesitation he wrapped his arms around her. She didn't resist.

Neither of them resisted once they made it to her

apartment a few blocks away. The click of the latch as the door shut behind them was like a starting gun. She tore at his clothes like a child ripping at a birthday present, and he matched her. They wanted each other naked. Her mouth tasted spicy from the liquor; her body was warm and smooth. He entered her and knew he wouldn't last long. And he didn't. Through his wincing he saw her looking up at him with compassionate pride in what she'd wrought.

Only after the first bout did he take the time to study her naked form. Her breasts were naturally pendulous, and bigger than they'd appeared under the T-shirt. He gently kneaded them, making the nipples stick out in earnest pleas for attention. He made his way down her toned stomach until he felt the soft curls of hair tickle his nose, and then he paused, drawing in her essence. He took his hands and cupped her smooth ass, running his fingers down the crack of it, probing, and anticipating a protest that didn't come.

They made love twice more before collapsing in two sweaty heaps on either side of the double bed. They lay breathing heavily, saying nothing until Veronica lolled her head toward Ash and asked, "How long had it been?"

"Too long," Ash replied.

"No, seriously."

Ash scratched his head in thought. "Over a year."

She laughed. "So I just got a year's supply, huh?"

Ash laughed, too. "More or less."

Then they stared at each other with their noses nearly touching, and her countenance turned serious. "What's wrong?" she asked.

"After what we just did you want to know what's wrong?"

"I don't mean sadness just now. I've seen sadness in your eyes all night. I'm wondering what's wrong."

"Nothing's wrong."

"Is it the war? Did something happen over there?"

"No."

Another silence followed. Veronica broke it with a question out of left field: "Have you ever killed anybody?"

For some reason when she asked it didn't irritate him as when the exec had asked the same thing a few hours before. She wasn't trying to draw some sort of vicarious thrill from his response like a perverse patron in the middle rows of life's theater. He sat up, rearranging a pillow at the small of his back. "What if I said yes?"

"I don't know." She sat up as well, tugging at the sheet to cover herself but ultimately letting it fall well below her breasts. "I've never been to war. I've never known anybody who has."

"Well, now you know me."

"Do I?" Her lips curled in a wry smile. "I don't feel like I do."

"There's not much to know, really," Ash shrugged. "What you see is what you get."

Veronica rolled toward him and wistfully said, "I don't think that's true, either. In fact, I have a feeling you may be the most complex man I've ever met."

Ash had always been a sucker for smart chicks. He felt himself stiffening again, and rapidly so. With a smile of his own he pulled the sheet aside, revealing his full extent, and said, "What you see is what you get."

And she straddled him.

23

After his East Coast weekend trip, Ash had mixed emotions about returning to Fairly. It was now obvious that he had no home at Roberts International, but he for damn sure didn't need the NROTC broken-toy project, either. What he needed was the sea and a challenging mission. What he got was a first-class seat on a plane bound for South Dakota with the promise of an uphill battle with misguided undergrads.

He had a couple drinks on the flight, just to loosen up, he told himself, and avoided conversation with the flight attendant who evidently didn't know what the word "no" meant. He didn't want to be an asshole, and if he'd been going any other place than Fairly for any other reason than picking up the mess left by Master Chief Fernandez, he might have been inclined to double down on his luck with the ladies at the moment. He'd spent a large part of the previous afternoon with Veronica, avoiding some of his family commitments. It was good, healthy sex, and it should have set the tone for follow-on engagements.

It didn't.

"You know," the woman sitting next to him said, "I do believe that flight attendant finds you attractive."

Ash looked at her.

"I'm probably butting in where I don't belong," she said, "but at my age, I really don't care."

Ash suspected "her age" was somewhat shy of seventy, but she was well preserved—slim and healthy-looking with an ageless grace. She wore a purple business suit and exuded the aura of a business professional. She played some kind of poker video game on her BlackBerry.

"You are butting in," Ash said.

She shoved out a hand. "Lauren Culpepper. Pleased to make your acquaintance."

Smiling a little at the sheer audacity the woman exhibited, Ash took her hand. "Ash Roberts."

"Well, then, Ash Roberts," the woman said, "how is it a young man, unmarried such as yourself, is turning down the attentions of a rather fetching woman?"

"I've got a lot on my mind."

"Of course you do. That's why you haven't said more than a handful of words since this flight began." Culpepper raised an elegant hand and signaled the waitress. "Miss."

The attendant hurried back, beaming at Ash. He started feeling uncomfortable, wondering if he was about to get double-teamed by the attendant and his matchmaking neighbor, and trying to figure out how to deal with it. The attendant had been bad enough by herself.

"Could I get two more drinks?" Lauren asked. "I'll have what my grandson is having."

Grandson?

"Yes, ma'am," the attendant said.

"He's getting married on Friday," Lauren bubbled. "To a truly wonderful girl." She smiled and took money from her purse, catching Ash's hand and holding it before he could take money from his shirt pocket. "Don't you think that's wonderful?"

The attendant took a second to answer. "Yes, ma'am. Wonderful." She turned to Ash. "Congratulations. I'll be right back with your drinks." She hurried away.

Lauren turned to Ash. "You do realize, of course, that she didn't mean a word of her congratulations."

"I do," Ash admitted. "It's also been my experience

that sometimes women like the idea of taking another woman's man."

"Not with his grandmother sitting next to him."

"If it works, I owe you."

Eyes sparkling, Lauren said, "If you weren't so obviously wound up in whatever it is you're thinking about, maybe I'd be flirting with you."

Ash laughed in spite of his dark mood. What a fascinating woman. "How do I know you're not flirting with me now?"

"Oh, you know I am," Lauren said in that husky smoker's voice she had. "But one of the things I've learned about young men is that all too often they're like dogs chasing after cars."

"How's that?"

"Why, even if you were chasing after me and caught me, you wouldn't know what to do with me."

Ash grinned and didn't know what to say.

"I've had young men before," Lauren said. "Left them laying in my dust all around the world. One of the advantages of living off of Daddy's money while Daddy's CEOs run the corporations."

The attendant returned with the drinks and placed them on cocktail napkins on the fold-down trays. She smiled at Ash but wasn't actively hitting on him now.

"During my years of traveling, I've discovered young men are trainable," Lauren confided. "You can show them where the equipment is and how to operate it, but they lack in confidence."

"Maybe you haven't found the right young man," Ash suggested.

"Now who's flirting?" She smiled at him. "See? I do know how this game is played. All you have to do is appeal to a young man's competitive nature." She sipped her drink. "You're all just too easy. Give me an older man, not older than me, but one with heart and a little experience. One who isn't quite so predictable."

"So there's a Mr. Culpepper?"

"Hell, no! I shot him myself when I caught him forni-

cating with the maid on the oak table my grandmother
Esther left me. That table had a good finish, I tell you.
Blood came right off it. But it took half of Daddy's lawyers to keep me from going to prison. I took my maiden
name back and have kept it ever since. Haven't had any
further inclinations toward marriage. I like the single life
just fine. If I want a husband, I'll steal one for a while."
She laughed at her own joke and Ash joined her. "So
what's got you so down in the mouth?"

"Work," Ash said, thinking that would be the end of
it. Nobody wanted to talk to someone else about work.

Lauren held up her empty glass. "Buy me another
drink and I'll let you tell me about it."

"Maybe I don't want to tell you about it."

"You do. You're ready to tell somebody about it.
That's why you've sat over there all knotted up. What
were you doing in New York?"

"Visiting family."

"God, that calls for a double."

Ash flagged the attendant down and ordered doubles.
He was starting to feel a little looser.

"If you ask me," Lauren said after the drinks came,
"family is way overrated. I mean, just getting born into
one gets you stuck in the damnedest of places."

"I know," Ash agreed.

The old woman shrugged. "But you take what you
can and make do. Take me for instance. If I hadn't been
born into the indolent rich, do you think I could have
gotten here by myself?"

Ash wasn't sure how to answer that.

"Of course not!" Lauren said. "And can you imagine
me as a scullery maid?"

Ash chuckled. He definitely could not figure that career choice for the woman seated next to him.

"See?" Lauren said. "That's what I mean. You can't
help being what you are. We're all made a certain way.
Seems to me our biggest struggles come from trying to
be something we're not. So my question is, what is it
you're trying to be, Ash?"

He thought about that for a moment, sipping his drink and buying himself time. "A United States Navy SEAL, I guess," he replied finally. There was no other answer.

Lauren frowned. "In the middle of South Dakota? She shook her head. "Hell of a place for a United States Navy SEAL."

"I've had a bit of bad luck," Ash admitted.

"We all have bad luck," she told him, patting him on the knee. "It's what gives us character. Trust me on that. If we didn't have the hardships we face in life, why, we wouldn't be interesting." She sipped her drink and regarded him. "I shot my cheating husband in Austin, Texas, laid him out stone-cold on my granny's dining-room table. Now maybe you've never heard of me, but everybody in Austin, Texas has. It caused some righteous problems in my life, I tell you. Tongues wagged. Everybody had an opinion. In fact, I had a hell of a time getting a date for the funeral."

Ash laughed. "You're pulling my leg."

Lauren held a hand up. "Swear to God. My hand on a stack of Bibles. Back in those days, a woman didn't show up at a social event unescorted. And the sheriff's deputies didn't count."

"Some first date," Ash said.

"Maybe." Lauren shrugged and sipped her drink. "It wasn't our last, I tell you. But he wasn't for me. Just somebody to pass the time with." She looked at him. "Let's talk about you. What are you doing in Fairly, South Dakota?"

Even though he had hoped not to, Ash told her most of it. When he finished, he was surprised. He wasn't one to provide a lot of information, generally.

"One thing I have to say," she told him, "you do have your work cut out for you. But you're made of the right stuff, Ash Roberts. My daddy, Mr. Culpepper, set store by such men as you, and I learned to recognize what Daddy saw in his friends." Her blue eyes twinkled. "You weren't always made for the straight and narrow, and you'll pay a higher cost of living than some, but you'll do best if you stick to your guns and do what you best know how to do."

"And what would that be?"

"Why, be a Navy SEAL, of course. I saw that look in your eyes when you told me what you were. A man like that, why, there ain't no other way for him to be."

Ash felt a little uncomfortable. "Sometimes," he said, thinking of Wild lying in that hospital bed missing half a leg, "you don't always get dealt a hand you can play."

"That's why you stick around for cards to the next one," she told him.

Lauren Culpepper stayed on the connecting flight to Las Vegas. She promised Ash that he'd see her on TV when she busted the bank at one of the casinos. Somehow, he didn't doubt her for a moment. He grabbed his carry-on and she bussed his cheek, making him feel as if he were six years old again going off to school. It was an interesting feeling but not too painful.

As he passed the flight attendant, she looked up at him with an arched eyebrow. "Leaving Grandma?"

"Gotta get a wedding gift," Ash said. "I'll catch up with her. Do me a favor and take care of her. You don't meet many like her."

"Sure," the attendant said.

Ash left the plane and walked into the terminal. As he passed a newsstand, he thought about what the old woman had told him, about being the best that he could be at what he wanted to be. He hadn't done that since he'd arrived in Fairly. He'd just been marking time, reliving the past—which he couldn't do a thing about—and pissing and moaning to himself about how bad it was. Well, the shit had surely hit the fan, whether he was really in need of some downtime for psychiatric reasons or Captain Napoli and his team had overreacted. Whatever the case, he'd been sent to Fairly to do a job.

He stopped at a newsstand and went inside to buy a legal pad. After all, he had to wait for his bags and it was a sixty-seven-mile drive to Fairly. Another stop netted him a big Styrofoam cup of coffee and a granola bar.

Down in baggage, he shouldered up against a set of lockers and waited. Taking a ballpoint pen from his pocket, he started making a to-do list of things that needed his attention. First and foremost, he needed to get his office squared away and get the mids on the right vector. Fernandez might have let some of them off the traces for too long to haul them back in, but Ash was going to be the one to have to make that call.

"CLEAN OFFICE," he wrote.

Secondly, he needed to know where the midshipmen stood as far as their NROTC training. What they'd covered, what they needed to cover. He also needed to investigate how they were doing in their other classes.

"ASSESS UNIT."

Thirdly, once he knew where everybody stood, Ash needed to make a plan of action to figure out how to get them where they needed to be.

"PLAN RECOVERY."

Fourthly, he needed to find a place to stay other than the sheriff's house, although Ash felt perfectly welcome staying there. The place was small and some of the things he was going to have to do to get his team organized weren't going to make a lot of folks happy with him.

"LOCATE HOUSING."

He sipped his coffee and looked over his list. It wasn't much yet, but it was a start. And any one of those steps might need to be broken down into a dozen different action paths to achieve his goal. He felt a little better.

Then, on the other hand, he could have been wasting his time. He was a SEAL in Fairly, South Dakota. It didn't get much worse.

The warning alarm rang and the light came on. Ash put his notepad away and watched as the conveyor belt jerked into motion. Luggage filled the belt and he started looking for his bags.

*   *   *

When Ash returned to Fairly, he stopped in at the sheriff's office, hoping to catch Bolo there. A young deputy with sallow skin and pimples asked Ash his business, then told him to have a seat while he checked to see if the sheriff was in. Ash sat, thinking it was pretty stupid to say something like that when the sheriff's cruiser was parked out front.

Less than two minutes later, Bolo came out of the office. "Hey, Ash. How was the trip?"

"I survived."

Bolo laughed. "Family'll do that to you." Then his face turned sober. "Visit your amigo?"

"Wild? Yeah, I did."

Bolo waited.

"He's doing good," Ash admitted. "Probably a lot better than I would be if I was in his shoes." *Shoe,* he heard Wild correct him, and almost smiled.

"That's good." Bolo looked at him. "Something I can do you for? Or did you already forget how to get around town?"

"Thought maybe I'd bend your ear for a minute."

Bolo nodded. "Got a diner around the corner. We can hoof over." The sheriff looked at the pimply-faced young man wearing a big cowboy hat and a deputy's star. "Cody, if anything goes wrong, you know where to find me."

"Yessir, Sheriff," Cody responded.

"And Cody?"

"Yessir?"

"Make sure it's something important this time. Something that can't keep."

The young man's face colored briefly. "You got it, Sheriff."

Ash followed Bolo out of the building and onto the sidewalk.

"He's a good kid," Bolo said. "His daddy was a deputy for a lot of years. Back in the days when the job didn't pay so good, and even while it didn't pay at all. He was shot down outside of town by bank robbers that were passing through. Cody's daddy pulled them over for a broken taillight; they gunned him down like they were Bonnie and Clyde. The sheriff then got them before they made the border." He shook his head. "Before my time."

"It's surprising he took up law enforcement with that track record," Ash said.

"Ain't it, though?" Bolo asked. "But Cody thinks he was born to the trade. Becoming a deputy's all he ever wanted to do. I'm just trying to keep him alive long enough for him to get some sense."

Maude's Dinner sat on the corner at the end of the block.

" 'Maude's Dinner'?" Ash read the sign.

"They misspelled it," Bolo said. "Her husband's work. Later, when people pointed it out to him, Fred said he intended it that way."

"Did he?"

Bolo shook his head. "Fred was illiterate, but a hell of a short-order cook. You should have seen the first menu. Loaded with selection and pet names, but you'd have had to be an expert in language to read it." He held the door open and ushered Ash inside.

The diner was small and compact. Booths lined one wall. Stools lined the grill on the other. A handful of old men sat at a few of the tables and watched ESPN on the television mounted in the corner. Ash and Bolo took a booth at the back.

A pregnant waitress with a blonde ponytail came over to them. "Afternoon, Sheriff."

"Afternoon, Maisie," Bolo greeted. "This is Lieutenant Ash Roberts. He's teaching at the university."

Maisie looked at Ash speculatively. "You're too young and too clean-cut to teach at the college."

Ash smiled. "I should be relieved or insulted?"

"Take your pick," she told him. She wrote on a piece of paper as she spoke. "Breakfasts here are good and we can fix them to go. The prices are reasonable and it beats eating that cardboard crap they serve at the fast-food places." She handed Ash the piece of paper. "That's the diner number. You want breakfast to go, call ahead thirty minutes. You got to ask for extra syrup for your pancakes if you want it. And the girls working the order still need to be tipped."

Bolo jerked a thumb at the young woman. "Maisie's a regular shrinking violet. Hard to get her to talk about anything."

Maisie stuck her tongue out at the sheriff. "Insults will get spit in your coffee when nobody's looking, Sheriff. You know that."

"I do," Bolo agreed. "That's why everything I say about you and this place is out of the goodness of my heart."

"What do you two gentlemen want? I ain't got all day to be lollygagging."

"Two coffees," Bolo said. "Black." He looked at Ash. "Did you eat?"

"This morning," Ash admitted. He'd completely forgotten about it when he'd reached the airport. "Had a liquid lunch on the plane and a granola bar at the terminal."

"A ham sandwich and an order of slaw," the sheriff added.

Maisie wrote it down and went away.

"I didn't come here for you to buy me lunch," Ash said.

"I know you didn't, but I don't want you eating a lot before tonight. Little Feather is laying out a big feed. I went home for lunch and found her peeling apples for a pie. The last thing I need to do now is show up without you. And eating two dinners ain't easy when one of 'em was made by my wife."

Ash grinned. "I didn't know I had dinner plans."

"You do now."

"All right," Ash said. It felt good, knowing that he had something more working in Fairly, South Dakota than a thankless task.

"So what brought you to my doorstep?"

"I'm going to do the job at the university," Ash said. "Train the cadets."

"Midshipmen," Ash corrected.

Bolo flipped a hand over.

Maisie brought the coffee and sat the cups down. "Sandwich'll only be two shakes of a dead lamb's tail."

"We ordered pork," the sheriff said.

She ignored him.

"So you're going to stick it to the midshipmen," Bolo said, turning his attention back to Ash.

Ash nodded. "I am. And Master Chief Fernandez. Going to make them sailors or bury them where they fall." He sipped the coffee and grimaced. It was scalding and almost unpalatable even by Navy standards.

Bolo laughed. "Careful with that. It's chicory. I take it you've never had it."

"No."

"Guaranteed to wake the dead," Bolo said. "It'll leave permanent scarring and raise hair on a frog." He sipped his coffee and grimaced a little. "I've been around it for years and still haven't gotten used to it."

"What is with you people and strong coffee around here?"

Bolo just smiled. "So you're here to tell me you're sticking it to the midshipmen because . . . ?"

"Someone may feel obligated to call you," Ash said.

Bolo's eyes narrowed. "You planning on physical violence?"

"Not if what you say about the chief is on the money."

"He's passive-aggressive all right. But doesn't mean he won't have a stupid spell now and again."

"I'm going to run them down into the ground," Ash said. "They're not going to have a minute to themselves that they won't be thinking of me. We're going to have a crash course in what it takes to be Navy officer material."

"If it doesn't kill them, it'll make them strong."

"Or make them quit."

Bolo studied him. "Them?" he asked. "Or you? You figure on pushing this assignment till it goes tits-up?"

Ash sighed and settled back in the booth. He looked at Bolo and thought about his answer. "I just saw my family this weekend. Talked to my father and my brother. Found out how disappointing it was to them that I was failing out of the Navy and still wouldn't consider being part of the family business."

"Big business. Plenty of room for one more Roberts."

That Bolo knew that told Ash that the sheriff was trusting only to a point. Evidently Bolo had done some background checking while he was gone. Or maybe even the night he'd stayed at his house. *Inquisitive bastard, huh?*

"Big business," Ash agreed. "It's just not my business. I went to the Naval Academy, and then decided I wanted to be a SEAL. Then I decided I wanted to be the best damn SEAL there ever was." He shook his head. "If I'm going to do this assignment, I only know one way to do it."

"Kick ass and take names." Bolo grinned and rubbed his whiskered face.

"Right," Ash said.

"I heard about Friday's little race. Beating Bruno Oslo in a run is big news around here. You keep that up, you're gonna be a hometown legend."

Maisie returned with a heavy plate containing a ham sandwich and cole slaw in a side dish.

Surprised at the hunger he suddenly felt, Ash dug in.

"You need to bring that appetite to the house tonight," Bolo said.

"I will," Ash said. "I plan on working up an appetite before dinner."

"Good. And if anyone from the university reports any *overzealous* acts committed by the new OIC there, I'll get around to investigating them. Eventually."

"Fair enough." Ash finished the sandwich and slaw, then drained his coffee, finding it had a much more pleasant taste with a meal.

The door at the front of the diner opened and Cody the deputy entered. He glanced around for a second, and then spotted the sheriff at the back. He crossed the floor with such intent deliberation that he drew every eye in the room.

"Sheriff," Cody said, placing both hands flat on the table, "I just got a call from Mrs. Jorgensen. She says she just rented a room to three men carrying handguns in belt holsters under their jackets."

Bolo rubbed his face with a big hand. "Did she say who these men were?"

"I got names, but they don't mean anything to me. I'll run 'em through NCIC if you want."

"You do that," Bolo said. "I'll take a run over to Imogene's. Call me on the radio if you find anything out." He laid money on the table to cover the bill.

"Shouldn't I come with you?" Cody asked.

"Not this time, son," Bolo said easily. "I need you to man the office. In case we gotta call in the off-duty personnel." He stood. "More than likely, this won't turn out to be anything."

Cody clearly wasn't happy about that, but he didn't say anything. He nodded, touched his wide-brimmed cowboy hat, and retreated.

"Mind if I ride along?" Ash asked. He wasn't ready to head to the university just yet. Riding along with the sheriff sounded like an interesting diversion.

"Don't you have enough problems?"

Ash stood. "Can you imagine how it would be? Me showing up to dinner and having to explain to Little Feather that you got Little Sheriff Bolo blown off because I had to go clean my office?"

"We call him the Enforcer," Bolo said with a grin.

Ash held up his hands in surrender. "Whoa. Too much information, Sheriff."

"Wouldn't be a pretty sight if you had to tell her we'd lost the Enforcer." Bolo sighed. "I've got a feeling I know what this is all about. I don't expect trouble."

"Then we won't expect it together." Ash liked the

sheriff. Bolo was a stand-up guy. "After all, you bought me lunch."

After a moment, the sheriff nodded. He led the way out the door.

24

"Imogene Jorgensen's got a twelve-room flop in the center of town along the main drag," Sheriff Bolo said as he drove the cruiser through Fairly's streets. "You probably passed it on your way in. Usually the rooms are reserved for people here on business who are going to be staying awhile. Insurance men. Landmen for oil and gas. Landmen for cable and cell tower easements. Hunters in from out of town. Those guys."

"Any of them ever come armed before?" Ash sat in the passenger seat of the cruiser and looked out the windows.

"Just the hunters. And they don't generally sport belly guns." Bolo drove with easy confidence, changing lanes effortlessly.

"So who do you think this is?" Ash asked.

"The ATF is showing an uncommon interest in Devon Hite."

"The leader of the Badlands Militia. You told me about him."

"Yeah, well, what I didn't tell you is that one of the ATF's agents went missing a few days back."

Ash thought about that, knowing that the sheriff was taking him deeply into his confidence. "Missing as in 'presumed dead.' "

"Missing as in 'can't find him anywhere.' "

"They think Hite killed him?"

"Or has him, or at least knows where the guy is."
Bolo stopped for a traffic light, then eased on through.

"What do you think?"

"I'm looking into it. Something like this, with it almost
sitting on top of the town, you need to go slow. The
ATF might not see it that way." Bolo looked at Ash.
"Waco and Ruby Ridge ring any bells for you?"

"They do. I was at sea during that time but there was
plenty of news about them." Waco and Ruby Ridge had
triggered federal intervention and resulted in loss of life.
In both instances, most agreed that the federal agencies
involved had overreacted.

"The chief special agent that I talked with was a guy
named Hank Howard," Bolo went on. "Seemed decent
enough and like he had his head on plumb. The problem
is, something like this can blow up and get past the local
handlers and reach national level."

"You think that's what's happening here?"

"God, I do hope not." Bolo turned left, drove in past
a Dairy Queen restaurant, and pulled into a parking area
in front of a small L-shaped motel. A sign out front read
JORGENSEN'S JOURNEY'S END MOTEL, and offered clean
rooms, HBO, Continental breakfast and the Internet.
"All the comforts of home."

The sheriff got out and Ash followed him into the
small office.

A tiny, wrinkled woman sat behind a scarred counter
that came up nearly to her chin. She wore a print dress
and carried a flyswatter in one gnarled hand. Her gray
hair was tied up in a bun and her glasses made her eyes
look too big. "Took your time getting here, Sheriff,"
she groused.

"It's the traffic, Imogene," Bolo said. "It's terrible this
time of year."

The motel office had a lived-in feel to it. Newspapers
and magazines hung limply in wire racks in the corner
next to dusty postcards. A small color TV set on a rolling stand played Court TV.

"Tell me about the guys you rented the rooms to," Bolo suggested.

The old woman eyed Ash suspiciously. "Who's the snot-nose?"

"His name's Ash Roberts," Bolo said.

"What's he do?"

"He teaches over at the college."

"Terrific," Imogene snarled, "you got gunslingers coming into town and you bring a schoolmarm. Don't that beat all."

Ash didn't know whether to be insulted or amused. He remained quiet. This was the sheriff's show.

"Imogene," Bolo said gruffly.

The old woman pulled out a floor plan of the motel. "There's four of 'em. All bundled up two by two like they was going on Noah's ark. I put them in Number Four and Number Twelve."

Ash peered at the floor plan. Number Four was at the juncture of the ·L. Number Twelve was at the opposite end.

"I thought I'd split them up," Imogene said. "Figured it would make it easier for you to investigate them." She peered over the sheriff's shoulder at Ash. "Of course, I was thinking you might want to bring some backup with you."

"We'll see," Bolo said. "What can you tell me about the four men?"

"They're young. Look like they're military or something. These guys are distant, you know. Didn't talk much. Not at all friendly. Started griping about the accommodations at once, talking about how they should have been put up somewhere else. Another one said these were just temporary quarters anyway. Quarters, like that. That was when I started thinking they were military."

"Maybe they are," Bolo said.

"Then why didn't they show me military ID when they checked in?" Imogene snapped.

"I don't know, Imogene."

"You know, Sheriff, I don't get the impression you're taking this seriously enough." The old woman's brown eyes turned definitely hostile.

"I'm here, aren't I?" Bolo sighed. "What ID did they show you?"

"Driver's licenses."

"From where?"

"Two are from Georgia, Atlanta and Columbus. One is from Nashville, Tennessee. And the last one's out of Los Angeles, California."

"Did they act like they knew each other?" Bolo asked.

"In case you weren't following the conversation, Sheriff," Imogene said, "I already told you they weren't exactly scintillating conversationalists."

Ash crossed to the motel window that looked out over the motel parking lot. Four guys from all over the United States. That didn't sound good. He glanced at the license plates of the five cars parked there. Two of them were from South Dakota, one was from Wyoming, and the other two were from Kansas. The Kansas cars were both Taurus models, more or less factory-made government issue.

"So they didn't talk much," Bolo observed. "Did they say how long they were staying?"

"They paid for two nights. Said they might stay longer. One of them said not if he could help it."

"Do you have home addresses for them?"

Imogene plopped down two registration cards on the countertop. Dutifully, Bolo took out a small notepad and started transferring information. "These addresses match the IDs?"

"Yes."

Bolo continued scribbling.

Ash got a bad feeling about what was going on. The military had operations like this, where one hand didn't know what the other hand was doing. He figured that if the ATF was operating in Bolo's backyard they should at least tell him.

"Don't you think that's strange, Sheriff?" Imogene asked.

"What's that?" Bolo closed his notepad and put it away.

"That the addresses they gave matched their IDs. I mean, most folks don't move all that much. But with them being young and male, and those being big cities, and not a wedding ring among them, you'd expect at least one or two of them had moved and hadn't gotten around to changing the address on their driver's license."

"Changing the address is the law," Bolo said.

"Pshaw," Imogene muttered. "If everybody obeyed the law, you'd be out of a job."

"Tell me about the guns."

Ash saw no movement in the two suspect units. Part of him was antsy now, feeling the call of adrenaline. But he respected the way Bolo handled the situation like a special-ops mission. Get as much information up front before anything went down. Once the wheels came off, it was pretty hard to put them back on.

"They're carrying long guns too," Imogene said. "They carried in cases from the cars."

"The same kind of case?"

"They looked like they were. Is that important?"

"I don't know. I'm just asking questions, Imogene."

"Well, if you go take a look, you'll know."

"I'm sure I will. So they had rifles . . ."

"Rifles. Shotguns." The old woman shrugged. "Something. It is hunting season up here, you know."

"I know."

"But that's no excuse for wearing holstered pistols into my place of business," Imogene said adamantly. "I got signage posted." She pointed at the signs on the big windows.

"All of them wore pistols?" Bolo asked.

"Two of them. I suspect the others were too. Men like that tend to hang out with others like them." Imogene handed the sheriff an electronic keycard. "This'll get you through those doors if you need to."

Bolo stepped over to the window with Ash. The sheriff quickly copied down all the license-plate numbers, but he only called in the ones on the Taurus models. A quick check with Cody confirmed that the cars were rentals out of Kansas City.

"It used to be a rental car had a rental tag," Bolo said. "Then everybody realized that the bad guys were using the rental plates to target out-of-towners. But you can still spot rental cars. This year's model or last, and usually a Ford Taurus or a Mazda 626 or a Dodge Stratus." He glanced at Ash. "This is probably nothing. You can wait here if you want."

"I'll tag along," Ash said. "Take notes. You never know when I might learn something that will come in handy."

Bolo grinned and slipped his sunglasses on. "I'll do the talking."

"Sure," Ash said. They went out the door together and it felt good to be moving, not thinking about everything he was going to have to do at Thaedt University. Even if the exercise was nothing, he at least had the jazz working for the moment. He thought about Wild, throwing himself into the rehab program because there was nothing else to do. Wild couldn't think about where he was going after he was released by Medical, so he had to concentrate on what was in front of him. Ash thought about that and kept it close.

Bolo moved quickly once he got under way. "We'll talk to the guys in Twelve," he said. "If something bad goes wrong while we're talking to the guys in Four, we end up boxed."

"Roger that," Ash said. He'd been thinking along the same lines.

The door to the unit was old, weathered, and scarred. Mismatched numerals identified the unit, and shadows in the paint showed where previous numbers had hung. Bolo put his right hand on his pistol, turned sideways, and glanced at Ash. Ash took the other side of the door, standing with his back to it. He couldn't help smiling at Bolo. *Burnt out, my ass,* he thought. *I live for this shit.*

Bolo smiled back, then his face became expressionless. He rapped on the door with his big hand.

"Who is it?" a male voice called from inside.

"Sheriff's department," Bolo replied.

"No one here called for the sheriff."

"You'll want to open this door," Bolo said.

Activity inside.

Bolo swiped the keycard, twisted the knob, and followed the door inside. He drew the pistol smoothly, sliding his forefinger along the trigger guard without putting his finger to the trigger.

Ash whirled and followed, aware he was without firepower of any kind. In SEAL training he'd learned to improvise, but there was a reason squads went in fully outfitted.

Two men were in the room. One of them sat at the small desk with a semiauto pistol, a Desert Eagle fiftycal by the looks of it, spread out on a towel. He wore a Beretta nine-millimeter in a shoulder rig and was pulling the pistol free of leather when Bolo aimed his own pistol in the center of the man's face.

"Bad idea," Bolo advised.

The man stayed his hand, but smiled up at the sheriff without concern. No emotion touched his flat gray eyes. He was slim but well built, maybe average height, give or take an inch. His partner sat on the bed taking apart an M24 7.62-millimeter sniper rifle. He wore a pistol on his hip. He hand started for it.

"Teddy," the first man said, his eyes never leaving Bolo's. "Leave that pistol where it is."

Teddy didn't move.

A shadow drifted into the doorway behind Ash. He was in motion before he knew it. A hand holding a Colt forty-five shoved through the door, intending to press the weapon up against the back of Bolo's head. Ash caught the gunman's wrist and slammed it against the door frame. The pistol popped free and Ash caught it by the butt on the way down. The pistol fell into his hand as if it were custom-fit. Setting himself, keeping hold of the captured wrist, Ash yanked the man into the room, throwing a hip into him and hauling the guy over. His opponent hit the ground hard enough to knock the air from his lungs with a painful thud. Ash knelt over the man, the pistol in his left hand as he pointed it at the man standing just outside the door.

The man outside had his pistol halfway out of its holster. His eyes were flat and hard as they locked on Ash's.

Remaining kneeling on the man he'd thrown, Ash looked at the man. "However you want to play this," he said softly. Warning bells pinged inside his head. The anger he'd experienced just a few short weeks ago aboard the Polish ship came roaring back at him. His finger slid over the trigger.

"Tom," the man at the desk said.

"Yeah?"

"Let it go."

"Sure." If the man outside the room had any problem standing down from the situation, it didn't show on his face.

"Put the pistol on the ground," Ash directed. "Slowly."

"Phil?" Tom asked.

"Do it. I believe we're up for an introduction to the local sheriff," Phil said.

"This is the sheriff?" Tom asked.

"Yeah. We were told about him."

That interested Ash. It made the situation either calmer or more dangerous. He didn't know which.

Calmly, Tom took out his pistol between his forefinger and thumb, and laid it on the ground.

"Step back," Ash commanded. "Lock your hands behind your head. Down on your knees."

Smiling, the man took three steps back, slid his fingers together behind his neck, and knelt. "I'll remember you," he said to Ash.

The tough-guy talk didn't scare Ash. There'd been a ton of that in the bases and ships where he'd served. But it did rake razor-sharp claws against the anger boiling inside him. He lifted his knee from the chest of the man beneath him. "You. Over on your stomach. Hands locked behind your neck."

"I like that idea," Bolo said. "Let's see if you two boys can't do that as well."

"You're making a mistake," Phil said. "We're not who you think we are." He made no move.

"Really," Bolo said. "Do you know who I think you are?"

"I've got a number you can call," Phil said. "I really think you should call it before you go any further."

"I'll keep that in mind," Bolo said. "Now you can either move out of that chair, or I'm gonna come move you myself. If I have to, gentle ain't going to enter the picture. I promise you that."

Reluctantly, Phil moved away from the desk, dropped to his knees in the center of the room, and locked his hands behind his neck. "It didn't have to be this way, Sheriff."

"Yeah it did," Bolo countered. "The minute you rolled into my town without so much as a phone call, it had to be this way."

Within minutes, Ash had helped Bolo bind the men's hands behind their backs with disposable plastic handcuffs from the cruiser. They sat along the back wall of the room and stared at Bolo without saying a word. After Phil had given the sheriff the number he insisted be called, he and his friends didn't speak again.

They were trained, Ash thought, and he felt certain that at least part of the training was military. Name, rank, and serial number. Just the way a special-ops warrior was supposed to handle getting captured. Of course, that wasn't the way it really went. When a man was tortured, he'd give up everything he knew. That's why his knowledge about an operation was compartmentalized and deliberately kept separate. *Need to know* meant exactly that. Looking at Bolo's prisoners, Ash got the impression that even they didn't know what their assignment was. Yet.

Bolo didn't make an immediate try to reach whoever was at the other end of the number Phil had provided. Instead, he turned his attention to the photo IDs and the serial numbers on the weapons, making sure the four men knew he was making a record of them. Their list was considerable. Weapons had been found in the other room as well, and more in the two cars. By the time Bolo and Ash had them all together, there were two sniper rifles and two handguns for each man. Metal ammo boxes held hundreds of rounds for each weapon.

"I don't suppose you want to tell me why you came to Fairly, South Dakota so well armed," Bolo said.

None of them answered.

Ash didn't have a problem putting it together. The four men looked like federal agents and they showed no fear of being arrested. That meant that if they weren't federal agents they were at least on a government payroll somewhere down the line.

"Tell me this isn't better than busting the master chief's chops over to the university," Bolo told Ash as he leaned against the desk.

"It does have a certain appeal," Ash admitted.

"Assholes," one of the men muttered.

Bolo grinned. "I do believe our guests are losing their professional aplomb." He paused. "Wait till after the first one pisses himself while we're waiting to hear from whoever they're working for."

25

Devon Hite stood on a hilltop and watched as his hand-picked tank crew put the T-72 through its paces. He wore an ear-throat communications rig one of the militia members had assembled from Radio Shack components. It was a little heavier than the gear he'd worked with when he'd still been with the Baron's Itch and later with Melvin C. Stewart's "Be Healed" program. But it got the job done.

Several other militia members stood in attendance, talking and laughing among themselves as if they were at a monster-truck rally.

Actually, the training course wasn't too far off from that today. A few of the members, after finding out what Hite wanted for the exercise, had managed to scrounge together a few old cars that no one wanted anymore. Wrecker drivers, Hite was certain, had taken some of them from where they'd been abandoned along the highways outside Fairly. All of them were POSes, pieces of shit, and beaters that wouldn't be missed.

Except for one. The flashy red Mercedes coupe belonged to the girlfriend of one of the state senators. It was a more expensive car than the senator's wife and daughter drove, and the girlfriend was younger than either of them. Hite had tasked a group to liberate the car over the weekend, deciding to give his tank crew a prize for their hard work.

"Are you ready?" Hite asked over the radio.

"Ready, General," Claude Thornton radioed back. He was in his early twenties, a farm boy who had seen his daddy's farm taken for nonpayment of property taxes after his daddy died. Claude, like a lot of other farmers who'd lost property and become part of the Badlands Militia, didn't understand why he was supposed to pay the federal government taxes on property his family already owned. That was un-American. In fact, some of them had pointed out, the United States used to *give* land away for free back when there was unsettled land. They'd started calling Hite "General" on Saturday morning. Hite didn't mind. In fact, he rather enjoyed the ring of it.

"Okay then," Hite said. "Time to rock and roll."

Down in the valley, which was tracked more heavily than a junkie's arms with tank threads, eight cars had been arranged in a vague oval. The pièce de résistance was the Mercedes sitting up on the hill a thousand yards away. The tank's gears engaged and the heavy treads bit into the earth. With a liquid snarl, the Russian tank lumbered forward. Claude and his crew took the metal juggernaut through the surrounding forest first. Brush and trees went down under the tank's cowling, leaving a mess of debris and torn-up earth in its wake.

They cut deep into the forest, which would be covered in the next couple days by crews Hite would send in to salvage firewood. He'd already filed with the DNR for the land to be turned into farmland. The Department of Natural Resources with its heavy-handed autocracy was another agency that ruffled the local feathers and swelled the ranks of the Badlands Militia.

"Okay," Hite said, watching the tank eat through the forest like some ravening predator, "bring her around."

"Aye, aye, General," Claude said happily.

Hite didn't bother telling the young man he was mixing the military branches. It didn't matter. They were making up their army now. If they wanted to "aye, aye" a general in their army, they damn well could.

The tank came around, throwing out clods of earth

and taking a new tack that left broken and uprooted trees in its wake. Gaining speed, the T-72 roared toward two cars parked end to end. When the massive tank slammed into the cars they spun outward, exploding safety glass from the windows. They were far enough away that the sound of the collision didn't reach the group of spectators for a few seconds. When it did, an excited cheer immediately drowned the noise out.

Hite grinned. He'd read about the abilities of the T-72, had even watched a few videos before making the purchase, but nothing could compare to watching the monster tank chew through vehicles and the land.

The tank crew stayed with the oval, busting through two more barriers formed of cars—simulating what would happen if law-enforcement personnel tried to stop the tank with their vehicles—then paused in front of a line of three cars. When the driver engaged the treads, the tank rose up off the ground at an angle sharp enough to allow it to crawl on top of the first car. The car couldn't hold the tank's forty-four metric tons and pancaked immediately. Lunging forward, the tank turned the car into an impromptu road, and then converted the two other cars as well.

Another ragged cheer went up from the crowd. Stories would be told tonight, Hite knew. And in the telling, the confidence his members had in the militia and what he was doing would take on a life of its own.

Finished with the race through the parked vehicles, the tank crew brought the massive vehicle to a halt. The T-72 locked down. The turret swiveled, pointing the 125-millimeter gun toward the Mercedes glistening on the hilltop a thousand yards away.

"Target acquired," Claude Thornton announced gleefully. "Requesting permission to fire, General!"

"Fire away," Hite responded.

Almost immediately, the T-72 belched a round that rocked the whole tank back. The detonation shuddered through the crowd and silenced them in awe because most of them hadn't seen the tank fire until today. A second passed, and then the round struck the Mercedes squarely, turning it into a fireball that flipped end over end and came down in smoking pieces.

The silence was maintained for a moment, carried on the shoulders of the sounds of the explosions that rolled after the sight reached the eyes of the watchers.

"It's dead," Hite declared in the stillness of the moment.

A savage cheer ripped from almost two hundred throats. Cowboy hats and baseball caps sailed into the air.

"Son of a bitch!" someone squalled. "Would you look at that?"

"Hell yeah!" someone else yelled. "That's what I'm talking about!"

"Let somebody come out here and try to take what's ours!" another man shouted. "We'll give 'em what for!"

En masse, the spectators loaded up into their pickups, jeeps, and motorcycles and drove down to gawk closer, descending like carrion birds to pick over roadkill.

Hite smiled. The tank would surely give his people something to take pride in, and feel secure about. And if push came to shove, Hite figured the Badlands Militia could shove just about as hard as anybody around. He walked back to his pickup and took out a jelly jar of peppermint tea, sipped, and thought about the possibilities as Claude Thornton and his group continued to run the tank around the exercise field. Several of the militia personnel caught hold of the tank's rear curtain and hopped aboard.

Damn fools, Hite thought. The farm had earthmoving equipment on it so an accident could be explained if medical attention was required, but he didn't want to deal with that. "Claude," he called over the headset.

"Aye, aye, General."

"Bring it back up to the warehouse. Let's tuck her in." The whining roar of a two-stroke motorcycle engine drew Hite's attention back toward the main house.

The motorcycle driver rode as if his life depended on

it. The Enduro bike got air several times, then landed a few feet away and came around in a skidding semicircle that threw dirt and rock for twenty yards.

"Something going on, Hector?" Hite asked as he recapped the jelly jar and replaced the tea in the truck.

Hector Dawkins, eighteen years old and lanky, unfurled from the motorcycle. He bounced his helmet off the ground and ripped off his dirt-smeared goggles. His face around the goggles was grimy and his beard was tangled with dirt and leaves. He loosed a huge squirt of tobacco as he walked over.

"Yeah, something's going on," Hector said angrily. "Them bastards done called in a strike team on us."

Hite remained calm. "What bastards?"

"The ATF."

"How do you know they called in a strike force?"

" 'Cause Sheriff Bolo's got 'em corralled at Imogene's motel. I tried to reach you on the two-way." Hector gestured at the pickup's whip aerial.

"It's been loud out here," Hite said. "I didn't hear it. Who told you about the strike force?"

"Hell, all you got to do is go into town right now. Sheriff's had them bastards holed up at Imogene's for the last hour or so. Everybody's talking about it."

"What were you doing in town?" Hite asked. He kept the men close to home for the most part. That way there was less chance of getting into trouble. The young ones, like Hector, sometimes when into Fairly to "get recruits" as they called it, but generally they just went there to drink and get laid.

"Had a friend who's thinking about joining," Hector said. "His dad's farm is about to get repossessed by the government for some loans he can't pay off. He's thinking that ain't right and wants to do something about it. I told him we had a place for him right here."

Hite nodded. "Did you get any names?"

"No sir," Hector said. He spat tobacco again. "I hightailed it out here as soon as I could. Want me to scout out the situation?"

"No," Hite said. But he was thinking maybe it was time for a visit to Fairly. But there were other preparations to make first. He keyed the headset and called, "Claude."

"Aye, aye, General," Claude replied enthusiastically. "Me and the boys, we were thinking we should have some kind of kick-ass call sign. Something that meant something, you know. What do you think about Iron Grinder?"

Hite grinned and shook his head. "Sure, Claude—"

"Iron Grinder, General," Claude interrupted.

"Okay, Iron Grinder, there's been a change in plans. Instead of taking the vehicle back to the warehouse, hide it at our secondary base. Stay with it there till I call you."

"Aye, aye, General. Iron Grinder out."

Hite turned back to Hector. "Get back to the house. Tell everybody we're going to condition yellow."

A serious look infused Hector's young face. "Condition yellow?"

"Yeah," Hite said.

"You really think them government people are going to attack us?"

"I don't know," Hite said. "I just want to be prepared."

Tension mounted in the hotel room as the clock hands slowly moved. Ash was having second thoughts about his impulsive decision to join the sheriff in his impromptu raid. But if he hadn't come, Bolo would have been outgunned, possibly even dead. Still, the call to action was hard to resist.

The sheriff lounged easily, sitting on the desk with his pistol in his lap as if he could sit there for another day or two. He chewed gum slowly and methodically.

One of the four cell phones on the desk pealed. Bolo scooped it up and answered, "Yeah." He paused. "No, Cornett can't come to the phone right now. He's tied up. I tied him up myself." He waited another moment.

"Me? I'm Sheriff Bolo. Tell Chief Howard he's going to have to pick these men up himself." The sheriff rolled his wrist over and checked his watch. "Tell him he's got twenty minutes to get here, then he can pick them up from the jail." He punched off the phone.

Cornett, Ash knew, was the name of one of the men sitting against the wall. None of them had any reaction whatsoever to the phone call.

"Well, that should stir the pot," Bolo said, putting the phone down and peering out the window.

One of the other phones rang immediately.

Bolo grinned mirthlessly as he reached for it. "Double-checking." He punched the answer button. "Sheriff Bolo. You're wasting time. Nineteen minutes." He clicked off without awaiting a response. Looking at Ash, he said, "If you want to bug out of here now, I wouldn't blame you."

"I'll stick," Ash replied. "Never like to see a job half done."

"I know what you mean."

The ATF agents arrived ten minutes later. They drove black Suburbans with heavily tinted windows that screamed *federal agents*. The three Suburbans fanned out in front of the motel, blocking the driveway and drawing the attention of the gawkers who already filled the parking lot at the Dairy Queen.

"Not exactly a low-profile operation out there anymore," Bolo observed. "I guess the ATF isn't going to be happy about that."

Another cell phone rang. After a quick inspection, Bolo discovered that this time it was his own. "Hello."

Ash watched through the window as the ATF agents fanned out. Most of them wore navy-colored windbreakers with BATF stenciled across the back in yellow.

"We might be a little late for dinner," Bolo said. "But I'm betting this will be a short meeting. We're on television?" He craned his neck over to the television on the stand, then picked up a remote control and flipped it on.

"I'll be damned." He cycled through the channels quickly.

Ash spared a glance at the television as well. Evidently the reporting crew was filming live from the Dairy Queen parking lot, judging by the angle. A slug line at the bottom of the screen announced: STANDOFF AT JOURNEY'S END.

"Imogene must be loving that," Bolo said. "She'll have stories to tell for weeks, and people will rent the rooms just to be here. You can't buy advertising like this."

On the screen a group of five men, three of them in riot gear and two of them wearing BATF windbreakers, walked toward the door of Number Twelve. Ash looked out the window and confirmed it. "Showtime," he said.

Almost immediately afterward, someone banged the door and yelled, "Sheriff! Sheriff Bolo!"

"My admiring public," Bolo said. He waved Ash into position on the side of the door that opened.

"How hard do you want to play this?" Ash still held one of the Beretta M92s they'd recovered. All of the weapons were military makes.

"Balls to the wall," Bolo said. "These assholes are treading on my turf after I already warned them." He looked at Ash. "You sure you're up for this?"

Ash knew the sheriff was wondering about the incident that had landed him in Fairly. And, truth to tell, maybe Ash was wondering a little himself. He still felt tense and jittery, and the anger surged in him without stop. For a moment he wondered if he'd ever get around it. Then he realized that even with it, he could still perform. It was just something to get used to.

"I'm sure," he said.

The door-banging ignited again. *"Sheriff!"*

"Coming," Bolo yelled back. He put his left foot up against the door, worked the locks, and swung the door open, sliding his foot back to act as a brake if he needed it. Lifting the pistol in his hand, he pointed it at the ATF agent's head. "Hello, Chief Howard. We can't keep meeting like this. It's a small town. People are going to talk."

Ash stood in a Weaver stance, left hand cupping his right as he held the Beretta locked on the opening.

"Son of a bitch!" The man in the lead squalled like a raped ape. "What the fuck is this?" But he stood rock-solid and didn't move.

"Personal party," Bolo said. "Invitation only. I'm going to speak with Chief Howard. So back the fuck away from my door."

"You pompous son of a bitch!" the man yelled. He started inside.

Uncoiling lazily, Bolo rapped the man between the eyes with his pistol butt and kicked him in the chest. The man shot back out of the doorway and landed flat on his ass at the feet of the three ATF agents in riot gear.

"That's not Chief Howard," Bolo explained. He pointed the gun at the other man. "This is Howard."

Howard stood in the doorway and looked down at the other man, who was fighting off the attempts of the three agents to help him up. The man cursed loudly and voiced dire threats.

"You coming in?" Bolo asked Howard.

Howard looked at the sheriff. "Can I smoke in there? Because if I can't smoke in there, I'm not coming in."

"You can smoke."

Howard took a last look at the downed agent and shook his head. Then he stepped inside the motel room and Bolo locked the door once more behind him. Howard glanced at the four men handcuffed against the walls. "Tough guys, huh? You're a bunch of puds is what you are." He took a deep breath. "Jesus Christ, you guys really screwed the pooch on this." He looked at Bolo. "Can I have that cigarette now? And I may need a fucking blindfold before this is over."

26

"Who was at the door?" Bolo asked.

Chief Special Agent Howard sat in a chair at the desk and took a long drag on his cigarette. He held the smoke for a moment before letting it pour out his nose. "That," he said after a moment, "was Chief Special Agent Mel Ferguson of the Seattle BATF."

"What's he doing at your get-together?" Bolo asked.

"Setting up party favors." Howard waved at the quartet of men handcuffed and sitting against the wall. "Chief Special Agent Ferguson is the senior ranking officer in the region. He decided, after it was known that I had an agent missing and Devon Hite was running the Badlands Militia, to take control of the situation."

"By sending in hired guns?"

Howard looked at the men. "They're supposed to be really good. Hostage-retrieval experts trained by the FBI for their HRT unit."

"The Hostage Rescue Team?" Bolo said. "No shit."

"Yeah, no shit."

Ash leaned against the wall with his captured pistol shoved in the waistband of his pants. For a small town, things were starting to get interesting. He glanced at the television, noting that the local channel had elected to stay live with the "developing story" although facts were in short supply. The camera revealed the ATF team standing outside their Suburbans in front of the motel. Chief Special Agent Mel Ferguson was pacing around holding a cell phone to his ear and a chemical icepack to his forehead. Blood ran down the man's nose.

"What were they supposed to do?" Bolo asked.

"Whatever Ferguson was inclined to tell them."

Bolo scratched a thumb along his whiskered jaw. "You went along with this?"

"It's Ferguson's party," Howard replied. "I was told to come along for the ride." He took another hit on the cigarette. "I think me being along was meant to rub my nose in the shit." He grinned. "It didn't turn out that way."

Bolo grinned back. "No, it didn't. But this ain't over yet. What's Ferguson like?"

"An arrogant prick with a chip on his shoulder. He handles the Seattle area. One of the largest ports in the United States with constant trade relations with Russia, China, and Japan. Want to bet how many weapons come in from those countries on Ferguson's watch?"

"Is he clean?"

"Straight as an arrow from all accounts," Howard said. "But dumb as a post."

"So he came down here from the big city to show you how to run your podunk town?"

Howard nodded. "That's pretty much the size of it."

Bolo gazed at the television, watching Ferguson pacing and shouting angrily into the cell phone. "This isn't going to go away easy, is it?"

"No."

Bolo sighed. "And I didn't make it any easier by hitting him."

"No. But I don't think you made it any harder, either. At least this way maybe he's got some respect for you."

"His kind doesn't come around to respect very easy."

Howard shrugged. "Maybe if you hit him again."

Bolo laughed, and Ash laughed too, though it wasn't a laughing matter. Howard joined in, along with two of the four guys they had handcuffed. Ash figured the one he'd gone up against was still nursing a grudge and the other was his partner.

After a moment, Bolo studied Howard. "Do you really think Hite has your missing agent?"

"Bobby Redmond?" Howard nodded. "I do."

"Is he still alive?"

Howard took another drag before stubbing his cigarette out in a disposable foil ashtray. "I don't know. I hope so. Bobby's a good kid. It would be a shame to lose him."

"Do you think Ferguson has calmed down enough to talk to?"

"You popped him on live television," Howard said. "If it's a slow news day, that footage may make national. He's going to hate your guts till the day he dies."

"Well then," Bolo said, "it's nice to know some things still last."

Devon Hite parked his pickup truck across the street from the Dairy Queen and the Journey's End Motel. Taking a pair of Bushnell binoculars from the glove compartment, he trained them on the motel and studied the action.

"All of those men are federal agents," Oscar Whitely said from the passenger seat. He was large and ponderous, but once he gave himself to something, he stayed the course the way few men did.

"What do you think they're doing here?" Curtis Ripley asked from the backseat of the king cab.

"At least they're here and not out at the farm," Hite said. He trained the binoculars on the motel's front door as it swung open. Sheriff Bolo stepped out and motioned to the agents. The guy holding the compress to his head walked toward the door.

"But they might be coming to the farm," Oscar stated.

Hite silently agreed. Maybe the idea of hanging onto Bobby Redmond after he'd been discovered spying on them had been a little too daring. It might have been better if they'd killed the ATF agent and dropped him down an abandoned well somewhere. Now they needed to hang on to him as a bargaining chip—and keep him out of sight so the ATF spies wouldn't see him around the farm, even though he looked very different now.

Hite got out of the truck and told the other men to wait there. He crossed the street to the Dairy Queen and went inside. All of the employees and customers were pressed up against the glass overlooking the motel, attentions divided between the motel and the television someone had brought up from the back. Hite went to the counter and waited till a young woman stepped over to wait on him.

"Can I get you something?" she asked.

"A Dilly Bar," Hite said. Those had always been a favorite. He couldn't remember when he'd last had one.

The employee got the ice cream from the freezer and rang it up.

Hite asked, "What's going on over to the motel?"

The woman watched the small portable TV on the counter. "Haven't heard yet. But it's the biggest thing to hit Fairly in years."

"Those Suburbans look like something government agents drive around in," Hite said, biting into the ice cream.

"They're feds all right," a young male manager in a stained tie said. His tone held disapproval. "I keep expecting to see Most Wanted rolling up any second."

"Why's that?"

"Imogene Jorgensen, she's the one that owns the motel," the manager said, "she said some of the guys there were carrying guns."

"No shit." Hite took another bite of ice cream.

"No, sir," the manager said. He pushed his glasses up his nose and looked serious. "Every now and again, we get hardened criminals running through Fairly. Had some bank robbers through a few years ago that shot up one of the sheriff's deputies."

"Killed him," one of the other employees said. "I went to school with his son. Tore that kid up pretty bad, I tell you."

"So who's in the motel room?"

"The sheriff. Some guy who's teaching over at the university."

"A professor?" That surprised Hite. He knew Bolo, but he didn't know why Bolo would walk a civilian into a dangerous situation. That didn't seem right.

"Yeah. Some new guy just arrived to Thaedt," said the employee who'd waited on Hite. "I bet he's about to poop himself right now. I know I would be."

"So why are the federal agents here?" Hite asked.

"I think they're looking for whoever's in that room." The manager smiled. "But Sheriff Bolo ain't gonna let them have whoever it is until he's through with them." He snickered. "The sheriff already hit one of those agents when he tried to duck into the room."

"Really," Hite said.

"That's exactly what happened."

Hite stood there and watched the television and ate his Dilly Bar. Things had definitely become interesting here in Fairly.

Spike sat at her computer and looked at the homework she'd brought in. Classes were a bitch. Living at a dorm, especially now that she couldn't count on the master chief's impromptu parties on a regular basis, sucked. It had been one thing to be behind on homework during volleyball season. Then she had an excuse. And if the team was up for a title, she had a get-out-of-jail free card for grades. Thaedt University liked pulling in the wins because there had been so few.

But now with the new lieutenant coming in as OIC, things were bound to get totally fucked up. Next thing she knew, she was betting he'd start handing out homework assignments as well. The only thing worse than trying to gut it out at college right now, and maybe the Navy after, was going to work at her mother's beauty parlor back in Peakner, the small town in Nebraska she was from. That would suck.

She looked at the heavy books on the desk and sighed. How could she screw off this much of the semester and expect to pull through? The task looked impossible. She wanted to go down to one of the local watering holes and drink beer until life looked good again. Or she just didn't care. Whichever came first was fine.

The only reason she'd joined the NROTC program was to get out of Nebraska and away from babysitting her four younger siblings and putting up with her mom's new boyfriend, who had moved in with his hunting dogs and his own troubles. The boyfriend, Dalton, was ten years younger than Spike's mom, and was looking more for someone to take care of him than for him to take care of her. As it turned out, Dalton fit right in with Spike's younger brothers and sister even though he was six years older than her.

Even then, she'd only been seventeen when she'd decided to join the NROTC. Her mom had had to sign for her. Until she'd brought the papers home, her mom hadn't known Spike had had an interest in military service. Actually, Spike still didn't know that she did. There seemed to be too many orders involved to suit her. She'd grown up around that. But the Navy at least offered her a way out of Peakner. And if Dalton hadn't been starting in with the groping and Spike hadn't told her mother—who had refused to believe a word of it— maybe those papers wouldn't have gotten signed.

Spike looked at the grade reports she'd pulled up on the computer. She'd made an F on her last Western Civilization test, which had been Friday while she'd been at the kegger with the master chief. Since the lieutenant's arrival, Fernandez had been more interested in taking care of his own ass than in looking out for hers. The master chief had never made the phone call to the Western Civ professor to get her an excused absence like he'd said he would. Now she was in danger of failing the class.

Fuck.

Spike leaned back in her chair. Somehow she'd gotten by during the last three years, but her grades had continued to cycle down. She didn't know why. They just had.

School was almost behind her and what the hell was she going to do with herself?

Someone banged on the door.

"Who the fuck is it?" Spike growled. Besides the F, she was PMSing.

"Chuck."

"What the fuck, Globe. Go bang on somebody else's door."

"I already did. You were next in line. You gotta see this."

"What?"

"It's cool shit, Spike. Could mean an end to our problems."

Spike looked at the F on her monitor and didn't think so. It would take a meteor impact or something.

"It's about the lieutenant," Globe said.

Spike blanked the monitor and walked to the door. She unlocked it and let Globe in. Just that amount of effort hurt her. She was beginning to think she'd have permanent damage from the new OIC's PT drills on Friday. Not even the most demanding volleyball coach she'd had had ever scheduled something like that.

Globe limped into the room, rubbing a quad. "You still hurting?"

"No," she lied. "I'm in a lot better shape than you guys."

He looked at her as if he didn't believe her.

She folded her arms and looked down at him, for once using every inch of her six-foot-one-inch frame. "What do you think is so important?"

"Haven't you heard about the standoff at the Journey's End Motel?"

Spike shook her head and regretted it. *Everything* was sore. She knew about the Journey's End Motel. She'd picked up out-of-town guys in bars around Fairly every now and again and enjoyed a few nights of physical release. Nobody at school, though, because she didn't like her personal life dragged around. She'd had enough of that growing up in Peakner.

"The sheriff's holed up in there with some fugitives."
Globe grabbed the television remote from the unmade
bed and switched on the set.

Spike was suddenly aware that last night's bra and
panties were lying beside the bed. She didn't feel uncomfortable around the rest of the guys talking trash, but it
was another thing for her personal business to hang out
there. Crossing over to the bed, she quietly kicked her
underwear under the bed.

Globe didn't notice a thing; his attention was solely
on the television.

"Don't you have a television in your room?" she
asked.

"Yes. I came down here because I thought you would
want to see this."

Spike blew out her breath. "Look, Globe, I got
homework."

"You?" He looked at her as if she'd just said the
world was going to end. "You never do homework."

I never flunked out of college before. She just locked
eyes with him. "You said this was about the new lieutenant. All you've told me is that the sheriff is locked in a
motel with some fugitives."

"Yeah." Globe smiled and waggled his eyebrows.
"But guess who's locked up in there with him."

"The lieutenant?"

"Yeah."

"No fucking way." Forgetting about her underwear
and the F in Western Civ, Spike sat on the end of the
bed and stared at the television.

"Way," Globe said, satisfied with the tuning. He sat
on the bed beside her. "Guess he's as crazy as the master chief said he was, huh?"

"I guess he is. But there's nuts crazy and there's this
type of crazy."

"The way it looks, the federal agents—"

"Federal agents?"

"Yeah. FBI or something."

"No fucking way."

Globe looked at her. "Maybe we could watch the television." He shifted his attention back to the set. "Anyway, looks like Lieutenant Ash Roberts just stepped into a bear trap with Sheriff Bolo. Looks like the FBI is about to go in guns blazing."

Spike doubled her fists up under her chin and rested her elbows on her knees as she stared at the tiny screen. If the lieutenant got shot and shipped out—she didn't really want him dead—then that would solve some of her problems. But it didn't take care of the F that had dropped her grade in Western Civ to failing.

27

"Who the fuck are you?"

Ash met Chief Special Agent Mel Ferguson's eyes and thought about his responses. An informed answer, maybe, or bury the needle at wiseass? Ash was undecided. Guys like Ferguson automatically got under his skin. The federal government agencies had more people in high-ranking positions who hadn't really come up through the trenches than the military. Senior officers who couldn't really lead troops were noticed in the military, and advances didn't just come solely through seniority. They rested largely on merit too. Ferguson was one of those guys who might never have had a meritorious day in his life.

"He's with me," Bolo growled.

Ferguson scowled at Ash, who stood his ground and remained unimpressed in the face of the other's hostility. Chief Special Agent Ferguson of the Seattle BATF didn't hold a candle to a ship's captain on a tear. Besides, it was hard for him to look threatening when he had a lump the side of a baseball between his eyes.

"We've got to get our stories straight," Bolo said. "That's a hell of a lot of press waiting out there for somebody to say something."

"We're not saying anything," Ferguson responded.

Bolo crossed his arms over his chest and sat with one haunch on the desk.

Ash admired the sheriff. From the first time he'd met

him Ash had liked the guy. Now the wild-assed, ballsy move Bolo had just played had deepened that respect. This was a guy, Ash knew, after Wild Willie Weldon's own roguish heart.

"Yeah we are," Bolo said. "This is my town. I run things here, and I say we're going to tell the press something. Give them some kind of story. What kind of story depends on you."

"Me?" Ferguson looked apoplectic.

"It does," Bolo said solemnly.

"Why did you arrest these men?" Ferguson waved over to the four men against the wall.

"Sir," one of the men said, "I really have to go relieve myself."

Ferguson sighed and looked at the stone-faced man. "Can't you hold it?"

"I have been." The man shrugged. "I can go on the floor. Doesn't make a difference to me."

Ferguson looked at Bolo, who didn't say a word.

Ash watched the unspoken interplay. It was a lot like an aggressive XO feeling out the boundaries of a new billet on board a captain's ship. Ash knew Bolo wasn't going to do a thing until Ferguson admitted control wasn't in his own hands.

"Did you hear him?" Ferguson demanded.

"I did," Bolo said.

"Well?"

"Well what?"

Ferguson sighed. "Christ on the cross, but you're a hard man."

Bolo nodded. "Obstinate. Stubborn. Set in my ways. Cantankerous. I've been called a lot of things by a lot of people."

"Can he go to the bathroom?"

"Sure." Bolo looked at Ash.

Ash went with it, knowing that Bolo didn't want to lose the upper hand by freeing the man himself or allowing Ferguson to assign someone to the task. Reaching into his pocket for his clasp knife, Ash cut through the disposable plastic handcuffs. The freed man muttered a neutral "Thanks" and went about his business. With the group split up now, Ash stood in the corner away from Bolo so they wouldn't be grouped together. It was an unconscious strategy that he didn't recognize till after he was already in place.

Howard set fire to another cigarette and watched the smoke curl to the ceiling.

"Why did you arrest these men?" Ferguson repeated.

"Because I got a report they were carrying concealed weapons. Then, when I found the sniper rifles, I decided that something more drastic was called for."

"They're working for me," Ferguson bellowed.

"Good," Bolo said. "We'll just step outside and tell the press there's been a misunderstanding. That men carrying concealed weapons and carrying sniper rifles—without proper identification—are working for you." He shrugged. "I can do that."

"They have proper identification."

"Not with them."

"I can show you authorization for them to be here."

"All right," Bolo said.

"Mel," Howard sighed.

"What?" Ferguson snapped.

Howard eyed his cigarette. "Let me play this out for you. You identify these men as ATF agents, or as special ops on loan from the FBI—and let's even say you make it stick and the paper on the arrangement doesn't fall apart—but what you might as well be doing is taking out paid advertisement to let Devon Hite know you're coming after his ass."

Ferguson glared at Howard.

"What?" Howard asked innocently. "Do you think that's a secret from anyone in this room?"

Ferguson again held the icepack to his forehead, which was looking red in addition to swollen now. "You should have left this alone, Sheriff."

"I take my job seriously," Bolo said. "You're not going to turn my town into a shooting gallery."

Ferguson peeled the curtain back from the window. "Son of a bitch," he said in exasperation. "Do you realize what a truly fucked-up mess this is?"

"Oh, yeah," Bolo said. "How does, 'Bureau of Alcohol, Firearms and Tobacco Brings in Hired Killers' sound to you?"

The man stepped back into the room from the bathroom. The sound of the toilet flushing gurgled into the room.

Probably a lot like that, Ash thought.

"I've got a missing agent somewhere over here," Ferguson said.

"Wrong," Bolo countered. "Chief Special Agent Howard has a man missing over here. You're just grandstanding."

Abruptly, Ferguson stepped into Bolo's space and tried to look tough. With the swollen forehead squeezing his eyes tight, he only pulled off looking like a scared weasel. "Don't go all high-and-mighty with me, Bolo. I had your jacket pulled. You aren't exactly clean when it comes to having dirty laundry. Does the Mi Chu Massacre mean anything to you?"

Bolo didn't back down. He leaned over the smaller man and went nose-to-nose with him. "It means a hell of a lot to me. I was there. I paid for my mistakes and they're out in the open. Want to ante up on yours?"

The men along the wall shifted, maybe getting ready to back their supervisor. Ash moved with them, shifting just enough to remind them they were still unarmed and he wasn't.

Ferguson glared back but broke the eye contact. "Fuck," he seethed, taking a deep breath. "Okay, what do you have in mind?"

"We do a handoff," Bolo said. "I tell the press that these men are fugitives—felons trafficking in stolen weapons—"

"Stolen weapons?" Ferguson looked as if he couldn't believe it.

"Munitions dealers. The press out there will believe

it. You'll sell them on it. I just happened to get lucky and catch them, after Imogene Jorgensen—make sure you mention her name because the town will eat that up—called in a tip."

"They're not munitions dealers."

Bolo was silent for a moment. "You're right. It would be much better if we tell them that these yahoos are hired government assassins."

Ferguson pushed his breath out and waved his hands in surrender. "All right. Munitions dealers."

"It'll sell," Bolo said. "We put pillowcases over their heads so they can't be identified. Maybe it'll save them a little embarrassment."

Ash watched the four men nodding among themselves.

"You tell the press that at this time you can't identify the men, that it's part of an ongoing investigation into a supply operation that might have terrorist ties," Bolo said. "I'll back you up on that."

"My God," Ferguson said. "Do you realize the attention that's going to raise?"

Bolo jerked a thumb at the television. "We're already there. The question is, what are we going to do about it?"

Ash appreciated the situation Bolo had engineered. When they'd first come through the door, he'd assumed the sheriff was just using a hammer when a slap would have worked. Now Ash saw that Bolo was taking no prisoners; the ATF would have to play according to his rules if they wanted out as gracefully as possible. It was a hell of a call.

"Okay," Ferguson said, "we say they're weapons dealers. Then what?"

"I turn them over to you—since it's a federal matter and I just dumb-luck walked into it—and wave good-bye as you all ride off."

Some of the weight seemed to lift from Ferguson's shoulders. "That's not so bad. Would have been better if you'd called and it hadn't come to this."

"Maybe," Bolo suggested, "if you'd have told me you had men in town it would have gone differently."

"I made a mistake," Ferguson said.

But it's one you're willing to make again, Ash thought, watching the man.

"Now, that will get you and these guys' tits out of the wringer," Bolo said, "so now I'm going to tell you what you're going to do for me."

Ferguson glared at Bolo.

"I'm keeping the IDs of these men," the sheriff said. "And their fingerprints. If I see them again in town, if *anyone* in town identifies them, I'm going to arrest them and make this even worse on you." He paused. "Do we understand each other?"

"Yeah," Ferguson grumbled.

"My town," Bolo said. "My rules. That's how it's going to be."

"I've still got—" Ferguson checked himself. "Hank has still got a missing agent."

"Let me work on that," Bolo said. "Howard can interface with me. If Bobby Redmond is still alive, we'll get him back to you."

Ash stood beside Bolo at the sheriff's cruiser. As soon as they had stepped out of the motel and guided the four men—once more in steel bracelets and now sporting pillowcases, purportedly to hide their identities so their co-conspirators didn't know how close the ATF was to them—Bolo had spoken briefly to the press, then stepped aside and left Ferguson with the question-and-answer session.

Even with his face swollen up, Ferguson was a natural in front of the cameras.

"How did you get injured?" one of the reporters asked.

"One of the men inside momentarily got away," Ferguson said. "Sheriff Bolo enlisted the services of a civilian to help him take these people down. The civilian wasn't used to handling a situation like the sheriff brought him into and one of the prisoners made a break. I got lucky and put him down." He grinned. "If we could show you the faces of these men, I'd show you what *he* looks like."

The audience laughed in appreciation.

Ash looked at Bolo and said, "Is it my fault for being inexperienced? Or is it your fault for dragging in a civilian that was unqualified for the job?"

"Hell," Bolo said, "I'll split it with you and buy you a beer after dinner. I did tell you Little Feather made a pie, didn't I?"

"Yeah."

"I'll pick up a gallon of ice cream." Bolo slid his sunglasses on. "You moved good in there."

"Thanks."

"If you need a second opinion for the Navy shrink, I'll be happy to write one up for you. Everybody's allowed to get tense when they're out in the jungle. It's part of what keeps you alive." Bolo looked at Ash. "What you did in there, if you hadn't been on your marks, you could have killed one of those men."

Or more, Ash thought but didn't say. He had been on his toes. He'd used just enough force and threat of violence to put down the threat and keep everybody intact. "Yeah."

"Or let one of them kill me," Bolo said, grinning sardonically. "I knew that guy was coming up behind me too late to do anything about it."

"You'd have done something," Ash said.

"Probably," Bolo admitted. "Would have shot the guys in front of me to hell and took my chances with the man at the door. Wouldn't have been a stellar move."

"I'd have given you a fifty-fifty chance." Ash listened to Ferguson's rhetoric again for a few minutes. "Think anybody's going to ask him why the ATF is out in force on such a calm day?"

"If they do, he'll just tell them he was out chasing down leads about weapons dealers." Bolo shook his head. "I've covered his ass as much as I care to right now. He's on his own. Can I give you a ride back to your car?"

Ash nodded and climbed into the cruiser.

Bolo dropped into place behind the wheel and keyed the ignition. Then he rummaged in the glove box and came out with a badge. "I'm deputizing you." He flipped the badge into the air.

Ash caught the badge in the air and felt the heavy weight of it. "I'm a deputy?"

"Honorary," Bolo said.

" 'Honorary' generally means no pay involved," Ash pointed out.

Bolo put the cruiser in gear and started forward. "I'll give you room and board here as long as you want it. I can't afford you. But having that star should help you . . . officiate matters with the master chief should push come to shove."

Ash didn't think he needed anything beyond his military rank to take care of that, but he understood what the sheriff meant. "Don't I have to say something?"

"Promise to keep my ass intact if it comes down to it."

"What about mine?"

"Keep it intact, too. Just remember the order: Save the sheriff's ass, then the deputy's ass. Order's an important part of an operation." Bolo looked both ways by the Dairy Queen and pulled out onto the street. "Damn." He slowed a little.

"What?" Ash asked.

"Evidently Devon Hite heard about the business at the motel," Bolo said. "He's in town at the Dairy Queen." He pointed at a dirt-covered four-wheel-drive pickup across the street. "That's one of the vehicles from the militia farm."

Ash resisted the impulse to look around for Hite. "If Ferguson sticks with the story you gave him, it might play out all right."

"Maybe." Bolo checked his mirrors. "But Hite is a survivor. He's one of those guys you could put into a nuclear wasteland and he'd find something to eat and a way to breed with the cockroaches for recreation."

"Do you think he has the ATF agent Howard is missing?"

Bolo nodded. "I do. Or knows where the body's buried."

"You do know Ferguson isn't just going to ride away from this."

"I know that too. That's why I deputized you. I've got six people working out of the sheriff's office. Two of them are nearing retirement. Three of them are like Cody, the young deputy you met earlier. And then I've got Mabel."

"Mabel?"

"Forty-year-old spinster who reads vampire romance novels and is the most deadly person I know with a twelve-gauge shotgun. She'll never win the hundred-yard dash and she'll outweigh most of the men she tangles with, but she'll never leave your side when you need her." Bolo signaled and made an easy turn. "What I'm saying is that none of my team is ready to handle anything like Hite and the Badlands Militia or the ATF if it comes to that. As long as you're in town, since you don't seem to be the type to walk away, I thought maybe I'd draft you into the service. And hope all we do is sit around in the evening and drink beer while we tell lies."

Ash dropped the deputy's star into his shirt pocket. "As long as we don't have to sit around and sing 'Happy Trails.'"

28

After retrieving his car from the sheriff's office, Ash drove to Thaedt University. He parked in front of Benjamin Hall and unlocked the main doors with the keys he'd been given. Making his way back to the NROTC offices, he waved to one of the janitors, then let himself in.

Master Chief Fernandez was in the office on the phone. He gazed at Ash with a heavy-lidded stare and didn't move. Ash thought about taking a more aggressive posture with the man and decided against it. Maybe the unexpected dalliance with Veronica had mellowed him. Or maybe the action back at the Journey's End Motel had taken some of the edge off.

While Fernandez continued his conversation on the phone, speaking so low that Ash couldn't hear him, Ash walked around the outside office. After a couple minutes, he started in with the cleaning he had planned. Outside, he went to the janitor and asked where the utility closet was. Once he found that, Ash returned to the NROTC office.

Fernandez was still on the phone.

"Chief," Ash said, "we need to talk."

Fernandez covered the mouthpiece. "I'm talking to my mother."

Ash counted to five. "Unless you're talking to her through a spiritual guide, that's not possible."

The chief looked at him.

"Your mother died seven years ago," Ash said. "That's in your record." The military personnel record followed a military man around his entire career and after. "You're off the phone—*now*."

Fernandez looked at Ash a moment longer, then said, "I'll call you back." He cradled the phone and leaned back in the chair, lacing his fingers over his impressive gut. "You're out of line. I'm—"

"'You're out of line, *sir*,'" Ash said in a tone of total command. "Or *Lieutenant*. Anything else insubordinate comes out of your mouth, Master Chief, and I'll see to it you're transferred into accommodations that are a little less comfy."

"Sir," Fernandez said grudgingly. "I'm on my own time."

"You're in the military," Ash said. "Your time has already been bought and paid for. You're on *my* time. In fact, if you want, you're even on overtime. Either way, we've got work to do."

"Sir," Fernandez said, "I just put in a full day."

"I'm sure you did," Ash said. "Now let's see if we can't get something productive out of it."

"I was about to go home."

"This is better," Ash said. "Saves me from calling you back in."

"Back in for what?"

"A GI party. We're going to clean this pigsty up. Call the mids and get them here."

"With all respect, sir, they've got homework to do."

"They can get it done later," Ash said. "Get them in, Chief. *Now*."

Devon Hite remained at the Dairy Queen until the black Suburbans left. He watched the action at the motel and on the television. After ATF Chief Special Agent Mel Ferguson had his say about the weapons dealers, the local channels stopped their live coverage and the story slowly ground to a halt. It had already been re-capped for the five o'clock news.

Despite how well Ferguson sold the story, Hite wasn't a believer. He finished up the coffee he'd purchased, then went outside and back to his truck. The other men, although they'd stretched their legs and seen to their needs, waited for him.

"Well?" Curtis asked.

"It appears Sheriff Bolo happened up on a quartet of weapons dealers," Hite said as he shoved the transmission into first gear and pulled out into traffic, which was still meandering by to watch the action at the motel.

"Do you believe it?"

"Maybe." Hite drove carefully. "For the time being, I want to keep everything at the farm separated. The tank stays hidden. All our primary armament remains hidden. In case we get a surprise visit, I want to be able to roll with it." He watched the traffic, thinking furiously. He'd gotten away with a lot. Hell, getting the tank into the country in one piece was an accomplishment that—to his knowledge, anyway—had never been done before. But maybe taking the ATF agent instead of arranging for an "accident" to happen had been pushing Lady Luck just one step too far. "I want to get a team inside the town, too."

"Somebody to keep an eye on things?" Curtis asked.

Hite nodded. "Use some of the new recruits that haven't been out to the farm much. Personnel we have that are strictly low-key. I don't want them active. Just listening."

"What are they listening for?"

"I don't think we're going to be alone for a while," Hite said. "So we'll run everything at the ranch in stealth mode."

The midshipmen hated him. Ash was as certain of that as he was that the sun would rise the next morning. They stood like a ragtag janitorial brigade in the outer office with brooms and mops and buckets close to hand. The air reeked of ammonia.

"With all due respect, *sir*," Bruno said as he grimaced at the mop he held, "this is a load of bullshit."

Hands held behind him, ramrod-straight and eyes cold, Ash stepped in front of the man. Bruno straightened automatically, trying to emphasize that he was still taller than Ash. He looked into the lieutenant's eyes.

"That observation didn't hold a note of respect in it," Ash commented.

Bruno glared at him.

"We can do this all night, buddy," Ash said.

After a brief second, Bruno glanced away.

Ash turned and walked down his charges and felt the true challenge of what lay before him. Leadership wasn't about busting down personnel; it was about building them up in the direction they needed to go. "We have a saying aboard ship that you'll come to know and love: a place for everything, and everything in its place. Once aboard ship you're going to be assigned a limited space for your things. Storage of your personal effects is going to have to be neat and tidy. Number one: You don't want them loose and rolling around because that's dangerous. Number two: If those things break or get lost, replacing them at sea is going to be difficult or expensive." He faced the unit. "You need to learn how to present yourselves and take care of your personal effects. We're going to start here tonight."

No one looked happy to be the recipient of such a personalized education.

"This office is how the rest of this campus sees you," Ash stated. He looked around. "You look cluttered and messy and unfocused. You're Navy officers in training. You're going to learn to be officers before you fulfill that capability. Do you understand?"

A handful of halfhearted "Yes"es came out of the forty young men and women crowded into the room.

"I didn't hear you," Ash barked.

"YES!" they responded.

Shaking his head, Ash pulled Globe out of the lineup. Ash figured that Globe, being interested in computers and used to the rules inherent in working with systems, would be the easiest to switch over. "Midshipman Enrich."

"Yes sir," Enrich said. He stood stiffly at attention.

"You will be my liaison throughout this task," Ash said.

"Yes, sir," Globe said, shoulders squared and eyes focused over Ash's shoulder.

"We're going to behave like we're aboard a ship," Ash said. "The correct response to your commanding officer is *'Aye, sir.'*" Do you understand?"

"Y-*Aye,* sir."

"Heh," Skinny whispered to the midshipman third next to him, "he said *'Eyesore.'*"

"Midshipman Skoskstad," Ash barked.

"Sir?" Skinny responded, wiping the smirk from his lips.

"Front and center," Ash said.

Reluctantly, Skinny stepped from the rest of the group. He suddenly didn't look so cocky and even paled a little.

"Thank you for volunteering for head duty," Ash said. He kicked one of the buckets with a toilet brush over to Skinny. "Feel free to make all the smart-ass remarks you want in there. But if I hear you, you're going to be cleaning latrines the rest of the week."

"Yes, sir."

"Midshipman Enrich," Ash said, "correct that man on his response."

Globe looked uncertain for a moment. "The response is *'Aye, sir.'*"

"Aye, sir," Skinny replied. From the corner of his mouth, he whispered, "Fuck you, Globe." Since Ash hadn't been looking at him at the moment, Skinny thought he'd gotten away with it.

"Midshipman Enrich," Ash said.

"Aye, sir."

"Please," Ash used the word like a weapon, delivering an instant field promotion to Globe on the spot, "inform

Midshipman Skoskstad that he is also assigned head cleaning efforts tomorrow night."

Globe hesitated.

Ash looked at him. "Do I need to choose another liaison?"

Swallowing, Globe said, "No, sir." Then he added, "Midshipman Skoskstad, you have head detail tomorrow night."

"The detail will be from nineteen hundred hours to twenty-three hundred hours," Ash said.

"You can't do that!" Skinny complained, breaking out of formation and turning toward Ash.

Ash turned and froze the midshipman in place with an icy glare.

"This is bullshit!" Skinny exploded. He looked back at the other students for support. It wasn't forthcoming.

"Shut up, Skinny," Fernandez snarled.

"This is *wrong*," Skinny complained. "He can't just come in here like some Hitler and just start telling people what to do."

Ash was in front of Skinny in two strides. "Step back in that line right now!" The voice Ash used had stopped twenty-year men in their tracks.

Flinching, Skinny stepped back into formation. He swallowed hard.

"Begging the lieutenant's pardon," Fernandez said.

Wondering if he was going to draw flak from the master chief now, Ash looked at the man. "What?"

"Requesting permission to take Midshipman Skoskstad to his duties, sir," Fernandez said. "If there's nothing more you need him to hear."

"One thing before you go, Master Chief," Ash said. He fixed Skinny with his eyes. "Have you ever read *Mein Kampf,* midshipman?"

"No, sir," Skinny replied.

"You will," Ash promised. "If you're going to compare me to someone, I want you well informed enough to make a judgment call like that. You will deliver, to me, a twenty-page report on your comparison of Hitler and his efforts in post–World War I Germany and what I'm doing here on my desk by middle of next week."

Skinny said, "Aye, sir."

"Requesting permission to leave, sir," Fernandez said. When Ash nodded, the master chief called Skinny out of line and walked from the room.

"All right then," Ash said, "let's get to work." He chose the seniors from among the group and designated them as leaders, then gave them their assignments.

Ash's cell phone rang. He drew it from his belt holster and answered as he stood. "Ash is up."

"Hey, buddy," Wild said. "How's it hanging?"

Leaning back against the wall in his office, Ash said, "Out in the wind at the moment."

"What's up?" Concern sounded in Wild's voice.

Ash closed the door to the office, shutting out the noise the midshipmen were making out in the main office. "Surprise field-day party."

"Fuck, man, you're bucking for chief-asshole rank." The grin was evident in Wild's voice. "You fucked with their party and now you're shitting on their downtime. What's next? Midnight PT drills in the rain?"

"If I have to." Ash peered out the window and saw the sky deepening into dusk. It had been a eventful day, but he didn't feel tired yet. More like . . . suspended. Hanging like a kite on the end of a string. "I've got to do something to get their attention."

"Running them into the ground Friday didn't do that?"

"I got their attention," Ash admitted. "Now I have to keep it." He took a deep breath and let it out. "This post, it isn't me, Wild."

"Fuck that," Wild said. "You're a goddamned Navy SEAL. Taught to survive anything God himself can throw at you on land, sea, and air. You just haven't found the handle on this yet."

"What's the handle?"

"Same handle as always, buddy. We do two things as

special ops: save people and blow shit up real good. As I recollect, you ain't there to blow shit up, so what have you been tasked to do?"

"Get my head together."

Wild snorted. "Bullshit. What you're there to do, Lieutenant, is save what's left of those middies. Get them on the right track after the master chief tried to poison them. This is a save. You just aren't looking at it right yet. If you buy into what the Navy doc lined you up with, I'm coming down there to kick your ass myself. With my brand-new leg."

"They've already got you fit for a prosthesis?"

"It came in today. I was up and around for fifteen minutes before they made me sit. Some bullshit excuse about needing to build up calluses before I use it too much."

"Damn, Wild, that's great."

"Oh yeah. The nurses on this floor are going to have to start hiding out. I get two legs under me, I've got all the traction I need to start cutting them out of the herd." Wild snorted with laughter. "This leg has got to be one of the weirdest things you've ever seen. Looks like something out of *Star Wars*. Supposed to give me upward of fifty percent of what I was able to do. If it's true, that's a damn sight more than most men have got to give."

Ash silently agreed with that assessment. "Have you given any thought to what you're going to do once Medical releases you?"

"Fishing," Wild said. "You see, I've got this buddy stuck up in South Dakota, which—according to one of the young nurses I've been talking to—has some of the prettiest lakes and rivers you'd ever want to see. Thought I'd come up and see him."

"Sounds good to me."

"In fact," Wild said, "I'm working on securing a weekend pass to get over that way. After that I'll have to report back here for the temporary hell they call rehab."

"Let me know when you get the trip locked in," Ash said. "I'll hook up with you at the airport."

"I can drive myself."

"Or I can pick you up and we can talk for about an hour without anyone or anything else getting in our faces while I drive us back from the airport," Ash countered.

"We could also make any number of stops along the way," Wild mused. "Not even take the straight and narrow back to wherever the hell it is you're stationed."

"We could do that."

"Okay, I'm sold. I'll give you a ring and let you know the particulars."

"Hey, Wild?"

"Yeah?"

"How are you *really* doing?"

"Piece of cake, man. I may have some aftermarket work done on the new foot. You know, so it doubles as a battery-powered sexual device for women."

Ash almost lost it, but figured that while he was in tough and tyrannical mode for the middies that it wouldn't be a good idea. "I got somebody you should meet while you're here."

"Don't tell me you're already shacked up. God, that'll kill me," Wild whined.

"No, but I did get laid in New York."

"After you saw me?"

"Yeah, but I was thinking of you the whole time."

"If you'd have been thinking of me, you'd have asked if she had a sister and let her know where I was staying."

Ash felt the weight of the deputy's badge in his pocket and grinned. "Got something else to tell you."

"What?"

"I made deputy."

"Deputy? Deputy what?"

"Deputy sheriff."

"You're fucking kidding."

Quickly, Ash detailed the events of the day, rolling in the background on Devon Hite and the Badlands Militia that he hadn't told Wild while they were together in Bethesda.

"Does this mean you're gonna be wearing one of those ten-gallon hats?"

"In case of an emergency, I could always use it for a condom."

"That's my line." Wild broke up into laughter and it sounded good, if tired.

They talked for a while longer, then one of the middies knocked at the door to ask a question. Ash hung up and got back to business. He thought about what Wild said, about this being a mission to save something—*someone,* and he figured maybe his friend was onto something.

Stepping into the outer office, looking at the dirty, sullen faces trained on him, Ash remembered how it felt going into battle in foreign countries to save people who didn't want to be saved. But he focused on the task at hand. Tonight he was going to save the NROTC offices.

"Gentlemen," Devon Hite said in the cool illumination provided by the generator-powered lights of the underground bunker they'd built as a secondary base, "at this moment we're going to act like we've entered a cold war. Active on all fronts." He spoke to the two hundred men filling the bunker. "We can only assume our enemy—the United States government—has deemed us a worthy opponent. And a threat to the way they do business."

Several of the men muttered in agreement.

"We've all seen over these past years, since 9-11 was *allowed* to happen," Hite went on, pacing in front of his troops, "that the government has found more ways to restrict Americans and take away our rights. Our *inalienable* rights. That's what this country was founded on. Now we find ourselves taxed to death, forced to buy oil from other countries for prices that should be a sin when we got oil of our own the government won't let anybody touch, and left without true representation in government."

"Hell yeah," someone yelled, eliciting support immediately. Moonshine made on the ranch had already started making the rounds through the men. "When's the last time your congressman shook your hand?"

"We've seen farms taken from hardworking families that have had to pay for that land over and over," Devon continued. "Every time somebody's father or grandfather dies, the rest of the family has to work together to ransom *their* land back from the federal government. A government that's supposed to be looking out for *our* needs."

"Well, they ain't doing that if they're bringing hired killers to town," someone else said.

"No, they're not, but that's why we built this base as a fallback position." Hite gestured toward the military guns and ammo lockers set into position along the wall. "If push does indeed come to shove, we're going to push back hard!"

The men cheered.

"Shit," somebody said, "what we ought to do is take the war to those mealy-mouthed sons of bitches! That would show them!"

Support for that possibility swelled inside the bunker till the rafters creaked.

Hite held up his hands for silence. Gradually the men calmed down. "We don't want to take the fight to them unless we have to. Once we do that, they're going to take everything away from us. This farm—the homes we've built here—will all be lost. We can fight the federal government; the only way we can win is to get the will of the people behind us. We have to be the blazing brand that leads the rest of our great country out of the shadows of ignorance the federal government has been feeding us all our lives."

Faced with the inevitability all of them reluctantly admitted was true, the men quieted and listened.

"During the next few days, we're going to watch ourselves and take care of each other," Hite said. "Nobody goes into town without someone with them. We take precautions at the farm. Nobody from outside comes in."

He paused to let that sink in. "Nobody talks about what we have here. Nobody talks about the munitions. Nobody talks about the tank. That's our ace in the hole."

"What if they attack us?" someone asked.

Hite walked through the group of men and clambered up onto the tank parked in the center of the bunker. "Then we fight back, gentlemen. Without reserve. We don't ask for quarter or mercy, and we give none. And we pray for deliverance from our enemies and the strength to stand against them." He remembered how Melvin C. Stewart had preached from the pulpit on "Be Healed." It wasn't all that different from playing to the crowds while he was with the Baron's Itch. Hite paced along the skirting on the tank, ministering to his congregation in the round. "I need you—all of you—to be at your best. Our enemies have sighted in on us, just as we knew they would, and now we need to stand tall." He put his hands together before him. "Pray with me now."

Every head in the bunker bent. Cowboy hats and John Deere ball caps were yanked from heads.

The Badlands Militia prayed as Hite led them.

29

Early Tuesday morning, Ash was out the door of Sheriff Bolo's home and in the rental car. Dressed in gym gear, he arrived at the park near the university. The sun was barely peeking over the eastern rim when he finished his stretching exercises and started running. Blood pumped, coursing through him, clearing his head.

Little Feather had prepared another big meal the previous night, barbequed ribs with potato salad, slaw, and homemade biscuits that had seemed to melt in his mouth. Then she'd offered thick slabs of red velvet cake and vanilla ice cream. Eating like that every night could be a problem, but Bolo seemed to be surviving it. Ash bet the sheriff was blessed with the same kind of metabolism that he had. Weight just didn't stick because he kept full days on the move. Unfortunately, the desk position at the university was going to make him pay a price if he let himself get sedentary.

Ash ran the first mile at an easy gait, just stretching everything out and letting his muscles warm. Then he poured it on for five more. He let his mind sail free, thinking about everything and nothing. The park was beautiful in the morning, filled with pines and poplar, flowers he couldn't name, birds he didn't recognize, gray squirrels and chipmunks. Those were things that couldn't be found at sea, and no port he'd been in lately had this kind of foliage. Fairly, South Dakota was peaceful in the mornings, he'd discovered over the last two days, and he liked that. Too much of it and it would become boring, though.

Monday evening, Wild had called to let Ash know the weekend looked good and he'd purchased the ticket to fly in Saturday morning and stay till the following Wednesday. A three-day pass and then some. The doctors had cleared him, as long as caution was taken with the new leg. Damaging the stump could set back recovery a few weeks.

The midshipmen were still hostile around him, but not openly so. Master Chief Fernandez was just marking time but not making waves, although his drinking had evidently increased. All things considered, the situation could have been better—but it could have been a hell of a lot worse.

The newest problem Ash had discovered was that several of the middies were in danger of failing this semester. Second and third class didn't overly concern him; they had time to retake the classes and set things aright. But four seniors, including Spike, were also on that list. They needed to be up and running by the end of the semester so they could enter the military. He didn't know what he was going to do about that yet.

He jogged another mile, cooling down, and felt revitalized. When he returned to his car, he found Devon Hite waiting on him, sitting comfortably on the concrete picnic table near the parking area.

The militia leader was clean-shaven except for the tuft of hair that bordered his bottom lip. He wore a faded Farm Aid T-shirt under a denim jacket, a Peterbilt ball cap, jeans, and scuffed work boots. He looked ready to go climb on top of a tractor and work the field. Except for his eyes. They were cold and steely.

"Good morning," Hite called out enthusiastically.

Ash slowed his approach to his car but didn't stop. "Good morning." He glanced around to see if any of Hite's followers were lurking around.

"I'm by myself," Hite said. He remained seated on

the picnic table, elbows resting on his thighs as he leaned forward.

"What can I do for you, Mr. Hite?" Ash asked.

"You know me?" Hite smiled, seeming pleasantly surprised.

Ash reached into the car and took a towel from his toiletry kit. "A lot of people around here talk about you." He wiped the sweat from his face and walked to the front of the car.

"I guess they do," Hite admitted. "There's not much that goes on in a small town that people don't talk about."

Ash waited, wondering what the hell Hite was doing bracing him like this.

"People also talk about the new instructor at the university," Hite went on. "I've heard you're not well liked at the Navy school."

"I don't imagine I am," Ash countered. "But I really don't think that's why I was sent here."

"What were you sent here for, Lieutenant Roberts?"

Ash hung the towel around his neck and hung onto it. If it became necessary, he could use the towel as a weapon. "To teach. To mold young minds."

Hite grinned. "Seems like we're in the same line of business."

"No," Ash replied. "I don't think we are."

"You don't like me, do you?"

"I don't know you well enough to dislike you," Ash said.

Hite laughed. "But you don't like what you've heard."

Ash held his gaze steady. "The potential is there."

"I guess maybe we're suspicious of each other, then."

"You're suspicious of me?"

Nodding, Hite said, "I am. Look at it from my point of view: I'm on the verge of getting persecuted by the federal government."

Ash didn't say anything.

"They've had an ATF agent watching me," Hite went on. "I know that because that ATF agent later went missing and a few days ago they came to my doorstep looking for him. That was the same day you arrived in Fairly."

Listening to the flat delivery of the information, Ash didn't know if he was supposed to feel threatened or not. "Coincidence."

"Is it?" Hite looked doubtful. "You see, the problem is I'm not a big believer in coincidences. I did a little checking into your background."

Everybody's a private eye with the Internet, Ash thought.

"I found out you were a SEAL."

"*Am* a SEAL," Ash said automatically. He regretted the impulsive reaction almost at once. He didn't have anything to prove to Hite, and the man could misconstrue the announcement.

"Understood." Hite paused. "A SEAL's a special breed of warrior. Goes in and works miracles behind enemy lines."

"I'm just here to teach," Ash replied.

"And you were an admiral's aide for a while," Hite said. "There was a big story about that. Then you went back to military operations. Why was that?"

"I'm not cut out to be a desk jockey."

A slow smile spread across Hite's lips. Morning sunlight gleamed on his shaved cheeks. "Yet here you are."

Ash knew he couldn't argue the logic Hite was insisting on using. *He's paranoid,* Ash thought. *But they really are out to get him.*

"Then, two days ago, I find out some FBI agents were in town," Hite said.

"The sheriff received a tip that resulted in the capture and arrest of wanted weapons dealers," Ash said.

"And you happened to be there."

"I did. I'm staying at the sheriff's house."

"I know." Hite grinned again. "I find that interesting too."

"Mr. Hite," Ash said, growing tired of the verbal sparring, "could I ask you to kindly get to the point?"

Hite slid off the picnic table and shot the cuffs on the denim jacket. "You're an outsider, Lieutenant Roberts, and you're a member of a government I don't much care for these days. I just wanted to get to meet you, that's all." Turning, he walked toward his dirty pickup. A rifle hung behind the seat in a mounted gun rack. He clambered into the pickup and started the engine. Then he rolled down the window and said, "You have a good day."

Ash stood there for a moment and watched the man depart. A warning buzzed inside him. Once the pickup was out of sight, he returned to the car and carefully went over it to make certain Hite hadn't taken the opportunity to plant a bomb. Even still, the itch of a sniper's scope between his shoulder blades didn't go away.

After a quick shower at the university gym, Ash stopped for breakfast at Maude's Dinner. The diner was filled with customers early in the morning. Heat from the grill rolled over Ash as he entered. Bacon and sausage popped on the flat grill. The heavenly smell of pancakes, biscuits, and hash browns filled the air. Ash took a deep breath and knew his cholesterol count had probably jumped fifty points. Bolo sat at a back corner table with Little Feather. The sheriff waved Ash over.

"Got time to sit?" Bolo asked.

"I didn't call ahead," Ash said.

"Then have a seat. You're going to be waiting a while. I'll buy you breakfast."

Ash said good morning to Little Feather, who had already finished her plate and was working on a cup of coffee. "If you two don't mind," she said, "I'm leaving."

"If I'm interrupting . . ." Ash said, starting to rise.

"Nonsense," Little Feather said. "I've been listening to him for years. I could use a break." She leaned over the table and kissed Bolo full on the mouth, eliciting a chorus of catcalls and whistles from the diner crowd. Little Feather looked at Ash and grinned. "He hates when I do that in public." Settling her purse over her shoulder, she walked out of the diner.

Bolo watched her with a combination of love and lust. "That," he said, "is a hell of a woman. In case you hadn't noticed."

"I had," Ash responded. "You're a lucky man."

"And there ain't a day goes by that I don't thank my lucky stars about that." Bolo cut up his ham and a soft-boiled egg, forking them in a stack and putting them on a piece of toast. "I was told Devon Hite was in town this morning. That he went out to the park where you ran yesterday and this morning."

A slim brunette approached the table, plopped down a coffee cup, and poured. She asked Ash what he wanted for breakfast and he told her. She made big eyes at him. "Are you having breakfast or shopping for groceries?"

"He's still growing," the sheriff commented.

The waitress smiled and went away.

"So," Bolo said, peering over the rim of his coffee cup. "Devon Hite."

Ash nodded. "I saw him. Spoke to him this morning." He bummed a piece of the sheriff's toast and a packet of strawberry jelly.

"And?"

"I don't know."

Bolo sighed. "This is like pulling teeth."

"I respond better to the bright light and the rubber hose."

"I feel a chorus of 'Happy Trails' coming on."

Ash held his hands up in surrender. "The truth is, I don't know what Hite wanted or expected." Quickly, as if he were doing a mission debrief, he laid out the encounter for Bolo. He finished just as the waitress arrived with the steaming plates holding his breakfast.

"Do you think he was trying to scare you?" Bolo asked.

"If he was, he didn't get the job done."

The sheriff leaned back from his empty plate and

sipped his coffee. "Maybe he was just taking your temperature. Your arrival could be viewed as suspect."

"Maybe." Ash dug into his breakfast.

Bolo eyed the plates. "Are we feeding you enough?"

"Yes. This is breakfast. It's a long time till lunch, and even longer till dinner."

"Let's just say, for the moment, that Hite was just getting the lay of the land."

"I think he was."

"Why go to you?"

"Because I seem to be getting involved in this."

Bolo grimaced. "That's my fault."

Ash nodded. "Partly. After all, I could have said no."

"I have to admit, after bumping into you at the barbershop, I wanted to meet you."

"To get an outsider's perspective on things?"

Shaking his head, Bolo asked, "Was it that transparent?"

"Actually," Ash said, "it didn't occur to me until just now. I've been wrapped up in my own problems." Then he halted his fork on its way to his mouth, gazing at the sheriff in wonder. "Son of a bitch. It wasn't just that. You wanted to get to know me, invited me to your house, so *you* could keep an eye on me."

Bolo didn't deny it. "You have to admit, it was awfully suspicious for you to come riding into town shortly after that ATF agent went missing. I don't agree with Hite on most things, but I do know the federal government sometimes gets overly interested in situations they shouldn't be poking their noses into. The ATF's response to the Badlands Militia is a prime case in point."

"My arrival here was coincidence," Ash said.

"I don't put much stock in coincidences," Bolo said.

Ash didn't know whether to keep eating or get up and walk out. He'd been played and hadn't even known there was a game on. "That's why you took me with you when you confronted the guys at the motel. You wanted to know if we knew each other."

"I'm a cautious man," Bolo said. "Also, I'm not stupid. If the wheels had come off of that thing at the motel, I figured you could back me up better than anyone I've got on staff. I'm not one to look a gift horse in the mouth. You were handy. And I believed in you. Still do." He paused. "Now get back to your breakfast."

"So which is it, Sheriff?" Ash asked. "You think I'm one of the good guys or one of the bad guys?"

Bolo leaned over the table and looked at Ash. "I like you and I trust you. Otherwise I wouldn't have you anywhere near my wife."

Some of the sudden anger and sense of betrayal Ash felt went away. He understood totally why the sheriff had done what he'd done. He turned his attention back to his breakfast and the other possibilities Hite's visit to him constituted. "If Hite's out checking his perimeters, that means he's planning something."

Bolo nodded. "That's what I was thinking."

"But what? Any move he could make right now would be stupid."

"Hite's not a stupid man," Bolo said. "He's not going to make a move. He's just wants to be ready for when the ATF makes one."

"They're still around?"

"Oh hell yeah. They think I don't know, but I do, only I'm pretending I don't. It's a little game we're playing." Bolo sighed. "The problem is, they really have a missing agent."

"You still think Hite has him?"

"I do. What's more, I think Howard and his buddies know something I don't about their agent." Bolo eyed Ash speculatively. "You up for a little action?"

"What kind of action?"

"I've been invited to go pheasant hunting on militia lands."

"I remember you telling me that."

"I'm thinking about taking Friday afternoon off. Maybe doing a little hunting. Want to tag along?"

"Recon?"

"I don't think those ATF boys are going to get their missing agent back on their own."

"You're going to help them?"

"If I can. If he's not already dead."

"You don't think he is?"

"No reason to believe so yet."

"And if we find the agent there?"

"We go back that evening, while most of the militia is tanked up on booze and looking for something soft to hold, and we break him out." Bolo smiled. "Kind of gets the juices flowing thinking about it, doesn't it?"

Ash had to admit that it did. The situation with the Badlands Militia was volatile, sliding treacherously close to full-on out-of-control craziness. Reconning an area that would undoubtedly be under the purview of hostile guns while in plain sight didn't have a lot to offer tactically, but for a SEAL jonesing for action, it was like honeycomb for a grizzly.

"Sure," Ash said. "I'll pencil it in."

30

It was a morning for visits. When Ash arrived at Thaedt University, an older man in a blue suit stood at the window, looking like a lizard warming in the heat of the sun through the glass. Ash entered the office, and the midshipman on duty came to attention.

"At ease," Ash said.

"Aye, sir." The midshipman sat back at his desk and put away the comic book he'd been reading.

Not quite literature, but least it's better than him checking out the porn sites, Ash thought. He turned to face the visitor, who approached him with his hand out.

Glasses framed his face, giving him a grandfatherly look, but the blue eyes behind them were hard and direct. A neatly trimmed gray fringe of hair made a horseshoe around his bald pate. A thin mustache ran to the corners of his mouth and lifted with his smile. He was a few inches short of six feet, but he carried himself confidently. In his early sixties, he was a little overweight but looked in good shape. His grip was strong and firm, and lasted just long enough. "Lieutenant Roberts?" the man inquired.

"I am," Ash declared.

"I'm Dean Williams. We haven't met and I thought we should. Is this a good time for you?"

It was quarter past eight. Ash wasn't scheduled in till half past, and even then the first two hours were dead time for him. Once the NROTC group was running smoothly, there would be little for him to do administratively.

"Now is fine, sir," Ash said. "Would you like to come into my office?"

"No, this will be good. I didn't want to take up much of your time. And you don't have to call me 'sir.' We're peers here at Thaedt. You can call me Al."

"Would you care for a cup of coffee, Al?" Ash waved to the coffeepot that now sat to one side of the office. He'd had a fake tree removed and put the space to better use.

"Please."

Ash poured coffee in two Styrofoam cups. Dean Williams helped himself to cream and sugar packets. At the desk the midshipman kept an eye on them.

Ash saw the dean look around the office. Navy posters hung on the freshly painted walls, carefully marked off for space to make a better presentation. Important government papers prospective applicants might want to see were prominently displayed. The bookshelves now held Navy books and pamphlets, biographies of key Navy personnel and volumes on Navy hardware and operations in past military engagements.

"I have to say," Dean Williams said, "that you've already made a number of changes around here."

"I couldn't have done it without the midshipmen," Ash said. The midshipman third class behind the desk looked over and nodded with pride. It had taken two nights to thoroughly clean the offices and bring them up to Ash's specs.

"Master Chief Fernandez didn't seem able to get this kind of response from your midshipmen. There were problems of chronic absenteeism, tardiness, and poor performance in class and on tests regarding your charges. I was also apprised about some recent underage drinking. I'd originally come over here to discuss those things with you."

"We're trying to improve."

"I can see that. But it's my feeling that the NROTC should never have sunk to the level that it did."

"I'm sure the master chief did the best that he could under the circumstances," Ash replied. "He was one man doing a two-man job. In a lot of ways, he was hamstrung with what he faced. We should be able to rectify that."

The midshipman looked over again.

"I see," the dean replied, rubbing his chin.

"I think you can continue to see improvements in this department," Ash said. "We're going to be something for you to take pride in."

"I believe you, Lieutenant."

"Call me Ash."

The dean smiled. "It was a pleasure meeting you, Ash. I look forward to getting to know you better. Do you play golf?"

"I do."

"We should play sometime."

"Let me know." Dean Williams shook hands again and departed.

"Wow," the midshipman at the desk said.

" 'Wow'?" Ash asked, stopping by the desk to check through the mail. He remembered the student's name. Midshipman Third Class Dave Kerby. Everybody called him Hawk. He was planning a military career in psy-ops.

"Aye, sir," Hawk said. "I've never seen the dean come in here that polite. He was always trying to rip Chief Fernandez a new asshole." He paused. "He treated you with . . . *respect*."

"Maybe it was because I treated him with respect."

"How? You guys hadn't even met until just now."

"By cleaning up this office and taking pride in being part of this school. That's what you do when you're part of a team."

"Why didn't you tell him it was all your idea? Why did you tell him we had anything to do with it?"

Ash sipped his coffee. "Because you did. Who do you think repainted those walls and vacuumed the floors?"

He waved the cup. "I have to give Skinny and the master chief props for the head detail, though. You could eat off that floor." He kept his tone light, hoping to pull the comment off as a joke, not knowing if it would take.

After a moment, Hawk nodded. "Team effort."

"Something like that. Only it's more." Ash paused to freshen his coffee. "We're in this together. Just like we were on a ship at sea. The way I look at it, we either all succeed or we all fail. There isn't room for Darwinism when we're building a team. There is no survival of the fittest in this. If we get divided, the predators have an easier time picking us off." While the midshipman was mulling that over, Ash crossed to the desk and pulled out his reading material. "Comic books?"

"Hey, it's a graphic *novel*."

"It has pictures."

"So do manuals."

Ash grinned. "Roger that." He tapped the comic . . . *graphic novel*. "Batman. At least you made a good choice." He walked back to his desk. "I don't mind you reading graphic novels at the desk. It's all about heroes and uniforms, right? Just make sure you keep the phone answered, the visitors addressed, and your homework done."

"Aye, sir."

Ash smiled at that. Little changes sometimes happened quickly. He already felt that he was working in a professional environment. Gazing around the bare walls of his office, appropriated from the master chief, who now worked from the smaller desk in the outer office, Ash was struck by the starkness of it. The office didn't hold a history or a personality. But that was all right. He wasn't planning on moving in. Just on getting the job done.

He dropped into the chair behind the desk and turned on the computer. He sorted through the files and looked at the midshipmen first class he'd marked for immediate followup.

Damn, they're in trouble.

Wild was right. This was a rescue mission. Ash just didn't know for sure how he was going to pull it off. If the students weren't willing, they were all screwed.

Spike sat morosely at a back booth at Harrigan's Pizzeria off Main Street and stared at the printout of the e-mail she'd gotten from Dr. Keller, her Western Civ professor. She'd written the best letter she'd known how to that morning and pleaded her case for a make-up exam. If she busted her ass over the next few weeks, she thought she could get a handle on the rest of her grades, but Western Civ was going to blow her out of the water. She hadn't been a sterling student the whole time she'd been at Thaedt, but she hadn't ever thought about failing out either.

Now that possibility was staring her in the fucking face. If she had to do another semester, she didn't know if the Navy would pony up the bucks. And she damn sure didn't have any savings to pay for it herself. Plus, she'd agreed on her entry date into the service. She wanted to scream because she didn't know how much trouble she was in if she didn't make it.

"Hey, Spike."

She looked up to see Globe approaching the table. As always, he carried his notebook computer with him. "Hey, Globe."

He put his backpack on the booth and looked at her again. "You remind me of a joke."

"Thanks," she said dully. "Like I really need that now."

"The one about the farmer who went up to the horse and said, 'Why the long face?' " Globe laughed at his own wit. Then he saw that she wasn't laughing with him. "You know, the farmer was talking to a horse. A horse has a . . . long face." He showed her with his hand in case she needed visual aid. "What's up?"

"Not my GPA," Spike said. "I'm flunking Western Civ."

Globe shrugged. "Hey, no biggie. You got another test or two, right?"

"One more. The next-to-last test was Friday. While we were at the master chief's kegger. He told me he was going to make everything cool. He didn't."

Globe leaned back. "He didn't plan on Lieutenant Roberts showing up."

"The lieutenant's arrival might have been somewhere in the memos he never bothered to read." Spike was angry, and the feeling was made even worse because she felt trapped by circumstances way out of her control. "Fernandez wasn't exactly the kind of guy who got things done." She groaned and leaned back in the booth. "Dammit, I knew I should have gone to take that test. I'd studied for it because I blew the last one. I *knew* the fucking material. I *had* to know it. I just didn't count on ending up at a kegger."

"If the chief had stayed in charge, he would have fixed it," Globe said. "He took care of us."

"A zero," Spike said. "Do you know how hard it is to make up a fucking *zero*?"

Globe hesitated, then shook his head. "No."

"Of course you don't." Spike slapped her forehead. "Look who I'm asking. Mr. Straight-A's."

"Hey," Globe said. "I made a B." He paused. "Once."

"In what?"

Globe looked even more embarrassed. "Seventh-grade gym class," he said defensively. "I had a thing about taking showers."

"Penis envy?"

"Nope. But then eighth grade came along and I got my growth spurt. Who knew a johnson could grow so much over one summer? I became a goddammed legend, is what I was."

"Bullshit."

"Not bullshit." Globe waggled his eyebrows at her. "Want to see?"

"Sure," Spike said. "And I'll show you the scariest thing a guy can see about his dick."

"Oh yeah? What's that?"

"The other end."

Globe recoiled, his mouth twisted in a pained O. "Owww! Ouch!" He put his hands over his crotch, then over his ears. "Lalalalalala. I can't heeeeaaaarrrr you." After a moment, he glared at her. "Jesus, Spike, don't ever say that to a man."

"Sue me."

"Look, I know you're bummed. Maybe you could talk to the prof and . . ."

Spike showed him the e-mail.

"Oh," Globe said. "You *are* fucked."

"Even if I ace the last test, which would be exactly the same chance as you have of getting even to second base with me, it wouldn't be enough."

Bruno arrived and dropped into his seat. "Grades?" He put his hands behind his head.

"Yeah," Globe said.

After a moment, Bruno said, "I'm in trouble in Criminalistics. Too much bullshit you gotta memorize."

"Criminalistics?" Globe said. "I didn't know you were taking that."

"We don't talk much about classes, brainiac. We don't exactly share the same interests." Bruno sipped his beer.

"What are you going to do with criminalistics in the Navy?" Globe couldn't leave it alone. "You should have been studying computers. Eveything's going to be high-tech."

"No matter where you go, Globe," Bruno said, "there's gonna be guys you gotta put in jail. I'm gonna be one of the guys who puts them there."

"Wow," Globe said. "You're going after criminals. Spike is worried about her grades." He shook his head. "After talking to you guys, I feel like I really missed that signpost up ahead."

"What the fuck are you talking about, Globe?" Spike asked.

"I entered the Twilight Zone and didn't know it," Globe said. "I mean, look at the two of you sitting around worrying about classes. Who knew?"

"Bite me," Bruno said. "Are we going to order pizza or what?"

"Where's Skinny and Boy?" Globe asked.

"Skinny's off someplace sulking with Fernandez. Boy's been waiting for one of his grades to post."

"Skinny's off with the master chief?" Spike asked.

Bruno nodded.

"I didn't know they were bosom buddies."

"Hey," Globe said to Spike, smiling, "if you ever need a bosom buddy, I'll—" Her frown pinned him like a bug on a collector's mounting board.

"They weren't," Bruno said. "Till the last two nights of latrine detail. I guess they've both got the lieutenant to bitch about."

"I don't think the guy is as bad as the master chief said," Globe said.

Spike and Bruno stared at him.

"No," Globe said earnestly. "I'm being serious here. Hawk, Midshipman Third Class Kerby?"

"You actually keep up with those guys?" Bruno asked in bewilderment.

"Hey, the guy totally rocks at Halo. You need a two-gunned threat at your side, Hawk's your guy. We've kicked ass all around the world over Xbox. And Splinter Cell? Don't even get me started."

"Terrific," Bruno said. "If we ever get invaded by aliens, we know who to call."

Globe showed Bruno a middle finger. "Fuck you, dildo breath. Anyway, Hawk said he was manning the desk this morning when the dean showed up."

"Dean Williams?" Bruno asked.

"How many other deans we got here?" Globe demanded. "Of course Dean Williams. Now shut the fuck up and let me tell my story. Please and thank you." He took a breath. "Anyway, the dean comes in and says how great the place is looking."

"He didn't say anything about the chief's kegger?" Spike asked. "I heard he found out about it."

"Not one word. But he says the offices are looking great. Then the lieutenant—"

"Brags about how he's kicking ass and taking names, right?" Bruno asked.

"No," Globe said. "He tells the dean that he couldn't have done it without us."

Spike couldn't believe it. "No way."

Globe nodded. "That's exactly what he did. Then he told Hawk that the way he saw it was we all win or nobody wins. That we're a unit and we have to pull together to make anything happen."

"Not quite the chief's 'every man for himself' and FTW attitude, is it?" Spike asked. FTW stood for Fuck The World.

"Don't you think you're being a little hard on Fernandez?" Bruno asked.

"He said he'd fix my Western Civ test," Spike said. "Did I mention I'm looking at a goddammed *zero*?"

At that moment, Boy arrived. Midshipman First Class Bryan Hendricks did *not* look like a happy camper. His face was flushed and his hair was in disarray. He stood in front of their table with his chest heaving. "All right. This has got to stop."

Spike drew back in the booth and looked at her two companions. She had no clue what Boy was talking about.

"What are you going on about?" Bruno asked.

"It's you, isn't it, you conniving bastard?" Boy exploded. People at two nearby tables picked up their pizza and moved away.

"Me what?" Bruno asked, getting a little angry.

"Do you know what's happened this week?" Boy demanded.

"Aside from the GI parties the lieutenant set up?"

"I've got two D's. *D's!* And I had everything locked. Only the history test turned out to be a multiple-choice nut-buster instead of an essay test, which I could have walked through, because the prof's pronging some new hot undergrad and needs his nights and weekends free, and the physics test turned out to be over the material I thought we *weren't* going to cover. On top of that, my girlfriend has missed her period! She never misses her period!"

"Boy," Bruno said gently, "I didn't have anything to do with the tests. And I didn't have anything to do with your girlfriend's missing period. Or any of her other grammar." He reached out to pat Boy on the shoulder.

Boy brushed Bruno's arm away. "You had to go and do it, didn't you? Even though I told you not to, you had to go and do it!"

"Do what?"

"Don't look at me so innocently!" Boy roared. "You've been praying to Geordie, haven't you?"

Geordie? It took Spike a moment to remember that Geordie was Boy's own personal angel who took his prayers straight to God's ears.

"Man, you've been jamming up Geordie's frequency," Boy shouted, "and I'm here telling you that you'd better knock it off!"

When the manager started over to their table, Spike knew the shit had hit the fan.

Master Chief Etan Fernandez leaned on the bar and added another empty shotglass to the stack he had in front of him. Even as drunk as he was, he still had a steady hand. The glass settled onto the others easily. The tavern was like hundreds of others he'd crawled through all around the world during his Navy career. Dingy walls, weak lighting, and air so thick with smoke it could be stirred with a stick. The television over the bar played ESPN, showing highlights from a baseball game. A handful of regulars held down the tables and chairs.

"Shit, Chief," Skinny said, barely able to hold himself up on the barstool, "how th'hell do you hold your liquor?"

"By her ears," Fernandez replied. "And I get a good

grip because I don't want her to get away till I'm done."
Then he laughed at his own joke. He knew from the
bartender's reluctant grin that it was one he'd heard too
many times. However, Skinny brayed out the laughter
of the truly drunk. "Fuck, Skinny, you are one messed-
up dude."

Skinny made a brave effort at sitting up straight and
focusing his eyes. Neither one of those things happened.
He finally gave up and slumped back over the counter.
"I am one *seriously* messed-up dude," he agreed. "But
it feels so fucking good not to be cleaning out urinals
that I don't care."

"I know what you mean."

"Being an officer blows," Skinny declared.

"It does," Fernandez said. He was forty-five years old
and hadn't bothered to mention to Skinny or any of the
others that he hadn't even had his high-school diploma
when he'd enlisted in the Navy. Only serious work and
time had moved him up the ladder to master chief. "You
sign up Navy as enlisted, you don't have to go through
all this bullshit."

"Well you're going through it now."

"That's 'cause I fucked up."

"How?"

"Got crossways with an XO at my last berth. I was
given the option of retiring or coming here." Fernandez
shrugged. "Thought I'd give South Dakota a try." He
lit a cigarette and blew out smoke. "You know what I
got to show for nineteen-plus years, son?"

"A hell of a pension."

"No, not yet. What I do have is four ex-wives and a
half dozen kids that haven't talked to me in years, that's
what." Fernandez stared at his reflection in the mirror.
He didn't like the way he looked. He'd gotten too old
and too fat, and he didn't know how to change any of
that. Flicking a finger at the bartender, he ordered another drink.

The bartender shook his head. "You've had enough
for the day, Chief."

Anger boiled up in Fernandez. "You're cutting me off?"

"I have to," the bartender said. "If I don't, I'll get busted, get fined, and lose my license."

"Fine." Fernandez took money out of his shirt pocket and threw a ten on the bar. "Let's go."

"That's a stupid rule," Skinny said. "If you can lift your arm, you should still be able to drink. When the arm doesn't come up, then it's time to quit." He jerked around on the stool and tried to get up. Then he looked at Fernandez. "I can't feel my legs."

"Shit," Fernandez said. He took hold of Skinny's arm and hauled it across his shoulders. Together, they staggered out of the tavern and into the waning afternoon light to Skinny's Miata. The red sports car had been a present from his absentee father, sort of a get-out-of-guilt-free car, Skinny had called it. The chief poured Skinny into the passenger seat, rifled his pockets for the vehicle's keys and uncomfortably settled his bulk behind the steering wheel. "Your place or mine?" the chief asked as he started the engine.

"Yours," Skinny said. "Too many people at mine. I don't want to be seen coming in shitfaced in case the lieutenant doesn't like it."

Figuring that was a pretty good idea, Fernandez shoved the transmission into reverse and shot out of the parking space, barely missing a large dual pickup truck. The driver honked his horn in indignation. Then Fernandez headed the car to his place. He maintained a rental cabin outside of Fairly that afforded him plenty of privacy.

"I've got a couple of bottles at my place," Fernandez said. "We don't have to get sober until we get ready to."

"Sounds great," Skinny said, but he was asleep by the time they waited out the red light.

Fernandez blinked blearily and concentrated on his driving.

31

Sitting in the quiet dark of the auditorium of the St. Paul BATF on Thursday morning, Chief Special Agent Hank Howard starved for a cigarette and listened to Mel Ferguson talk. Since they'd returned, Ferguson had been chafing at the bit to do something, anything to move against Devon Hite and his people, and to overturn Sheriff Bolo's interference. Ralph Trimble, the agent Ferguson had assigned to figure out the logistics of the ATF raid, held center court. A digital image of the Badlands Militia farm—*compound,* as Ferguson kept calling it—showed on the large board. Trimble used a laser pointer to designate areas.

"I put this together through the aerial recon we've done through LEO satellites," Trimble was saying. Getting access to the low-earth orbit satellites had been a major coup for Ferguson. "With everything we had available to us, I was able to get a pretty good picture of what it's like inside their compound."

Compound, Jesus Christ. Howard thought if he heard the farm called that one more time he was going to puke. He'd seen the farm and it wasn't a fortified structure. It was a place where people raised their kids and said they defied the American government, all the while accepting free inoculations for their children as well as income-subsistence programs. Ferguson and the others talked about the farm as if it were a staging platform for world domination.

"Lay it out for us," Ferguson encouraged. Although three days had passed since Bolo had rapped him with the gun barrel, Ferguson's head still looked swollen and was mostly purple with swatches of yellow and green mixed in. From the way he ate Motrin, Howard knew Ferguson had a persistent headache. "Tell them what we have."

"What we have," Trimble said, "is a major grouping of buildings here." The laser pointer touched briefly on the main house, the outlying structures and the big warehouse. "There are a few lesser ones outside the perimeters of the main area, but I feel like we need to concentrate on these."

"What about the women and children?" Howard asked, and then damned himself for speaking up. He'd promised himself he wasn't going to, but he'd been basically sitting on his hands since Monday. "They're living in those areas, too."

"Hey," Ferguson said, shrugging and spreading his hands, "*we* didn't suggest they abandon the rest of the world and go off to live with a fringe lunatic."

"I think we can minimize the losses there," Trimble said.

"Son of a bitch!" Howard exploded, standing up. " 'Minimize losses'? What kind of bullshit is that, Trimble? Those are kids we're talking about." All of them knew kids existed in the ranks of the Badlands Militia. They'd all seen pictures of them, playing and in the outdoors classes the women taught. "You're talking about killing women and children?"

Trimble stared at him blankly, as if Howard were speaking a foreign language.

Turning, Howard looked at the rest of the group. "Am I the only one who sees what's about to happen if you guys attempt this?"

Ferguson stared at him coldly. " 'You guys'?"

Howard remained silent. The dice were already rolling, sent spinning by his outburst.

"By that, Chief Howard," Ferguson said, his eyes

squinting below his big purple bruise, "do you mean to set yourself apart from the rest of us?"

Forcing himself to speak calmly, Howard said, "I didn't sign on to the Bureau to become a murderer."

Ferguson leveled a finger at the wall projection. "They have one of our agents. For all we know, he may be dead now because we fucked around this long with those people."

"We don't know—"

"We know they had Agent Redmond," Ferguson said. "*I* know they had him. A week ago when you were there. Devon Hite walked Agent Redmond by you as a joke. Made you look totally stupid in front of his redneck buddies." He squinted at Howard again. "Doesn't that piss you off, son? If it doesn't, you must have mosquito-sized balls."

Barely containing the anger that swirled around inside him, Howard faced the table and knew the lines had been drawn. "We don't even know that Redmond is alive."

"Is that what you want to tell Agent Redmond's family?" Ferguson asked. "That we're not going into that compound and kicking ass because we think the bad guys have already killed him? Because if you do, I don't want anything to do with that."

"We need more information."

Ferguson nodded. "We do. We're not going to get it. Those men *your* sheriff busted out of the motel were supposed to infiltrate the compound and get that information for us." He ticked off points on his fingers. "Whether Bobby Redmond was still alive. Where he was being kept. What would be the best course of action to get him out of that place in one piece."

Howard didn't believe Ferguson. Those men had been stone killers. They'd been contracted to kill Devon Hite and rescue Bobby Redmond if they could. "You're talking about innocent lives," Howard said weakly.

"I am," Ferguson agreed. "Bobby Redmond was— *is*—one of those innocents. I want him out of harm's way, too. Maybe by rescuing him, we can rescue some of those others Devon Hite has brainwashed. More than that, we can cut this cancer out now before it gets any bigger." He drummed his fingers on the desktop. "Now sit down and behave or I'm going to ask you to leave the room while the adults talk."

For a moment, Howard was torn, not truly knowing what to do. Then he decided that it was better knowing more than knowing less. Even if he didn't like it.

Silence hung heavy and thick in the auditorium for a moment.

"How soon can we be ready for Operation Moonstalker?" Ferguson asked.

"The National Guard unit tells me they can be in position tomorrow night at twenty-three hundred hours," Trimble said. "That late at night, the women and children should be in bed. We'll go in quiet. According to the numbers I've crunched for the tactical op, we should be able to secure the area in minutes and get the hell out of there with Redmond." He paused. "The innocents, if you want to believe there are any at that location, should be at minimal risk."

"There is always some collateral damage on an operation of this magnitude," Ferguson said, staring straight at Howard. "That's just the price of doing business."

Howard felt another wave of nausea shudder through him. In all his years at the ATF, he'd been involved in two gunfights. Neither of them had had over a dozen bullets fired. Nobody had died or even been wounded in either one. Sitting there in that chair at that table, he felt as if he were watching nuclear winter blowing in. It was arriving tomorrow night at twenty-three hundred hours and there wasn't a damn thing he could do about it.

A knock sounded on the door to Ash's office. He took his bloodshot eyes from the computer monitor and said, "Come on in."

Hawk opened the door. "Your twelve o'clock is here, sir."

"Thanks." Ash looked at his notes. The twelve o'clock appointment was Midshipman First Class Ingrid Hansen. His first appointment of the day had been Skinny, but neither he nor the master chief had yet put in an appearance for the day. "Send her in." He pulled up the file he'd started on her.

Spike came in wearing her NROTC uniform. Ash hadn't implemented that change, but he'd set the tone by wearing his own. Most of the other forty students had already made the changeover. For some of them, maybe, it was sucking up, but he felt others had simply wanted to start taking pride in who they were.

Ash stood and waved to one of the two chairs in front of his desk. "Have a seat."

Spike sat. She looked tense and withdrawn.

"Getting enough sleep?" Ash sat and leaned back in his chair.

"I'm not partying, if that's what you mean." Spike's tone was defensive.

"That wasn't what I meant," Ash said. "You just look tired, that's all."

She sat with her hands in her lap, her backpack to one side on the floor. "Late-night studying. I'm cramming for a couple tests tomorrow."

Nodding, Ash said, "Understood." He focused on the computer monitor. "I'm going to cut to the chase. Save us both some time. Academically, you're floundering."

"Yes, sir, I know, and the last thing I need from you is a load of fucking guilt." As though shocked by her own response, Spike nervously added, "Sir."

Ash looked at her. "I know that's the last thing you need from me," he said. "And the last thing I need to do is waste my time if you're going to scupper yourself. If you're going to continue goofing off, I'm going to let you hang by yourself. There are other students that aren't goofing off that could use some assistance." He let that hang for a moment.

"Assistance, sir?" Spike looked confused.

"I'm putting together a study group," Ash said. "An intervention. My review of scholastic-achievement records shows that we have some of the best and brightest students here at Thaedt. I'm going to fund some tutoring for the students that need—and *want*—it."

"Tutoring, sir?" Spike said that as if it didn't compute.

"Yes," Ash said. "I think we can help each other get through the rest of the semester. If that's what you want."

Swallowing hard, Spike said, "Yes, sir. That's what I want. You see, my mom owns this beauty shop back where I'm from. She didn't want me to come out here or join the Navy, or even leave town for that matter. But that town, that beauty shop—it's a dead end." She took a deep, shuddering breath. "I want more out of life than she ever had. And growing up where I did, how I did, there's no way I can get it on my own. I've never been a great student, but I've always gotten by. Until lately." She broke off, unable to go on.

"What happened lately?" Ash asked gently after he let a little time pass. He was surprised by the genuine emotion he saw in the young woman. With her being one of the master chief's hardcore hangers-on, he'd expected the conversation to be of a more combative nature.

She shook her head. "I don't know." Tears ran down her cheeks. "I think . . . maybe I got *scared*."

"Scared of what?"

"Failing." Spike shrugged. "Proving my mom right." She cleared her throat. "You see, I don't know if I can be a Navy officer. A lieutenant. Be in charge of anything. I was my mom's babysitter for years, and then I was her assistant at the beauty shop. The only way I escaped that was by signing up for the Navy. It seemed like the Navy offered more chances to see the rest of the world."

"You do get that chance," Ash said.

"I'd always hoped so. But this year, I just didn't want

to deal with failing. It seemed easier to flunk here than get tossed from the Navy."

"Being an officer isn't easy," Ash said, "but you do get help. The Navy doesn't set you up just to watch you fail."

"That's not how Chief Fernandez presents it."

"The chief's view of things is slightly skewed. In my experience," *Which got me here,* Ash couldn't help thinking, "the Navy takes care of their own." Just saying that seemed to remind him of everything he'd been through with the military. Maybe the event that had triggered his reassignment here hadn't been a pleasant circumstance, but being adrift in the wilds of South Dakota and off a ship had given him a perspective he hadn't had in a long time.

"Even if they do," Spike said, "it's too late."

"Why?"

"I fucked up. Blew off a Western Civ test last Friday."

"While you were at the chief's party?"

"Yeah."

Ash nodded. "Maybe you could try to talk to the professor."

Reaching into her backpack, Spike pulled out a printed paper and handed it to him. "I tried."

Ash read the terse response.

"I think the prof knew where I was. Or he found out," Spike said.

Ash laid the paper aside and looked at her.

"There's only one test left," Spike said. "Even if I scored a hundred on it, I won't be able to pass."

"Were you ready for this test?" Ash asked.

"Yes."

"Are you still ready?"

She blinked at him. "Yes. I studied for this one. I knew I had to pass it. I didn't have a choice."

After a brief consultation with his planner, Ash picked up the phone, set it to speaker function, and dialed. "Give me a minute."

Spike started to leave.

"No," Ash said. "Have a seat."

"Dean Williams' office," a bright and cheery voice answered.

"This is Lieutenant Ash Roberts of the NROTC here on campus," Ash said. "I'd like to speak to the dean."

"Let me see if he's busy." The phone clicked as the connection was put on hold.

"What are you doing?" Spike cautiously sat back in her chair.

"Magic," Ash told her with a smile. "It's what we do in the Navy, Middie."

The phone clicked again and the woman said, "Here he is, Lieutenant Roberts."

"Good afternoon, Ash," Dean Williams said.

"Good afternoon, Al," Ash said. "Do you remember telling me if there was ever anything you could do for me to just give you a call?"

"Yes." The dean sounded wary now.

"I'm calling in a favor, if I could," Ash said. "I've got a student, Midshipman First Class Ingrid Hansen."

"I'm not familiar with her, but that's not surprising, given the number of student body here."

"I understand that. The problem is that she missed a test she needs to make up."

"Then she needs to talk to the instructor."

"He won't let her make it up," Ash said.

"I see. Why not?"

"Because she was one of the ones at Chief Fernandez's off-campus parties."

Spike's eyes widened at that.

The dean was quiet for a moment. "Then I have to tell you, Ash, I don't see why I should run the risk of angering one of my professors over a student that didn't think enough of him to show up for his test."

"I couldn't agree more," Ash said.

"I'm glad."

"However," Ash said, "that test was last week." He looked at Spike. "Midshipman First Class Ingrid Hansen is in a different place this week. She's going to be out of here at the end of the semester and embarking on her Navy career. She's come to that realization and there's nowhere else she'd rather be."

"She blew off the test."

"Yes, sir."

"And now she wishes she hadn't."

"Yes," Ash said quietly, reading the fear in the young woman's eyes.

"Do you know how many college students are in that same boat?"

"No. I'm dealing with this one because she has put her heart in the right place."

"This week?" The dean sounded doubtful.

"We have to start somewhere, Al. We've all had those periods where we needed help. *I'm* asking for your help today."

"Do you think she has changed that much?"

Ash looked at Spike, who looked totally frozen. "I give you my word, Al. She's not only ready for the test, but she's going to do well."

The dean hesitated. "Ash, I've got to be honest, if I hadn't seen the changes you've already made in those offices, I wouldn't even consider this."

"I appreciate that."

"Hold on for a minute."

Ash waited.

When the dean came back on, he said, "All right. Have her show up at the testing center at three today. She'll be given the test then."

"Thank you."

"Don't make me regret this, Ash. Going over a professor's head, especially this one, is a difficult thing."

"I won't. Thank you again. And if the Navy can do anything for you, let me know." Ash punched off the connection and looked at Spike.

"I can't believe you just did that," she whispered.

"We've turned a corner since last week," Ash said. "The dean was in. He saw the work that you people did.

It makes a difference. You'll find that people have a tendency to give to those people that give back."

"But he wouldn't have done it for me. The dean did it for you."

"I wouldn't have asked or put my head on the block if I wasn't willing to take a chance on you," Ash said. "You just need to be ready by three o'clock."

"Aye, sir," Spike said. "I will be."

Hawk rapped on the door again and stuck his head in. "Your twelve fifteen is here, sir."

Ash stood, feeling good about the weight that he'd seen lifted from Spike's shoulders. He offered his hand and she took it, then stepped back and fired off a salute with tears still fresh on her face.

"Give 'em hell, Spike," he said.

"Aye, sir." The young woman squared her shoulders, turned smartly, and walked from the door.

One down, Ash thought. He thought he might be feeling his own load lighten.

Midshipman First Class Bryan Hendricks passed Spike in the doorway.

"You asked to see me," Ash said.

"Yes, sir," Boy said. Anger mottled his face. "I've got a problem."

Ash motioned him to one of the chairs. "What's the problem?"

"It's Bruno."

"What about Bruno?"

Boy hesitated. "He's praying to Geordie, Lieutenant."

" 'Geordie'?" Ash repeated.

"Yes, sir," Boy said. "Ever since I told Bruno about Geordie, Bruno's been praying to him."

"So?"

"It's messing me up," Boy said. "Bruno's crowding up the signals with his own pathetic whining." He drew a deep breath. "It's got to stop!"

32

Betraying one's coworkers at the ATF was harder than Hank Howard had believed it might be—not from an emotional perspective, because he didn't agree with the small-minded bastards concerning how the Badlands Militia needed to be dealt with, but from a logistical one. Mel Ferguson didn't trust him as far as he could throw him and was keeping a watchful eye over him. When Howard left BATF headquarters in St. Paul, he noticed almost immediately that he had somebody following him. *Son of a bitch,* he thought as he cupped his hands and lit a cigarette. The guys doing the tail job weren't exactly trying to be covert about their task. They sat, in their cheap suits and wraparound sunglasses, in an unmarked car bristling with radio antennae and watched him. Since he didn't know either of the guys, he assumed they were out of Seattle Division and had been brought in by Ferguson, who had populated the St. Paul office with several of his people.

When he was once more surrounded in a nicotine-rich environment, Howard started thinking, all the while giving the appearance of going over his notes. If Ferguson had a tail on him, it was a given that his home phone and his cell phone were tapped. Unless he felt like shit-canning his career, which he wasn't about to do over the likes of Devon Hite, he wasn't going to call Sheriff Bolo over those devices. At the same time, sending in the National Guard at night into an area loaded with women and children and standing by while it became a fire-free zone wasn't something he could live with. And Bobby Redmond's chances of survival weren't going to be improved.

No, the way Howard looked at it, Redmond and those women and children only had one chance at emerging unscathed from the coming goat-rope. And that rested solely with Sheriff Dominic Bolo and his new buddy, the NROTC university lieutenant, who thankfully just happened to be a SEAL. Howard knew about Lieutenant Roberts because Ferguson had insisted on having the man's background checked after he'd backed the sheriff's play at the Journey's End Motel. The Navy had been closemouthed about why such an elite warrior would be stationed in South Dakota, but they'd given the lieutenant high marks. But something about the profile didn't add up.

Howard put his Day Runner aside, lowered his sunglasses, and put the transmission into drive. After looking both ways, he pulled out onto East Seventh Street and headed downtown. The unmarked car pulled smoothly into the lane behind him, not even trying to be coy about it.

No stealth mode, Howard thought. *So if I accidentally lose them in heavy traffic, I look suspect. That's fucking great.* Plus, he'd bet that the second he went off the grid he'd get a phone call from Ferguson or one of his subordinates and they'd ping him by GPS through his phone. Howard figured he was just fortunate they hadn't put him under house arrest.

Of course, Howard hadn't risen to chief special agent without knowing how to cut corners. Ferguson had gotten by on being an asshole and wielding a big stick. That worked if a guy didn't mind the asshole label. Honest-to-God brinksmanship required subtlety.

At six p.m. the downtown traffic was a bitch, all stop-and-go, but Friday night would be worse with the exodus from the burgeoning metropolis to the small towns and lakes with their boats, Jet Skis, fishing gear, and well-stocked coolers. Howard was an old hand at negotiating it, though. He was slowed by having to keep the tail car locked onto him.

He found a parking space downtown and went into Delvecchio's, one of his favorite Italian restaurants. It was a hole in the wall where the cooks spoke only Italian and slaved relentlessly for Frankie Delvecchio's hard-nosed mama, who was from the Old Country and ran the kitchen like a Swiss watch. The décor hinted at an uptown groove, but was strictly faux pas. Frankie had done a lot of the carpentry work himself, using pre-shaped molding that held grapes, leaves, and wine bottles in raised relief. Of course, Mama Delvecchio had insisted on hand-painting the images, which had driven her son crazy but now lent the restaurant some of its Old World atmosphere.

A young waiter with broken English took Howard to one of the small tables. Howard flashed his ID. "I need to see Frankie."

A little worried, the waiter headed to the back.

The two ATF agents tailing Howard came in and stood around till another waiter showed them a table.

A few minutes later, Frankie showed up, looking at once dapper and dangerous. Howard didn't know what Frankie's whole story was; he probably never would. They'd first crossed paths when one of Frankie's cooks had been running guns. The St. Paul PD had wanted to wrap Frankie up with the charges, too, but Howard had interceded, kept Frankie out of the boilover, and ended up taking down a Chinese gang called the Copper Dragons who were moving a hundred AK-47s and thousands of rounds of ammunition through the Twin Cities. It had been a big bust. Frankie and Howard hadn't exactly been best friends since, but Howard ate there, Frankie gave him a price break, and the two swapped information and bet on the Vikings together. Best friends cost too much, but Frankie and Howard had a working relationship.

"Hank," Frankie said, smiling. "How you doing?"

Howard smiled back, stood and shook Frankie's hand. They sat down at the table together. There was enough crowd noise around them that Howard felt comfortable talking in a normal tone of voice. "I'm doing good, Frankie. How's Mama?"

Frankie frowned. "Meaner than a snake if you ask me. But you ask me in front of her, you're going to get a different answer."

Howard laughed and then lowered his voice, saying, "I got a problem."

Leaning in a little, Frankie said, "What?"

"The two guys in the corner?"

Frankie didn't even look. "Yeah. The suits. They look like twins of you. Only younger, better groomed, and handsome."

"You're all heart, Frankie."

Grinning and shrugging, Frankie said, "Hey, what the hell are friends for, you know?" He paused. "These guys, they watching over you for some reason?"

"Yeah."

"You want them there?"

"Not exactly."

"You need out the back way? That can be arranged. Let me know what they're driving, it'll never leave the lot."

"It's not like that," Howard said. "I need to make a phone call, but I think my phones are tapped."

Frankie frowned. "By who?"

"I'm doing an end run around an asshole who thinks he's my boss. I need to get hold of a guy who's going to get crunched in a crossfire he doesn't deserve, let him know the shit's about to hit the fan. But if I get caught, I could lose the job at the Bureau."

Frankie grinned. "You lose your job, you could come work for Mama."

"Welfare would be easier." Both of them laughed, then Howard asked, "Can you hook me up with a phone? I don't want those guys to know I got it."

"Sure." Frankie rose from the table. "You want me

to order dinner for you? Mama's got some great angel-hair pasta tonight." He kissed his fingers and flung them into the air, the stereotypical Italian gesture.

"Sure," Howard said. Two minutes later, he had an appetizer plate of bread in front of him. One waiter had dropped a cell phone into his lap while another deposited an appetizer in front of his watchdogs. Howard hung the earpiece over his left ear, out of sight of the two agents, and dialed Sheriff Bolo's cell number.

On the third ring, the sheriff answered gruffly, "Bolo."

"It's Hank Howard."

"What can I do for you, Chief Howard?"

"It's what I can do for you." Howard sipped his drink. "First off, you can't contact me. I'm being watched by Ferguson. I'm pretty sure he has my phones tapped. I get caught talking to you, my pension takes a major hit."

"All right."

"Couldn't just sit by and not tell you, Sheriff," Howard said. "Ferguson is planning an armed invasion of the Badlands Militia tomorrow night."

"How the hell did he get a warrant for that?"

"We have photographic evidence that Bobby Redmond, at least last Friday, was being held by Devon Hite and his people."

The sheriff was silent.

"We don't have a lot of time to mess around here, Sheriff," Howard said.

"Someone should have told me," Bolo said.

"Do you think Hite would have given Redmond up? Think about it. If Hite admits to having Redmond now, or having had him and killing him, everything he's worked for there is toast. Hite knows that. This is what always happens to these sorts of guys: They get too cute by half. His only choice has been to keep his mouth shut." Howard leaned back in his chair and rubbed his eyes tiredly. He wasn't faking the fatigue. Using periph-eral vision, he caught sight of the two agents sitting eas-ily and enjoying the bread, chatting up two of the cute waitresses Frankie had undoubtedly sent over as distractions. After this, Howard knew he was going to owe Frankie.

"Okay. Chances are, Bobby Redmond isn't alive," Bolo said.

"I know that. I think Ferguson is counting on that too, the bastard. Until Redmond's body turns up, he gets to assume Hite still has him in custody."

"Why are you telling me?" Bolo asked.

"You're an ex-Green Beret," Howard said. "You've buddied up to a Navy SEAL. Shit, together you should be an unbeatable tag team. You know the territory over there. I'm not one to tell you your business, but I'm thinking maybe if you hauled ass over there and got Bobby Redmond out of the bad guy's clutches, maybe we could save a lot of people."

"Interesting proposition," Bolo growled.

"Either that or invest in body bags."

"If I should have a problem . . ."

"Don't. That's all I can tell you." Howard toyed with the bread. "Like I said, you can't call me. I don't want to lose my job over somebody else's fuckup. But I don't want to see those women and kids hurt either."

"All right," Bolo said.

"I know this sounds chickenshit, Sheriff," Howard said, "but it's the best I can do."

"That's fine. I appreciate the heads-up." Bolo cut the connection.

Howard took the earpiece off and dropped it onto the phone. He wondered what Bolo really thought of him, if he thought he was a real chickenshit or if he understood. Then he tried to put that out of his mind because it would only mess with his head to the point where he couldn't stand himself. The waiter had been covertly watching him and came over at once to bring a glass of wine and take away the phone. "Tell Frankie thanks," Howard told the waiter.

"Yes sir."

Howard sat there with the Italian music in his ears and said a little prayer. Just in case it helped. He wasn't a terribly religious man, but at times like these, it never hurt to try.

When Ash arrived back at Benjamin Hall in the early evening, he was surprised to find the offices filled to overflowing with midshipmen. They sat in the hallway with books and laptops open, with book bags nearby, and tall Styrofoam containers of coffee at their sides. Ash stood for a moment, not believing what he was seeing.

Spike uncoiled from the floor and stood, squaring her shoulders. "Attention on deck!" she said.

Immediately, the midshipmen rose to their feet. A few other young people Ash didn't recognize pushed uncertainly to their feet as well.

Surprised, Ash returned, "At ease." He looked at Spike. "Midshipman First Class Hansen, do you want to tell me what's going on?"

"Scholastic intervention, sir." She gazed at the midshipmen around her, looking a little perplexed herself.

"By my count, there must be sixty or seventy people here," Ash said. "Only forty midshipmen are currently enrolled." And only fifteen of those had shown up at Wednesday night's intervention.

"Yes, sir," Spike said. "It turns out a few of us had friends. The word got out about what we were doing. The intervention, I mean. It appears some people can help, and others need help themselves." She shrugged. "When they started showing up, Globe and I decided we could divide them up and spread the wealth. Everybody gets a chance to tutor and a chance to be tutored. Globe and I put them into groups according to subject matter."

At best, Ash had figured maybe ten or a dozen midshipmen would show up. The ones that were truly in trouble. Curiosity might have brought a few others. Or the hopes of getting laid. Ash remembered what college had been like. "Good call, Spike. However, this could strain our ability to be hosts."

"Not to worry. Globe and I rounded up extra coffee-pots and coffee. We should be able to keep up with the demand."

"All right." Ash looked at Globe. "Know any good pizza places that deliver to the college?"

"Good *and* deliver?" Globe mused. "Usually those are mutually exclusive."

"Settle for deliver," Ash directed. "Negotiate the best price you can for . . ." He looked at Spike. "How many pizzas?"

"Fifty," she answered.

"Fifty pizzas," Ash said. "Don't ask for orders. Divide up the selections as best as you can."

"Excuse me," Globe said, looking a little sheepish, "but this is end of the month."

Ash just looked at him, not understanding.

"End of the month," Globe repeated as if that had special meaning.

"He means you're not going to find a lot of students with money tonight," Spike translated.

"Understood," Ash said. "This is on me. Make it happen."

"Yes, sir," Globe said.

"And pass the word," Ash told them, "no alcohol."

"Yes, sir," the two midshipmen replied.

Ash fixed his gaze on Spike. "How did we do in Western Civ?"

Smiling, Spike gave him a thumbs-up. "An A or possibly a high B. I knew the material."

"Good work."

"Thank you. For the compliment and the chance, sir."

"No worries," Ash said, "Now point me at the poli-sci group."

Spike pointed. "Once Globe and I handle the food arrangements, I'll be right there."

Ash made his way over to the group, introduced himself, and sat cross-legged on the floor. He asked for a book and one was eagerly thrust into his hands. They told him which sections they were currently covering.

He was surprised at how easily the material came back to him.

The phone rang and he plucked it from his holster, standing and stepping away from the group for a moment. "Ash is up."

"Catch you at a bad time?" It was Bolo.

"This is fine. Catching up on a little homework at the university. Got something?"

"Interesting phone call," Bolo said. "From our friend at the alphabet group. He says they're planning on a raid out at the farm tomorrow night at eleven. Unless their missing agent turns up."

"What are the chances of that happening?"

"Slim to none."

"That's about what I had figured," Ash said. "If they put together a raid, a lot of people are going to get hurt." The BATF didn't have a sterling record as far as urban assaults went.

"That's why I thought I'd call you," Bolo said. "Find out if you're still up for tomorrow."

"I am," Ash said, wondering if he was going to end up trapped between the Badlands Militia and the ATF. It wasn't a pleasant thought.

"You're late," Master Chief Fernandez said as he swayed drunkenly in the door leading to his bedroom. "C'mon, Skinny, crawl outta bed. We got to be moving." He stumbled into the living room where Skinny slept on the ratty couch the master chief had purchased from a secondhand store.

Skinny lay facedown in a pillow.

Struggling to focus his eyes, Fernandez looked outside. It was dark. Damn, with all the sleeping he'd been doing, he'd have thought it was morning by now. A glance at the clock on the wall told him it was eleven fourteen. He looked back outside. Shit! No way was it dark at eleven-fourteen unless there was an eclipse, and he'd have known about an eclipse. If it was dark, that meant it was dark *again*. They'd slept the day away.

"Goddammit," the master chief muttered. They'd been drunker than he thought. He reached down and caught hold of the sleeping midshipman's shoulder, then shook him. "Skinny. Wake up, shipmate."

Skinny didn't move.

Suddenly, Fernandez realized that he couldn't tell if Skinny was even breathing. Who the hell slept facedown in a pillow? The master chief remembered when his kids had been small that was one of the things his wives had always told him to watch for when they left the babies with him. Don't let them sleep facedown.

"Skinny." Fernandez shook the prone midshipman again. Then the chief realized he was standing in puke, cold puke that stuck to his foot. Panic streaked through him then, fired by stories of college frat-house parties that came with body counts caused by overdrinking and alcohol poisoning. Seemed like none of the college guys could hold their liquor anymore, or knew when to quit. *Son of a bitch.* Had Skinny lain there and died on that miserable secondhand couch? Fernandez closed his fist more tightly around Skinny's shoulder and shook him harder. "Skinny!" Fear sailed through the master chief, rattling his molars.

Suddenly, Skinny snuffled and jerked away from the older man's grip. "Goddammit, Derek! You fucking prick! Leave me alone or I'm gonna tell Mom!" Crusted puke surrounded his mouth and stained his shirt.

"Skinny!" Fernandez roared, partly from irritation and partly from relief. "On your feet!" Then he relied on the one thing that would get a college student up and going. "You're late for class! There's a test today!"

Reluctantly, Skinny sat up. His hair, moussed by puke, stuck out in all directions. He folded his arms across his chest and belched. "Th' fuck, Master Chief?"

"We gotta make a command decision," Fernandez said.

Skinny sat unsteadily on the couch. "What?"

"You missed class. I missed work."

Skinny shrugged. "Don't care."

"Neither do I. I'll call in sick tomorrow for today, make it retroactive. That means tomorrow's Friday. We gotta decide if we're gonna sober up or keep drinking."

With furrowed brow, Skinny considered the options. Fernandez could almost see the neurons firing. "Stay drunk. Getting sober's too painful just to think about."

"That's the spirit." Fernandez went to the kitchen and checked his liquor supply. Two empty bottles lay in the sink. *Shit! We were at it hard last night . . . this morning. Whatever the hell it is.* A brief tour of the refrigerator revealed only a six-pack of beer. "Bad news, shipmate. We got to make a beer run."

"You got beer."

"This is the last of it. We're gonna need more."

"Okay." Skinny stood and noticed the puke on his shirt, then on the floor. "Oh. Shit. I thought I only dreamed that."

"No sweat. When it dries, I'll vacuum it up. Be easier to handle then. Coming?"

Skinny pulled the offensive shirt away from his body. "Can I borrow a shirt?"

Fernandez got an extra T-shirt from his room and fired it at Skinny. After a quick change, they headed out the door.

"How's my hair?" Skinny asked, raking a hand through it. "Feels funky." He was swaying as he stood.

"Looks fine to me," Fernandez said. "Let's go."

Out in the driveway, they found Skinny's Miata parked behind the chief's nine-year-old SUV. The sports car's bumper had crumpled the trash can.

"Shit, did I do that?" Skinny asked.

"Yeah," Fernandez said, even though he'd been the one to drive home.

"Sorry about that, Chief."

"No sweat."

"Maybe you better drive."

"Sure." Fernandez fished the keys out of his pocket and started for the driver's side.

Skinny had been patting his pockets. He blinked blearily at Fernandez. "You got my keys?"

"I took 'em away from you after you murdered my trash can."

"Oh. Yeah. Thanks." In a drunken, shuffling gait, Skinny made it to the passenger side and folded himself into the seat.

Fernandez fired the sports car up and let it warm for a moment. He cracked open two beers and handed one to Skinny. The midshipman took it and slurped. The master chief upended his own and drained it in one long swallow, then fired the empty in the direction of the trash can. He cracked open another, then shoved the car in reverse, cranked up the stereo on a classic-rock station, and backed out.

On the highway, Fernandez gazed around at the moonlit landscape. Away from Fairly, the darkness was complete. Open plains tracked the highway on either side. Stars lit up the heavens. The air even tasted sweeter. With the radio blaring and a cold beer in his hand, it was about as close to nirvana without the open sea as the master chief had ever been.

He wasn't expecting the buck deer to cross the highway in front of him. Skinny saw the deer before he did, shouting and pointing. Fernandez caught a brief glimpse of the deer, rack spread wide as tree branches, before he twisted the Miata's steering wheel. The sports car slewed out of control but couldn't come around quickly enough. Low as it was, the car caught the deer at the knees, lifting the two-hundred-pound animal up so that it skated across the hood and smashed into the windshield. The safety glass gave way at once, dropping into Fernandez's lap in chunks the way it was supposed to. Then the deer came through as well, slamming hard into the master chief's chest.

The Miata left the road at over seventy miles an hour. It screamed through the underbrush, hit a tree with the left front fender and flipped. Fernandez's senses swam, but through it all, he felt the weight of the deer against his chest. The Miata landed on its side and the grinding roar of the crash filled Fernandez's ears. He couldn't breathe. The deer was too heavy. He tried to push it off and couldn't, couldn't even feel his arms. He tried to shout for help, but if any sound came out, he never heard it.

Abruptly, his vision narrowed to one tiny pinprick of light. A few seconds later, that light was extinguished.

33

The whirling lights of the emergency vehicles marked the crash site along the highway. Ash had no problem finding it. A sheriff's deputy waved a baton and brought him to a halt. The deputy was young under the brim of his cowboy hat, but he looked pale and haggard beyond his years now. Ash rolled his window down.

"I'm sorry, sir," the deputy said. "There's been an accident. I'm afraid you can't go through right now."

Ash held up his Navy ID. "I'm Lieutenant Ashton Roberts. Sheriff Bolo is expecting me."

"Yes, sir. We were told you were coming." The deputy looked up and called out to another deputy, who dragged one of the sawhorses away. "Go right through there. Park next to the sheriff's car."

Ash pulled through and parked, but he was on autopilot. The call had come from Bolo scarcely ten minutes ago. Ash had still been at the intervention going on at Benjamin Hall. After he'd gotten the news, he'd started moving, but hadn't mentioned the accident or the fatality to any of the midshipmen. He got out of his car with a sense of dread and moved toward the area where rescue workers with flashlights tramped through the woods.

Besides the sheriff's deputies, Fairly's four-unit fire department, and two ambulances, three eighteen-wheelers were parked at the sides of the highway. One of the deputies intercepted Ash. "Who are you?"

"Lieutenant Roberts," Ash answered, never breaking stride. "Those are my people in there."

"I'm sorry to hear that," the deputy said.

"How bad is it? The sheriff said there was a fatality, but he didn't know who it was." Ash didn't wait for a reply. He scrambled down the side of the highway berm and walked across the field toward a grove of trees. Jagged and splintered branches marked the path the vehicle had taken when it left the highway, leaving the white meat of the trees exposed.

"There's a fatality," the deputy agreed. "The other man was thrown from the vehicle." He hesitated. "I have to tell you, Lieutenant, he's pretty messed up. The EMS guys had to bring him back twice." He nodded up the embankment. "They're working on him now, trying to get ready to transport. Hospital staff is getting ready for them, but we don't see much of this. Not like they do in the big cities."

"I understand." Ash found Bolo standing beside the wreck. Firemen tramped through the brush, putting out small fires with fire hoses.

"You might want to take just a second to gather yourself," the deputy warned. "This is pretty bad. It's bad enough when you see something like this, but it's even worse when it happens to someone you know."

"I appreciate that, Deputy." Ash kept moving. He didn't bother explaining that he'd been in combat, that he'd seen friends die while they were standing right beside him, or watched helplessly as brothers in arms were blown up and scattered like broken dolls in a violent war zone. The deputy, judging by his youth and trepidation, had never borne witness to the kind of horrors Lieutenant Ash Roberts had seen in his career.

Bolo turned around at Ash's approach. The sheriff kept from shining his flashlight in Ash's eyes. "Fernandez is dead," Bolo said. "I didn't know that when I called you."

Ash took a deep breath. "What about Skinny—Midshipman First Class Skoskstad?"

"He was thrown from the vehicle sometime after it left the road." Bolo shone the flashlight back up the embankment. "Don't know where, exactly. Maybe the traffic specialists can figure it out. Didn't look like he was wearing his seat belt."

"That's his car," Ash said. He knew that from the records he had on the midshipmen. "Was he driving?"

"No. Fernandez was driving."

Ash looked down and saw moonlight glint on metal. A lone beer can, totally undamaged, lay in the wake of the wreck. "What happened?"

"Deer stepped out in front of them," Bolo said. "Out here, it happens. Every now and again it might be a bear. When you're driving at night, you need to stay on your toes." He paused. "They were drinking, Ash. Both of them. Had what was left of a six-pack in the car."

Ash nodded, not knowing what to say. "They were both absent today. I should have come looking for them."

"Why?" Bolo asked.

"Maybe I could have prevented this."

Bolo dropped a heavy hand on Ash's shoulder. "Fernandez was an accident waiting to happen. You couldn't have stopped that if you were God, which you ain't." He paused and looked into Ash's eyes. "You've been in combat. You've seen things that could have been prevented and things that couldn't. There's a certain wisdom in knowing which is which. What happened here tonight, that was something that couldn't have been helped."

Ash knew that was true. Just as he couldn't have stopped Wild from losing part of his right leg to a roadside bomb in Anbar Province. But it didn't stop him from wishing he could change any of it. "Where's the master chief?"

"Still in the car. They haven't been able to get him out yet."

Ash moved toward the front of the vehicle, glimpsing the crumpled deer astride the bowed hood of the Miata.

"Ash." Bolo held onto his shoulder. "It's bad. You can wait to do this."

Looking back at the sheriff, Ash shook his head. "I can't. He was under my command. When you lead men, you see them through to the end." He walked toward the car and Bolo fell into step with him.

At the front of the car, in the light Bolo provided, Ash saw one of the most macabre sights of his life. He knew immediately that the deer had gone up onto the Miata's hood and then crashed through the windshield. But what surprised him was the fact that the deer's shattered antlers had crunched through the chief's chest and pinned him to the bucket seat. Fernandez's frozen expression was one of horrified shock. Blood leaked from his mouth.

"Antlers broke during the collision," Bolo explained. "Made them sharp as knives. From the looks of it, one of them drove straight through Fernandez's heart. I don't think he felt a thing. He was probably dead on impact."

Ash hated calling Skinny's parents. Notifying a family about a loved one's injury—or worse, death—was one of the more difficult parts of the job, and the possibility that he might have to do something like that while in South Dakota had never entered Ash's mind. The school assignment was a no-brainer task, punishment or medicinal or mistaken, depending on how he wanted to view it. Nothing like this was supposed to happen.

The phone calls went about as expected. Skinny's parents were divorced. His mom had remarried a guy who came across with all the feelings and emotional complexity of an ice cube. The father was an alcoholic—or so one of the faculty had related—and the guy started a crying jag that Ash had a hard time keeping himself distant from. The mother and stepfather were flying out. The father was locked up in a psych ward in the middle of a thirty-day observation.

Master Chief Etan Fernandez's fourth ex-wife had

agreed to sign the papers to see to it his remains were buried in Houston, where the chief was originally from. The ex-wife also didn't sound as if she was going to go to the ceremony but thought that her kids would be able to if they wanted because Houston was close.

Sitting in the hospital waiting room, Ash shifted his mind into neutral. Bolo had come by to check on him, but there was a lot of paperwork to tend to. Ash knew that if he fell somewhere along the way, either through a bullet, an IED, or an accident, his family would take care of his body and see to it that he went out in style. Of course, it would be a Roberts International production with the assistance of the U. S. Navy, but it would be done.

Other people occupied the chairs around him. None of them looked at ease or rested. A television played in the corner, but no one was watching.

"Lieutenant."

Looking up, Ash saw Spike, Globe, Bruno, and Boy all coming through the door. A few other midshipmen were with them.

"We just heard," Spike said, sitting beside Ash.

Ash pulled on his professional face, knowing they'd suffered a loss and would need some guidance now.

"Is it true?" Spike asked. "Is Fernandez . . . dead?"

"Yeah," Ash answered. "He is."

"What about Skinny?" Bruno asked.

"He's in the ER," Ash said. "He's alive. They're still working on him."

Spike looked at him. "He's going to be all right, isn't he?"

Ash saw the desperation in her eyes, saw it mirrored in the eyes of the others. He wanted to tell them everything was going to be fine. But he couldn't. *You can't lie to them and keep their trust.* He shook his head. "I don't know."

They were quiet for a moment, then Boy said, "Maybe we could pray. You know. Just a prayer. We can ask

Geordie." He looked at Bruno. "Something like this, man, we can all pray to Geordie."

"Sure," Ash said. He didn't know if prayer helped and had never been big on it himself, but he knew that it gave some people hope and stability. "You say it, Boy." They linked hands and lowered their heads.

"Lieutenant Roberts."

Ash looked up at the sound of his name. A man in green scrubs stood in the doorway of the waiting room. Crossing the room, Ash took the man's hand. "I'm Roberts."

"Dr. Eugene Horton," the man said. He had a firm, confident grip and a broad face, and looked clear-eyed even at two in the morning. "I've been working on Gerhardt Skoskstad."

"Yes, sir," Ash said.

"I understand you're the closest thing there is to family here."

"I'm his officer-in-charge," Ash replied. "I've talked to his parents. His mother and stepfather are on their way here but won't arrive till morning."

"He's resting now," Horton said.

Ash felt a small knot in his stomach unravel. "I'll call them and let them know that."

"That young man was in bad shape when the ambulance arrived with him," Horton went on. "He's suffered two broken legs, a broken arm, a half dozen broken ribs—one of which punctured a lung, but we've taken care of that—and multiple fractures and contusions. He's got almost four hundred stitches in him, sewing up lacerations as well as repairing the damage we did trying to put everything else to rights."

"Then he's going to be all right?"

"Given time, physically, he should be fine. The only problem we're having right now is that he's unresponsive. We haven't been able to wake him up, but we don't really need to at this point. Maybe after a few hours' rest, till some of the immediate trauma in his body subsides, he'll wake on his own. We'll just have to wait to see if that happens." Horton paused a moment. "Most people don't survive what he's been through."

"I understand that."

"But he's young," Horton went on. "That plays in our favor, so keep that in mind. If there's anything you need, don't hesitate to ask. I'll be monitoring his condition."

"Thank you, Doctor," Ash said. Then he turned and walked back to the group of midshipmen anxiously awaiting word. "I've been here almost a week," he told them, "and I haven't found out if there's an all-night place that serves coffee at two in the morning."

"Shouldn't we stay here?" Spike asked.

"They have my number," Ash said. "If anything happens, the hospital will call. Until then, we're going to exhaust ourselves here. For the moment, we know all there is to know. We need to regroup."

"There's a truck stop out by the highway," Globe said.

"Fine," Ash said. "Let's go there."

The truck stop was just short of a historic building. Over the years of its existence, the place had been refitted and rebuilt, added to and restructured, finally ending up with a wall as a demarcation between the truck-stop side of the business and the all-night café. Shelves and circular racks in the convenience store side held shirts, mugs, and vanity plates advertising South Dakota and Mount Rushmore. The stock ran the gamut from snacks to replacement parts for CB radios and cell phones. There were even GPS devices and computer software.

Ash herded his group to one of the larger tables in the back of the café, under a mounted buffalo head. A chubby waitress took their order and went away.

"How did the intervention go?" Ash asked, to break the silence that had descended over the group. A twangy country song bleated through the cheap speaker mounted in the ceiling.

"Most of them were still at it when we left," Spike said.

"That's good. Are you getting any feedback from it?"

"They appreciated the pizza."

Ash smiled. "I figured on that."

"But you can't feed them all the time."

"I can't?"

"No. If you feed them all the time, they're going to keep coming. But it's going to be for the food, not the study group."

"How do you know that?" Ash asked.

Spike shrugged. "That's the way it was with my brothers' and sisters' friends. Once I started preparing food around the house, it seems like I had everybody's kid over." She looked at him and understanding dawned in her eyes. "But you already knew that, didn't you?"

"Yes," Ash said, "I did."

The waitress arrived with cups and a pot of coffee. She passed the cups around and left the pot.

"So why did you feed them tonight?" Bruno asked.

Ash sipped his coffee. "That's a good question, Bruno. Why did I feed them tonight?"

They were all silent for a moment. Ash was determined not to make it any easier for them. They had to learn to stand and think on their feet.

Then Boy said, "It's simple marketing. The pizza tonight was advertising. Just a way of getting people talking about what was going on."

"Yes," Ash admitted. "The same way overseas soldiers often carry chocolate bars into hostile territory to give to kids."

"But why do that?" Bruno asked.

"I don't know," Ash said. "Why would I want to do that?"

Globe narrowed his eyes suspiciously. "To add warm bodies to the mix. The lieutenant knew we couldn't cover all the tutoring we needed done. Tomorrow night, there will be even more of them. We don't have to feed them, but it might be better if we could. We got a lot of help tonight that we wouldn't have gotten on our own." He paused. "How are we going to feed them?"

Ash shrugged. "That's your problem. I've got a system in place for you to utilize. You're going to have to find a way to sustain it at its present size and richness. That's one of the problems of command."

"You did it for more reasons than that," Spike said.

Ash grinned at her, glad they were able to talk about something other than Skinny lying up in ICU. "What else could there be?"

"The students that came tonight are going to talk," Spike said. "More than just other students are going to hear about it. The professors are going to hear about it, too. Maybe they won't get involved in the meetings, but they might be more . . . accessible to whatever we need."

"If they're not, Dean Williams might hear about this and take an interest as well," Globe added. He grinned and shook his head. "Man, you *are* twisted."

"The deeper into rank you go," Ash said, "the more devious you become. You don't have to beat the other people around you; it's the system you have to get over on. You don't break the rules of engagement and you can't alter the terrain where you have to fight your battles, but you can *change* the rules to become friendlier, or move the combat to an environment better suited to you. It's Sun Tzu."

They looked at him.

"What you're doing here, with the scholastic intervention, only works if you're *trying* to square yourself with your work. If it's a smoke screen to get out of it, you might fool them for a while. But, eventually, they'll know it and you'll be further behind the eight ball than you were."

They were quiet for a while, thinking about what he'd said. Ash could see the gears turning. Even then, though, he knew their thoughts weren't far from Skinny and the master chief.

"What happened tonight," Bruno finally said, "is totally hosed up."

"It is," Ash agreed quietly.

"Sitting back drinking with the master chief last Friday," Bruno went on, "I didn't see it coming to this." He shook his head. "Not even when I knew Skinny was hanging out with the master chief Tuesday night after latrine detail and both of them were getting loaded at one of the local watering holes. The master chief just seemed . . . *invincible,* you know? Larger than life."

"I know," Ash said quietly.

"Why didn't you jump the master chief's ass on Friday?" Globe asked. "We were all wondering."

Ash thought about his answer. "Command is a tricky thing," he said finally. "It's one thing to be aboard ship with a full crew at your back. You bring a new sailor on, that sailor knows his ass is grass if he steps out of line. If the captain doesn't break a boot off in him, one of the crew will. Officer or enlisted. Doesn't matter. They're making waves on a ship that's already working." He paused. "But walking into a situation where *you're* the odd man out?" He shook his head. "That's different. If I'd attacked the master chief, that would have thrown all of you into protective mode. He's been with some of you a couple years. I was the FNG."

"FNG?" one of the sophomores asked.

Bruno hammered the bill of the guy's Twins baseball cap. " 'Fucking New Guy,' 'tard," Bruno growled. "Damn, act like you been there."

"I had to handle things more calmly," Ash said. "When you strike is as important as how you strike."

"What about if this had happened on your ship?" Spike asked.

Ash looked at her. "This wouldn't have happened on my ship."

She nodded.

"Besides that, I believe in *leadership,* not *fear,* as a command tactic. If I can't get you to believe in me, in what I think and why I think that, I'm doing something wrong." Ash shrugged. "Not every officer believes that, but I do. I've built teams, SEAL teams, that went in and kicked ass all around this world. I've made some of the best friends a man can make by being that kind of officer." He sipped his coffee. "You people are fortunate. You're going to get to meet one of them this weekend."

"This weekend?" Globe asked.

"Yep. I've got permission to take you on a field exercise," Ash said. "We're going to the gun range and I'm going to provide instruction. If you get really lucky, Wild will help instruct." He'd set the shooting range up for two reasons. Only one of them had anything to do with the NROTC students. Looking over their records, he'd seen that all of the midshipmen had been on the range and that most of them had qualified for a shooting medal.

"What are we going to do about Skinny?" Spike asked.

"Whatever we can," Ash said. "During the time we can't help him, though, we've got to go on with our lives. Speaking of which"—he rolled his wrist over and looked at his watch; it was almost four—"most of you have class at zero eight."

A few scattered groans sounded, and someone said, "Couldn't we call in after everything that's happened?"

"We could," Ash agreed. "But we put tonight in getting ready for tomorrow. Let's hit it tomorrow and plan on getting some rack time tomorrow afternoon. If anything changes with Skinny, I'll let you know."

34

"Lieutenant."

Ash looked up from his desk and saw a third-class midshipman standing there. It took him a moment to remember the guy's name. "What is it, Ferret?"

"Sheriff Bolo's here to see you, sir. Says you were expecting him." Ferret's small stature and close-set eyes had earned him his nickname. Rumor had it that he had pulled off the biggest panty raid in Thaedt University history, though it had never been proven.

"I am. Send him in." Ash shoved aside the paperwork he'd been doing. The Navy demanded a lot of forms when one of their own died in the line of duty. And even though he'd been drunk and away from work without leave, Master Chief Etan Fernandez still fell under that heading.

Bolo walked into the office and closed the door behind him. "Well, you look like shit."

"It's good to see you too," Ash replied with a grin.

Bolo dropped into one of the chairs in front of the desk. "Did you get any sleep last night?"

"I catnapped in the chair here, and then gave up this morning, took a shower, and started over."

"Little Feather said you didn't come in last night," the sheriff said. His eyes were red-rimmed, but like Ash, Bolo had learned a long time ago how to function on little to no sleep.

"Got tied up dealing with the fallout," Ash admitted.

"I checked over to the hospital. They said Skoskstad is still in a coma."

Ash nodded. "Don't know if that's good news or bad news yet. The doc said Skinny would be better off sleeping. As long as his body decided that on its own without responding to something they can't fix."

"I didn't know if you still felt like going pheasant hunting after everything· you've been through," Bolo said.

"You haven't had any more contact with Howard?"

The sheriff shook his head. "He said that was the only time he was going to call unless something changed. He hasn't called, so I'm thinking the ATF raid scheduled for twenty-three hundred hours is going to take place. If we're going to stop it, we've got to get ATF Agent Bobby Redmond out of harm's way."

"All right." Ash pushed up from the desk. "You're ready to go now?"

"Yeah. Little Feather packed us a picnic basket."

Ash deposited his duffel bag in the backseat of the sheriff's cruiser, taking care not to knock over the wicker basket covered with a red-and-white-checkered cloth that already sat in the backseat. He straightened and looked at Bolo across the top of the car. "That's a picnic basket."

"I told you." Bolo shook his head and looked a little embarrassed. "It doesn't exactly present a manly image, does it?"

"I thought you were just speaking figuratively." Ash took another peek at the picnic basket. It was still there. "Damn, we could use that for bear bait in Jellystone National Park."

"Get in the damn car," Bolo growled.

Ash opened the passenger door, dropped into the seat, and pulled the seat belt around him. Then he reached into the back and grabbed the picnic basket. When he uncovered it, he found the basket crowded near to bursting with sandwiches wrapped in wax paper, chips, pickles, apples, and bananas. There were even individually wrapped blueberry muffins.

"The sandwiches are chicken salad and roast beef." Bolo put the car in gear and took off. "They should be marked, she said. She also sent two large Thermoses. One with coffee and the other with lemonade."

"All we need is a tent."

"Shotguns are in the back. Maybe carrying one will make you feel more manly."

Ash couldn't help grinning. After everything that had happened last night, and the action that potentially lay before them today, the thought of the picnic basket struck him as funny. He held up a sandwich. "Wax paper. Old school."

"I know." Bolo waved a dismissive hand. "I told her to use baggies, but she insists that wax paper keeps the sandwiches fresher. Personally, I like the wax paper. Kind of gives it a personal touch, but I know baggies would be easier for her."

"Do you know the last time I ate sandwiches wrapped in wax paper?" Ash asked.

Bolo looked at him over the top of the sunglasses. "You're serious?"

"Yeah." Ash was a little surprised. "I guess I am."

"When?"

"I was eleven. At one of the summer camps my parents sent me to. There was a kid there. Emery or something like that. His mom made peanut butter and jelly sandwiches for parents' day, and they were wrapped in wax paper. Folds creased sharp, just like these. During the camp, we didn't get peanut butter and jelly sandwiches. Not nutritional enough, or maybe the cafeteria manager didn't like them. That day, though, I remember thinking they were the best sandwiches I'd ever eaten."

"Because of the wax paper?"

Ash shrugged. "I guess so."

"I'll do you one better." Bolo drove one-handed, as calmly as if they were going out for a Sunday drive instead of spying on the Badlands Militia. "I used to live down the alley from the grocery store when I was ten. A *real* grocery store. You wanted cold cuts, sausage, or cheese, they sliced it right there for you. My mom would leave me money during the summers while she was working. I'd go down to the grocery store, buy enough bologna and cheese to make a couple sandwiches, four pieces of bread, a pickle, an ice-cold Pepsi and a Superman comic book. Mrs. Tatum would put mayonnaise on the bread for free. I'd wrap those sandwiches in the white butcher's paper Mr. Tatum sliced it in, and go crawl up in a tree house I'd built in the backyard and read that comic book. Those bologna and cheese sandwiches and that Pepsi were the best things you could ask for in the middle of a hot summer day."

Looking at the sheriff, Ash found it hard to imagine Dominic Bolo as a ten-year-old. "Want a sandwich?"

"Yeah."

Ash passed them out, then poured black coffee into two Styrofoam cups. He bit into a chicken salad sandwich that sent his taste buds scrambling. He chewed with true gusto, and then swallowed it down with coffee. He didn't talk until he'd finished the first sandwich, then noticed that Bolo had already finished his own.

"You realize that we may not get a warm welcome from Devon Hite," Ash said as he unwrapped a second sandwich for the sheriff.

"We will," Bolo said, accepting the sandwich. "Whether Hite likes you or not, I'm the sheriff. I can make his life all right, or I can make things difficult. At this point, with the ATF breathing down his neck, I'm certain he'll take an easier way if one comes open around him."

Forty minutes later, Ash sat drinking a final cup of coffee as the sheriff pulled to a stop in front of the Badlands Militia compound. Three guards dressed in similar attire and carrying rifles came out to meet them.

"Something I can do for you?" one of the men asked.

"Devon Hite told me I could go pheasant hunting on farm property," Bolo said.

The man hesitated for just a moment, then said, "Wait right here." He turned and went into a huddle with his buddies.

"Deciding who's going to make the call to Hite," Bolo said. "You'd think they'd already have that figured out in advance."

"They probably don't get many visitors," Ash said. He talked easily, but he felt the tension tight as coiled wire inside him. He hadn't seen Hite since that morning at the park track, but he was certain the militia leader hadn't dropped his suspicions about him.

After a few more minutes, the man returned. "You can go on up, but I'm going to have to have your weapons."

"It's going to be hard to go hunting without a shotgun," Bolo pointed out.

"Yep." The man spat a stream of tobacco onto the dirt road. "Everything's okay at the main house, you'll get your shotguns back. We'll keep the others."

Bolo reached down and popped the trunk latch. "Shotguns are in the rear. Be careful with them. One of those was my daddy's." He passed his pistol through the window.

"We know our way around guns," the man said contemptuously.

A few minutes later, they were once more en route to the main house, led by a driver in a huge four-by-four pickup that rocked threateningly along the trail as if it were going to fall over. A foxtail and a small Confederate flag flew from the whip antennas for the CB radio.

"Nervous?" Bolo asked.

"No," Ash said. "My asshole always puckers like this after chicken salad."

The sheriff laughed. "Don't feel like the Lone Ranger. I'm wound up tighter than a nine-day clock. But it's more over the fact that Ferguson and his ATF boys might jump early than at anything Devon Hite might do."

But as they neared the main house, then tension inside Ash went away the way it always did when he was past the point of no return. He was cool, calm, and collected. There was none of the jittery feeling or anger he'd experienced when boarding the *Polska Marholvski* in the Gulf.

Devon Hite stood with a group of armed men in front of the main house. The militia leader put on a big grin when he saw the sheriff. "Howdy, Sheriff." He turned his cold, dead eyes to Ash. "Lieutenant Roberts."

Ash followed Bolo's lead and climbed out of the cruiser.

"Hello," Bolo said. "I've come to take you up on your invitation to go pheasant hunting."

"That's what I'm told." Hite's eyes swiveled to Ash. "Surprises me that you'd be here after what I heard happened last night."

Ash felt the anger boil up in him then; he didn't trust himself to speak.

"I persuaded him to come," Bolo said. "Hanging around the hospital, when there ain't anything you can do, you can drive yourself crazy. Thought I'd bring him with me and air him out a little."

Hite smiled again. "Nothing better than wide-open places to lift the weight of the world off a man's shoulders, I always say." He nodded to three men standing nearby. "Cletus and his brothers, Tom and Leroy, will be happy to guide you."

And keep an eye on us, Ash thought.

"They is up yonder," Cletus whispered excitedly. He pointed ahead and squinted beneath his stained Ford baseball cap. He looked at Ash and Bolo. "They is three, maybe four of them. I seen 'em just for a second, then they was gone into the brush."

Ash nodded and brought the Remington Model 870 shotgun from his shoulder. He flicked the safety off and moved forward through the brush, alert to any sudden movement. For three hours, Ash and Bolo had followed Cletus and his brothers through the woods east of the farm's main buildings. Ash and Bolo had kept up a quiet conversation, just anecdotes about military life and interesting things they'd seen while on their tours of duty. Servicemen learned to talk when there was nothing to say, sharing borrowed stories or inventing new ones on the spot because there was downtime in the job. Now that skill served as a protective cover. It also drew in Cletus and his kin, who also had interesting tales to tell of the local area, and legends that had been passed down for generations. Somewhere in that, though, they'd all gotten caught up in the hunt.

"Call them dogs over here," Cletus said.

Tom, the lanky one, gave a low whistle. The two bird dogs the brothers had brought along instantly converged on the spot and started stealthily picking their way through the brush. The two English setters worked together well.

Moving quietly, Ash heard the pheasant tracking through the brush. He slowed, not stopping, but moving easily through the tall grass and brush across the uneven ground. The heavy weight of the two pheasants he'd brought down earlier swung against his leg. Bolo had already bagged four.

A moment later one of the English setters froze, one front leg lifted and locked, tail ramrod-straight and head down to show he'd gotten a hit.

"Okay," Cletus said excitedly. "He's all over them."

Without warning, two pheasants launched from the ground. Reddish-brown and sleek, trailing long tail feathers, with the distinctive ring around their necks and red faces, the birds drummed the air like heartbeats and tried to escape. Cletus fired too early, cutting the tops of the brush in his haste.

"Goddammit, Cletus!" Tom yelled. "Hold your water! You nearly shot my dogs!"

Cletus banged off another round that simply tore a hole in the air.

Ash breathed out and waited. He and Bolo had been taking turns firing the first shot. It was now the sheriff's turn again. Bolo fired and the lead pheasant twisted in mid-flight, tumbling down with wings broken by shot. Immediately, Ash shifted his aim to the second pheasant. Someone else fired, but missed the bird. Leading the pheasant a little, Ash slid his finger over the trigger and squeezed. The shotgun's butt slammed against the pad on the shooting vest Bolo had brought for him. Instantly, the pheasant pinwheeled and dropped as Ash racked the shotgun's slide. He had the semiauto feature turned off for the moment, preferring to clear the weapon himself since there were so many people—and some of them not as experienced as he would like—in the hunting party.

"Damn, but that's some fine shooting!" Cletus complimented. He moved forward through the brush. The final two pheasants erupted in front of him. Cletus squalled and fell back, discharging his weapon into the air.

Smoothly, Bolo brought up his shotgun and waited. Ash led the lead bird and fired, dropping it. The sheriff fired on the heels of his shot, knocking the second bird from the air.

"Son of a bitch!" Cletus yelled as Ash's dead bird dropped heavily on him.

"Hey Cletus," Leroy yelled. "Can you find that bird now?"

"Fuck you, Leroy," Cletus replied. But he reached down and plucked the dead pheasant from the ground by its neck and shook it in triumph. "You boys are done over your limits. Now you gotta share."

"Sure," Bolo said, reloading automatically.

Ash did the same. He'd noticed during the hunt that the sheriff had never let himself cycle dry. Ash hadn't either. By law, the reservoirs had to be plugged so that only three rounds could be chambered at any time. Neither of them, apparently, had liked the idea of being without a weapon while in the company of Hite's three "guides."

"You ready to head back?" Bolo asked Ash.

Ash nodded. During the past three hours, although they'd been "led" by their guides, Bolo and Ash had managed to walk in the direction of the highway to the east. That was where Bolo had thought they would come in that night once it got dark. Their recon had confirmed Hite didn't post any guards or electronic surveillance. The militia leader evidently believed in the force he had on hand at the main buildings.

"You can't go yet," Cletus whined as he stuffed the dead bird into the bag at his waist. "Hell, we ain't hit Leroy's limit yet. And you've seen the boy can't hit the broad side of a barn."

"Fuck you, Cletus," Leroy said.

Bolo and Ash laughed. Despite their own motivations for hunting, the humor of the situation wasn't lost on them.

"Maybe we'll pick up Leroy's quota on the way back," Bolo suggested.

"Fuck you too, Sheriff," Leroy said sullenly.

"Wow, Spike! What's the occasion?"

"Piss up a rope, Globe," Spike said as she joined the midshipmen first class at the pool table in the back of the Long Branch Saloon at seven that evening. Still, for all that Globe's comment rattled her, she felt good. She didn't dress up that often, and when she did she liked to be noticed. She wore tight-fitting jeans, Doc Martens, and a low-cut maroon sweater that showed off her cleavage. A few heads had turned to follow her, and she felt good about that, too. It was all right to be one of the guys, but sometimes she wanted to be female.

Bruno, Boy, Globe, and three other midshipmen held down one of the four pool tables. Smoke hazed the air under the low-hanging lights. Locals, farmhands and blue-collar guys who worked at the local businesses occupied the other tables.

"Haven't been keeping up with your laundry?" Bruno snickered.

"Actually," Spike said coolly, "I felt like showing you guys up. Maybe you might try wearing something other than jeans and a concert T-shirt when you go out."

"Hey," Bruno said, pulling the shirt down so everyone could see it, "this isn't just any concert T-shirt. This is a Grateful Dead T-shirt. And it's signed by Bob Weir, whoever he is. I swiped it from my old man."

"Oh," Spike said sweetly, "then it's a historical artifact."

The others laughed.

Bruno rolled his eyes and gave up, turning his attention back to the pool game.

"Has anybody heard anything about Skinny?" Spike said. Following the lieutenant's advice, she'd put in rack time after classes and had only just gotten up.

"He's holding steady," Globe said. "Hasn't come out of the coma yet. Dr. Horton seems to feel pretty good about everything, though."

"Does the lieutenant know?" Spike asked.

"He's the one that told me. Told me to disseminate the information among the troops." Globe shrugged a little self-consciously. "It's the first time since I got here that I actually felt like one of the 'troops.' " He made quotation marks in the air with his fingers. "Felt pretty good."

"Yeah," Bruno said as he lined up his shot. "I have to admit, a lot's changed this week." He paused. "I miss Master Chief Fernandez, though. That guy knew his way around a dirty joke." He shot and missed whatever he'd been aiming for. Cursing, he looked up at the ceiling. "C'mon, Geordie, have you deserted me or what?"

"Hey," Boy said. "Knock it off. Geordie doesn't answer pissant requests involving pool shots."

"He should," Bruno grumbled. "This could cost me ten bucks."

"You know," Spike said, "this week has got me thinking—maybe it's Skinny, too, and the master chief—

but none of us really have that much more time together here." She looked around the group and could tell by the expressions that they'd been thinking along the same lines. "I mean, we finish us this semester, we're going to be moving on into the Navy."

Globe nodded.

Spike wrapped her arms around herself. "I've been wondering if I'm really ready for that. The situation in Iraq is still going on, and there are a lot of other places the Navy is watching over. I was reading the Internet just a couple days ago and learned that China is deploying long-range nuclear weapons that are submarine-based. According to the article, those missiles can be fired at targets all throughout the United States." She paused. "That kind of made me wonder if I was ready to take on that kind of responsibility."

"That's not what we're going to be doing when we go in," Globe said. "The Navy has the Pentagon and Joint Chiefs and admirals to make all those decisions. We're just going to be following orders."

"Maybe," Spike admitted. "But there's more to it than that." She looked around at them. "We found that out yesterday when we got the call about Skinny and Master Chief Fernandez. Once you step into this life, it's going to affect you and change you. Maybe a lot."

"Hey," Bruno said, "maybe you just need to lighten up a little, Spike." His voice was easy and calm, and he evidently meant no foul. "We'll get around this. We've got each other."

"Once we leave here, though, that's no longer true."

"Bullshit," Globe said. "Look at the lieutenant and his friend Wild. Coming in tomorrow and they haven't seen each other much. But they're friends. Maybe a couple hundred years ago when sailors boarded ships they didn't see each other or talk to each other much, but this is the twenty-first century. We've got phones and e-mail. If we're not in each other's lives after this, it's because we don't want to be." He paused. "We'll still be together." He shrugged. "I guess that's another thing

the lieutenant was getting at with his intervention sessions. We'll *always* have each other."

Silence hung over the table for a minute, then a raucous voice said, "Are you guys gonna shoot pool or are
you gonna jabber all night?"

Looking up, Spike spotted one of the rough-hewn men
from the Badlands Militia standing nearby. The guy was
young and hard-looking, his hair shaggy and his beard
unkempt. He wore a stained ball cap advertising the
local feed store and a plaid shirt. Five of his buddies
stood behind them.

"This table's taken, buddy." Bruno used his stick to
point at the rolls of quarters on the end by the coin slot.

"Fuckin' college students," the guy muttered.

Bruno started to take a step forward. Spike moved
into his path, planting her backside against him to block
him. "Don't," she said. "Let him walk away." She knew
Bruno was on edge. They all were. The thing with
Skinny and the master chief was hard to take.

"Gonna let your girl do all your fightin', college boy?"
the man demanded.

"He's half drunk," Spike said. She was surprised to
see the guy there. Usually the Badlands Militia didn't
come into Fairly. "Let it go. If Skinny needs us tonight,
we need to be there."

"This is fucked up, Spike," Bruno growled.

"Ignore him." Spike put steel in her voice even
though she talked quietly.

After a minute, the man hurled a few more curses,
questioned Bruno's manhood, and walked away with his
buddies in tow.

"Son of a bitch," Bruno spat.

"We're here to relax," Spike said. "Let's work on
doing that." She stepped away from Bruno. "I'm going
to go get a beer. Want anything?"

Bruno shook his head. "I'm good." He turned his attention back to the pool game.

Spike went to the bar, cutting through the tables and
the crowd. When the bartender asked what she wanted,

she asked for a beer. While she was waiting for the beer, looking in the long mirror behind it, she saw the Badlands Militia guy come up behind her and shoulder his way in beside her at the bar.

"Hey darlin'," he purred.

Spike ignored him.

In the mirror, the guy frowned. "Hey, you don't have to be all pissy with me."

Looking at him then, Spike asked, "Are you going to get the message any other way?"

"Look," he protested, "I just wanted to ask you to dance, that's all. I didn't mean to show up your boyfriend."

"Yes, you did."

He blinked at her for a moment, then shrugged and grinned like a mischievous little boy. With his looks, the act probably usually took him wherever he wanted to go. "Yeah, I did. But he had it coming."

Spike looked away from him.

"So what about that dance?" he persisted.

"No," Spike said, aware now that Bruno had her on his radar and was watching from the pool table "Just one little dance," he coaxed. "To show there's no hard feelings."

"All right." Spike let him lead her away from the bar, hoping he would cool it after the song and go away. If he just wanted the pride points in front of his buddies, she was willing to give them if it would keep her friends out of it.

The guy could dance. She knew that immediately from the way he moved. The song carried a raucous beat and a baritone singing about how wild Texas women were. In the middle of it, Spike's dance partner started rubbing his denim-encased erection against the inside of her thigh. She pulled away from him.

"Where are you goin'?" he asked, pulling her back to him.

"I don't want to get to know you *that* well," Spike told him, levering a forearm up in front of her and trying to break his grip. She couldn't do it. Before she could try again, he ran a hand up the front of her sweater and started massaging one of her breasts. In that split second, the act reminded her of her mother's boyfriend. A surge of adrenaline gave Spike the strength to push free. When the guy stepped toward her, she slapped his face hard enough to turn his head.

Action came to a grinding stop out on the dance floor.

Grinning, the guy wiped blood from his mouth. "Damn, little girl, you truly shouldn't ought to have done that." With blinding speed, he backhanded her.

Spike's knees turned to Jell-O. Before she knew it, the floor was coming up at her. She caught herself just short of smashing face-first into it. On her knees, right ear ringing from the blow, she looked up at him. He was grinning down, opening his big mouth to say something else he probably thought was cute. Spike doubled her fist and threw an elbow into his crotch, thankful that his tight jeans outlined the target so well. She connected and heard him yowl.

His buddies started forward and one of them grabbed her. She didn't know what they were going to do to her. But whatever it was, they didn't get the chance to do it. Bruno led the midshipmen into them, lowering a shoulder into the first one and mowing him down the way he did the offensive line in football. Then Bruno turned and punched the man holding Spike. When he staggered back, Spike stepped free.

The man she'd hit in the crotch came up faster than she'd expected. Snarling curses, he ripped a broad-bladed hunting knife free of his boot and started for Bruno's unprotected back. Without even thinking, Spike was there, grabbing the guy's knife hand and ramming her head into his face before he even knew she was there. She held on to his hand and managed to kick him in the crotch three more times. Somewhere in there, he released the knife and fell onto the floor in a fetal ball.

Then chaos broke out all around the bar.

35

Surprisingly, the NROTC armory was well supplied in the way of firearms, and—with the shooting exercise scheduled for tomorrow—Ash had just the excuse for going through its contents. Although he and Bolo had agreed their search for ATF Agent Bobby Redmond was going to be as nonaggressive as possible, Ash still dressed to kill. After throwing in body armor and NOMEX masks to disguise Bolo and him in the dark and protect their faces somewhat from bullet fragments and indirect hits as well as fire, he took a SIG-Sauer P226 nine-millimeter and a .357 Magnum revolver from the armory, spare magazines for the SIG, and plenty of jacketed ammunition for both. Adding an M4 rifle and extra magazines and rounds, he picked up two pairs of night-vision goggles, two sets of load-bearing suspenders to handle the gear—the extra for Bolo if he didn't have an equivalent—light-amplifying binoculars, and a medical kit. On second thought, he threw in a half dozen smoke grenades and flash-bangs. In case the party got out of hand, he could always use a little disorientation.

He put all of the gear into his duffel and left the armory at quarter past seven, slightly ahead of schedule. The sky was just turning black and it would be full dark by the time they reached the Badlands Militia. He was nearly to his car when Hawk caught up to him in the parking lot.

"Lieutenant."

Without pausing, Ash used the electronic key to open the rental's trunk. He swung the duffel in and closed the trunk, then looked at the young midshipman. "Yes."

"Something's happened," Hawk said.

Ash instantly thought of Skinny still lying in a coma in the hospital. Then he shoved that from his mind. If something had happened to Skinny, the hospital would have called him. "What?"

"Some of the midshipmen were in a bar fight downtown," Hawk said. "Spike. Bruno. Globe. And some of the others. At the Long Branch Saloon."

Ash couldn't believe it. He could vaguely remember where the bar was from his trips downtown to Maude's Dinner. "With who?"

Hawk shook his head. "I don't know, sir. All I heard is that there was a fight. Somebody said it might have been with some of the guys from the Badlands Militia."

"All right," Ash said. "I'll handle it."

"Yes, sir. I thought you would, sir."

Confused, Ash slid in behind the steering wheel and started the engine. His cell phone rang. He answered, "Ash is up."

"It's me," Bolo said. "I thought I might tell you—"

"That some of my midshipmen were involved in a bar fight?" Ash pulled out of the parking lot and headed for downtown Fairly.

"News travels fast," the sheriff commented.

"It's a small town," Ash agreed. "Anybody hurt?"

"A few lacerations, a few bruises. Nothing that will send anyone to the ER. The problem is, we're on a tight deadline as it is," Bolo went on.

"I'm listening."

"I think we can use this to our advantage," the sheriff said. "We put in an appearance, dress them down, and send them home. Your people got into a fight with some of the young hotheads from the Badlands Militia."

"Confirmed?"

"Oh yeah. None of Hite's top-tier muscle, but some of his guys all the same. After we kick 'em loose with a warning, I figure they'll go back to the farm, maybe sit around and tell everybody how tough they are."

"While they're telling stories, we go in and snatch Redmond." Ash couldn't argue the deviousness of the plan.

"You got it in one. Those guys get to be part of our camouflage."

"I'll be there in just a minute."

"See you then."

"Looks like another Shotgun Saturday Night," Chief Special Agent Mel Ferguson observed.

Looking through the dusty front windshield of the ATF Suburban, Hank Howard had to agree. Three sheriff's cruisers sat with their light bars blazing in front of the Long Branch Saloon. A crowd had gathered as well.

"Pull over there," Ferguson told the agent driving.

Howard watched through the window and craved a cigarette. He checked his watch. It was seven twenty-six p.m. Only three and a half hours remained before the raid on the Badlands Militia was scheduled to take place. *And now Sheriff Bolo's going to have his hands full, goddammit!* Howard's stomach flipped and lurched sickeningly as he thought about all the coming bloodshed. Ferguson hadn't backed down on his decision once. Everything was set up and ready to play out.

A moment later, Bolo's cruiser pulled to a stop in front of the bar. The sheriff got out and immediately pushed the crowd back. The deputies and bouncers had gotten control of the combatants.

"Some of those are Badlands Militia people," Trimble said. Since he'd organized the strike force operations brief, he would know.

"Hite?" Ferguson asked tensely.

Trimble took out pocket binoculars and swept the group sitting out in the middle of the street. "He's not there."

"Good. We'll still be able to catch him at the compound." Ferguson tapped the dashboard. "Okay. I've seen enough. Take us around this and let's get going. I want to be in place early."

Howard sat calmly and watched as Bolo stepped out of his car. The ATF chief special agent swallowed hard, thinking the only chance to circumnavigate Ferguson's planned invasion had just disappeared.

Ash admired the way Bolo defused the situation. With the Badlands Militia involved and the Thaedt NROTC on the opposing side, so that it looked as if the townspeople were trapped in between, things could have escalated instead of calming down.

"What happened here tonight," the sheriff thundered, walking along the boardwalk in front of the Long Branch Saloon, "is a crock. I'm not going to put up with it in my town." He looked at the militia and the midshipmen with a hard eye. "Not for a damned New York minute, I won't."

"Sheriff," one of the militiamen said, "it weren't our fault. They started it. Billy Roy asked that bitch over there"—he pointed his chin at Spike—"to dance, an' she up an' slapped his face out on the dance-room floor. She had no call to do that."

"Mabel," the sheriff barked.

Immediately, a woman deputy built along the lines of a refrigerator stepped away from one of the cruisers. Her uniform was crisp; her boots were polished. She wore a handgun that looked like small artillery and Ash thought it was a Desert Eagle. Probably a fifty-cal. "Yes, Sheriff," she said.

"Arrest Buck there and take him down to the jail," Bolo said. "Charge him with disturbing the peace, destruction of private property, interrupting the sheriff while he's talking, and I'll think of some others to tack on."

Buck started to protest. Mabel rapped him on back of the head with her PR-24 combat baton in a manner that reminded Ash of military security personnel. Buck closed his mouth but didn't look happy about it. Mabel handcuffed him and put him in the back of one of the cruisers.

"Anybody else want to interrupt me and spend the night in jail?" Bolo demanded.

No one said a word.

"Good," the sheriff said. "Now it's time to put this foolishness aside. All of you all that were involved in this fracas"—he jabbed his fingers at the militia and the midshipmen—"give your names to the deputies and get on back to where you belong or I'll run you all in. You're still going to be liable for your actions here tonight, as well as the damages you caused. I'll be in touch." He took a deep breath. "Now get out of my sight."

Ash had to admit that the sheriff gave the office flair. Not many men could have bullied that many people into doing what he wanted them to do without machine gunners covering his every move.

The midshipmen spotted Ash in the crowd and came over to him. "It wasn't our fault," Bruno protested. "Those bastards came in spoiling for a fight. One of those guys sexually assaulted Spike."

Ash looked at her. "Are you okay?"

She frowned and held herself self-consciously. "I'm fine. It wasn't anything worse than a really bad first date with a frigging octopus. Guy just wouldn't keep his hands to himself."

"They can't get away with that," Globe said. "I mean, they came in there like they could just walk all over us."

"It'll be all right," Ash said, grimly aware that time was running out on his and Bolo's plans. "We'll deal with this tomorrow. For now, just get on back to the dorms. Catch up on rack time."

Grumbling, they headed for their cars out in the parking lot.

When they cleared out of the situation, Bolo and Ash were twenty minutes behind their agreed-upon timetable. They made ten minutes of it up on the drive to the Badlands Militia farm.

*   *   *

"Do you know how to use this gear?" Ash asked, handing over the night-vision goggles.

"Does a bear shit in the woods?" Bolo growled. "Maybe this is a small town, but I do yearly training with the SWAT teams in Pierre. And I haven't forgotten everything I learned in the Green Beret."

"Fantastic," Ash said as he shucked his clothing for the black Dockers and black turtleneck he'd packed for the infiltration. He dropped the clothing into the dirt and scuffed them around. Bolo did the same with his own clothing. Most people figured to disappear in the dark all a man had to do was wear black. But that wasn't true. The night was made up of varying degrees of darkness. The brown and gray smudges from the dirt were a quick fix.

They were parked behind a copse of hardwood trees off the highway east of the Badlands Militia farm. Traffic this time of night was sparse, Bolo had said, and Ash felt confident the cars couldn't be seen from the highway or the farm. They'd brought both vehicles in case one of them failed to start. Redundancy was one key to surviving special ops. Single-point failures were always a red flag in a plan.

Dressed again, Ash pulled on the load-bearing suspenders and the NOMEX hood, then placed his gear. The nine-mil rode at his hip and he carried the .357 Magnum wheel gun under his left armpit. Then he divided the grenades between himself and Bolo.

"Grenades?" the sheriff asked.

"If you don't use 'em, bring 'em back," Ash told him. "Flash-bangs and smoke. Just trying to layer in some confusion and concealment if we need it."

Bolo frowned at the hood. "I don't care for the mask."

"Your choice," Ash said. "They're flame-retardant and bullet-resistant. Heavy, yeah, but they usually help deflect a knife slash, but not a puncture."

"Blunt trauma will scramble your eggs if you take a bullet in the face," Bolo said.

"Oh," Ash said. "I forgot." He looked at the sheriff. "Try really, *really* hard not to get shot in the head. I thought you'd learned that in the Green Beret."

Bolo looked at him. "You know, if you didn't look like Zorro or something, I'd be offended."

"Put the mask on," Ash urged. "You get to be my faithful sidekick." He reached into the rental car's trunk and took out a package of disposable cable ties big enough to double as handcuffs. "You ready?"

Bolo took a quick breath and let it out. "Yeah." He pulled on the NOMEX mask and lifted the mini-M14 range rifle he carried as his lead weapon. "Let's do it."

"Want me at point?" Ash asked.

"You think you're good enough to run it without getting us killed?" The sheriff held out a clenched fist. "Odd on three. Go."

Ash shook his fist with the sheriff. On the count of three, he stuck out one finger. So did the sheriff. "Even," Ash said, waggling his finger. "I got point." He turned and headed for the fence. He took out wire cutters and clipped the barbed-wire strands near one of the posts. Reaching into the medical kit, he took out tape and ran a quick white line around the pole. Looking back at Bolo, he said, "It's on our right going in."

"Coming out, it's on our left," Bolo said. "I got it. C'mon, you're killing the clock."

Cradling the M4, Ash jogged through the woods, avoiding the open areas where the moon burned down on the tall grass of the rolling plain. He didn't go too fast and he used the trees for cover. Twice he scared rabbits out of hiding and they bolted through the grass. Another time he came up on a deer and was past it before the animal knew he was there.

Forty-five minutes later, only six minutes behind schedule now, Ash pulled up and dropped to one knee. He rested the M4 on the ground and held the barrel with both hands as he breathed deeply to charge his lungs with oxygen. Bolo was at his heels. Together, they looked out over the farm.

Cars were parked all around the main house and the outlying buildings. The staccato throbbing of electric generators filled the night as they supplied power to the buildings. Orange glows showed the positions of men out smoking in the dark. Several of them kept walking back and forth between the buildings. A couple dozen kids chased fireflies just outside the lighted areas.

And this is where Ferguson wants to bring the ATF shock troops, Ash thought sourly. Women and kids were going to get caught in the crossfire. This was stupid on both counts. Ash didn't assign guilt just to the ATF; he also assigned the bulk of it to Devon Hite, who had chosen to place noncombatants in the center of the struggle. But the strategy was an old one. Since the birth of villages and towns, the people who had gone there to live among others had always been used to slowly encroaching forces. Those people had nowhere else to go and everything to fight for, even when they didn't agree with whoever the encroaching force was after.

"Well?" Bolo whispered.

Ash rolled back his sleeve and checked his watch, careful to keep the face pointed toward his chest so it couldn't be seen. He hadn't seen any lookouts posted, but those were generally the ones who spotted invading forces.

Half past nine. They had an hour and twenty minutes to secure ATF Agent Bobby Redmond and let the ATF know. For a quick run to the grocery store, it was all the time in the world.

"Too many buildings to investigate in the time we have left," Ash replied. "We're going to have to shave the odds."

"Agreed." Bolo looked around. "We need a man alone."

"Or two men," Ash said. "We can take two men quietly." They waited in the darkness as the minutes slipped by.

At twenty-one fifty-eight the mothers called the children into the community barracks where the kids were kept and more of the lights were turned out. Blue glows from television sets supplied by signals from satellite dishes played against the windows. Most of the men went inside, complaining about the mosquitoes and wanting to watch television.

"Closer," Bolo whispered in Ash's ear.

They worked their way closer to the main buildings, staying away from the big house where everyone seemed to gather. Voices splintered the quiet of the night, punctuated by laugh tracks. Five minutes later they reached one of the buildings that housed the generators. Glancing through the window, Ash saw two men pouring fuel into the generator tanks. They smoked cigarettes during the whole process and Ash kept expecting the building to blow at any moment. When they were finished, they headed toward the door.

"I'm telling you, Jed, they ain't gonna do nothin'. It's just a bunch of talk is what it is. Why, the sheriff come out here to go pheasant hunting today. If anything was gonna go on, he'd have said something."

"I hope you're right, Tucker," Jed said. He took a beer from his overalls pocket and cracked it.

Ash pointed at the men. Bolo nodded. Together, quiet and swift as morning fog, Ash and the sheriff lifted from the ground and went in pursuit. Ash reached the door before the two men did. He let the first one pass, then stepped in behind the second and roped an arm around Jed's neck, shutting off his wind. Ruthlessly, Ash pressed the blade of a fighting knife up against the man's neck.

Bolo slipped up behind the first man and duplicated Ash's move, only he screwed the muzzle of his pistol into the man's ear and hissed, "One word and I empty your brainpan. You understand?"

The man nodded.

Ash and Bolo walked them backward till they reached the rear of the building. Confident that the sound of the generators laboring would help cover whatever noise they would make, Ash shoved his prisoner facedown on the ground. Keeping his SIG pointed at the back of the man's head for emphasis, Ash told him to put his hands behind his back. Working one-handed, Ash lashed the man's hands together with one of the plastic ties, pulling it only taut enough to secure without cutting off blood supply. Another tie secured the man's feet.

Bolo did the same to his man.

Kneeling, knowing he was a fearsome sight in the NOMEX hood, Ash grinned at their prisoners. The problem with the generators, though, was that the noise also prevented Bolo and him from hearing anyone creeping up on them. Ash didn't want to waste time.

"What the fuck do you want?" Tucker asked.

Without a word, Bolo slapped the man across the face hard enough to jar his head against the ground. "Speak only when we ask a question."

"We only need one of you alive," Ash told them. "The other is expendable. Cooperate and we let you live. Don't help us and we'll kill you right here and take our chances with the next set." They wouldn't do that, of course, even though Ash and Bolo were trained to kill in cold blood if the situation called for it. But the militia members didn't know that. In fact, all the propaganda about the federal government that Hite had told them was coming back to haunt them now. "Nod if you understand."

Both men nodded.

"Good. Maybe both of you will wake up in the morning." Ash paused. "I want to know where the ATF agent is. I want to know what Hite has done to Bobby Redmond."

Jed started to open his mouth.

Ash slapped the man. "I didn't tell you that you could speak, did I?"

Frightened, the man shook his head. He looked about ready to cry. Ash felt bad about that. He wasn't there to terrify people. His job was all about securing objectives.

"Is Redmond alive?" Ash asked. "Nod or shake your head."

Both men nodded.

Thank God, Ash thought. If the agent's body had been disposed of there would have been no way of calling off the doomsday Ferguson had planned. "Is Redmond on the farm? Nod or shake your head."

Both men nodded again.

"Can you both tell me where? Nod or shake your heads."

Again the nods.

"Good. Now, Jed, you get to talk. I'm going to ask you 'Where?' and you're going to tell me in a quiet and polite manner." Ash looked at the man. "Where?"

"Under the stable," Jed said in a quiet, polite voice. "There's a basement."

"How do I get there?"

"Fourth stall from the south end. There's a hidden trapdoor under the straw."

"Any alarms?"

"No."

"Because if there are," Ash said, "I'm going to put a bullet through your head."

Jed shook his head.

Taking out his knife again, Ash cut the plastic tie binding the man's legs together. "Let's go."

36

Nearly half past ten p.m.

Ash walked behind his prisoner, the SIG-Sauer at the ready. The pistol was more for psychological threat. He wasn't excited about shooting someone about now. Not that he wouldn't to save his or Bolo's life, but a single shot could bring the whole encampment down on top of them.

Jed led the way, staying behind the buildings and taking advantage of the stables. The pungency of livestock filled Ash's nostrils as they slipped in the back way. The throbbing noise of the generators sounded more distant but louder trapped inside the stable's cavernous interior. A fluorescent light above each set of doors at the ends of the barn put out a soft glow that almost met in the middle, leaving a patch of darkness that made it look as if bites had been taken out of either side.

"Here." Jed pointed to the second stall on the right.

"Where?"

"Center of the stall."

Guiding his captive into the paddock, Ash sat him down in one corner and resecured his feet with one of the plastic ties. Bolo slung his weapon and retrieved a pitchfork. He shoved the tines through the straw and muck and struck wood. The rest of the barn floor appeared to be earthen.

Working quickly, Bolo scraped away the top layer of muck. As he studied his surroundings, Ash realized the paddock hadn't been used and the straw was perfectly clean. A steel ring mounted in the center of the rectangle of wood glinted. Bolo caught hold of it and pulled, lifting the door up from its recesses. Narrow stairs led downward.

"Me first," Bolo said. "You stay up top and keep a lookout."

Ash nodded and passed over the med-kit he'd brought.

Bolo took a flashlight from his own kit and headed down the stairs. Leaning down into the hole, Ash saw the ATF agent huddled and chained to an iron-framed bed against the wall in a room about eight by eight, probably the dimensions of the cell Devon Hite was going to spend the rest of his life in for kidnapping a federal agent.

"He's alive," Bolo called back, then turned his attention to the prisoner. "Going to need something to get rid of this chain. Bolt cutters, maybe."

Holding the SIG in one hand and the pen flash in the other, Ash went to a toolbox in the center of the stable. A quick search turned up a pair of hoof trimmers that looked heavy enough to cut through chain. Leaning back down into the hole, Ash passed them over.

"How is he?" Ash asked.

"Drugged. Beat up. He's been through it." Bolo applied the trimmers, growled with effort, and snapped through the links. "He's not going to make it on his own."

Dammit! Ash had known going in that transporting the agent might be a problem. But at least if he was alive there was a chance of calling off the ATF strike force.

"I need some rope," Bolo called up.

Ash found that easily and passed it down. He watched as the sheriff secured a loop around Bobby Redmond's chest and passed the end up.

"Use it to keep him steady," Bolo said.

Nodding, Ash holstered the SIG and took a double-fisted grip on the length of rope. "Ready."

"Here we go."

Redmond was groggy. He fumbled for the steps and started up. From the way he was swaying, he would never have made it to the top under his own power. Ash hand-over-handed the man up, then caught hold of an arm and extracted Redmond from the hidden cellar.

The young agent's face was strangely distorted. Using the pen flash, Ash discovered that someone had done some reconstructive surgery, maybe to keep him hidden and maybe to make it harder to identify the body later. Hite was a sick bastard, sicker than Ash had figured he was. Bolo came up from the cellar.

Ash looked at his watch. Thirty-six past. They were running out of time. He looked at Bolo. "There's no way we can do this quietly."

"No guts, no glory," Bolo said. "They've put him through it. He can't walk. We're gonna need a vehicle to get him out of here in one piece." Together, he and Ash each looped one of Redmond's arms across his shoulders and walked him toward the rear door.

"I'm going to try for one of their trucks," Ash said. "It's only a short drive to the front if we go that way. If we weren't under the time crunch, we could take Redmond out of here slowly. If we weren't so far from town, maybe escaping with him over fifty miles of highway wouldn't be so bad. But somewhere out there, Ferguson has got the National Guard. All we have to do is get out of the farm alive."

"Agreed," Bolo said. "I don't want to be here when the ATF turns this into ground zero."

"I'll be back," Ash said. He walked out into the shadows and rounded the building. Fewer militia people were out in the common grounds now. Slinging the M4, he walked to the nearest pickup, one not new enough to have antitheft devices. He leaned in through the open window and removed the dome-light cover, then the bulb. He climbed in. Using his penknife, he quickly bared a hot wire and a starter wire. They sparked when he twisted them together, and the motor turned over.

Slipping the truck into first gear, he placed the M4 in the seat next to him, let out the clutch and rolled forward.

"Hey!" someone shouted. "That's my truck!"

Ash didn't hesitate. He wheeled around in a tight semicircle and drove toward the rear of the barn. Several other people were shouting behind him now. He skidded to a stop behind the barn and got out with the M4 in his hand. "Company's coming!" he shouted to Bolo.

"Heard them. Damn, but you need to work on your stealth technique." Bolo hustled Redmond forward, having to support most of the agent's weight. Ash grabbed Redmond's other arm.

"Hey!" someone shouted behind them. "*Hey!* Somebody's got the agent out of the barn!"

"Loudmouth," Bolo said. He caught hold of the truck's tailgate latch and popped it open. Together, he and Ash muscled Redmond's almost dead weight into the bed.

Men rushed toward them. Shots cracked and ricocheted from the truck cab, punching through the glass.

Ash wheeled and fired a short burst over the heads of the men. As far as he was concerned, all of Hite's people were rednecks with their hearts in the wrong place. None of them were hardened criminals the way Ferguson thought they were.

In response to the M4's roar, the militia members dove to the ground, gripping it for their lives.

"Let's go," Bolo said.

Ash hauled himself into the cab and slipped behind the steering wheel. As he got the vehicle rolling he freed his SIG, tucking it under his right thigh in case he needed it. Rounding the barn, he got his bearings and roared straight for the main road leading out of the farm. Lights flared along his back trail, letting him know pursuit from other vehicles was already under way.

"Sheriff," Ash called, looking at his watch. It was eight minutes before eleven.

"Yeah."

"Time to call Howard and get him to have Ferguson

stand down." Ash concentrated on his driving, whip-sawing across the narrow dirt road, juddering across washboard hardpan that rattled his teeth and nearly sent him out of control. He hung on; the finish line wasn't much farther ahead.

Hank Howard's phone rang as he listened to shots cracking in the distance.

"What the hell is going on over there?" Ferguson demanded. They were in the back of a large RV that had been gutted, covered in armored plate, and made into a mobile operations command vehicle. Surveillance was provided by several wireless cameras set up around the compound and from cameras worn by the national guardsmen. The computer techs manning the equipment cycled through the camera feeds as Ferguson watched over their shoulders. He pointed at one of the screens. "There. That one. Stay with that one."

Looking at the screen as he fumbled for the phone, Howard saw a jacked-up pickup truck powering down the narrow road as if it was being chased. Other vehicles roared after it. Bright flashes showed on the screen—muzzle flashes. "Oh shit," Howard whispered as he hit the TALK button. "Howard."

"Howard! This is Bolo!"

Howard turned away from the computer screens. "I hear you, Sheriff."

Ferguson turned to glare at him.

"Ash and I have your missing agent," Bolo said. "We're in the truck leaving the farm." His voice broke and sounded out of breath, as if he were being beaten to death as he was talking.

"We've got you on-screen, Sheriff," Howard said. He moved to the computer monitors and pointed, speaking to Ferguson. "That's Sheriff Bolo. He's got Agent Redmond with him." Turning his attention back to the phone, Howard asked, "How's Redmond?"

"He's hurt, but he's alive," Bolo said, voice rising and

falling. "Tell Ferguson to call off the strike teams. Women and children are all over inside that place."

Howard lifted his eyes to meet Ferguson's. "I've got Bolo on the line. He and Lieutenant Ash Roberts entered the farm earlier on a search-and-rescue mission. They've got Redmond. He's still alive."

"You knew they were planning this," Ferguson shot back, hot gaze pinning Howard.

"There's no reason to continue with this," Howard said. "We're done. Just have the guardsmen hold the line at the highway."

"You told them what I was going to do," Ferguson went on.

"There's no reason to go any farther with this."

"You told them *when* we were going to do it," Ferguson said. "That's why they're in there right now."

"Goddammit!" Howard roared. "Don't you hear a word I'm saying? We don't have to do this!"

Ferguson lashed out unexpectedly, knocking Howard's cell phone from his hand. He leaned down to the microphone that linked him to all available units. "This is Chief Special Agent Mel Ferguson. Commence Operation Moonstalker. *Now!* Take it all down!"

When he saw the national guardsman standing on the other side of the gate Devon Hite used to keep the rest of the world at bay, Ash felt a moment of triumph thrill through him. They'd done it. Slipped ATF Agent Bobby Redmond right out from under the noses of the Badlands Militia without doing anything more than leaving a couple of guys bruised up and a little scared. Then all of that triumph drained out of him when the guardsmen on the other side of the gate opened fire.

Bullets ripped into the truck's hood and smashed through the windshield. As Ash ducked for cover, both front tires went flat, torn to shreds by the rounds. Ash held on to the steering wheel, feeling the rims shudder and jerk as they rolled across the road. Out of control, he skidded through the front gate to the farm and butted up against one of the national guard's jeeps. Sitting up, Ash was subjected to an intense white light drilling into his eyes. He could feel the weapons pointed at him as shadows moved through his peripheral vision.

"Hands on the dash!" someone yelled. "Do it now and you won't die!"

Out of breath, midsection bruised from the sudden stop, Ash put both his hands on the steering wheel. He kept his face in plain view. "I'm Lieutenant Ash Roberts of the United States Navy!" he bellowed. "I'm a friendly! Hold your fire!"

Two assault rifles pointed at Ash. The ruby discs of laser sights rested on his chest. Light streamed through the windshield and hurt his eyes. In short order, the men hauled him from the truck cab, threw him on the ground and bound his feet together and his hands behind his back. They left him lying on his face. Seconds later, Bolo and Redmond joined him.

Gunfire tore holes in the quiet of the night. Men and women screamed in terror.

Feeling trapped and helpless, Ash had no choice but to lie on the ground and listen. He couldn't hear enough from the screams or the abbreviated radio contact coming through the radios of the two men that guarded them to get a sense of what was going on. He put his face into the dirt and tried to shut it out. Something had happened. Somehow Hank Howard hadn't gotten the message that they'd taken Redmond into custody. Rolling his head to the side, he looked at Bolo.

The sheriff was facedown on the ground as well, but his eyes were closed and tears turned his cheeks muddy. Ash knew that Bolo wasn't completely on that farm or near that battle. Part of him was back in Vietnam, at Mi Chu, listening to the screams of innocents. Ash knew a warrior's wars were never truly far behind him.

Clad in body armor, his breath rasping against the helmet's mask, Hank Howard followed the national guardsmen out of the truck and through the farm. Powerful flashlights raked the buildings and moved rapidly across the bodies lying between the vehicles. Many of them had been caught out in the open. Most of them, thankfully, were men, but here and there Howard saw dead and wounded women and children. The youngest was a boy, no more than two or three.

Seeing the dead youngster, Howard gave in to the nausea swirling through his stomach. He cracked open the mask and threw up. One of the young guardsmen did the same thing.

"Goddammit!" the young soldier said, wiping his mouth with his sleeve. "Goddammit, they didn't have to make us kill them!"

Howard didn't say anything. He didn't fault the militia members. He faulted Devon Hite and Mel Ferguson. Both of those men had known it would come to this. In fact, each of them—for reasons of his own—had wanted this to happen. Each of them had also wanted to win, to prove his point. Howard knew that wasn't going to happen now.

He took a handkerchief from his pocket, blotted his mouth, took a fresh grip on his pistol, and kept moving through the swirling layers of smoke that drifted over the area. The guardsmen were going door to door now, knocking, throwing in canisters of CS, and then clearing each building. The tear gas was designed to debilitate without leaving any permanent damage.

The action went quickly now. The living members of the Badlands Militia—men, women, and children—were herded into the parking area in front of the main house. They were quickly bound hand and foot.

A motor shrilled to Howard's left. Spinning in that direction, he brought his pistol up and stared as eight headlights and fog lights aboard a pickup suddenly barreled down on top of him. Howard fired two rounds, putting them both through the windshield, though he didn't think he'd hit the driver.

Careening wildly, the pickup missed Howard by inches, only because he dove for cover. He swiveled on his hip, braced his right elbow in his left hand, and started tracking the fleeing vehicle's tires. Without pausing, the pickup driver drove into a small group of militia people who had their hands up, knocking most aside but leaving one sprawled on the ground. The pickup finally came to a halt against the huge bulk of an earthmover parked next to the barn. The man got out, dragging a shotgun behind him. Before he could bring it to his shoulder, yelling curses the whole time, several rounds from the rifles of the guardsmen struck him and left him on the ground.

Sonofabitch! Howard thought as he looked over the scene. The carnage he saw around him was worse than anything he'd imagined Ferguson was capable of. He took a deep breath to calm himself but couldn't keep his hands from shaking. In all his years with the Bureau, he'd never been through anything like this.

"You okay, sir?" A guardsman grabbed Howard by the shoulder and straightened him. The young soldier's face was tense and pale.

"I am," Howard said. But he knew he was lying.

Then the soldier was gone and the killing continued.

Devon Hite ran up the stairs of the house he shared with his five wives. He'd been in bed with two of them when the warning about the abduction of Bobby Redmond had rung out. He'd pulled on a pair of jeans and gone outside, yelling over the radio to get some sense of what was going on. Then the attack had come. He'd chased the women and the children, some of them his, into the cellar below.

The United States government had come for him. Even though he'd told all his men that would happen one day, Hite had never truly thought they would. Worst-case scenario, after Waco and Ruby Ridge, he'd felt certain the government would find some way to ambush him in court. That would only have drawn more people to his cause in the long run. He looked forward to confrontations like that. Of course, he'd prepared for war, just in case.

As he fed a magazine into the CAR-15 he'd picked up from a local gun and knife sale, then had modified for three-round burst, his thoughts flew to the T-72 tank they had at the hidden bunker. If they had the tank now, the battle outside would go much differently. But he'd believed the ATF would have negotiated a warrant for his arrest or for search and seizure of weapons before a situation would have come to this.

Barefooted, dressed in jeans and a flak jacket he'd picked up at the same sale, Hite ran to one of the second-story bedrooms. Other people lived in the house with him. Everything at the farm was shared. Lights from below strobed the room as he rushed inside and took up a position at the window. Kneeling, he brought the CAR-15 to his shoulder and took aim at a shadow running across the open area. He led it slightly, and then squeezed the trigger.

The bullets slammed into the running man and knocked him sideways. A flashlight beam fell over him briefly, revealing the now-bloody face of Gerald Tompkins, one of Hite's militiamen.

"Shit!" Hite snarled, taking aim again. This time he had one of the guardsmen in his sight. He squeezed through two three-round bursts, cutting into the soldier's knees below the body armor. Then, when the man was on his stomach, his helmet rolling a few feet away, Hite punched three bullets through the man's head and left him sprawled limply on the ground.

For a few short minutes, Hite went unnoticed in his sniper's nest. He brought down two more guardsmen. Then someone caught sight of him. Bullets ripped into the window frame and tore loose a confetti of splinters that sprayed over him. Hite ducked and slithered away to the bedroom across the hall.

Footsteps pounded up the stairs to Hite's left. He took cover in the doorway, still seated, and swung the assault rifle toward the sound of the running feet. A face appeared for an instant, and then ducked back.

"Devon, dammit! It's me!"

"Come ahead, Ben," Hite called after recognizing the man's face. He shifted the CAR-15 back into the room.

"Thought you were going to take my head off," Ben grumbled as he came up the stairs carrying a Marlin thirty-thirty lever-action hunting rifle.

"You should have called ahead." Hite took up a position beside the window and peered out.

"Didn't know if you were still alive." Ben folded himself into position on the other side of the window. "These bastards are cutting us to pieces."

"I know."

"You told us this could happen." Ben shook his head. "I just didn't see it. Not without us doing something to set 'em off."

"They're afraid of us," Hite replied. But he knew he hadn't believed the government would send in troops. "The fear in them just got too strong."

"We need to get out of here," Ben said. "Live to fight another day and all that."

"I know."

"We can get lawyers now," Ben went on. "We can't stand up to 'em out here, we'll take our chances in court. Even if we lose, we're going to bring more people over to our side. If the government's gonna attack us, them other groups gotta see that one day they'll attack them, too."

Hite knew that was true. Many of the militia groups used paranoia for fuel. But as he knew tonight, that paranoia was real. Hite's mind was on more than lawyers, though. He still had the tank out there. From the day he'd found out the T-72 was on the market till the day it arrived, he'd dreamed of what the tank could do. No one had ever run a tank against the government shock troops before. Now it was time to see how those teams would fare when the war was brought to them.

"All right," Hite said. He nodded toward the back of

the house. "The woods start right back there." The woods started less than thirty feet from the house. His wives kept a small vegetable garden in between the house and the trees. The ground was soft enough to break his fall from the second floor.

Before they could move, a gas canister exploded through the side window and plopped into the center of the floor. For a moment, Hite thought he was dead. Then, instead of exploding, the canister started spewing white gas. At the first whiff, Hite's sinuses and eyes started burning. Tears spilled down his cheeks as his vision blurred and he started hacking and coughing almost at once. He forced himself up and through the back window. Outside, he ran quietly, staying low across the slanted roof. He carried the CAR-15 in both hands.

"There's a man on the roof," someone shouted.

The roof vibrated under Hite's feet. Counter-vibrations told him Ben had followed him from the room. Hite hoped the guardsmen had Ben in their sights, not him. Shots rang out. For a moment he thought he'd surely be hit. Then he heard Ben yelp in pain behind him and slam into the roof.

At the end of the roof, Hite couldn't help looking back. It was human nature. Or, at least, it was his nature. Ben tumbled in a loose sprawl down the roof and landed in a heap on the ground. Maybe he was dead. *Another martyr to the cause,* Hite thought. Then he turned and leaped from the roof's edge. The drop was only a little more than ten feet. He landed on his feet, the assault rifle still tight in his hands. He ran again, breathing hard now, his eyes and his lungs still stinging from the damned tear gas that had flooded the room.

He was only a few feet short of the trees when the spotter lights fell over him. Four ruby laser spotting lights danced on the ground before him, letting Hite know he was covered from several sides.

"Stop!" a commanding voice shouted.

Hite considered for only a moment. He didn't want to die. He didn't want to be a martyr. He wanted to be the man that mourned the martyrs and called for a day of reckoning against the United States government. That man would live longer. And be famous. Maybe even be a national leader himself one day.

But the trees were so close.

He plunged into them, dodging to escape the spotter lamps and the laser sights. Branches whipped at his face. His chest felt too tight; he couldn't catch his breath. A guardsman rose up from the darkness ahead of him, rifle leveled.

"Halt!" the man shouted, but Hite was already firing and the soldier was already firing. Lightning flickered in the man's hands. Sledgehammers slammed against Hite's chest, knocking the wind from him. Off balance, he tumbled into the brush and tried to get up. He was on his knees, hunting for his rifle, when the guardsman reached him. Mercilessly, the man stroked Hite with the stock of his M4.

A comet exploded inside Hite's head.

37

Ash sat cross-legged on the ground next to a National Guard ten-ton truck and watched flames from the burning building lick the dark sky. Bolo sat beside him. Neither of them said much. There was nothing to say. Every now and again, someone inside the farm yelled in pain or fear. None of the Badlands Militia was fighting back now and the invasion had turned into a rescue.

Ambulances from several counties had arrived. EMTs ran rescue missions into the farm, separating the wounded from the dead. Reporters from several news agencies had arrived as well. After a while, a gray-haired man in a blue suit parked a car nearby and approached the sheriff. The guardsman standing sentry blocked his path for just a moment, but the man flipped open his wallet and the young soldier stood down. The man stopped in front of Bolo.

"Sheriff," the man said.

"Doc," Bolo acknowledged.

"You all right?" The man leaned over Bolo and did a quick inspection in a thoroughly professional manner. "You appear to be all right."

"I am," Bolo said. "Dr. Peter Watson, this is Lieutenant Ash Roberts. Ash, Doc is a good friend."

"You doing okay, son?" Doc asked in a gentle voice. Looking at the man closer up, Ash figured that Doc Watson was in his late sixties or early seventies. His hair was gray. Round lenses reflected the flames in the distance. His grip was surprisingly strong.

"I am," Ash responded.

"Good. That's good." Doc glanced back at Bolo. "Why do they have you trussed up?"

"The FBI doesn't much like us," Bolo answered. "I thought you were retired."

"I was. I am." Doc lifted his shoulders and dropped them. "I just had to come out . . . see if I could help or if anybody needed it. I'm just an old warhorse. Something bad happens, I come on out. I don't know any other way to be." He shook his head. "The media is making a mess of the reporting."

"You can always count on them for that," Bolo said.

Doc unfolded a knife. "Let me see your hands."

"Aiding and abetting, Doc?" Bolo asked.

"Are you a criminal?" Doc bent over with a little trouble.

"No."

"Going to be charged with anything?"

"I don't know."

"Plan on fighting it if you are?"

"Every inch of the way," Bolo said.

"Then I'll take my chances," Doc replied. He sawed the disposable cuffs off the sheriff's wrists.

"Hey," the young national guardsman said, stepping over quickly. "What the hell do you think you're doing?"

Doc stood erect, half a head taller than the young soldier. "Stand down, Corporal," the old man barked. "These men are not enemies."

"Yes, sir," the soldier said, backing a step away.

"I'm taking full responsibility for them."

The soldier went away.

Ash knew that if he or Bolo tried to leave the area the soldier would doubtless call for reinforcements. He held out his hands when the sheriff waved to him. Bolo cut through the disposable cuffs. It was a relief to have the plastic off his wrists. Prickles of returning sensation fired through his fingertips. Bolo cut his own feet free, and then handed the knife to Ash.

"Doc was First Marine Division in Korea," Bolo stated quietly. "He was one of the survivors of Chosin Reservoir."

Ash sawed at the restraint around his ankles. He knew about Chosin. It was one of the bloodiest battles of the Korean War, and still an example of the most savage small-unit engagements in history. The American forces had been routed and left miles of dead, enemies as well as their own, in the bitter snow and freezing waters and mud.

Moving slowly, Doc sat with them next to the over-sized truck tires. He reached into his pocket and took out his cell phone. "You might give Little Feather a call," he said to Bolo. "Let her know you're still alive."

Bolo took the phone, hesitated a moment, and dialed.

Ash sat quietly, wondering how bad it was going to be.

Hank Howard walked through the dead zone. Despite the fact that the national guardsmen held the area now, Howard was still gun-shy. He chain-smoked, taking care to keep his spent butts in his jacket pocket. God only knew how forensics would deal with all the chaos spread out around him, but Howard knew they had already been called onto the scene and would have to reconstruct events as best as they could.

God, what a nightmare, Howard thought. He gazed down at a dead little girl staring sightlessly up into the night. She was maybe ten or eleven. The bullet that had killed her had punched through her heart. During the past hour and a half Howard had seen seven dead kids, fourteen dead women, and thirty-six dead men. He thought they were all different, but maybe he'd seen some of them more than once. He'd walked around in circles a lot, trying to figure out what the hell it was he was supposed to do.

He couldn't help feeling that this was his fault. If he had gotten Bobby Redmond back *before* Mel Ferguson had gotten involved, none of this would have happened. *And Redmond might be the one who was dead now,* he told himself in almost the same breath. *Devon Hite had set up this war. It's his fault.* Howard tried to believe that, but he struggled with it. Ultimately, it was all their faults. It should have stopped before it had come to this.

Tenderly, Howard knelt and closed the little girl's eyes with his fingertips. Her skin was already cool to the touch.

Ash tensed as Mel Ferguson made his way to them. Quietly, Ash stood, his arms at his sides. Bolo and Doc Watson stood with him, presenting a solid front.

Ferguson stopped and glared at the three of them. "Did you release these men, corporal?" the ATF agent demanded.

"Sir," the corporal said politely, "I did not. The civilian with them did that, sir."

"And you allowed it?" Ferguson gave the man a hard look.

"No, sir. I chose not to interfere with the doctor's actions. They were not permitted to leave this area. They didn't try."

Cursing, Ferguson turned his attention to the three men. "You will not discuss anything that transpired here tonight," the ATF chief said.

"You had no reason to invade that farm," Bolo growled. "We called. We had your missing agent in custody."

"For all I knew," Ferguson said, "you were part of Hite's happy band of homicidal maniacs. I went with the plan I had in place, and I have to admit I wasn't sure we were going to succeed." He drew a deep breath and smiled. "But we did. We *really* did."

"You murdered women and children," Bolo growled.

"Collateral damage." Ferguson gave a small sigh. "There was some loss of life. You can't do this kind of operation without breaking a few eggs." He paused and stared into Bolo's dark gaze. "Everyone here on the farm was a target, Sheriff. That couldn't be helped. In the darkness, with the terrain . . ." He let the rest remain unspoken.

"You chose the time and the place, you bastard," Bolo said.

"Wrong!" Ferguson shouted. "I didn't choose for Hite to take his little group of miscreants and live apart from the rest of us. I didn't decide for them to capture an ATF agent and hold him hostage. You don't just get to walk away from this country, Sheriff. Even living out here, Devon Hite and the Badlands Militia still reaped the fruits of what the United States has to offer. Who do you think puts miles of safe country between their pissant farm and someone else that would do them harm?"

"That's not how they see it," Bolo said.

"Fuck them!" Ferguson said. "Let them try living apart in China. Or Russia. Or some third-world nation. See how they like living somewhere that people drop like flies when sickness invades or somebody else decides they want to be king of the world." He paused and took a breath. "But not *here*. Not on lands fought and paid for by true patriots and true dreamers. I'd be happy to airdrop their asses anywhere else they want to go, but they can't stay here."

A news helicopter thundered by overhead, immediately warned off by a National Guard helicopter.

"I love this country," Ferguson said. "I won't see a few pockets of resistance sour or undermine what we're doing here. I thought maybe you'd understand that."

"There were other ways," Bolo said.

Ferguson breathed hard, obviously in the grip of strong emotion. "You don't understand."

"Yeah, I do," Bolo said quietly. "You wanted to play God, and playing God isn't free. Those people have paid the bill."

Ash was surprised when Ferguson actually threw a punch. Despite the evening's events, Ash believed the ATF chief still had command of himself.

The blow hurtled at Bolo's face. The sheriff never flinched, but his left hand came up and caught Ferguson's fist. The *smack* of the impact was loud. Bolo held onto Ferguson's hand, trapping it in midair.

"We're leaving," Bolo said. With slow deliberation, he pushed the ATF chief's hand back and away. "Now."

Ferguson stood there breathing hard for a moment. Then he said, "Corporal."

"Yes, sir," the young soldier replied.

"Let them go."

Bolo led the way away from the ATF chief. At first, Ash figured they were in for a long walk back to their cars, but the Fairly sheriff's office had responded as well. Bolo had Deputy Mabel drive them back to their cars. Doc joined Bolo.

Bolo stood outside his cruiser and looked at Ash. "I don't feel like taking this home just yet."

Ash didn't either. He couldn't imagine going back to the campus or Bolo's house and quietly turning in. His stomach still churned and his heart still pounded a little faster than average. None of what had happened was right. Something had to be done, but not what Ferguson had orchestrated. Freeing Bobby Redmond, who had been transported to the hospital in Fairly and was currently doing well, had been a start.

"Me neither," Ash said.

"I know a bar out on the highway on the other side of Fairly," Bolo said. "I'll show you the way." He climbed into his cruiser with Doc on the passenger side, and Ash followed.

Gus Iverson, an old man with a walrus mustache and a laugh like an AK-47 on automatic, owned the Highway Tavern, so named because it was located on the highway. He knew hundreds of bad jokes and laughed at the conclusion of each.

Less than an hour after his arrival at the bar, Ash was working on a serious drunk, the first he'd had in a long time. He noticed that he and Bolo tended to get shitfaced in the same way, just quietly relaxed as if they were sipping tea. However, Doc and Gus turned out to be obnoxious, constantly bantering and exchanging jokes. They leaned over the bar like two grade-school boys out of sight of the teacher.

Ash's attention, like that of the sheriff, was riveted on the television behind the bar. The news coming out of the Badlands Militia farm was frenetic and filled with speculation.

"Bureau of Alcohol, Tobacco and Firearms Chief Special Agent Mel Ferguson assures me," a young female reporter said, "that the Badlands Militia had a veritable armory on site." The wind blew her long blonde locks and fire burned behind her.

" 'Veritable armory,' " Bolo said, and his words were only slightly slurred. "If you count squirrel guns and hunting rifles, which everybody in this neck of the woods owns."

The camera cut to footage of men wearing BATF gear and national guardsmen carrying weapons out of one of the buildings. The rifles and pistols were laid on tarps in the middle of the ground.

"What precipitated the attack tonight?" the news anchor asked.

"Chief Ferguson is declining comment at the moment," the reporter said, "but the rumor I've heard is that the BATF came in after one of their own. Suspected leader of the Badlands Militia Devon Hite is believed to have captured a young BATF agent and has been holding him hostage."

"Is the agent all right?"

"He is," the reporter confirmed. "He's been taken out of the area to a hospital. It's believed he's at Fairly. We're following up on that and if we get any more word, we'll let you know."

"What about Devon Hite?"

"Hite was taken into custody," the reporter said.

"Now there's a surprise," Bolo said. "I didn't think

Hite would survive. I figured that Ferguson and his team would kill him."

Ash silently agreed.

The reporter and anchor talked for a little while longer. Footage rolled of Hite's days with the Baron's Itch and "Be Healed." Other footage rolled of people who were for and against the Badlands Militia. The news, Ash decided, was slanted. None of the interviewees in favor of the militia seemed to be articulate or well informed, just knee-jerk separatists who had a skewed view of what the federal government was.

"At present, Hite is being held under BATF supervision somewhere in Fairly," the news reporter said.

Ash looked at Bolo. "Did you know that?" The sheriff had remained in contact with his deputies who were on the outskirts of the Badlands Militia farm.

Bolo shook his head, and then drained his glass. "No, I surely did not."

"Doesn't make sense," Ash said. "They should get Hite out of the area."

Gus came over and drew another beer for the sheriff, then added a shot of whiskey. The bar had closed some time ago, but Gus hadn't minded staying open for them.

"They should," Bolo agreed. "But Ferguson's going to milk this for as much publicity as he can. If he took Hite to Pierre or one of the bigger cities in the state, even back to Minnesota and St. Paul, he'd lose some of the attention he's getting now." He paused and downed the whiskey shot. "Plus, remaining on site here he can take care of any loose ends." He looked at Ash. "Like making certain the BATF hostage doesn't remember who actually saved him. Or watching over a sheriff or a Navy SEAL that might be inclined to give their stories of what happened."

Ash and Bolo had already discussed that possibility. In the end, it was their word against the BATF chief's. Neither of them wanted the grief bucking the federal agency would cause.

"Your friend's coming in later this morning, isn't he?" Bolo asked.

Blearily, Ash rolled his wrist over and looked at his watch. It was twenty past three in the morning. Wild's plane was scheduled to land at nine. He had time to crowd maybe four hours' sleep in between. "Yeah. I'd better be going." He reached into his pocket for money.

"Oh no you aren't," Gus said, coming down the bar again. "Ain't neither of you two fit to drive. You aren't leaving here. I got cabins in the back where you can bunk up."

Ash wanted to argue, but he knew it was the alcohol talking. He thought he could probably drive—hell, he'd been in worse shape in the past, and Fairly wasn't exactly a bustling little metropolis—but the idea of stumbling into Little Feather's home drunk in the middle of the night was unappealing. Not to mention the possibility of being caught doing so by the media.

"All right," Ash said. "Show me the way." He just wanted to put tonight behind him.

Pain ripped Devon Hite out of the darkness. The throbbing filled his head; it felt as if it would blow his eyeballs from their sockets. He couldn't move. Something restrained his hands and feet. Opening his eyes hurt. First it was the movement of parts actually working, and then it was the stabbing ferocity of the light burning on the ceiling above him. He knew instantly he wasn't in jail. Gazing around, he decided he was in a hotel, in the bathtub in the bathroom. Television voices came through the open bathroom door. He couldn't remember being brought here from the farm. The last thing he recalled was the rifle exploding into his face. His mouth was puffy and swollen and his front teeth felt loose. He still tasted the coppery flavor of blood when he swallowed.

Looking up between his arms, he found metal handcuffs securing his hands to the faucet assembly. Manacles held his feet. He pulled on the handcuffs, putting his weight into the effort. The chain grated along the faucet but didn't come loose because there wasn't enough slack to get it over the knobs. If he tried, he thought maybe he could break them off, but the operation wouldn't be quiet.

As if to underscore that, two young guys in casual wear filled the bathroom door. They carried pistols in shoulder rigs.

"Hey asshole," one of them said with a cocky grin. "Looks like you're about washed up."

Hite didn't say anything. It was hard keeping quiet, but he didn't want to give them the satisfaction of a response. He relaxed back into the bathtub. The soap by the sink on the other side of the bathroom advertised the Carriage House Hotel, Fairly, South Dakota.

"You ask me," the other man said, "we put him in the wrong facility." Both of them laughed at the joke.

They taunted him for a few more minutes, but Hite just lay back in the bathtub and worked on breathing. He'd learned a long time ago that when nothing else seemed to be going right, he could always do that. Inside his mind, he retreated back to the days when he'd played with Baron's Itch, letting the music match the throbbing pain in his head.

They hadn't killed him. They hadn't taken him out of Fairly. And no matter what they had done at the farm, the ATF hadn't gotten all of his people. Hite figured he still had a chance, and he intended to make them all pay when he did. He breathed deeply, letting the music thunder inside his mind.

38

Ash stood awaiting the passengers filing off of Flight 1187 from Minneapolis. The three and a half hours of sleep hadn't helped; he still felt hung over. If he'd been meeting anyone but Wild at the airport, he would have been tempted to leave a message that he wasn't coming and sack out for a few more hours.

Bolo had been up and gone by the time Ash awakened. Gus Iverson had confirmed that the sheriff had shaved, showered, and put on a fresh change of clothes he had in his cruiser. Ash had had to settle for the clothes he'd taken off in favor of the black outfit he'd worn on the raid on the farm. A quick phone call to Bolo had let Ash know the sheriff was dealing with the fallout from the raid. Hite hadn't been well liked around the town, but now he was a folk hero next to the ATF. The national news had picked up the local story and was having a field day, as well.

The crowd wandered past Ash, heading for the baggage carousel, the rental-car agencies, and the cab stands. Other people, singly and in groups, met the arrivals and went off. When the crowd thinned, Ash began to wonder if something had happened to Wild or if something had come up, or why Wild hadn't called to let him know he'd missed the flight. Ash could only imagine Wild trucking through the airport and not surrendering to assistance. That wasn't how Wild was made.

Then Ash saw him.

Wild wore casual clothing, gray Dockers and a burgundy Dri-Fit mock tee that showed off his upper body. He looked like a surfer, all moussed blond curls and bright smile. During his hospital stay, he'd lost some of the tan he normally kept, but he looked fit, healthy. Wraparound sunglasses with bright metallic gold lenses were pushed up on his head. Earbuds for an iPod lay coiled around his neck. He talked with a young flight attendant who looked like a hard-body herself and it was obvious what was going on.

Ash grinned. Wild was back.

After a minute, the flight attendant took Wild's cell phone and punched in a number. She walked away, hips working beneath her dress. Wild stood and watched her go.

"Making friends?" Ash said.

Wild turned and smiled broadly. "The docs told me to play nice. Otherwise they'll increase my rehab. Personally, I think the nurses don't want to let me go."

"Too bad your friend had to leave. Maybe you could have gotten better acquainted."

"Maybe *longer* acquainted," Wild said, "but not better. Would you believe she didn't even get my name while we were in the bathroom together?"

Ash looked at his friend. "No way."

"I mean, if we hadn't had to be quiet in the back of the plane—kind of on stealth mode, you know—whose name would she have been yelling out in the throes of passion?"

Shaking his head, Ash didn't doubt it for a moment. He remembered the lifestyle Wild had enjoyed when they'd reconnected at the Pentagon. Ash had been certain then that the women and late nights were going to do to Wild what enemy fire hadn't been able to do.

"And did you see her walking away from here?" Wild asked. "I mean, she was *throwing* it. That was a definite challenge, man. She's not through with me. If I'd had to take much more of that, I wouldn't have needed this prosthetic." He slapped his leg. "Hell, I could have walked out of here on my woody!"

"So when do you see her again?" Ash asked.

"Monday night. She's got a layover. I told her I'd have a place." Wild looked at Ash. "I do have a place, right?"

"I've been staying with the sheriff," Ash said.

"Hope he doesn't embarrass easy."

"We're not staying with him. I scored a couple cabins for us."

Wild's eyes gleamed. "Stand by for heavy rolls, then. Wall-to-wall Wild. There's not much more a woman could want. I'll have to call her and see if she has friends."

"I think I can manage my own entertainment."

"Dude," Wild said, shaking his head, "that invitation wasn't for you. *I'm* the one that's been locked up in the hospital. I'm working a five-day liberty. I can exhaust myself. I've got a professional rehabilitation team waiting on me when I return to Bethesda. I didn't come out here to make their jobs easy."

"You carry as much luggage as a woman," Ash griped as he pulled Wild's fourth suitcase from the carousel.

"Hey, it's a lot of work to look this pretty," Wild argued. "Besides, I didn't know what the local flora and fauna had to offer. Country girls. Punk girls. Rock and roll. Business types. You get out in these small towns, you find all kinds. I wanted to dress appropriately. This is *not* going to be a dry five days."

Ash could believe it. Wild didn't move with quite the same grace as he had before his injury, but the moves were there. He was balanced and agile on the artificial limb. The only thing that seemed off at all was the ankle work. There was a hinge joint, which allowed some movement, but it wasn't the same as the natural joint.

"I move good on it," Wild said, noticing Ash's interest. "Not as good, but I'm getting there. The main problem is the load-bearing. That's just not possible at the moment. The docs tell me I'll get there. I'm not going to make liars of them." He paused. "But it won't be easy."

"Good to know," Ash said, but he knew that both of them were dodging the obvious question of what the infirmity was going to do to Wild's career. Wild was good at computers too, but he hadn't gone through SEAL training to be a desk jockey.

"What I'm saying, homo, before you get all Walton's Mountain on me, is that we're going to need help with the luggage," Wild said. "I don't want the one-legged man to have to ask for it."

"So I'm supposed to look old and incapable?"

"Dude," Wild said, "look at you. You came to pick me up at the airport hung over and in clothes you slept in. You ask me, that's old and incapable. At least your pants are dry."

"You know," Ash said, "I was thinking maybe I'd planned a day that would be too strenuous for you. Now—I find I just don't care. And if the mids make fun of you because you can't keep up, don't come crying to me."

"So what's on tap?"

Ash looked around and spotted a skycap, waved the guy down, and pointed to the four pieces of luggage.

"We had a hairy night last night," Ash said.

"I saw the news. It looks like the ATF screwed the pooch royale."

"They did, I'm afraid. But that's another story. First I thought we'd take the mids on a little live-fire exercise."

"Out in the Wild, Wild West?" Wild grinned. "Dude, what are you going to shoot at? Tin cans or rattlesnakes?"

"Actually, there's an outdoor gun range near the airport. Police and sheriff's departments in the area use it to train personnel. Supposed to be good. Moving targets, popups, that kind of thing."

"Sounds like fun."

"Yeah, I figured we could show the mids how a tough-guy SEAL handles his ordnance."

"With both hands. It's big ordnance."

"I thought maybe you could hold a cigarette between your teeth," Ash said. "I could shoot it. You can do it with or without the blindfold. But I have to tell you, I don't think they'll be as impressed if you use the blindfold."

It only made sense that Wild would come with his own weapons. One of the pieces of luggage was filled with an arsenal of pistols, a takedown sniper rifle, and an assortment of combat and clasp knives. He'd flipped it open on one of the beds in the motel they'd rented near the range. Transporting weapons through the airline was legal as long as they were declared.

"Afraid they were all out of weapons in South Dakota?" Ash asked.

"Like I said, the news has been full of the Badlands Militia," Wild said.

"That's just an excuse."

"It is." Wild sat on the bed and took out a ninemillimeter. He ejected the magazine, and then filled it with rounds from one of the several boxes he carried. Once the magazine was filled to capacity he inserted it into the pistol, worked the slide to chamber a round, then ejected the magazine and filled it to capacity once more. He put the pistol on safety and snugged it into a shoulder holster. "They didn't let me play with my weapons while I was in the hospital." He smiled and shrugged. "Well, I guess I could have played with the old pink torpedo, but I'd rather *have* that played with." He used the remote control and checked the menu. "News or porn?"

"I get a choice?"

Wild looked at him. "I know there's something you're not telling me. The militia thing popped last night. You show up in yesterday's clothes, hung over, and smelling like wood smoke and cordite."

"You don't miss much."

"There's some things I can do by Braille," Wild assured him. "So what's it going to be? Local news to keep up with the militias? Or *Debbie Versus the Anal Intruder?*"

"News."

"These cabins you rented?" Wild changed channels to the local news. "Do they get cable? Or do we have to buy a stash of porn before we go there?"

"I don't know."

"You got a number so we can call and check, right?"

"I do." Ash glanced at the television. The local news was still filled with the Badlands Militia invasion.

"Go take a shower. You can borrow some of my clothes. Unless you want to show up looking like shit in front of the mids."

Ash knew Wild was right. Inside the shower, he turned the water up to near scalding and relaxed as clouds of steam filled the bathroom. Standing braced against the shower, he let the water rush over his body and take away the aches from the night before. His wrists and ankles still bore bruises from the disposable restraints. Nightmares had threaded through his dreams last night, mixing up the faces of those he'd seen dead in other places with those he imagined dead at the farm. The number of men, women, and children was at twenty-six. Five of them had been less than sixteen years of age. The youngest had been two. What Ferguson had authorized was unforgivable.

"You okay in there?" Wild shouted through the door.

"I'm fine," Ash said.

"Then hurry up and we'll talk about it."

Mechanically, Ash showered.

The door opened and Wild came in. "I'm putting some stuff out for you to use, essentials. And by essential, I mean they're essential for you to use if you're going to be around me." He left.

When Ash finished with the shower, he dried and looked at the array of deodorants, body sprays, mousse, and other things that he couldn't identify. For a guy trained to live in the mud and eat insects and raw pig entrails, Wild took his grooming seriously. A special-ops guy couldn't do that in the field, though. Cologne or gel was a dead giveaway that could get a man killed.

Wild had also left clothing—denim cargo pants covered in pockets and a skin-tight blue muscle shirt with NAVY stenciled on it in highway yellow, as well as underwear and socks—on the counter. Ash shaved quickly and dressed.

"Damn if you don't look more human," Wild said when Ash returned to the room.

"I feel it, too."

"Then talk to Uncle Wild. Let me know all that's wrong."

Ash started to speak but stopped when the news went to a story about the previous evening's battle. Together, they listened as the reporter spoke about the "arguably unprovoked" attack on the Badlands Militia farm where "overanxious" national guardsmen had gone toe-to-toe with "settlers" in an effort to free a captured ATF agent who was rumored to have been kidnapped but might have wandered off on his own. About halfway through the feature, a knock sounded on the door.

"You want to get that?" Wild asked. "Save me from getting up?"

"Sure." Ash answered the door and found a Chinese-takeout delivery person standing there. She was in her twenties and stunning to boot.

"On second thought," Wild said, getting up from the bed, "I ordered it. I should pay for it."

"Sure." Ash backed off and watched Wild work his magic. With his surfer good looks and innate charm, he had a phone number *and* a date before he paid for the delivery.

"Gonna be a busy five days," Wild commented as he carried the cartons of food to the small table by the window.

"I see that," Ash said. "I'm beginning to wonder if you're going to have time to visit."

"I have to stay busy while you're teaching school," Wild protested.

Ash left the room long enough to go next door to the convenience store and pick up a twelve-pack. When he returned, Wild had the food spread out on the table.

Wild sat in his chair, then pulled up his right pants leg and unstrapped the prosthetic, taking it off and tossing it onto the nearest bed. He massaged his stump but, for the first time since Ash had known him, seemed a little self-conscious. "Kind of unnerves you, doesn't it?"

"It's different," Ash said. "That's all. It'll take some getting used to. But you're still you, Wild. That's all anybody could ask for."

"I know." Wild returned his gaze full measure. "I could be bitter about this. The docs are expecting it at some point. But I'm not going to let myself. You can get trapped in bitterness and you'll never take another step. I'm going to take steps. I don't know what's in store for me, but whatever it is, I'm going to be standing to see it coming. One leg or two, I was trained to be a Navy SEAL. When they bury me, that's what they'll be burying: a SEAL."

Ash passed a beer over before cracking one open for himself and offering a toast: "SEALs."

"SEALs," Wild said, clinking his can.

They downed the first one in a rush, and then worked on the meal as Ash told his story.

"You and Sheriff Bolo had the ATF guy out of the line of fire before the Bureau went in?" Wild asked when Ash had finished recounting last night's events.

"We did."

"Then Ferguson called the strike because he wanted to make a point."

Ash nodded and picked through his fried rice and mu shu pork. He surprised himself by having an appetite.

"Guy's an asshole," Wild said.

"Government's full of them. That's no secret to you and me."

"You know what the problem is, don't you?" Wild asked.

"With what?"

"The militia issue?"

Ash only halfway expected Wild to be serious about his answer.

"The world's getting too big for a lot of people," Wild said. "It's coming at them too fast. Over the television. Affecting their jobs. Causing havoc with the prices they pay for everyday things like gasoline, milk, eggs, and bread. Utilities. The world is becoming a global market-place. Buying and selling truly knows no boundaries now. It was one thing when local stores started getting affected by Internet businesses that undercut their prices on electronics and everything else. But now everything seems like it's getting affected by things most people have never really heard of. Jobs are being outsourced to foreign countries. Major industries are shutting down here because the price of business has gotten too great. Now the jobs that these guys thought would last them all their lives is gone. Dust. And they don't know why. Hell, here in the West in these small communities, every-body was tied to the land. As long as you had the land, you were going to be all right."

"Now that isn't true either," Ash said.

"No," Wild said. "It isn't. Granddad was lucky to keep the farm. Few other people were, after him."

"You sound like you understand this."

"It's easy to understand," Wild said. "This kind of thing has happened all throughout history. Businesses and industries change civilization. And when those busi-nesses and industries undergo changes, it's going to hit the populace, too. But these people can't just step away from the government. What they need to do is start edu-cating themselves about what they need to do."

"A college course isn't—"

"I'm not talking about a college course or a PhD There are plenty of MBAs in business driving cabs. They have to realize that expectation has to meet preparation.

The world is changing too fast. Even the way you and I grew up, Ash, that's different than what today's elementary-school kids are going through. There's no way they're going to have the same lives their parents did. But that's what their parents expect and what they train these kids to expect. You've got to be prepared to learn something new every day. Circumstances change on a dime these days." Wild gestured to the prosthesis lying on the bed. "I'm facing some of those changing circumstances myself. Life isn't exactly going to be what I thought it would be. But I'm going to make it the best that I can. Nobody gets the life they had yesterday if their life has changed irrevocably. Otherwise it wouldn't be irrevocable. That's the choice everybody ultimately has."

Ash thought about that. For all his shallow, superficial interests, Wild had a deeper grasp on things than most people would have expected, and it was made deeper by his wound, no doubt.

"You did the best you could last night, Ash," Wild said. "You don't get yesterday back, and when you were doing what you could, that was all you could do. The thing is, what do you do from here?"

Ash sighed. "Whistle-blowing doesn't pay well."

"Not to mention the fact that you probably couldn't prove it," Wild added. "Unless this guy, Redmond, could swear on a stack of Bibles that you and Bolo rescued him before the firefight started. Even if he was willing to do that and possibly sacrifice his own career, which I doubt, from what you say about him, I'm sure a case could be made that he wasn't in his right mind. So what does that leave you with?"

"Taking care of the NROTC unit," Ash said. "Just like I was sent here to do."

"Right. You got one mid in the hospital—can't remember his name—"

"Skinny."

"Skinny," Wild repeated. "You'll need to see your people through that, whether Skinny makes it or not."

Trust Wild to be that blunt. "And you're working a man short since the master crashed. I'd say you've got your work cut out for you."

"You're right."

"Of course I am." Wild cracked open another beer. "The delivery girl?"

"Yeah?"

"She has a friend. They hang out at a place called the Drumbeat. They'll be there at nine o'clock tonight. What say we go show your mids how to shoot, tuck them in, and come back here to try our luck?"

"Sounds like a plan," Ash agreed. But he couldn't help watching the footage still spilling across the television. He still felt that he had unfinished business out there.

39

There is something therapeutic about a shooting range, Ash thought. It wasn't the destruction or the loud noise, or the adrenaline or the anticipation of targets popping up from the ground. Those were great, too. But they weren't the relaxing part of the exercise. The relaxing part was a lot like bowling: simply trying to do the same thing over and over until it was right every time and came naturally.

The course was a grinder, requiring shoot-and-cover techniques, frequent magazine changes, and constant assessment of the situation because some of the popups were civilians and some had hostages. Ash and Wild took turns walking the mids through the exercise. Whoever wasn't guiding was back at the shooting table securing control of the weapons. No one was armed but the two people on the course.

The range was located four miles out of town and was surrounded by trees and hills. No one moved within those hills. It was laid out over a one-hundred-yard square.

During the time they were on the range, the forty midshipmen—thirty-nine with Skinny out of the mix— were totally his. Master Chief Fernandez had occasionally taken them to indoor shooting ranges where they'd learned to handle, fire, and clean the weapons they'd used. Almost half of them had hunted before and knew the basics of firing while under cover.

They shot for nearly four hours, and then loaded up for the return to Fairly. During the range time, Ash had watched the midshipmen relaxing and enjoying themselves. Competition started up concerning scores and performance, aided and abetted by Wild's merciless taunting. They had to take it, though, because Wild outshot every one of them. In fact, he'd outshot Ash two out of three times, though their scores were incredibly close. Ash had hesitated on two hostage situations and Wild had blown right through them without hesitation.

"Hey, people," Wild called, standing among them with his gold lenses glinting in the sun, "you did good out here today."

A round of applause followed. Ash just grinned and shook his head. Leave it to Wild to come in and win over a bunch of college kids in a few hours.

"I'm thinking we're Navy issue," Wild said, walking smoothly in front of them, "so that means we're not done yet. Do you have a pizzeria in Fairly worth my attention?"

"Harrigan's," Spike said immediately. "Best damn pizza in town."

"All right," Wild said enthusiastically. "Now we're talking." He glanced at his watch. "It's seventeen thirteen now. We'll meet at Harrigan's at eighteen thirty. Pizza's on me."

A chorus of applause met the decision immediately.

On the way back to the car, Ash noticed Wild limping slightly. "How are you holding up?" Ash asked.

"I'll be fine. We've got an hour of downtime on the way back." In the car, Wild peeled his pants leg back and examined the bandages on his stump. "No blood. Just pain. That's a good sign. If everything holds together, all I'll have to do is toughen up."

"They don't come any tougher than you, Wild."

"Yeah, well, we're going to find out, aren't we?"

As he started the car, Ash reflected on their friendship. When they'd worked together while Ash had been an aide to Admiral Garrett's office, he and Wild had been forced to saw off and steal a dead man's hand to get into a protected area. That had been insane, but both of them had borne up under it. Now they were both being tested in ways they'd never imagined. There was no telling what next year held in store.

"Don't think about it, homo," Wild said.

"What?"

"You're not feeling the stump, you sick bastard."

That inanity, so classically Wild, cracked Ash up. "I was just thinking," Ash said when they'd regained their composure, "about what might happen the next time we get together."

"You're looking too far ahead," Wild said, sinking into the seat and pretending it was more comfortable than it was. "We have tonight, girls, and a lot of alcohol between us and tomorrow. Don't even look for next year."

Claude Thornton rode in the T-72 in the back of an eighteen-wheeler he and his team had lured off the road less than an hour ago. Sitting inside the tank inside the trailer, Claude couldn't help but think of that old story about the wooden horse the Greeks had given whoever it was they were fighting. Not that they were giving the eighteen-wheeler to anyone, but, inside it, the tank was hidden in plain sight. He sat in the driver's seat and wiped his sweaty palms on his pants.

He reminded himself that he was on a military operation—Operation Crowbar—and he was a professional when it came to running the tank. No one else in the Badlands Militia had the same skills he did. Tonight he was going to prove that. He keyed the headset and spoke into the mike. "Hey Hauler, how's it looking?"

"We're clean and green, Puncher," the reply came. "Pulling downtown in Fairly now. We'll be kicking the doors open soon."

"Understood," Claude said. Then added, "Over and out," because he wanted to sound professional. He wiped his sweaty hands again. All his life he'd been a video-gamer. Eye-and-hand control was everything, the skill set that separated life and death. Tonight was going to prove no different.

At present, nearly all of the national guardsmen still on assignment to the ATF were out at the farm. That gave the Badlands Militia at least forty minutes to wreak havoc with the town that had stood idly by and let militia people get killed. Claude had barely gotten away last night and had lost two buddies he'd grown up with. He could have ended up just as dead as they had.

But he hadn't. He'd regrouped with the other survivors and gotten a plan together to come into town and rescue Devon Hite. They'd found out from their contacts that Hite was still being held by the ATF in Fairly at the Carriage House Hotel. If they waited much longer, there was a chance that the feds would move Hite somewhere else beyond their means.

And with the way the search was progressing at the farm, everyone felt certain the tank would be found sooner, not later. So they had to go tonight.

"You know we're not going to win this war," Truman Diller said. He sat at the gunner position, manning the smoothbore gun. Like Claude, he'd only been out of high school for a couple of years. Neither of them had graduated, but they'd spent extra years failing at it.

"Not here to win it," Claude said. "We're here to make a statement. Same as that fucker Ferguson keeps saying on the TV."

They were fully loaded tonight, carrying forty rounds of ammo, an equal split between frag rounds and HEAT. The frag rounds were for antipersonnel and the High Explosive Anti-Tank rounds were for vehicles as well as buildings. A HEAT round could punch through another main battle tank, a helicopter, or an enemy bunker.

"Quiet," Cooter Rogers said above them. He was in the commander's seat, filling out the three-man crew that operated the T-72. With the autoloader for the rounds, the fourth traditional tank position was unnecessary.

"Puncher," Hauler called back a few minutes later, "you're at your twenty. Land rover, do you copy?"

"Land rover copies," a man replied. Land rover was the designation for the team assigned to get Devon Hite out of the hotel. "Land rover is in position." Meaning they were already inside the hotel.

The eighteen-wheeler came to a halt.

"Puncher," the truck driver called, "start your engines."

Claude started the big V12 power plant and listened to the rumbling growl as it sat inside the trailer. "Puncher is operational," he said, and he couldn't wait for the party to begin.

Fred Jackson stepped into the lobby of the Carriage House Hotel with his hand wrapped tightly around the silenced pistol in his pocket. He was not quite thirty years old, sharp-jawed and angry. Two of his younger brothers had died in the attack on the farm last night. He knew he could never look his old man in the eye again if he didn't deal out some vengeance.

Hazel Morton, the night clerk and the organist for the Lutheran Church, was on duty. She was sixty and blue-haired. She took one look at Fred and knew he was trouble. Her blue-veined hand shot for the telephone. Fred took his pistol from his pocket and shot her four times, putting each round through her chest. She staggered back and sat down, dropping the phone on the desk. Fred dropped the magazine and reloaded from his pockets. He had extra magazines, but there was time. He was a patient hunter. A dozen men fell in behind him, all of them armed.

Devon Hite was kept on the third floor toward the middle of the building. The ATF had taken the conference room at the corner nearest Puncher's position. Ferguson was currently being interviewed on television. Fred had seen the advertisements for the interview earlier that day. The ATF man seemed to enjoy talking, but he never really said anything. Fred figured that was because the government didn't want him telling the truth.

At the third-floor landing, Fred stepped out into the hallway with the pistol extended before him. Two ATF agents guarded the door in front of the room where Devon Hite was being held. Fred shot both men twice in the head—something the Army had trained him to do before he got caught dealing in black-market goods— dropping them before they could do more than try for their guns. Blood stained the wall behind them and they dropped to the floor. He put one more round through each of their foreheads to make sure.

Reaching the door, Fred shucked the partially used magazine for a fresh one. He tried the knob and found it locked. Swiftly, he went through the dead men's clothing and turned up a key-card and a handcuff key. He inserted the card and the lock translated, clicking open audibly. Twisting the knob, he followed the door inside.

Two more men sat inside, TV blaring as they watched the live interview with Special Agent Mel Ferguson in his hotel room down the hall. They looked at Fred, who shot them. The first man died, spilling his dinner in his lap, and the second man actually had his fist around his pistol and was diving to the floor when a bullet entered the top of his head.

Fred stood inside the room and waited for a moment. It felt good killing again. After he'd gotten a taste of it in Iraq, coming back home and hunting hadn't been the same. When he was satisfied that every ATF agent in the room was dead, he entered the bathroom.

Devon Hite lay in the bathtub.

"We've come to get you out of here," Fred said.

"Of course you have," Hite replied. He jerked at the chain that held his manacled hands.

Fred posted guards, and then knelt with the key. He opened the manacles around Hite's hands, then his feet. Hite needed help to crawl out of the tub.

"Arms and legs are asleep," Hite said.

"Figured they would be," Fred said. "But we got to be moving. Claude's down below with the tank."

"The tank?" Hite looked amazed.

"Yeah." Fred grinned. "Figured we might give Fairly a little back of what they let us get. We need to get out of this building. The ATF boys are at the end of the hallway. That's the tank's first target."

Hite grinned back and started moving. Fred covered the retreat to the stairwell. "Puncher, we've got him. You've got a clear field of fire."

In the tank Claude asked, "Did you hear him?"

"I did," Truman replied. "Get us out of here."

"Hauler," Claude said, throwing the tank into gear with both treads, "open 'er up."

A moment later, the rear of the trailer opened. Claude guided the tank forward, rolling onto the heavy, rein-forced beams they'd used to load the tank into the trailer. The T-72 rolled down the ramps and into the alley.

"Son of a bitch!" Cooter yelled. "Watch the gun! Watch the gun! You're not clear!"

Too late, Truman tried to stop and swing the turret around. The big gun caught the wall of the mechanic shop at the side of the alley and punched through the brick and mortar.

"Goddammit!" Cooter yelled. "If you've bent that gun . . ."

"That gun was designed to take more punishment than that," Claude said. He locked down the left tread and brought the tank around. Unfortunately, that brought the tank into the garage as well. The spinning treads ate through the brick and mortar like acid, chew-ing through the whole corner. Claude grinned like a loon. He was a fucking building killer in the tank.

"Get me a shot," Truman said.

"Coming up," Claude shouted over the din of the rocks and mortar falling over the tank. *Damn but I'm going to hate abandoning this.* The tank was proving to

be better than every video-game fantasy he'd ever had.
He turned the T-72 toward the Carriage House Hotel.

"Hang on," Truman said. "I can take a shot from
here."

Claude gripped the handholds while the turret lifted.

Ash leaned back in the booth and marveled at Wild.
He sat in front of the mids, effortlessly spinning story
after story. Some were his own and others were borrowed, but they all had the mids engaged.

"What's the weirdest thing you've ever had to do?"
Globe asked.

Wild rubbed his chin over that one. Despite the fact
that he was still being rehabbed and had put in an active
day, he didn't show any signs of slowing down. "The
weirdest thing. Hmmmm." He smiled and looked at Ash.
"I'll have to give that one to Lieutenant Roberts."

"Hey," Ash said, holding up his hands defensively,
"tell your own stories."

"Last year, the lieutenant was assigned to the Pentagon," Wild said, ignoring Ash's guidance. "He caught
wind of an espionage op running beneath the noises of
the boys in the E-Ring. Of course, he invited me in. It
got pretty hairy, to say the least. In fact, at one point,
we had to saw off a dead man's hand and use it to get
into a restricted area."

"That's gross," Spike said.

"Yeah," Globe said. "Gross but not weird."

"As it turned out," Wild continued, unperturbed, "the
scanner we had to access not only scanned for prints,
but also for body heat. That's when the lieutenant had
the bright idea of warming the dead hand in the
microwave."

The mids were riveted.

Ash hadn't exactly had nightmares about the incident,
but he hadn't forgotten it either.

"Do you know what setting you use to warm an ampu-
tated hand up to body temp?" Wild asked, grinning. He

had them. They sat on the edges of their seats. "Steak. Twenty seconds."

"No way," the mids chorused.

"Way," Wild told them. "The problem is, you can only warm that hand up a few times before it swells up like a man allergic to shellfish."

"Then does it blow up?" Bruno asked.

Wild sipped his beer. "Don't know. We never had to test it that far."

A sudden impact sounded outside but not far away.

"What the hell was that?" Globe asked.

A moment later, Ash heard another grinding noise, one he'd heard a few times overseas when ground-pounders had come in behind the SEALs on an operation. He looked at Wild. "That sounded like a tank."

Wild nodded and rose to his feet. "Hell yeah. Do you have tanks here in Fairly?"

"No."

"Wonder if the ATF guy brought them in?" Wild jerked a thumb over his shoulder at the television set that showed Ferguson being interviewed.

"For what?" Ash said, getting up.

"Beats me."

Just then, Ash heard the unmistakable *whumph* of a main battle tank's big gun.

Nauseated with the whole thing, Hank Howard got up from the ATF interview and let himself out of the room. Ferguson didn't seem to notice him, totally focusing on the question he was circumnavigating about last night's violence, but Howard knew there would be hell to pay later. This was Ferguson's moment of glory and he wasn't going to let anyone miss it.

Out in the hall, Howard took out his cigarettes, shook one out, and lit up. Then he noticed the bodies lying in the middle of the hallway in front of the door where Devon Hite had been kept. Drawing his service weapon, Howard ran forward, knowing from looking that it was too late to help the two men. He peeked inside the room and saw another two men dead there as well.

He noticed the blood trail leading to the stairwell. Somebody had stepped in the blood of the dead agents on their way back out of the room. Howard reached for his radio and keyed the mike as he ran for the stairwell door. "Listen up, dammit! Somebody just broke Devon Hite free! There are four dead agents—" Before he could say another word, the world suddenly came apart. A concussive shock wave lifted him from his feet and slammed him against the stairwell wall.

Claude watched the destruction through the view port. The 125-millimeter round weighed over fifty pounds leaving the big gun, but it hit like a wrecking ball at the other end. Slamming into the third-floor corner conference room that had been identified as the place where the ATF agents had gathered, the frag-HE round detonated almost immediately, unleashing the steel balls that formed a jacket around the high-explosive charge. There couldn't have been much left of whoever had been in the room. The corner of the building no longer existed. Only a gaping hole filled with smoke and fire remained.

Truman whooped with glee. "Okay, find me another target, dawg."

Claude pulled the tank out of the alley and onto Main Street. There was no reason to remain in hiding anymore. The treads churned, tearing holes in the pavement that cracked under the tank's raw tonnage. No longer spread out over the long frame of the eighteen-wheeler trailer, the tank was a hazard just driving across most of Fairly's streets.

Roaring out of the dark alley, Claude didn't slow down for traffic. A late-model pickup slammed into the T-72 and stopped, hardly jostling the massive attack vehicle. A subcompact car slid up under the front of the treads. The tank mounted the small car, and then smashed it flat.

"Oh man!" Claude said. "This is much cooler than I

thought it was going to be! And I thought it was going to be pretty fucking cool!" He shifted, gaining speed now.

"There's Harrigan's!" Truman shouted. "I washed dishes for that old bastard for months! Take it out!"

Claude slowed the left tread and sped up the right, turning left and aiming straight for the pizzeria. He was whooping and laughing.

Then two men stepped from the restaurant. The blond one lifted a pistol and took careful aim.

"Too fucking bad, surfer boy," Claude crowed. "You brought a pistol to a tank fight." He cackled with glee.

Calmly and coolly, though, the man stood his ground and fired again and again. Without warning, one of the rounds sparked off a corner of Claude's viewport and screamed inside the tank. Something nipped at his ear. He reached up and touched the mangled remains of his ear, feeling hot blood coursing down his neck.

"Son of a bitch!" Claude screamed. "He shot me! He fucking shot me!" In fear, he steered away.

"Hey!" Truman protested. "What the fuck do you think you're doing?"

"He shot me through my viewport!" Claude still felt the blood running down his neck.

"Well close it, you dumb bastard!" Cooter yelled. "Use your instruments!"

Claude closed the viewport and switched on the camera. He'd trained to do that while at the farm. In seconds, with the tank's operation feeling even more like a video game, he was more confident, a rolling juggernaut of destruction waiting to happen to Fairly, South Dakota.

40

Still not believing what he'd just seen, Wild fighting off a forty-plus-ton iron monster with a nine-millimeter pistol, Ash stared at the tank as it crossed the street and rammed through a line of buildings. Most of the businesses had closed at five, and some of them had closed at noon because it was a Saturday. None could withstand the tank bearing down on them, and were quickly reduced to heaps of rubble.

Ash turned to Wild. "Don't tell me. You watched *Patton* again recently."

Wild grinned at him. "No. But I figured any asshole who didn't know enough to close his viewport during battle might not be used to being under fire either. I'm thinking I was probably right."

"You're damned lucky is what you were," Ash said.

Wild nodded more soberly. "Couldn't let them run through the pizzeria. Too many families in there."

"I know." Ash stared at the tank lumbering through the city.

"Who do you know that would want to drive a tank through this sleepy little town?" Wild asked.

"Lieutenant," Spike called from inside the pizzeria. "It's on the news."

Ash zipped back inside and glanced at the television.

". . . from someone just inside Fairly, South Dakota," the reporter was said. "There are several reports from residents of the small town near the Badlands Militia that involve a tank running amok throughout the town. We've got a crew en route . . ."

"Lieutenant," Boy called out. He stood at one of the windows, peering down the street.

"What?" Ash asked with more irritation than he intended. He needed time to think.

"The tank," Boy said, pointing. "It's turning around."

A few blocks away, the Soviet weapon *was* turning around.

"Quick!" Ash said. "Get everybody out of here! Now!"

In seconds, the pizzeria became even more of a madhouse. A little less than half of the customers remained inside Harrigan's when the tank fired again. The *whumph* trailed the screaming round that detonated against the two-story office building next door. The building came tumbling down in a rush of masonry. The detonation was close enough to blow the windows out of the pizzeria.

"Hasn't got our range," Wild said. "It's hard firing a tank at short yardage."

"Yeah, well, all they have to do is get close," Ash replied. "Horseshoes and hand grenades, remember?"

"I do." Wild helped a woman to her feet and ushered her out the door. "We need a plan. You've still got weapons out in your car."

"Yeah, but small-arms fire isn't going to do much against that tank."

"I don't think the tank is going to be all of our worries." Wild allowed Ash to go through the rear exit of the pizzeria before him. In the next instant, another round scored a direct hit on the restaurant, bringing it down and rupturing the gas lines to start fires that flared against the night. The concussive wave knocked everyone behind the building to the ground. Screams of frightened men, women, and children filled the air. "And they're getting better at the range."

"Spike," Ash yelled.

Spike looked at him. She was disheveled and scared,

but she was holding together. "Aye, sir." The reply was automatic.

"I need two groups," Ash said. "One to get the civilians clear of this area and the other to the university to make a weapons run. Spike, get these people moving. Globe."

"Aye, sir," Globe responded.

"Weapons run. I need grenades, antitank weapons—LAWs, whatever you can find—and body armor. As much as you and your team can carry."

"Aye, sir."

"Move out."

Globe went.

"And a Barrett sniper rifle," Wild yelled after him. "With armor-piercing rounds."

Turning to Spike, Ash said, "Four-man teams. Do not engage these people. Stay moving. Find civilians and get them to safety."

"Safety? Where?"

"Somewhere underground. A place that tank can't go."

"There's an old fallout shelter near the train station."

"Use that. Stay on foot and hide as much as you can. If the older people and kids can't keep up, commandeer vehicles."

"Aye, sir." Spike moved at once, barking out orders as if she'd been born to it.

"That leaves you and me," Wild said.

Ash grinned. "We're bait."

"Maybe I should help with the women and children."

"Haven't you ever wanted to hunt a tank?"

"From an Apache helo? Maybe. From a Hummer loaded up with an antitank gun? Possibly. You and me from that rented POS you're driving while armed with popguns? No fucking way."

"More of a challenge," Ash said.

"You're just trying to impress the mids. You hated the story I told about the hand, didn't you?"

Another 125-millimeter round crashed through the air,

causing Ash and Wild to go to ground again. The round struck a dress shop two buildings away and started another rash of fires. Thankfully, most of Fairly's downtown sector was deserted at this time of night on a Saturday. Most of what was actually being lost was property, not lives.

"I wasn't actually thinking about popguns," Ash commented. "There's a convenience store a block over. I was thinking about poor man's napalm."

"Fire isn't going to slow that tank much," Wild said.

"If we get a chance to get it inside that tank, it could."

"They were reporting this live on Fox News. All we have to do is live till reinforcements arrive."

"Ready to give up the glory, Wild?"

"Damn," Wild said in amazement. "I can't believe I just said that. It's that damn rehab. Gets you so you limit yourself. Hell no, I don't want to share the glory. Let's go bag us a tank."

"The car first."

"Why?"

"Because it has our weapons." Ash led the way back to the street.

"You should really have thought about getting another car."

"Wasn't planning on pulling off a cavalry attack when I took it," Ash said. He paused at the edge of the crumbled remains of the pizzeria, watched as the tank rumbled by, then dug out his key and ran for the car. He opened the driver's-side door, slipped behind the steering wheel, unlocked all the locks and the trunk, and had the engine running by the time Wild grabbed a bag containing guns and ammo and dropped into the seat.

"There was a time when you couldn't beat me," Wild said, rummaging through the bag.

"There will be again," Ash said. Without warning, a burst of auto-fire raked the front of the car and pocked holes in the windshield. Ash floored the accelerator, pulling out across the debris that littered the street. An

SUV whipped by in front of them. Men hung out the sides, bristling with weapons. "Militia!"

"I see them." Wild punched rounds into pistol magazines by feel as Ash sped through the streets. "I presume we're taking the long way around to this convenience store?"

"Since the guys in the car are coming back and you're still working reloads, yeah."

"Man, you do provide some excitement when you're around."

"You should see me when I'm not stressed by combat and can give it my full attention," Ash told him.

Wild slapped a nine-millimeter into his hand. "You're locked and loaded."

"You?"

"Getting there." Wild slipped an M4 from the rifle case. "Unlike you and the NROTC, I don't leave my weapons empty." He took out a magazine and shoved it into the assault rifle. "Thing that sucks is that this rifle is single-action to qualify me for ownership here in the States." He swung over the backseat.

Ash drove, cutting between the buildings like a man possessed. "Say when."

"When," Wild replied. He slid over the seat into the back and shoved the rifle out. "Keep it straight for a second."

"They're going to have an easier time shooting us."

"At least until I learn how to shoot around corners, yeah."

Ash gazed into his rearview mirror and watched as Wild shot, calmly and methodically. Brass flipped into the backseat. Abruptly, the side mirror exploded into a million pieces, shattered by a stray round. "Wild."

"Keep it steady, dammit."

"It there wasn't building debris overlaying the potholes in the street, maybe I could."

"Bitch, bitch, bitch," Wild said, then fired again.

A pickup truck loaded with armed men screamed onto the street from an alley. Shots rang out and a handful of them tore into the side of Ash's rental and broke out more windows. Ash jerked the wheel, dodging away from the new arrivals.

"Shit," Wild exploded. "I thought you were going to hold steady."

"If I had, we'd be dead now." Ash took another hard right turn, peeling into a cross street.

Wild struggled to take a shot again. "How many people did you say were in the Badlands Militia?"

"The sheriff didn't have exact numbers."

"I bet they were low."

Ash ignored that and took out his cell phone. He flipped through the address book and pulled up Spike's cell number, then punched TALK.

Spike answered. "Lieutenant."

"How are you doing?"

"No casualties so far."

"I need a spotter," Ash said.

"A spotter, sir?"

"Someone who can keep an eye on the tank. I need to know where it is." Ash flinched as bullets cut through the already-shattered windshield. Glass rained down over him as wind rushed at him. Headlights shined to his left and let him know the pickup was jockeying for position.

"I can do that," Spike said.

"No," Ash said. "Not you. You have your orders. Someone else. Tell me who."

"Boy."

"Get him on it then."

"Aye, sir."

Ash closed the phone and looked at the intersection coming up. "I'm going to try something."

"Joy," Wild said, shoving another magazine into his rifle. "I've picked off two guys in the car and still haven't hit the driver."

"You still get points. Given any thought to the tires?"

"I thought they were out of season."

"Hold on. I'm gonna sacrifice the rear of this car and

hope that we stay mobile." Ash pulled hard left as he jammed on the brakes. Before he even came to a stop, he'd shoved the transmission into reverse. He put his foot flat on the accelerator and shot backward.

"Oh *shiiiiiittttt!*" Wild yelped.

"I knew you'd like this," Ash said. The SUV shot by untouched, but the car rammed the pickup and crunched to a stop. Even strapped in, Ash almost slid free. The air bag deployed and pinned him against the seat. Bringing up his pistol, he fired through it, sending the bullet out the shattered windshield. He unstrapped the seat belt and stepped onto the street, raising the nine-mil. Wild rolled free on the other side.

A couple of the guys in the truck tried to return fire, but Ash's and Wild's marksmanship from almost point-blank range was merciless. The militiamen died in seconds.

The SUV came back around at them.

"Time to go," Wild said, jamming another magazine into his weapon.

"I'm out," Ash said, dropping the empty pistol into the passenger seat.

"I got you," Wild said. "Just get us out of here."

Ash put the car in gear and stomped on the accelerator. The dead weight of the pickup, plus the dead weight of all the would-be Badlands bad men in it, held them fast for a moment, then—with a tortured rasp of metal—released. Fishtailing, Ash drove straight for the SUV. At his side, Wild fired again and again. As the vehicles passed, Ash pulled slightly into the SUV, hard enough to knock the other vehicle aside.

In the rearview mirror, which was cracked in three places but somehow miraculously remained, Ash watched as the SUV drove into a parked car and stuttered to a stop.

Without a word, Wild took the pistol and reloaded it. "Well, that was fun."

Ash's phone rang. He scooped it up and answered. "Ash is up."

"Where are you?" Bolo asked.

"Running for my life," Ash answered. "What about you?"

"Playing pin-the-tail-on-the-donkey with a tank."

"Sounds fun. I would have been playing that except I got sidetracked by the damn militiamen that followed it in. I don't suppose I have to ask who brought the tank into Fairly?"

"The word I get is that the militia broke Hite out of ATF custody right before the tank started blowing shit up."

"We have reinforcements on their way," Ash said.

"The first of them should get here in about twenty minutes," Bolo said. "By the time they arrive, the town will be leveled and the Badlands Militia members will have vanished. Everybody was out securing the Badlands Militia farm."

"Guess they missed the tank, huh?"

"Yeah."

"Would this be a good time to bring up my benefits package as a volunteer sheriff's deputy?" Ash asked. He got his bearings and found the convenience store. It looked different with all the lights off, and it wasn't on fire like a couple of buildings next to it.

"Sure, I'll get the elves on it."

Wild dropped the pistol back into the passenger seat, then added three more in quick succession. Shit, nobody reloaded like Wild Willie Weldon.

"Any suggestions about the tank?" Bolo asked.

"I'm working on it," Ash said. "I sent some of my midshipmen on a weapons run to the school."

"What kind of ordnance do you have up there?"

"Enough, I hope."

"I've got another idea."

"I'm listening." Ash parked the car at the convenience store.

"That ATF agent we rescued?"

"Bobby Redmond," Ash said, picking up one of the

nine-millimeters and taking two extra magazines Wild gave him.

"Yeah. I talked to him this morning. Got to know him a little."

"You've been busy."

"Not all of us are honorary deputies."

"That's why you make the big bucks." Ash looked into the convenience store.

"Pumps are still working," Wild said, holding a dripping nozzle in one hand over a pool of gas. "We need containers."

Ash tried the door and found it locked. He slammed the nine-millimeter's butt against the glass and shattered it. "Redmond," he reminded. "I know you didn't call to reminisce."

"He's a UAV pilot."

"Unmanned aerial vehicle? And?"

"And," Bolo said, pausing slightly. "And I was thinking, since I have his equipment in impound—"

"You have his equipment?"

"While you were still sleeping this morning, I was doing detective work. I decided that if Ferguson was going to sell us down the river, maybe I could make a case for the position of overkill the ATF has been on since this mess started. I broke into Redmond's garage at the rental property he was staying on. I found a couple of UAVs. Thought maybe they would be great material evidence."

Ash strode into the darkened convenience store, followed immediately by Wild.

"Feels kind of creepy doing this, doesn't it?" Wild asked. "Like something out of *Night of the Living Dead*." He was only halfway joking.

"What I was thinking," Bolo said, "was seeing if Redmond could operate one of those UAVs and fly it into the tank."

"And have it smack against the tank like a bug against a windshield?"

"And load it up with enough dynamite to where it smacks back," the sheriff said.

"You have dynamite?"

"Confiscate some every now and again. Guys like to go fishing who don't like to bait hooks. And I keep some on hand to blow up occasional moonshine stills. I think I've got enough to do the job. I just need a distraction while I get Redmond out of the hospital."

"Wild and I plan on being distracting," Ash replied. "Go get Redmond. We're working on the tank." He folded the phone and put it away.

"Are you through gossiping?" Wild asked.

"It was the sheriff. The ATF guy, Redmond—"

"Is a trained UAV pilot. I got that."

"The sheriff's got his UAVs."

Wild smiled. "Nice."

More explosions sounded in the background, letting them know the tank was still delivering nonstop carnage.

"Get the soap," Wild said. "I think I've got our containers." He grabbed a half dozen grape-juice bottles mocked up to look like wine bottles, stopped at the counter to turn on the pump, and went outside. He opened the bottles and emptied the contents.

Ash picked up three half-gallons of dishwashing detergent.

"Get these going," Wild said. "I'll get more bottles."

Working swiftly, Ash poured the bottles a third of the way full of detergent. While Wild was pouring out the new bottles, Ash pumped the others full of gasoline, then went to work on the next six. Wild stuffed cloth napkins into the filled bottles and shook them vigorously. When they were finished, they had a dozen Molotov cocktails primed for destruction.

"Gotta get lighters," Ash said.

Wild opened his pocket and showed a dozen disposable lighters inside. "We're ready, amigo. Now let's go find us a tank."

41

Devon Hite shoved a forty-five caliber pistol into the back of his waistband and ran his cold gaze over the town. Several buildings downtown were burning. He'd lost his farm, but that wasn't going to be the only loss if he had anything to say about it.

"People are going to remember this," he told Fred and the other men with him. "What you're looking at here, it's the first true blow struck in the name of freedom since that shot heard 'round the world at Lexington and Concord. We're going to win our lives back, gentlemen. And you've all helped contribute to the cause." He stepped up into the truck. "We can go underground after this, where the feds can't find us, but we're going to grow a new nation of people who will rally to our cause."

"Hell, yeah," someone said.

Fred handed Hite an M14 that had been modified to fire on full auto and a bandolier of clips for the weapon. "We don't have much time," Fred said.

"Then we'll make the most of it," Hite said. "Do you know where our escaped prisoner is?"

"Redmond?" Fred looked puzzled. "He's in the hospital."

Hite nodded. "Let's go there. I hate leaving unfinished business."

"Ash is up."

"Lieutenant, can you hear me?"

"I can hear you, Globe," Ash answered as he drove through the streets looking for the tank.

"Mission accomplished, sir," Globe said. "I packed everything I thought might be useful."

"Good job."

"Where do you want to meet?" Globe asked.

Ash turned hard left and thought about it. "Downtown seems to be the center of activity, corner of Main and Oak. The armory is there." Of course, the armory wasn't used for anything these days except as a skating rink, and a bingo and dance hall for seniors. Still, the old building had been well put together back in the 1940s, when people felt certain they were going to be bombed any day of the week. It would stand up to a hell of a lot of damage before it went down.

"I'll see you there."

Ash called Spike: "How's it going?"

"We've got most of the downtown area clear," Spike returned.

"Good. Meet Globe at the corner of Main and Oak."

"The old armory?"

"Yes. We're going to try to establish a fallback and hold position there. Get hold of the other first-class midshipmen and make this happen."

"Yes, sir."

Speed-dialing once again, Ash called Boy. "Where's my tank?"

"Down by Coggins' Furniture Store."

"Don't know it."

Boy was silent for a moment. "Two blocks west of Maude's Dinner."

"Got it. Do you know how many militia vehicles are involved in this?"

"I've counted five others besides the tank," Boy replied. "I don't count them unless I've seen them before, but the number might still be off."

"It gives us working numbers to deal with," Ash replied. "That's all I'm looking for. You're doing well. Just keep Geordie in the loop." He closed and put away the phone, then dropped his foot harder on the accelerator.

Fairly had become an urban hell. Fires raged through the buildings. Even if all of the businesses had insurance—and *enough* insurance—Ash didn't know if everyone would rebuild. Fairly would never be the same again, and that made him angry.

"Stay loose," Wild said quietly. "If you over-invest in this, you're going to be setting yourself up for failure."

"I know." Ash took a fresh grip on the steering wheel and sped toward the tank. Less than thirty seconds later, they rolled up on it. He didn't know if the tank was out of ammo or was just conserving it for the moment, but it wasn't firing. However, it was still chugging through buildings like a brick-and-mortar carrion feeder. "Ready?"

"Born ready," Wild said, picking up one of the Molotov cocktails. He lit the dangling cloth napkin jammed into the bottle's neck and leaned out the window. "Go!"

Ash drove, coming up close on the tank. From only a few feet away, Wild threw the Molotov cocktail. The bottle spun end over end for a moment, the flaming wick burning the whole way, then smashed to pieces against the T-72's turret. Flames followed the soap-laced gasoline over the fighting vehicle. The soap caused the fire to stick to the metal, holding the gasoline with it.

The turret turned and took aim from fifty yards out.

"Incoming!" Wild yelled.

Ash cut the wheels hard left as the HEAT round flew past them and cored a hat store. Flaming hats scattered across the sky like burning stars when the secondary charge blew in an ear-shattering explosion. The car rocked from the force of the blast and debris rattled over it. Ash turned down the side street. "From behind again or from the front this time?"

Wild lit another Molotov cocktail. "From the front. I feel like doing that jousting-knight thing."

Ash made a right, raced up three blocks—certain he was getting ahead of the tank—then made two more rights, doubling back the way he'd come. The tank was now directly ahead of him. Smoke and flames roiled up from its burning metal hide. Like a brontosaurus, the T-72 lumbered through a mini-mall complex, leaving a trail of broken buildings.

"Do it," Wild urged, pushing himself out to sit in the window. He held the Molotov cocktail in one hand.

Ash sped forward, hoping he could get under the gun. The round *whooshed* by overhead, missing them by a few feet, but to Ash they felt like inches. Then Wild threw the second Molotov cocktail. This one arced high, then came down on top of the tank, smashing and leaving a flaming pool on the front of the vehicle under the main gun.

This time when Ash passed, two Badlands Militia vehicles swooped onto his back trail.

"Company," Wild said grimly.

"I see them." Ash pulled out his phone and called Globe. "Globe."

"Here."

"Are you in position?"

"Yes."

"I'm coming in with two bogeys on my tail."

"Bring 'em," Globe replied. "Which direction are you coming from?"

Ash turned right, figured out his cardinal points on the compass, and said, "From the south. I'll go right by your position." He checked the rearview mirror and saw both vehicles pursuing him. The headlight on the pickup winked out when Wild fired the rifle.

"Goddammit," Wild snarled, then readied himself for another shot.

"Roger that," Globe said. "I had one of the others pick up some roadblock spikes from the university's security offices too. After you pass, we're going to throw those across and see if it doesn't alleviate pursuit."

"Copy," Ash returned. "Good call. Keep your eyes open. We're coming through." He kept the accelerator down and made the final turn, skidding onto the street that ran right by the old armory.

"If we play this right," Wild said, "we can break their backs right here. The tank's coming too."

"I'll be happy if we just live through this," Ash said grimly. He saw the shadows of the midshipmen at the side of the street. As soon as he was by the armory, he turned and skidded sideways.

"Fill your hands," Wild said, dumping two pistols into Ash's lap.

The two pursuit vehicles didn't hesitate, roaring in front of the armory and just barely illuminating the back of the midshipman who had draped the strip of road-block spikes across the street. The spikes punctured the tires at once, blowing them out and reducing them to shreds. Out of control, both pickups jerked across the debris strewn over the street.

Wild was out of the car at once. He had a flaming Molotov cocktail in his right hand, which he flung at the nearest vehicle even before it came to a stop. The fire-bomb arced through the window of the cab and exploded inside. The occupants died immediately.

Ash's phone suddenly rang. His head swiveled around, catching sight of the tank six blocks away and the truck that flanked it. Ash suspected it was one of his midshipmen calling in with a warning about the tank. Before he could answer the phone, before he could warn Wild, before he could move, the tank's main gun belched.

An instant later, the world spun around with sickening ferocity and his consciousness faded.

"Do you have it?"

Listening to the sheriff's gruff voice over the telephone cradled between his ear and his shoulder, Bobby Redmond looked at the UAV control station set up in his hospital room. He still wore his gown and his face throbbed from the plastic surgery. Despite the drugs in his system, Redmond felt like death warmed over. But his mind was his again, snapped back to normal by the pressure of his colleagues He made himself keep going only because he knew more people were going to die if he didn't. Sheriff Bolo had been very clear about that.

The instrument panel showed the diagnostics of the UAV he flew. The laptop computer showed the uploaded video from the cameras mounted on the craft. Bobby saw the chain-link fence of the holding compound where the sheriff had stowed his equipment. Using the joystick, he caused the UAV to lift almost vertically from its mooring and skate over the razor wire at the top of the fence. Then he was once more in his element, flying toward the destination Sheriff Bolo had given him, using only instrumentation until he recognized the landscape. He was looking for a tank. Damn, how hard could that be?

"I have it," Redmond said, growing more confident with his skills even though he felt partially zonked.

"You're looking good," Bolo said.

Once clear of the fence, Redmond went to full throttle on the UAV, causing it to streak across the town. The terrain blurred in the camera array. He ignored the images, but he caught enough of them to be shocked at what he saw. It looked as if bomb—no, *several* bombs—had gone off downtown.

A tank, he reminded himself. He was so amped and drowned in painkillers that he missed it.

"Back up," one of the two ATF agents guarding him said. "You just flew right by it."

"I did?" Redmond asked groggily.

"Yeah."

How the hell could you miss a tank? But Redmond brought the UAV around. He glided right by the armory, narrowly missing the building.

"Careful," Bolo said over the phone. "You bump anything hard with that payload and whatever chance we have of stopping that tank is gone."

Redmond concentrated, willing some of the effects of the anesthetic out of his system. Then he saw it: a tank covered in dancing flames. *How the hell did I miss that?*

Now that he had it in his sights, though, he headed straight for the T-72.

Recovering from the blast, partially shielded by the smoking remains of the rental car, Ash pushed himself to his feet. Then he nearly coughed up a lung trying to get his breath back. He hunted for the pistols he'd had and only succeeded in finding one of them in the debris. He didn't see Wild anywhere.

"Son of a bitch," Wild wheezed.

Turning, Ash found Wild rising like the dead behind him. Embers clung to his clothing and danced in his tangled blond locks. Dirt and smoke grimed his face, mixing with the blood from a cut over one eye. Somehow he'd managed to hang on to both his pistols.

"That was almost a direct hit," Wild said. He squinted through the smoke at the tank. "You've got to admit, they're getting better with that thing."

"Yeah, well, we're not here to hand out critiques," Ash reminded him. "And they're reloading."

"That can't be good. Time for a distraction. Back away from the car." When Ash moved away with Wild, the other SEAL fired into the car's backseat. The rental didn't blow up, as it probably would have done in a movie, but the backseat was suddenly filled with fire from the Molotov cocktails. "Run!"

The fire *whooshed* out of car like a monster that had escaped its cage, lighting up the area. It also lit up the UAV that flew overhead.

"Kamkaze time!" Wild yelled, diving for the pavement.

Ash followed suit, then watched as the UAV wheeled around, nearly slammed into the armory, and headed back toward the tank, which was now bearing down on their position with all due haste. The gunner's hatch opened on the top and a man grabbed hold of the fifty-cal mounted antiaircraft gun.

At that moment, the UAV slammed directly into the tank. The explosion was loud, concussive. Ash hugged the ground, watching in stunned fascination as the T-72 turned to burning scrap in front of his eyes. The right-side tread came apart and flapped like the loose sole of a tennis shoe. The turret hung at a rakish angle. Flames licked at the surface of the tank's exterior. Even the reactive armor hadn't prevented the damage the UAV's payload had carried.

"If anybody survived that," Ash shouted, barely hearing himself over the deafness that resulted from the explosion, "we're taking him to Vegas."

"No shit," Wild agreed, wiping at his bloody nose. "Hell, after that I'm thinking maybe we should take *us* to Vegas."

"It takes a lot to be a teacher these days," Ash said. "Man, you wouldn't believe the work you take home with you." He took out his cell phone and called Boy. "Boy, this is Ash. What do you see?"

"Tank's dead," Boy said. "All blessings be to Geordie. And most of the other vehicles are down or gone. But there's a green truck streaking for the hospital. It's parking at the ER now. I saw it with the tank earlier."

Ash swapped looks with Wild. The volume on the phone was loud enough that Wild heard Boy over the ringing in his ears. "Understood," Ash said. "Call Spike and Globe. Have them set up search-and-rescue efforts."

Ash broke the connection and called Bolo. "We need wheels," he told Wild. "We've still got one rat loose in the maze."

Wild nodded and ran for the parking lot of an all-night launderette.

"Bolo," the sheriff answered.

"We've identified a green truck headed toward the hospital that was sighted with the tank," Ash said.

"I'll see you there," Bolo said.

Ash folded his phone and sprinted after Wild, hard-pressed to keep up with him even with the prosthetic foot holding his friend back. Finding an older pickup, Wild smashed the window and unlatched the door. If there was anyone inside the launderette to complain, no one came forward. By the time Ash crawled in on the passenger side, Wild already had the engine hot-wired.

"Who's at the hospital?" Wild asked.

"Maybe they're taking someone there."

"We're going to play it like they aren't." Wild whipped the pickup out onto the street, slewing the back end around and sliding sideways around the burning wreckage of Ash's rental.

"The ATF agent," Ash said. "Bobby Redmond. He's probably the guy who flew the UAV, too."

"So they're going there for payback or to take a hostage."

"Either seems far-fetched." Ash pointed and called out directions to the hospital. He was amazed at the damage that had been done to the town in only a few short minutes.

"The hospital seems to be their destination," Wild said. "With all the other ATF guys probably dead, Redmond might be the biggest hostage around."

"He's also the one that knows Bolo and I had him off the farm *before* Ferguson called for the attack."

"Maybe Hite is planning on a sequel," Wild suggested.

Ash shook his head. "Nope. He doesn't get a sequel." His phone rang. "Ash is up."

"Just got a call through dispatch," Bolo said. "Hite and his people are inside. An orderly called me when she recognized him. Hite wanted to know what room Redmond was in. When he got the answer, he killed the duty nurse."

Damn, Ash thought. "What room is Redmond in?"

"Four-thirteen. I'm at the front entrance now," Bolo said. "Wear a white hat so I'll know you."

"Roger that, cowboy," Ash said.

Wild skidded the borrowed pickup to a halt at the ER entrance. Two EMTs were working on a fallen comrade, but they cowered back when Wild and Ash stepped from the pickup with guns in hand.

"Friends," Ash said, holding the pistol up. "What happened?"

"It was Hite," one of the EMTs said. "He just gunned Ted down on the way in. Didn't even think twice."

Stepping up the pace to a jog, Ash ran into the ER admissions area. An orderly lay sprawled on the tile floor with his face shot away.

"Son of a bitch," Wild murmured. His eyes hardened. "We're not taking any prisoners on this run."

Ash didn't say anything. He wasn't as vindictive as Wild could be, but he wasn't going to hold back either. "Do you see a fire alarm?"

"Here," Wild said, pointing at the wall on the other side of the elevator.

Ash tripped the alarm.

"Like locking the barn door after the cows are already out, isn't it?" Wild asked.

"The fire alarm shuts down the elevators," Ash explained, heading for the stairwell. "They'll have to use the stairs."

"So will we," Wild said.

Ash glanced back, remembering only then how hard the climb was going to be on Wild. Before his injury, the distance wouldn't have been anything.

"Go," Wild said. "If I fall behind, don't wait on me."

Ash zipped into the stairwell and started climbing at once. Wild struggled to keep up but fell behind. The prosthesis wasn't the same as a real leg. Maybe Wild would get better with it later, but for now he was limited. By the time Ash reached the fourth-floor landing, Wild was a floor below, still ahead of where an average guy would be.

In the hallway, Hite and four men muscled Bobby Redmond into motion. The young ATF agent wore a hospital gown and leads to various medical equipment and IVs dangled from him. They all turned as Bolo shoved open the stairwell door at the other end of the hallway and shouted, "Put down your weapons, you bastard!"

Roping an arm around Redmond's neck, Hite hid behind his prisoner and opened fire immediately. The sheriff fired as well, and one of the militiamen dropped, then gunfire knocked him back into the stairwell.

Ash went through the door at once, taking a two-handed grip on the nine-mil. He shifted his aim from Hite to one of the militiamen, who was lifting his CAR-15 to his shoulder to aim at the fallen sheriff. Ash centered three rounds on the man's back.

Hite turned immediately, whirling Redmond in front of him again. Hite's two companions pointed their weapons at Ash and opened fire. One of the rounds hit Ash in the side and knocked him sideways. Stumbling, he nearly tripped over Wild, who threw himself into the room on his belly, both pistols extended before him. Wild fired his weapons dry, targeting one of the men beside Hite, then the other. He was already ejecting the empty magazines when he looked at Ash and said, "Shoot the sonofabitch already."

Hite had his pistol pointed at Redmond again. "Come any closer and I'm going to kill him."

"Kill him," Ash said, lifting his pistol before him, "and you won't have time to kill me." Without another word, he broke into a run, going straight at Hite. Hite didn't hesitate—confident in the cover he had from his hostage—and shifted his weapon to aim at Ash.

The pistol jumped in Hite's hand. Ash felt the wind of the big slug skate past his face. Less than twenty feet separated them. The exposed portion of Hite's face beside Redmond's neck could have been covered by a playing card, revealing only one eye. He fired again and the round struck Ash in the center of his bulletproof vest, stealing his breath and breaking his stride. Ash remained fixed on his target, managing two more steps as Hite's hand came down into the ready position from the recoil. Hite screamed.

Less than ten feet away now, Ash fired once. The bullet caught Hite square in the eye and removed a chunk of bone as it exited his skull. The militia leader dropped to the floor. Redmond, no longer held up by his captor, fell as well, but he hadn't been hit.

Sucking in air, Ash put a hand to his side and felt the warm blood leaking out of him. He didn't think the wound was enough to be fatal. Turning, he checked Wild, who had both weapons recharged and was using the wall to climb back to his good foot.

"I'm cool," Wild said, holding the pistols at the ready. "Check the sheriff."

A quick inspection of Redmond revealed that he was all right, just woozy from the medication. Bolo was already trying to get to his feet when Ash reached him. Blood stained his pants and shirt where he'd been hit in the right thigh and in the left shoulder.

"You all right?" Ash asked.

"I'm leaking," the sheriff replied.

"At your age they say you can expect that," Ash said.

"If you hadn't just shot the bad guy," Bolo threatened, "I wouldn't let you get away with that." He ejected the partially spent clip and put in a fresh one. Together, they walked back to where Hite lay on the ground. "Is he dead?"

"You know," Wild said, using his prosthetic foot to roll Hite's head over to reveal the massive exit wound in the back, "a mind is a terrible thing to waste." Then he grinned his irrepressible grin. In spite of the pain, Ash matched him.

EPILOGUE

". . . After Saturday's unexpected attack by the Badlands Militia," the news reporter standing in the middle of Fairly, South Dakota's nearly demolished Main Street was saying into the camera, "this sleepy little town is already on its way back to reclaiming its former glory."

Watching from the barbershop, which had miraculously been left standing, Ash shook his head. *Former glory. What about all the people who died here?* Including the ATF agents who'd been relentlessly murdered, one hundred and eighty-two people had lost their lives in the attack. Adding to that the lives the ATF had taken in their attack, the number was well over two hundred. Add the number of friends and families, and thousands of lives were in upheaval at the moment.

"Damn," Sven the barber said, looking up at the television in the corner that was carrying the live broadcast. "I'm about ready to step outside and throw rocks at that son of a bitch if I hear 'sleepy little town' one more time."

Ash silently agreed. All over Fairly, earthmovers worked to clear the damage and debris. Volunteers from several counties and other states had descended into the town to help put things right. Ash helped himself to the free coffee Sven kept on hand for the volunteers—most of the other businesses were doing the same—said goodbye, and stepped back out into the morning sunlight. He wore jeans and a muscle shirt and carried a hard hat.

"Good morning, Lieutenant Roberts," the hardware-store owner next to the barbershop said. She was in her seventies, wrinkled as a prune from the sun, and hardened by a lifetime of work. She swept the sidewalk off in front of her store.

"Good morning, Mrs. Danvers," Ash replied.

"You feeling better?"

"I am," Ash said. The bullet had gone cleanly through his side and missed hitting any major organs. He'd been lucky. But maybe he'd been due some luck. "Thank you for asking."

"You get to feeling tuckered," the old woman said, "you come on over to my store. I got air-conditioning in the back that'll cool you down. And I just made up a batch of lemonade that's better than that rat poison Sven is calling coffee."

Ash smiled. "I'll do that, Mrs. Danvers." He continued down the street to where Maude's Dinner was still serving free breakfasts to the volunteers.

A car rolled to a stop at the curb beside Ash. When he glanced over, he saw Sheriff Bolo sitting behind the wheel of the cruiser. His left arm was in a sling.

"Where are you headed?" Bolo asked.

"Around the corner," Ash replied. "With the university being temporarily closed for the next couple weeks, I thought the midshipmen would volunteer their services. We're digging Bascombe's Plumbing out from under debris today. Should be a lot of salvage there we can use to repair leaks in some of the buildings."

"Hop in. I'll save you some steps."

Ash did.

"I talked to Hank Howard just a few minutes ago," Bolo said.

"Yeah?"

"He's going to back up Bobby Redmond's story that he was clear of the farm before the invasion. It might cost him his job and his pension with the Bureau, but he doesn't care. He just wants to wash the guilt off his hands. Down deep, I think he's a decent human being."

Bolo shrugged. "If Ferguson had lived, maybe it would have been different. The media would have had a whipping boy then." He paused to round the corner. "This way, with Ferguson's intentional attack on the farm out in the open, maybe the federal government will feel the need to step in and do something for the survivors of the attack."

"That would be helpful."

"The mayor got an interesting phone call from a public-relations person at Roberts International," the sheriff went on. "It appears the corporation is going to send some men and materials into the area to help with the rebuilding."

Ash felt good about that. When he'd asked his father Sunday, two days ago, he hadn't known what the answer was going to be. Ash made it a habit not to ask for anything from his father because that put him in the position of owing him. And Ashton Roberts III never forgot who owed him. Possibly there existed the chance that Ash IV would have to do something for the corporation—or his father, since they were essentially one and the same—at some point in the future. Maybe he and his father weren't on the same page when it came to his career, but it was good to know they shared some of the same traits. His father hadn't balked a bit about sending aid.

"Any idea how that happened?" Bolo asked.

"Not a clue," Ash replied. "I've heard that Roberts International has a humanitarian side."

"Yeah, well, they're not known for it," the sheriff replied. He stopped the car where Bascombe's Plumbing had been. All that remained was a huge pipe wrench hanging from a signpost. "What about you?"

"What about me?"

"What are you going to do? After all of this, I'm sure you've proved to the Navy that you're not ready for a rubber room."

"If I have," Ash said, "they haven't called." He paused, looking at the midshipmen working in lines to haul debris from the ground floor of the plumbing shop. Across the street a big yellow earthmover lowered its bucket and scooped out the shell of a building, then dropped it into a dump truck. "I think I'm going to hang around here for a while. Finish polishing these midshipmen up and see if I can't help them get a handle on their Navy careers. Maybe get a few more pheasants before the season is over."

"Not exactly the life of adventure you're looking for," Bolo said.

"No," Ash admitted. "It isn't. But it will be again."

"Now you're talking," the sheriff said.

"Besides, if I need any real excitement, I've got my position as honorary deputy sheriff to fall back on."

"I hope that's not nearly as exciting as it has been." Bolo scanned the workers. "Where's your buddy?"

"Wild?" Ash looked around too, noticing for the first time that the SEAL wasn't in the middle of things. That was generally where he expected Wild to be. "I left him here."

"He looked like he was getting around okay." Bolo eased out of the cruiser and stood. "Getting around better than me, actually."

Ash silently agreed. During the past few days, Wild had pushed himself and paid for it at night, but the leg and the prosthesis were holding together. He was even in negotiations to get an extension on his leave, once he got checked out at a Navy hospital.

Walking over to Spike, Ash said, "Where's Wild?"

Spike waved to the earthmover across the street. "There."

Ash looked again but didn't see Wild. "There where?"

"On the machine," Spike answered. "He asked one of the construction people to show him how to use it."

"While I've been gone?" Ash couldn't believe it.

"Yeah," Spike said, grinning. "Wild also got a date."

"With the construction guy?"

"With the construction *woman*," Spike said. "You don't have to be male to run earthmoving equipment."

"I knew that," Ash replied. He crossed the street to where a slim young woman in overalls and a tank top stood watching the earthmover. She had a pair of leather gloves in her pocket and held the chinstrap of a hard hat in her hand. "Excuse me."

She turned to look at him with the bluest eyes Ash had ever seen. "Yes?" she asked.

"Is Wild Willie Weldon up in that thing?" Ash asked.

"Wild?" The girl smiled. "Yeah. He is. Isn't he doing great?"

Ash watched the earthmover dump another load of debris into the back of the waiting dump truck. "Yeah. Terrific."

"He really knows his way around equipment. He's got big hands."

Suddenly, the earthmover stopped moving earth. The door on the cabin flew open and Wild stepped out. "Ash!" He waved. "You gotta come up and try this, dude! This is one of the coolest things I've ever done!"

Ash cupped his hands and shouted over the loud diesel engine to be heard. "Later! Knock yourself out!"

Wild crawled back into the cabin and set the machine into motion again. Ash watched him work the earthmover with careless abandon, as if he'd been doing it all his life. Standing there, Ash let go some of the concerns and worry he had about his friend. Even missing part of a leg, Wild was going to land on his feet. They both were. They were Navy SEALs and landing right side up was part of the job description.

Wild moved forward and slammed the bucket into a broken wall that stood two stories tall. The impact shattered the wall and brought it down. Even over the rumble of grinding masonry, Wild's triumphant yell echoed over the street.

"You know," the woman said, "some men just never outgrow their Tonka toy phase."

"No," Ash agreed. And for a time he was content just to watch Wild work. War would call him back, and he'd be ready when it did.

Signet (0451)

THE AIDE

by

Ward Carroll

Navy SEAL Ash Roberts has taken up a new
position at the Pentagon as aide to Vice
Admiral Brooks Garrett, assistant principal to
the Joint Chiefs of Staff.
He sees and hears all. But what he's just
discovered about his new boss is a secret too
dangerous not to expose-one that threatens the
security of America, and the future of the brave
men and women who fight in her name.

0-451-21551-6

Available wherever books are sold or at
penguin.com

S495